45307312

TWELFTH
EDITION

Kendall Hunt
publishing company

D0782123

PURPOSE,
PATTERN,
& PROCESS

LENNIS POLNAC
ARUN JOHN

Contents

PART 1: PURPOSE 15

3: PERSUASIVE WRITING 63

4: REFERENTIAL WRITING 89

PART 2: PATTERN 121

5: CLASSIFICATION 123

7: NARRATION 201

8: EVALUATION 257

PART 3: PROCESS 283

9: IDEAS 285

10: DETAILS 293

11: FOCUS 301

14: STUDENT WRITING   441

CREDITS   461
INDEX   465

Preface

This book explores the processes writers engage in when they write. In particular this explanation focuses on how the purpose of the writing and the patterns of organization used to develop the content affect how those writing processes work. An understanding of how purpose and pattern affect process allows students and other writers to develop a better understanding of the many different options available to them when they have to create documents of all sorts.

As in previous editions of this book, we have based the organization and much of the content on the theories developed by James Kinneavy in his groundbreaking work *A Theory of Discourse*. Kinneavy's theory is especially useful as a way of organizing a composition course. It gives students a comprehensive theoretical framework that allows them to explore a variety of different kinds of writing in a systematic way and to make informed decisions about their own writing.

The "Introduction" defines the basic terminology used in the book. In addition, it shows how the three concepts—purpose, pattern, and process—are interconnected.

Part I, "Purpose" (Chapters 1 through 4), covers four kinds of writing defined by the purposes of the message—expressive, literary, persuasive, and referential. Each chapter presents a further classification by discussing four perspectives of expressive writing, four approaches of literary writing, four appeals of persuasive writing, and four focuses of referential writing. Examples of each type of writing are analyzed for their distinctive characteristics. In addition, these examples provide students with models for imitation.

Part II, "Pattern" (Chapters 5 through 8), covers the four basic patterns of organization—classification, description, narration, and evaluation. The chapters dealing with classification, description, and narration include a number of variations of the basic patterns. Three kinds of classification (organizing by categories) are included in Chapter 5: formal classification, comparison and contrast, and definition. In addition to physical descriptions (of people, of places, and of things), Chapter 6 includes two other methods of arranging parts within a whole: division and analysis. Finally, Chapter 7 on narration includes three alternative patterns of organization by time order: narration of event, narration of process, and cause and effect. These additional organizational patterns in Chapters 5, 6, and 7 provide writers with a variety of models for imitation and analysis. Furthermore, the four chapters that discuss the patterns of organization (5–8) include examples of writing that combine each purpose with each pattern. The examples of the combinations are analyzed according to the characteristics of the purposes discussed in Chapters 1–4 and the principles of organization presented in Chapters 5–8.

Part III, "Process" (Chapters 9 through 12), covers the process of writing by explaining four necessary activities—getting ideas, creating details, focusing writing, and refining the language. Each chapter provides suggestions for accomplishing those activities. In addition, each chapter in Part III includes guidance for doing research and reporting the information. Chapter 12 offers some basic advice on mechanics, grammar, and usage.

Part IV, "Additional Readings and Student Writing" (Chapter 13), provides thirty selections that illustrate the principles discussed in the earlier parts of the book. Selections with similar content are grouped together. At the end of each reading are questions that can be used for class discussion and writing assignments of five types: personal, research, persuasive, analytical, and investigative. The suggested writing assignments encourage students to create original content.

We would like to thank the many colleagues and students who, over the years, have contributed to the development of this work. We invite comments and suggestions from faculty and students who are currently using this book.

Lennis Polnac
Arun John

Introduction

Writing is the natural, and no doubt inevitable, consequence of our ability as humans to speak and to use language. With the creation of writing, civilization began to develop more rapidly than it ever had before because people were able to gain access to more information. In fact, in many ways writing made progress possible. Before writing had been developed, information could only be transmitted orally, and the amount of knowledge that could be passed along from one person to another in that way was necessarily restricted by the limitations of human memory. Writing gave human beings a powerful tool. It allowed them to make use of the knowledge accumulated by previous generations as well as to benefit from the wisdom derived from other cultures. At the same time, writing made it possible for people to add to their store of knowledge systematically.

Now, as a result of this process of preserving and passing along information in written form, a vast body of data, which is still continuously expanding, can be found in libraries, museums, archives, and various other repositories of knowledge throughout the world. This enormous reservoir of the collected knowledge and wisdom of the ages, recorded in written form, makes up the fabric of our modern world and enables our various social institutions—business, industry, science, technology, government, education—to function and to progress continually.

The high level of technological development that we enjoy today is the result of the continuing increase in the amount of information available to our society, and at the base of it all is the written word.

Ironically, even though our world in the twenty-first century is more advanced technologically than it has been at any time in history, in some ways we seem to have devalued writing. Letter writing seems to be a lost art in the age of the smartphone; time that people may once have devoted to reading is now spent watching movies and TV and playing video games. Yet in other ways the ability to communicate clearly and effectively in writing continues to be an important, if not an essential, skill in our hi-tech world. As we become more and more dependent on computers, our ability to manipulate written language becomes ever more crucial. In many ways, our use of electronic communication—e-mailing, texting, using social networking sites, and blogging—is making writing more important than it has ever been. As a result, more than ever before, those who read well and write effectively will have a decided competitive advantage in today's society.

In this textbook we will look closely at how writing works by examining the processes that we all go through when we create written communications. Specifically, as the title of the book suggests, we will consider how the purpose of any piece of writing and its pattern of organization fit into the writing process and how an understanding of that process can help us write more effectively.

Any communication, whether it is written or oral, will have a purpose. It would be impossible to conceive of a message that did not have a purpose. Even though we may not always be aware of it, whenever we communicate, a purpose controls practically every aspect of writing: how the message is created, what details are included and excluded, and how those details are organized.

In addition to its purpose, any message we create will have a pattern of organization. When we generate details, we must arrange them in some way. That arrangement will depend on both the purpose of the message and the subject matter being addressed.

Finally, we can think of writing as a process, a series of activities we go through each time we create a message. These activities vary, depending on the personality, work habits, and experience of the writer. In general, however, the process involves selecting a topic, defining a purpose, generating details, and organizing them. An understanding of how this writing process works will enable any writer to have more control over the final product.

PURPOSE

Anytime we speak or write, that communication will have one of four purposes: to express the self, to entertain, to persuade, or to explain. Writing that reveals the self of the writer is **expressive**; writing that entertains is **literary**; writing that attempts to convince an audience is **persuasive**; writing that explains a topic is **referential**.

Each of the following examples illustrates one of these four purposes.

1. I hate cats. They're always in the way. Sometimes I'd like to get rid of every cat in the world. They're such slobs, always lying around. Good for nothings. Cats. You can have 'em.

2. The cat moved stealthily through the shadows, making no sound. It crouched, entirely immobile, its tail twitching rhythmically, watching a bird that cavorted in the grass, oblivious to the impending danger.

3. Cats are adorable, fluffy animals that make wonderful pets. They love to be rubbed and petted, and when you pet them, they make a purring sound to show their affection. Get a cat and you'll never be lonely or unloved again.

4. The cat is a domesticated carnivore that has been a popular pet for centuries. It is a curious, often affectionate animal, but somewhat independent. Although it is often kept to rid a house of mice, it will kill birds, snakes, and lizards as well.

You will notice that each example above, even though it addresses the same general topic, is different in content, organization, and style. The differences occur in part because each example has a different purpose. Example 1 is expressive; 2 is literary; 3 is persuasive; 4 is referential.

These four purposes can be explained in terms of the Communication Triangle (Fig. 1).

All written messages have four elements: a writer, a reader, a topic, and words. Each one of the four purposes emphasizes one of the elements of the Communication Triangle. Expressive writing emphasizes the writer. Literary writing emphasizes language structures. Persuasive writing emphasizes the reader. Referential writing emphasizes the topic (the subject matter).

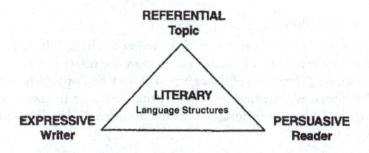

FIGURE 1   The Communication Triangle

The purpose is like a *filter* through which every word to be included in the written communication must pass. Such elements as humor, imagery, objective words, jargon, emotional language, and slang are included in or excluded from any particular piece of writing depending on what purpose is at work. For example, when writing up the results of an experiment, a scientist would select language that is neutral as opposed to language that is emotionally charged. A writer creating a poem would probably select figurative imagery and avoid technical language. It is the purpose that controls a writer's choices about what kinds of words and devices of language to use in a composition.

DEFINITIONS AND CHARACTERISTICS

Any particular piece of writing will have distinctive characteristics that reflect one of the four purposes.

Expressive Writing

Writing that has an expressive purpose is the most personal of all writing. It communicates an impression of what the writer is like. Expressive writing is about the writer, and it reveals how the writer looks at the world. Examples of expressive writing are diaries, journals, and personal letters. Expressive writing is also called personal writing.

Literary Writing

The literary purpose produces writing that is meant to be entertaining, or in some way pleasing to the reader. This kind of writing creates an aesthetic response in the reader because of the way the writer has structured the language. Short stories, novels, plays, poems, and humorous essays are examples of literary writing. The term creative writing is often used in referring to literary writing.

Persuasive Writing

Persuasion is an effort on the part of the writer to change the reader's mind about some issue and in some cases to move the reader to take some action based on a conviction of the rightness of the writer's position. Some examples of persuasive writing are political pamphlets, advertisements, and op-ed articles. The terms rhetoric and polemic are often used in discussions of persuasion.

Referential Writing

Referential writing has as its purpose to explain a topic. That focus on the subject matter creates a need for accuracy and clarity. As a result, writing that has a referential purpose will usually be somewhat more formal than writing that has one of the other purposes. Textbooks, news stories, and business letters are examples of referential writing. Referential writing is also called expository writing.

In Chapters 1, 2, 3, and 4 we will examine each of the four purposes in more detail by looking at four major characteristics of each. For each purpose we will discover how writers present the *main idea*, how they provide *substantiation* of the main idea by the elaboration of detail, how they provide *authentication* of those details, and how they make choices about the *language* to be used.

COMBINATIONS AND DISTINCTIONS

Not every piece of writing fits neatly into these categories. Most writing will have characteristics of more than one purpose. Some persuasive writing may be made up of parts that are purely referential; some literary writing may have some elements that are persuasive. Usually, however, we can identify a primary purpose. That is, most of the characteristics of the work will reflect one of the four purposes. If characteristics of another purpose are present, they can be regarded as secondary.

We can also think about the concept of primary and secondary purposes in a slightly different way by visualizing the communication triangle as a three-dimensional figure (a tetrahedron, also called a triangular pyramid) with the elements of the message (the writer, the reader, the topic, and language structures) at the four corners.

Any given work, depending on the relative influence of each of the elements, can be located somewhere within that solid figure. The location would depend on how much of a subordinate (secondary) purpose is present in the work. We can see these relationships between the primary (dominant) purpose and other subordinate purposes in a number of readings throughout this textbook (Fig. 2).

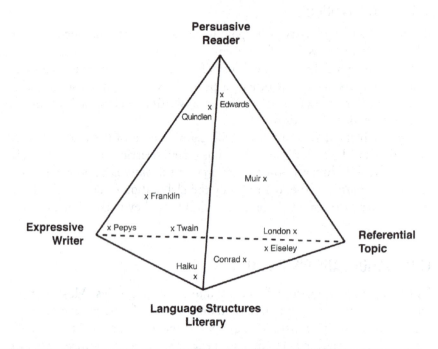

FIGURE 2   The Pyramid

Works with a primary expressive purpose like Samuel Pepys' "Diary" in Chapter 1, Benjamin Franklin's "The Arduous Project of Arriving at Moral Perfection" in Chapter 6, and Mark Twain's "Two Ways of Viewing the River" in Chapter 5 would be located in the corner of the figure close to the writer. Both Franklin's and Twain's works, however, would be located on the line toward the reader because they are both autobiographical and so are meant to be read by a wider audience than a diary is. Twain's work, because of his use of literary descriptions, would be located more toward the center of the figure than would Franklin's.

Literary works like the four Haiku in Chapter 2, poems of three lines creating a highly compressed text, and that, as a result, focus the attention of the reader on the language itself, would be located in the corner of the figure close to language structures. Joseph Conrad's "The Passage" in Chapter 2, although it has a primary literary purpose with an obvious focus on language structures, especially in the descriptive passages, would be located along the line toward the topic (subject matter) because the content of the work reflects an attempt to create an accurate depiction of the world as it is.

Jonathan Edwards' "Sinners in the Hands of an Angry God" in Chapter 3, a sermon designed to elicit emotional responses from the audience, although obviously persuasive, also has a great many literary devices and so would be located close to the corner at persuasive writing but along the line toward literary writing. Anna Quindlen's "The Death Penalty's False Promise: An Eye for an Eye" in Chapter 3, is also clearly persuasive, but her personal responses and her use of extended narrative examples would locate the work toward the center of the pyramid between the line leading to the writer and the line leading to the topic.

Works with a primary referential purpose like Jack London's "The San Francisco Earthquake" in Chapter 7, Loren Eiseley's "How Flowers Changed the World" in Chapter 7, and John Muir's "Where the Sequoia Grows" in Chapter 4 would be located in the corner of the figure close to the topic (subject matter). London's article is for the most part a traditional news article, a more or less objective account of an event, but it has a few first person authorial intrusions that would move it slightly along the line toward the writer and expressive writing. About eighty percent of Eiseley's article is purely referential, but the last twenty percent records a personal experience related to the topic and has a smattering of literary devices. As a result, Eiseley's work would be located further along the line toward the expressive than London's and slightly toward the line leading to literary writing. Muir's article would be located along the line toward the reader because the subject matter requires that the writer demonstrate to the reader logically that the interpretation of the evidence is a valid one.

As you can see, this way of looking at the various relationships among the purposes allows for a more sophisticated understanding of a text because we are made aware of the many nuanced connections between dominant and subordinate purposes. Keeping in mind those subtle connections as we read and write enables us as readers and writers to gain additional insight into the texts we interact with. So, looking at a text is not just a matter of putting it into a rigid category, but rather seeing the work as a fluid interconnected series of influences from several purposes. One purpose will always be primary (dominant), but the other three are always potentially present and to varying degrees influence how we create our own texts and how we read texts created by others. In any text there is always a writer, a reader, a topic, and language structures.

Maintaining a balance between competing purposes is sometimes tricky. Some combinations of purposes may create awkward readings. For example, it would probably not be appropriate to include an expressive response like "Wow, I loved this experiment," in a lab report. Literary devices and emotional language would be inappropriate when the primary referential purpose is purely factual or if a work requires logical proofs to demonstrate the validity of the argument.

The term argument is often used when we talk about writing that has either a referential interpretive focus or a persuasive rational appeal. Although both forms involve argumentation, the requirements for authenticating each form differ drastically. The kind of proof required for a referential thesis is not the same as the kind of proof that will suffice for a persuasive claim. For example, an argument that *too much stress can cause health problems* would be very different from an argument that *we should reduce stress in our lives*. The first, a referential thesis, would demand demonstrable evidence with a high probability of certainty to validate the assertion. Scientifically validated studies would be required. The second, a persuasive claim advocating that the audience take some action, would not require an argument that had a high level of certainty. Whatever the audience would accept in support of the argument would be enough. Although evidence used to prove the referential thesis might be part of the persuasive argument, it would not be essential to success of that argument. For some people, the evidence that stress may cause health problems might not be important enough to convince them to reduce stress in their lives. If they valued family highly, however, they might be convinced by an emotional appeal from another family member. So, it is important, when we think about arguments, that we distinguish between referential arguments and persuasive arguments because the kind of support demanded for each is quite different. We lose precision and accuracy when we fail to pay attention to those distinctions.

Writing is not an isolated phenomenon; it is controlled by the circumstances surrounding its production, by the writer's motivations, and by the expectations of any potential readers. All texts are determined by context, both the immediate situational context that has prompted the writing and the broader cultural context that gives any artifact meaning. Many cultural norms go beyond the immediate historical situation and involve traditions, both literary and social, that provide boundaries for both writer and reader. Our understanding of a text, then, depends on our understanding of both the social context and the cultural traditions influencing it.

PATTERN

Whenever we create details, we arrange them in some way. Patterns of organization are ways of structuring our experiences and perceptions. They reflect the different ways we think about the world around us. We may classify, describe, narrate, or evaluate. With **classification** we organize by putting things into categories; with **description** we tell what something is like; with **narration** we record events; and with **evaluation** we make value judgements. Which of the four patterns we use in any given piece of writing is affected by the nature of the topic, by the purpose, and by the situational context.

Although generally one dominant pattern will be used to organize the entire work, several different patterns may be, and usually are, present in a single piece of writing. For example, narrations usually have some descriptive elements in them. The categories of a classification system may be developed by description, narration, or further classification. Evaluations necessarily involve the use of another pattern: the subject to be evaluated must be presented to the reader by means of narration, description, or classification.

Each of the following examples illustrates a different pattern.

1. There are many kinds of cats. Most people are familiar with the popular breeds, such as Persians, Himalayans, Siamese, and the American Shorthair (sometimes mistakenly referred to as "alley cats"). These breeds, and other less familiar kinds of cats, can be grouped into three general classes: longhairs, shorthairs, and Rex. The longhairs include the ever popular Persians and Himalayans. Siamese and the American Shorthair, as well as other less well-known breeds like Burmese, Abyssinian, Russian Blue, and Manx, are included in the shorthair category. Finally, the Rex, a new breed, has hair that is somewhat short but which is also wavy.

2. Our cat has four white feet, but the rest of her fur is solid black. She is a small cat, dainty and retiring, shy around people she doesn't know. She has a small, squeaky voice.

3. The cat crept along the fence staring intently into the vines that grew along the edge of the yard. It could see something that I couldn't. Suddenly it froze, tensing its body and twitching its tail. Then it jumped forward and seemed to have trapped something with its paws. After a moment it began hopping around and slapping the undergrowth with its claws. Finally, it pounced at the bottom of the fence as the elusive prey apparently escaped.

4. Himalayans make great pets. They are playful and somewhat unpredictable. Their long fur is so soft that it feels like an expensive fur coat. The only drawback to Himalayans is that they leave that wonderfully soft fur on everything they touch.

In each example above, cats are presented in different ways because the writing is organized in a different way. Example 1 is organized by classification; example 2, by description; example 3, by narration; example 4, by evaluation.

The four basic patterns of organization are shown by the diagram below (Fig. 3).

We can think of the patterns of organization as different ways of seeing the subject matter depicted by the writer. Both description and classification represent the subject matter as a static reality, like a snapshot frozen in time. Narration creates a dynamic picture because the details presented change from one event to another. Evaluation is also dynamic because the judgments made are based on assumptions about how the subject being evaluated functions or behaves.

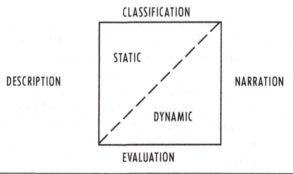

FIGURE 3   Patterns of Organization

DEFINITIONS AND CHARACTERISTICS

In addition to purpose, any piece of writing will also have a pattern, or patterns, of organization. These patterns help make writing understandable and predictable to the reader.

Classification

When we classify, we are organizing the details of our writing into general categories of things. Classification is the arrangement of the details of a subject into classes or kinds. The organizing principle for classification is the **relationship between categories in a system.**

Description

Description is an attempt to make the reader understand how some physical reality or concept is structured. The most obvious use of description is to show physical relationships in space. Space order shows how the different parts of the whole description are related to each other. The organizing principle for descriptions is the **relationship between parts within the whole**.

Narration

Narrations tell a story. All narrations show how events are related in time, so they are arranged in time order. One event follows another, and the resulting sequence of events can be seen as a whole narrative. The organizing principle for narration is the **relationship between events in time**.

Evaluation

When we use evaluation, we make judgments about the subject being evaluated. That is, we say that it is relatively good or bad, or something in between. The organizing principle is the **relationship between values and judgments**.

COMBINATIONS AND DISTINCTIONS

For each purpose, any pattern of organization or combination of patterns may be used. For example, a paper with a persuasive purpose may achieve that purpose through the use of description, classification, narration, or evaluation. Remember that *all writing will have both purpose and pattern of organization*. Patterns are often combined. Descriptions are frequently combined with narratives, especially literary narratives. The categories in a classification system may be developed by further classification and definition, but they may also be developed by narration and description. As you will discover in Chapter 8, any subject being evaluated must be presented to the reader by one of the other patterns of organization.

PROCESS

Writing is not always easy. In fact, it usually never is. In his poem "East Coker," T. S. Eliot observes that writing is "a raid on the inarticulate/with shabby equipment always deteriorating. . . ." These images capture some of the inevitable struggle that most writers go through. At times it does seem that writing is almost like a battle between the writer and the language.

We must drag each word, kicking and screaming, onto the page and try to make it fit. If the words don't work the way we want them to, we throw them out and find new ones.

When we sit down to write, each of us goes through a process, a certain way of generating ideas, arranging them, and putting them into written form. Although this writing process varies with each individual, some basic elements are always present. The process is recursive. That is, the various parts are repeated again and again so that the whole process moves from one element to another, back and forth. It looks something like the diagram in figure 4.

When we write, we have an idea we want to communicate to our readers, and that idea usually suggests a general purpose (either to express the self, to entertain, to persuade, or to explain a topic). We also define the purpose more specifically by creating a main idea, a specific statement of what the writing is about. (In expressive writing the main idea is a *self-definition*; in literary writing it is a *theme*; in persuasive writing it is a *claim*; and in referential writing it is a *thesis*.) The general purpose and the main idea, then, enable us to generate details that we put into writing. After, or even while, we generate the details, we begin to organize them by using one or a combination of the patterns—classification, description, narration, and evaluation.

This organizing process may make us generate details that we left out when we first began. And this additional organizing and inventing may actually cause us to change our purpose (the main idea or the general purpose or both) and that may in turn cause us to recognize that we need different details that must also be organized and reorganized. So we continually repeat the parts of the process—organizing, generating details, and reorganizing—until we feel that the paper is finished or until we run out of time and have to hand it in. If details are added, they may affect the organization or the purpose. If we move some material from one place to another, we may also change our purpose somewhat.

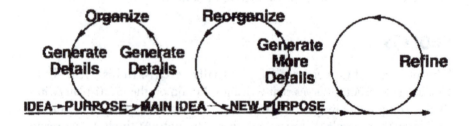

FIGURE 4   The Writing Process

There are no rules governing this process. The parts of the process may occur in a different order, or there may be more or fewer of them, depending on the experience of the writer and the nature of the writing task. Writing a technical report, for example, would certainly involve a more complicated process than writing an interoffice memo.

The process may occur mostly on paper (or on screen) or almost entirely in the mind, depending on the personality of the writer. That is, some people put down everything they can think of and work through a great many drafts. Others may do most of the editing in their heads before they put a single word on paper. Most of us probably fall somewhere in between these two extremes. Though we alternate between thinking and writing, we will tend to follow all the steps of the process fairly completely.

In general, writers who are more aware of the process will have more control over their writing. As a result, a simple awareness of the steps of the process is a powerful tool.

DEFINITIONS AND CHARACTERISTICS

Even though the nature of the process (or, more accurately, processes) is unique to each individual, there are four discrete kinds of activities that most writers accomplish: getting ideas, generating details, focusing the details, and refining the content. These four activities may occur in any order, or even simultaneously; however, most writers tend to perform each of the four in the order outlined here.

Ideas

The writing process begins with ideas, and even though ideas are all around us, writers sometimes have difficulty coming up with one that is workable or shaping it so that it can be presented in written form.

Details

The details arise from the idea and are controlled by the general purpose and the main idea (specific purpose) of the work. In the initial stages of the process, the writer may generate content sporadically, almost at random, some of which may later be discarded. But it is often necessary to create more content than can actually be used in the final product.

Focus

As more and more content is generated, the work will inevitably begin to have a focus. During that process of focusing, the writer will begin to settle on some patterns of development for the work. Some of those arise naturally from the nature of the topic. At other times, the writer will make conscious decisions to employ a particular method of development.

Refinement

Even though most writers are primarily interested in generating details and in organizing those details in the early drafts, they usually do some refining all along. For example, even in an initial draft many writers will tend to spell most words correctly, insert punctuation where they think it should go, and make decisions about style. Toward the end of the process, this kind of activity will increase.

COMBINATIONS AND DISTINCTIONS

Of course, not everyone uses the different parts of the process in the same way. Some writers may do most of the composing in their minds before putting it down in written form. Others may write down everything they can think of and then revise extensively by creating a great many drafts. The number of drafts may vary greatly, but most writers will create more than one.

Even though the writing process as it has been presented here is dominantly recursive, it also has some linear aspects. That is, the process repeats itself while at the same time moving from beginning to end, from initial draft to final draft. It is helpful to be aware of both aspects.

PURPOSE
Part 1

Expressive Writing
Literary Writing
Persuasive Writing
Referential Writing

Expressive Writing

T he desire to express ourselves with words seems to be an intrinsic part of human nature. Indeed, the urge to communicate who we are as individuals may be basic to the way we think. The noted psychologist Abraham Maslow has suggested that the highest of all human needs is the need for self-actualization, that is, understanding who we really are and acting on that understanding. Expressive writing would seem to be a manifestation of that need for self-actualization and, at least to some degree, a means of achieving it. Expressive writing allows us to engage in a process of self-exploration and self-discovery, to find out who we are and even, perhaps, who we are going to be.

The dominant feature of all expressive writing is that it reveals the writer's identity and individuality. Everything in an expressive work reflects those perceptions and attitudes unique to the person who created it. Each subject addressed is considered, not on its own terms, but rather in terms of how it fits into the writer's personal vision of things. What we see when we read expressive writing is, in essence, a depiction of the mind of the writer, a subjective representation of the world according to the creator of the message.

Examples of self-expression include not only writing by individuals—like diaries, autobiographies, and personal letters—but also documents that are more public and are often collective expressions of a group consciousness, like creeds, declarations, and manifestoes. No matter what forms self-expression may take, however, all of them have certain characteristics in common. In practically any example of expressive writing, we can see these same general features: self-definition, emotional responses, an expression of values, and subjective language.

GENERAL CHARACTERISTICS

- A self-definition is formulated or suggested.
- Emotional responses are made.
- Values are expressed.
- Subjective language is used.

SELF-DEFINITION

Defining the *self* is an integral part of the ongoing process of expressing ourselves and trying to understand who we are. A self-definition in expressive writing may include one or more of the dimensions that make up the writer's identity. When any of those facets of the writer's personality are revealed, a self-definition is the result. No matter what the definition is, it reveals how the writer sees the self. We may define ourselves in any number of terms that are most significant to us at the time. For example, statements like

"I am an American,"
"I am an extrovert,"
"I am a woman,"
    and
"I am a rebel"

reflect aspects of a self-definition.

There is no formula for defining the self. Creating a self-definition occurs naturally when we examine our thoughts and feelings. The simple revelation of the writer's thoughts and feelings may suggest a self-definition. Indeed, it would be impossible to record thoughts and feelings without, at least partially, defining the self as well. A self-definition is implied by what we choose to say, what thoughts and feelings we choose to reveal. For example, an essay that involves a discussion of "my education" would suggest that the writer thinks of himself or herself as a student. Such a discussion might, in fact, lead to a specific definition of the self, like "I am a student."

How we see ourselves, and define ourselves, is determined in part by past experiences, the culture we live in, the specific circumstance that produces the occasion for self-expression, and the many individual needs, desires, and fears that control our perceptions, attitudes, and beliefs.

In addition to our conception of ourselves at the present moment, we all have some vision of ourselves in the future—what kind of job we want to have, what kind of house we want to live in, what kind of car we want to drive, or what kind of clothes we want to wear. Such projections of ourselves into the future form a part of the idea of who we will be and who we want to be. The process of self-definition and the articulation of a value system may give rise to, and may actually shape, our goals—those things we want to accomplish either immediately or in the long term. For instance, someone who says, "I am a student," would value things associated with that self-definition. As a result, we wouldn't be at all surprised to hear a "student" say, "I'm going to stay in school until I get a degree," a statement of a goal reflecting the values of a person whose self-definition is "I am a student."

EMOTIONAL RESPONSES

Self-expression reveals the writer's emotions. These emotions are expressed with emotional words as well as exaggerated or imperative language such as exclamations, commands, or sweeping generalizations. Very often the personality of the writer or the situation being written about, or both, provokes an emotional response.

Emotional Language

The writer may reveal emotions directly by using words like *love*, *hate*, *hope*, or *fear*—words that express emotions. Through this language, the inner world of the writer is revealed to the reader.

In addition, the writer may use words that have strong connotations. Connotations are the associated, emotional meanings of words. (Denotations are the literal dictionary definitions.) Some words have positive connotations; that is, they create good feelings in most readers. Others, that have negative connotations, create unpleasant feelings in the reader. For instance, the words *thrifty*, *stingy*, and *economical*, although they have similar meanings, have very different connotations.

Exclamations

An exclamation is a sentence that expresses strong feeling, like "I love this place!" (These sentences are usually followed by an exclamation point.)

Commands

A command is an order or a direction like "Take this away." (Notice that there is an implied *you* at the beginning of the command, so that the sentence means, "You take this away.")

Sweeping Generalizations

Generalizations are statements that include a great many individual cases. A statement like "Everybody likes baseball" is a sweeping generalization because it doesn't allow for any exceptions. Obviously the statement can't be literally true, but in expressive writing such a statement may be an accurate reflection of the feelings of the writer. In addition to *everybody*, words such as *all, everything, everyone, none, no one,* and *nothing* may create sweeping generalizations.

EXPRESSION OF VALUES

The responses we have to events in the world around us shape and are shaped by what we value. Generally speaking, values are those principles, standards, or qualities considered worthwhile or desirable by an individual or a society. We couldn't understand ourselves fully or express the true nature of our identities without understanding the values that influence us. Our values tell us who we are, affect how we see the world around us, and control how we respond to it.

When we say that something is good or bad, or use some synonym for degrees of *goodness* or *badness*, we are revealing values. Superlatives, words that end in *-est*, also indicate that a value judgment is being made, as in the statement, "That's the great*est* book I've ever read." The writer's system of values, either stated explicitly or implied by the judgments made, is present in all expressive writing. Whether those values represent an individual response or the demands of the culture, they are a part of the writer's expression of the self. Values control self-definition. Values are also connected to emotional responses. When we value something, we are likely to respond to it emotionally.

Attempts at self-definition are invariably connected to a discussion of values and are frequently couched in the terminology of values. The self-defined student who values education highly might say something like

"Getting an education is a great opportunity and opens many doors," thus revealing a part of the larger value system.

SUBJECTIVE LANGUAGE

The subjective nature of expressive writing can be seen in the writer's choice of words and phrases. This stylistic feature is part of the revelation of who the writer is.

One of the first things we notice when we read a piece of expressive writing is the first person pronouns (*I, me, my, mine, we, us, our, ours*). The use of these pronouns is consistent with the subjective nature of the self-expression. It would be hard to imagine a piece of expressive writing without these first person pronouns.

Since the self is the dominant element in expressive writing, most of the language used reflects the writer's personality. The writer is expressing his or her identity. The writer's own particular way of using language (called an *idiolect*) controls the selection of words. As a result, expressive writing may have informal features like slang expressions and a conversational style. These characteristics may appear because they are a part of the writer's personality; they honestly express the writer's identity.

Slang and Dialect

Slang expressions are those words and phrases that have special meanings in certain cultures and subcultures. For instance, someone may say that something is *cool*, referring not to its temperature, but to how desirable it is.

Dialect usually refers to regional or social variety in the use of certain forms of language, especially if they deviate from standard usage (although strictly speaking, standard usage is also a dialect). In personal writing, we tend to use language that we are comfortable with, the language we used as children or the language we use in casual conversations with close friends and relatives, even though those forms may not conform to the rules of standard usage.

Conversational Style

A conversational style has a naturalness of tone and ease of expression that helps the writer to communicate emotional reactions. In other words, the conversational style sounds like conversation, as if the writer were speaking aloud spontaneously without thinking too much about such things as word choice, sentence construction, or the particulars of standard usage.

AN EXAMPLE

The following excerpt from John Graves' book entitled *Hard Scrabble* illustrates how the writer's value system and his emotional responses work to create a self-definition. Graves, in creating a definition of himself, also projects goals for the future. In this autobiographical work, Graves gives us a look at his farm in Somervell County, Texas where he has made a transition from urban to rural life. His record of that transition gives us a glimpse of Graves' identity as it has been shaped by the hard scrabble land of central Texas.

THE WAY

JOHN GRAVES

Nothing else on the place generates quite as much friction with the order of things as goats do, though nearly all the Syndrome's activities generate some. Chickens are proverbially attractive to carnivores, but ours at present, a hen house and yard not having been built, are scrub games, true Darwinian fowl that roost here and there in the barn and get along without even being fed anything except what they can steal by pecking holes in sacks or can glean from larger animals' feed. Sneaking nests in cubbyholes, chasing grasshoppers far out into the pastures, they have managed to raise some chicks and to increase a little every year despite the good red-yolked brown eggs the children find by searching and bring to the house, and the young roosters we take for meat, and an occasional specimen grabbed and eaten by a gray fox that lives up the horse-trap's fenceline. I have intentions of doing battle with this fellow if I ever get the chance, but I rather like him too and somehow never have a gun around when I catch a glimpse of him. For that matter his toll is minimal; the games can fly like quail and even the cockerels I kill for the table have to be shot sportingly in the head from a distance, with a twenty-two. . . . They could probably cope with hawks too, for when buzzards fly over low they give the hollow hawk-warning call and dart for cover. One man I used to know had a gamecock that would fly up in the air to meet and fight a diving hawk, which I daresay the hawk found disconcerting. . . . But sadly hawks are not much of a problem these days, DDT and other sweet agents of profit and progress having decimated their numbers in a brief few years, since in the late fifties I saw the great "hawk storm" on White Bluff. I miss them and am glad to see the few that still show up, nor would I shoot one now if he killed every chicken I have.

Deer love the winter grainfields and graze them hard at times. Here on the creek there aren't yet enough to worry much about, and an occasional loin or haunch of venison is recompense for what damage they do. But at the Soft Scrabble place a few miles south, near big ranches where the current deer explosion is centered, they are already making it nearly impossible to raise certain crops. Though I leased the tract for hunting to friends last winter to hold down depredations a bit, the hunters' light legal take affected them not at all, and at the height of the season a neighbor counted fifty in one bunch amid the ruined oats and vetch I had sowed to make spring hay. . . .

Rabbits have sometimes been rough on the vegetable garden's lettuce and things, but a good tight poultry-wire fence now keeps most of them out, and predators hold their numbers down, so that maybe by not shooting the gray up the fence I am just swapping an occasional fowl for lettuce and cabbage and greens. Coons, barred access to our garbage by dogs at the house, climb over the garden fence at the wild end, and for two or three years made it impossible to harvest any sweet corn—ripping it off the stalks just before it was prime, eating some ears and discarding others scornfully on the ground. I tried lanterns and ticking clocks and cans of urine and other O. F.-recommended techniques but they did no good, and at last I put a sheepdog bitch down there one night, which led to a fine, squalling, barking battle at four in the morning, three grown coons and the bitch and the bitch's son Blue, and me dancing around in my shorts with a flashlight and a club.

But I don't really dislike coons that much—not at all, in fact—and when the big tough boar specimen that did not survive the battle had been buried shallowly amid my ravaged corn (where he would be, like Old Speck the erstwhile goat-killing dog, a fertility in the soil, a dying and reborn god), I found by accident what seems to be a peaceful solution for the problem. As the smell of coonish mortality seeps gently roundabout in that area of the garden, it serves as a reminder to other trespassing coons of their own mortality. Like their human brethren they appear not to care for such reminders and thenceforth stay away, at least till the smell dies out. Nor do you have to resort to further coon-murder to get hold of a corpse to bury; a stretch of morning highway will often yield one or two, freshly slaughtered by last night's passing cars.

(There is perhaps a problem about what to say to acquaintances who may come along and catch you scavenging dead things from the roadside, but an O. F. learns furtive swooping skill in such activity, and a certain amount of shamelessness. He finds it possible to feel not only unashamed but proud of something like a heaped pickup-load of chicken poot. . . .)

The Way's real Sunday punch at vegetable gardens, though, is delivered by bugs. Squash bugs, stink bugs, cabbage loopers, hornworms, cutworms, army worms, nematodes, grasshoppers, crickets, cucumber beetles of two sorts, aphids of a dozen, leafhoppers, corn earworms, pill bugs, Colorado potato beetles, root maggots, and any number of other such skillful and hungry destroyers . . . All true O.F.s distrust poisons, and hence from year to year we base new hopes on Rodalian "organic" approaches and concoctions—ladybugs and mantids, fireplace ashes, garlic-and-pepper water, companionate plantings, compost and mulch and garbage and manure to firm up the plants' resistance, mineral oil, salt water, beer. . . . Some work surprisingly well at times, and at other times none seem to do much, and impurity invades the O. F. and maybe he guiltily slathers some poison around, but even then of nonresidual sorts, preferably the old botanicals like rotenone and nicotine and sabadilla dust. Or maybe at such times he just lets the bugs take over, or replants enough stuff for them and him both.

This excerpt shows how an expressive purpose reveals the author's value system and how that value system is connected to the author's emotional reactions and a self-definition. Graves reveals a value system based on minimum human impact on nature. Emotional responses like "I rather like him [the fox] too" and the implicit self-definition *I am a nature lover* are closely associated with his value system.

FOUR KINDS OF EXPRESSIVE WRITING

All expressive writing has the general characteristics discussed above, but can be further divided into four groups, each with characteristics different from the others. Each one creates a different perspective on the process of self-expression. They can be called personal, autobiographical, ritual, and interpersonal.

THE PERSONAL PERSPECTIVE

Personal self-expression, which includes diaries and journals, is the least restrictive and perhaps the most characteristically expressive of all the forms of expressive writing. It has four identifying features.

- Immediate impressions and perceptions are recorded.
- Matters of importance to the writer are dealt with.
- The nature of the self is explored.
- Associations are made and/or episodes are recounted.

Immediate Impressions and Perceptions

Diaries and journals are usually records of the daily experiences of the writer. As a result, they reflect a sense of immediacy more than the other forms of self-expression. The writer records impressions and perceptions of ordinary, everyday things and common events.

Matters of Importance

The writer deals with ideas and beliefs he or she thinks are of the utmost importance. Things that may, upon reflection, seem trivial, nevertheless seem important at the moment they are recorded. If the writer considers something to be important, then it is important. Each individual's value system determines what is important for that person.

Exploration of the Self

In personal writing, the general characteristic of giving a self-definition usually involves an examination of motives and desires, often explained in terms of values. An understanding of the values that underlie motives and goals is an essential part of self-exploration. That kind of understanding can provide important clues for understanding actions, thoughts, and emotional responses.

Associations and Episodes

Because personal writing tends to focus on recent experiences, it follows a pattern of development that reflects the working of the writer's consciousness. Our mental processes usually follow a stream of consciousness—thoughts, impressions, memories, and ideas connected by personal associations. When this process is put down in writing, as it is in a diary or a journal, the result is usually associative. That is, one idea suggests another.

Even when a narrative is recorded, it may well be in the form of a disconnected series of episodes.

AN EXAMPLE

From 1660 to 1669 Samuel Pepys kept a secret diary in a shorthand he devised. In his diary he recorded many of the events of his life. Now it is one of the most famous diaries in English literature because of the candor with which it reveals life in seventeenth-century England. The following excerpts give an idea of its content and illustrate the characteristics of personal self-expression.

DIARY

SAMUEL PEPYS

July 1, 1660 (Lord's day.)—Infinite business, my heart and head full. Met with Purser Washington, with whom and a lady, a friend of his, I dined at the Bell Tavern in King Street, but the rogue had no more manners than to invite me, and to let me pay my club. This morning come home my fine camlet cloak, with gold buttons, and a silk suit, which cost me much money, and I pray God to make me able to pay for it. In the afternoon to the Abbey, where a good sermon by a stranger, but no Common Prayer yet.

October 13, 1660.—I went to Charing Cross, to see Major-General Harrison hanged, drawn, and quartered; which was done there, he looking as cheerful as any man could do in that condition. He was presently cut down, and his head and heart shown to the people, at which there was great shouts of joy. It is said, that he said that he was sure to come shortly at the right hand of Christ to judge them that now had judged him; and that his wife do expect his coming again. Thus it was my chance to see the King beheaded at White Hall, and to see the first blood shed in revenge for the King at Charing Cross. Setting up shelves in my study.

January 1, 1662.—Waking this morning out of my sleep on a sudden, I did with my elbow hit my wife a great blow over her face and neck, which waked her with pain, at which I was sorry, and to sleep again. . . .

October 2, 1662.—At night, hearing that there was a play at the Cockpit, and my Lord Sandwich, who come to town last night, at it, I do go thither, and by very great fortune did follow four or five gentlemen who were carried to a little private door in a wall, and so crept through a narrow place, and come into one of the boxes next the King's, but so as I could not see the King or Queen, but many of the fine ladies, who yet are not really so handsome generally as I used to take them to be, but that they are finely dressed. Then we saw *The Cardinall*, a tragedy I had never seen before, nor is there any great matter in it. That company that come in with me into the box were all Frenchmen, that could speak no English; but, Lord! what sport they made to ask a pretty lady that they got among them, that understood both French and English, to make her tell them what the actors said.

January 6, 1664 (Twelfth Day.)—This morning I began a practice, which I find, by the ease I do it with, that I shall continue, it saving me money and time; that is, to trimme myself with a razer: which pleases me mightily.

August 7, 1664 (Lord's Day.)—My wife telling me sad stories of the ill, improvident, disquiet, and sluttish manner, that my father and mother and Pall do live in the country, which troubles me mightily, and I must seek to remedy it. . . .

October 16, 1665.—. . . God knows what will become of all the King's matters in a little time, for he runs in debt every day, and nothing to pay them looked after. Thence I walked to the Tower; but, Lord! how empty the streets are and melancholy, so many poor sick people in the streets full of sores; and so many sad stories overheard as I walk, everybody talking of his dead, and that man sick, and so many in this place, and so many in that. And they tell me that, in Westminster, there is never a physician and but one apothecary left, all being dead; but that there are great hopes of a great decrease this week; God send it! . . .

September 2, 1666 (Lord's day.)—Some of our maids sitting up late last night to get things ready against our feast today, Jane called us up about three in the morning, to tell us of a great fire they saw in the city. So I rose and slipped on my night-gown, and went to her window; and through it to be on the backside of Marke-lane at the farthest; but, being unused to such fires as followed, I thought it far enough off; and so went to bed again, and to sleep. About seven rose again to dress myself, and there looked out at the window, and saw the fire not so much as it was, and further off. So to my closet to set things to rights, after yesterday's cleaning. By and by Jane comes and tells me that she hears that above 300 houses have been burned down tonight by the fire we saw, and that it is now burning down all Fish Street, by London Bridge. So I made myself ready presently, and walked to the tower; and there got up upon one of the high places . . . and there I did see the houses at the end of the bridge all on fire, and an infinite great fire on this and the other side the end of the bridge; which, among other people, did trouble me for poor little Michell and Sarah on the bridge. So now with my heart full of trouble, to the lieutenant of the Tower, who tells me that it begun this morning in the King's baker's house in Pudding-lane, and that it hath burned St. Magnus's Church and most part of Fish Street already. . . .

September 5, 1666.—I lay down in the office again upon W. Hewer's quilt, being mighty weary, and sore in my feet with going till I was hardly able to stand. About two in the morning my wife calls me up, and tells me of new cries of fire, it being come to Barking Church, which is the bottom of our land. I up; and finding it so, resolved presently to take her away, and did, and took my gold, which was about £2350, W. Hewer and Jane down to Proundy's boat to Woolwich; but, Lord! what a sad sight it was by moonlight to see the whole city almost on fire, that you might see it plain at Woolwich, as if you were by it. There, when I come, I find the gates shut, but no guard kept at all; which troubled me, because of discourse now begun, that there is plot in it, and that the French had done it. I got the gates open, and to Mr. Shelden's, where I locked up my gold, and charged my wife and W. Hewer never to leave the room without one of them in it, night or day. So back again, by the way seeing my goods well in the lighters at Deptford, and watched well by people. Home, and whereas I expected to have seen our house on fire, it being now about seven o'clock, it was not. But to the fire, and there find greater hopes than I expected; for my confidence of finding our office on fire was such, that I durst not ask anybody how it was with us, till I come and saw it not burned. But going to the fire, I find, by the blowing up of houses, and the great help given by the workmen out of the King's yards, sent up by Sir W. Penn, there is a good stop given to it, as well as at Marke Lane end as ours; it having only burned the dial of Barking Church, and part of the porch, and was there quenched. I up to the top of Barking steeple, and there saw the saddest sight of desolation that I ever saw; everywhere great fires, oil-cellars, and brimstone, and other things burning. I became afeard to stay there long, and therefore down again as fast as I could, the fire being spread as far as I could see it; and to Sir W. Pen's, and there eat a piece of cold meat, having eaten nothing since Sunday, but the remains of Sunday's dinner. . . .

September 17, 1666.—Lay long in bed, talking with pleasure with my poor wife, how she used to make coal fires, and wash my foul clothes with her own hand for me, poor wretch! in our little room at my Lord Sandwich's; for which I ought for ever to love and admire her, and do; and persuade myself she would do the same again, if God should reduce us to it. . . .

May 31, 1669.—. . . And thus ends all that I doubt I shall ever be able to do with my own eyes in the keeping of my Journal, I being not able to do it any longer, having done now so long as to undo my eyes almost every time that I take a pen in my hand; and therefore, resolve, from this time forward, to have it kept by my people in long-hand, and must be contented to set down no more than is fit for them and all the world to know; or, if there be any thing, I must endeavour to keep a margin in my book open, to add, here and there, a note in short-hand with my own hand.

And so I betake myself to that course, which almost as much as to see myself go into my grave: for which, and all the discomforts that will accompany by being blind, the good God prepare me!

You can see in these excerpts that Pepys communicates both the insignificant and the momentous happenings of his daily life. He selects those details that are important to him. Such apparently trivial incidents as beginning the practice of shaving himself (January 6, 1664), accidentally hitting his wife in the head (August 7, 1664), and going to the theater (October 2, 1662) are recorded along with accounts of such historically significant events as a hanging (October 13, 1660), the plague (October 16, 1665) and the great fire of London (September 2, 5, & 17, 1666). But at the particular time they occurred, even those seemingly inconsequential details were important enough to Pepys for him to record them.

Many of those details of daily life reflect values and goals. Some of the passages can be regarded as attempts at self-exploration, self-definition, and a statement of goals for the future. Notice particularly the entry of February 25, 1667 in which he expresses his love and admiration for his wife. Also, in the last entry (May 31, 1669), he reflects on his journal and his failing eyesight.

Throughout the diary, the entries illustrate the associative and episodic structure of personal self-expression. He recounts three separate narratives on July 1, 1660. On October 13, 1660 he comments on the apparently trivial event of setting up shelves in his study after he has recorded a rather unsettling description of the hanging of Major General Harrison.

THE AUTOBIOGRAPHICAL PERSPECTIVE

Autobiographical writing is seen in autobiographies, memoirs, and reminiscences. Such writing results from a consideration of and a reflection on major events in the life of the writer. Although the content is much like personal writing, the events are given more order. The presentation is not as random as it is in journals and diaries. The following specific characteristics are apparent.

- Experiences from the past are recounted.
- Significant events in the life of the writer are explored.
- An effort is made to explain the writer's personality or character.
- The writer's past actions are rationalized or justified.

Experiences from the Past

The writer of autobiography may look to the distant past as well as to the immediate past. An adult may relate events from childhood. An understanding of the self, as it relates to a person's formative years, provides a basis for explaining recent actions and current values.

Significant Events

In looking back over past events, the writer of autobiography will select those events that are the most significant, those that, for some reason (perhaps because of subsequent events), retain an importance in the writer's memory. These memories may be focused on significant places or important people, for example.

Explanation of the Writer's Personality

The writer of autobiography may make an attempt to explain his or her identity and perhaps tell how that identity developed as a result of significant events. The events and experiences of the past form a pattern that adds up to the present personality.

Rationalization of Actions

Since the gap between the time when the events occur and the time when they are recorded is greater in autobiographical self-expression than it is in personal writing, the goals and values of the writer may have changed. Consequently, there is an effort to make the past actions fit into the present value system. When experiences from the past are recalled, they may be somewhat distorted by time and changed by the process of recording them.

AN EXAMPLE

In the following excerpt from Book I of *Confessions* written by Jean Jacques Rousseau in 1783, we can see how a significant event from Rousseau's childhood is explained and rationalized in light of his values as an adult. Through his recollection of the event, we get a better understanding of Rousseau's personality. The characteristics of autobiographical self-expression are clearly illustrated in the selection.

THE END OF CHILDHOOD

JEAN JACQUES ROUSSEAU

One day I was learning my lesson by myself in the room next to the kitchen. The servant had put Mademoiselle Lambercier's combs in front of the fireplace to dry. When she came back to fetch them, she found one with a whole row of teeth broken. Who was to blame for the damage? No one except myself had entered the room. On being questioned, I denied that I had touched the comb. M. and Mademoiselle Lambercier both began to admonish, to press, and to threaten me; I obstinately persisted in my denial; but the evidence was too strong, and outweighed all my protestations, although it was the first time that I had been found to lie so boldly. The matter was regarded as serious, as in fact it deserved to be. The mischievousness, the falsehood, the obstinacy appeared equally deserving of punishment; but this time it was not by Mademoiselle Lambercier that chastisement was inflicted. My uncle Bernard was written to and he came. My poor cousin was accused of another equally grave offence; we were involved in the same punishment. It was terrible. Had they wished to look for the remedy in the evil itself and to deaden forever my depraved senses, they could not have set to work better, and for a long time my senses left me undisturbed.

They could not draw from me the desired confession. Although I was several times brought up before them and reduced to a pitiable condition, I remained unshaken. I would have endured death, and made up my mind to do so. Force was obliged to yield to the diabolical obstinacy of a child—as they called my firmness. At last I emerged from this cruel trial, utterly broken, but triumphant.

It is now nearly fifty years since this incident took place, and I have no fear of being punished again for the same thing. Well, then, I declare in the sight of heaven that I was innocent of the offence, that I neither broke nor touched the comb, that I never went near the fireplace, and had never even thought of doing so. It would be useless to ask me how the damage was done; I do not know, and I cannot understand; all that I know for certain is, that I had nothing to do with it.

Imagine a child, shy and obedient in ordinary life, but fiery, proud, and unruly in his passions: a child who had always been led by the voice of reason and always treated with gentleness, justice, and consideration, who had not even a notion of injustice, and who for the first time becomes acquainted with so terrible an example of it on the part of the very people whom he most loves and respects! What an upset of ideas! what a disturbance of feelings! what revolution in his heart, in his brain, in the whole of his little intellectual and moral being! Imagine all this, I say, if possible. As for myself, I feel incapable of disentangling and following up the least trace of what then took place within me.

I had not sense enough to feel how much appearances were against me, and to put myself in the place of others. I kept to my own place, and all that I felt was the harshness of a frightful punishment for an offence which I had not committed. The bodily pain, although, severe, I felt but little; all I felt was indignation, rage, despair. My cousin, whose case was almost the same, and who had been punished for an involuntary mistake as if it had been a premeditated act, following my example, flew into a rage, and worked himself up to the same pitch of excitement as myself. Both in the same bed, we embraced each other with convulsive transports: we felt suffocated; and when at length our young hearts, somewhat relieved, were able to vent their wrath, we sat upright in bed and began to shout, times without number, with all our might: Carnifex! carnifex! carnifex!

While I write these words, I feel that my pulse beats faster; those moments will always be present to me though I should live a hundred thousand years. That first feeling of violence and injustice has remained so deeply graven on my soul, that all the ideas connected with it bring back to me my first emotion; and this feeling, which, in its origin, had reference only to myself, has become so strong in itself and so completely detached from all personal interest, that, when I see or hear of any act of injustice— whoever is the victim of it, and wherever it is committed—my heart kindles with rage, as if the effect of it recoiled upon myself. When I read of the cruelties of a ferocious tyrant, the crafty atrocities of a rascally priest, I would gladly set out to plunge a dagger into the heart of such wretches, although I had to die for it a hundred times. I have often put myself in a perspiration, pursuing or stoning a cock, a cow, a dog, or any animal which I saw tormenting another merely because it felt itself the stronger. This impulse may be natural to me, and I believe that it is; but the profound impression left upon me by the first injustice I suffered was too long and too strongly connected with it, not to have greatly strengthened it.

With the above incident the tranquillity of my childish life was over. From that moment I ceased to enjoy a pure happiness, and even at the present day I feel that the recollection of the charms of my childhood ceases there.

In this selection Rousseau looks at an event from his past—an unfair punishment for a misdeed he was wrongly accused of. It is an event that affected him dramatically and changed him significantly, so much so that he says that with that event "the recollection of the charms" of his "childhood" cease. The significance of the event is understood retrospectively.

THE RITUAL PERSPECTIVE

Ritual self-expression includes not only documents that are individual and personal (e.g. wills and prayers), but also writing that is the collective expression of a group (e.g. creeds, declarations, and manifestoes). All self-expression with a ritual perspective has the following characteristics.

- The self is presented in terms of an agreed upon value system.
- A repetitive or parallel structure is used.
- The importance of the document is emphasized.
- Traditional language and/or traditional forms are used.

An Agreed Upon Value System

The content of ritual self-expression conforms to whatever set of values the writer has adopted. Those values usually tend to reflect a value system agreed upon by a culture or a society.

The following example, "The Apostle's Creed," illustrates such a set of values, values and beliefs found in the doctrine of the Catholic Church. The document, many centuries old, is a collective affirmation of the traditions of the Christian faith.

> I believe in God the Father Almighty, Creator of Heaven and earth; And in Jesus Christ, His only son, our Lord; Who was conceived by the Holy Ghost, born of the Virgin Mary, suffered under Pontius Pilate, was crucified, died, and was buried; He descended into hell; the third day He rose again from the dead; He ascended into Heaven, sitteth at the right hand of God, the Father Almighty; From thence He shall come to judge the living and the dead. I believe in the Holy Ghost, the Holy Catholic Church, the communion of saints, the forgiveness of sins, the resurrection of the body, and Life everlasting.

Repetitive or Parallel Structure

Repetitive or parallel writing structures very often reflect and underscore the group's value system. Repetitive words, phrases, and sentence patterns reveal the ritual nature of the writing and emphasize what the writer considers to be important. Repeated words or phrases focus the reader's attention on key elements of that value system. Notice the repetition of the word "I believe" in the example above.

Importance of the Document

Ritual self-expression is most often solemn. This tone emphasizes the importance of the document to the group and to the culture as a whole. The subject matter of such writings has great significance to the people who preserve the traditions on which the works are based.

Traditional Language and Traditional Forms

Certain words and phrases that have special meanings are used. This traditional language makes us aware that the document itself is important. Works of this kind use language that has appeared over and over in similar documents previously and that reflects the values of the traditions that have produced those works.

AN EXAMPLE

In Benjamin Franklin's will we can see that the distribution of his estate reveals not only his loyalty to his family and friends but also his feeling of responsibility to certain institutions that exist for the public good.

Wills, even though they tend to be highly formalized, reveal a set of values at the core of a person's belief system. Franklin's will gives us an intriguing look at the mind of one of the most original thinkers in Revolutionary America.

THE LAST WILL AND TESTAMENT OF BENJAMIN FRANKLIN

BENJAMIN FRANKLIN

I, Benjamin Franklin, of Philadelphia, printer, late Minister Plenipotentiary from the United States of America to the Court of France, now President of the State of Pennsylvania, do make and declare my last will and testament as follows:

To my son, William Franklin, late Governor of the Jerseys, I give and devise all the lands I hold or have a right to, in the province of Nova Scotia, to hold to him, his heirs, and assigns forever. I also give to him all my books and papers, which he has in his possession, and all debts standing against him on my account books, willing that no payment for, nor restitution of, the same be required of him, by my executors. The part he acted against me in the late war, which is of public notoriety, will account for my leaving him no more of an estate he endeavoured to deprive me of.

Having since my return from France demolished the three houses in Market Street, between Third and Fourth Streets, fronting my dwelling-house, and erected two new and larger ones on the ground, and having also erected another house on the lot which formerly was the passage to my dwelling, and also a printing-office between my dwelling and the front houses; now I do give and devise my said dwelling-house, wherein I now live, my said three new houses, my printing-office and the lots of ground thereto belonging; also my small lot and house in Sixth Street, which I bought of the widow Henmarsh; also my pasture-ground which I have in Hickory Lane, with the buildings thereon; also my house and lot on the North side of Market Street, now occupied by Mary Jacobs, together with two houses and lots behind the same, and fronting on Pewter-Platter Alley; also my lot of ground in Arch Street, opposite the church-burying ground, with the buildings thereon erected; also all my silver plate, pictures, and household goods, of every kind, now in my said dwelling-place, to my daughter, Sarah Bache, and to her husband, Richard Bache, to hold to them for and during their natural lives, and the life of the longest liver of them, and from and after the decease of the survivor of them, I do give, devise, and bequeath to all children already born, or to be born of my said daughter, and to their heirs and assigns forever, as tenants in common, and not as joint tenants. . . .

All the lands near the Ohio, and the lots near the centre of Philadelphia, which I lately purchased of the State, I give to my son-in-law, Richard Bache, his heirs and assigns forever; I also give him the bond I have against him, of two thousand and one hundred and seventy-two pounds, five shillings, together with the interest that shall or may accrue thereon, and direct the same to be delivered up to him by my executors, canceled, requesting that, in consideration thereof, he would immediately after my decease manumit and set free his Negro man Bob. . . . I also discharge him, my said son-in-law, from all claim and rent of moneys due to me, on book account or otherwise. I also give him all my musical instruments.

The king of France's picture, set with four hundred and eight diamonds, I give to my daughter, Sarah Bache, requesting, however, that she would not form any of those diamonds into ornaments either for herself or daughters, and thereby introduce or countenance the expensive, vain, and useless fashion of wearing jewels in this country; and those immediately connected with the picture may be preserved with the same.

I give and devise to my dear sister, Jane Mecom, a house and lot I have in Unity Street, Boston, nor or late under the care of Mr. Jonathan Williams, to her and to her heirs and assigns for ever. I also give her the yearly sum of fifty pounds sterling, during life, to commence at my death, and to be paid to her annually out of the interests or dividends arising on twelve shares which I have since my arrival at Philadelphia purchased in the Bank of North America and, at her decease, I give the said twelve shares in the bank to my daughter, Sarah Bache, and her husband, Richard Bache. But it is my express will and desire that, after the payment of the above fifty pounds sterling annually to my said sister, my said daughter be allowed to apply the residue of the interest or dividends on those shares to her sole and separate use, during the life of my said sister, and afterwards the whole of the interest or dividends thereof as her private pocket money. I give the right I have to take up to three thousand acres of land in the State of Georgia, granted to me by the government of that State, to my grandson, William Temple Franklin, his heirs and assigns forever. I also give to my grandson, William Temple Franklin, the bond and judgment I have against him of four thousand pounds sterling, my right to the same to cease upon the day of his marriage; and if he dies unmarried, my will is, that the same be recovered and divided among my other grandchildren, the children of my daughter, Sarah Bache, in such manner and form as I have herein before given to them the other parts of my estate.

The philosophical instruments I have in Philadelphia I give to my ingenious friend, Hopkinson. . . .

I give to my grandson, Benjamin Franklin Bache, all the types and printing materials, which I now have in Philadelphia, with the complete letter foundry, which, in the whole, I suppose to be worth near one thousand pounds; but if he should die under age, then I do order the same to be sold by my executors, the survivors or survivor of them, and the moneys be equally divided among all the rest of my said daughter's children, or their representatives, each one on coming of age to take his or her share, and the children of such of them as may die under age to represent and to take the share and proportion of, the parent so dying, each one to receive his or her part of such share as they come of age.

With regard to my books, those I had in France and those I left in Philadelphia, being now assembled together here, and a catalogue made of them, it is my intention to dispose of them as follows: My "History of the Academy of Sciences," in sixty or seventy volumes quarto, I give to the Philosophical Society of Philadelphia, of which I have the honour to be President. My collection in folio of "Les Arts et les Metiers," I give to the American Philosophical Society, established in New England, of which I am a member. My quarto edition of the same, "Arts et Metiers," I give to the Library Company of Philadelphia. Such and so many of my books as I shall mark on my said catalogue with the name of my grandson, Benjamin Franklin Bache, I do hereby give to him; and such and so many of my books as I shall mark on the said catalogue with the name of my grandson, William Bache, I do hereby give to him; and such as shall be marked with the name of Jonathan Williams, I hereby give to my cousin of that name. The residue and remainder of all my books, manuscripts, and papers, I do give to my grandson, William Temple Franklin. My share in the Library Company of Philadelphia, I give to my grandson, Benjamin Franklin Bache, confiding that he will permit his brothers and sisters to share in the use of it.

I was born in Boston, New England, and owe my first instructions in literature to the free grammar schools established there. I therefore give one hundred pounds sterling to my executors, to be by them, the survivors or survivor of them, paid over to the managers or directors of the free schools in my native town of Boston, to be by them, or by those person or persons, who shall have the superintendance and management of the said schools, put out to interest, and so continued at interest forever, which interest annually shall be laid out in silver medals, and given as honorary rewards annually by the directors of the said free schools belonging to the said town, in such manner as to the discretion of the selectmen of the said town shall seem meet. Out of the salary that may remain due to me as President of the State, I do give the sum of two thousand pounds sterling to my executors, to be by them, the survivors or survivor of them, paid over to such person or persons as the legislature of this State by an act of Assembly shall appoint to receive the same in trust, to be employed for making the river Schuylkill navigable. . . .

During the number of years I was in business as a stationer, printer, and postmaster, a great many small sums became due for books, advertisements, postage of letters, and other matters, which were not collected when, in 1757, I was sent by the Assembly to England as their agent, and by subsequent appointments continued there till 1775, when on my return, I was immediately engaged in the affairs of Congress, and sent to France in 1776, where I remained nine years, not returning till 1785, and the said debts, not being demanded in such a length of time, are become in a manner obsolete, yet are nevertheless justly due. These, as they are stated in my great folio ledger E, I bequeath to the contributors to the Pennsylvania Hospital, hoping that those debtors, and the descendants of such as are deceased, who now, as I find, make some difficulty of satisfying such antiquated demands as just debts, may, however, be induced to pay or give them as charity to that excellent institution. I am sensible that much must inevitably be lost, but I hope something considerable may be recovered. It is possible, too, that some of the parties charged may have existing old, unsettled accounts against me; in which case the managers of the said hospital will allow and deduct the amount, or pay the balance if they find it against me.

My debts and legacies being all satisfied and paid, the rest and residue of all my estate, real and personal, not herein expressly disposed of, I do give and bequeath to my son and daughter, Richard and Sarah Bache.

I request my friends, Henry Hill, Esquire, John Jay, Esquire, Francis Hopkinson, Esquire, and Mr. Edward Duffield, of Benfield, in Philadelphia County, to be the executors of this my last will and testament; and I hereby nominate and appoint them for that purpose.

I would have my body buried with as little expense or ceremony as may be. I revoke all former wills by me made, declaring this only to be my last.

In witness thereof, I have hereunto set my hand and seal, this seventeenth day of July, in the year of our Lord, one thousand seven hundred and eighty-eight.

B. Franklin

Signed, sealed, published, and declared by the above named Benjamin Franklin, for and as his last will and testament, in the presence of us.

Abraham Shoemaker, John Jones, George Moore.

Franklin defines himself in several ways at the beginning of his will, as a printer, as a diplomat, and as a politician. His values are revealed both by his possessions and by the people he leaves them to. The language of the document reflects the traditional wording of wills, a repetitive form indicating how the decedent's estate should be handled. Because it is a legal document, the will is of obvious importance.

THE INTERPERSONAL PERSPECTIVE

Although, at first glance, *interpersonal self-expression* might seem to be a contradiction in terms, it is an appropriate name for personal correspondence and friendly letters because this kind of writing involves a relationship between two people, and while the message is addressed to another person, it is, at the same time, a revelation of the writer's *self*. It is because of the close relationship between the two people involved that such writing tends to be expressive. The writer feels free to open up to the other person. Interpersonal self-expression has the following characteristics.

- Matters of mutual interest to the writer and reader are addressed.
- An ongoing relationship is revealed.
- A level of intimacy is established or maintained between the writer and reader.
- A personal or social obligation is fulfilled.

Matters of Mutual Interest

The content of interpersonal writing focuses on topics that the writer and reader have in common. A bond between the two is created by shared values or shared experiences. The interpersonal communication itself intensifies the bond by contributing a new set of shared experiences and by reinforcing the values the correspondents have in common.

Ongoing Relationship

Since the communication in friendly letters usually occurs because the two people involved are living apart and perhaps because they have been separated for a period of time, the content of such writing may involve asking and answering questions. There is an implicit assumption that the correspondence will be ongoing and that the questions will probably be answered at sometime in the future. Even if no questions are asked, there is an implicit expectation of a continuing dialogue.

Level of Intimacy

Depending on the relationship between the writer and the reader, a certain level of intimacy is established or maintained. Because of this intimacy, the writer feels comfortable sharing emotional responses with the reader. At times, if the people involved are intimate enough, they share a private language known only to the two of them.

Personal or Social Obligation

Letters between two friends may fulfill a social obligation between them. Expectations are created and fulfilled by the correspondence. Just as a conversation between two people assumes certain rules of etiquette, so does interpersonal correspondence.

AN EXAMPLE

Georgia O'Keeffe was one of the most important American Modernist painters of the 20th century. She was known for her dramatic images that included skyscrapers, flowers, and Southwestern landscapes. The following personal letter reveals O'Keeffe's spontaneous emotional feelings and illustrates how interpersonal self-expression involves a sharing of those feelings.

LETTER TO ANITA POLLITZER

GEORGIA O'KEEFFE

[Canyon, Texas, 11 September 1916]
     Tonight I walked into the sunset—to mail some letters—the whole sky—and there is so much of it out here—was just blazing—and grey blue clouds were rioting all through the hotness of it—and the ugly little buildings and windmills looked great against it.
     But some way or other I didn't seem to like the redness much so after I mailed the letters I walked home—and kept on walking—
     The Eastern sky was all grey blue—bunches of clouds—different kinds of clouds—sticking around everywhere and the whole thing—lit up—first in one place—then in another with flashes of lightning—sometimes just sheet lightning—and sometimes sheet lightning with a sharp bright zigzag flashing across it—.
     I walked out past the last house—past the last locust tree—and sat on the fence for a long time—looking—just looking at the lightning—you see there was nothing but sky and flat prairie land—land that seems more like the ocean than anything else I know—There was a wonderful moon—
     Well I just sat there and had a great time all by myself—Not even many night noises—just the wind—
     I wondered what you are doing—
     It is absurd the way I love this country—Then when I came back—it was funny—roads just shoot across blocks anywhere—all the houses looked alike—and I almost got lost—I had to laugh at myself—I couldnt tell which house was home—
     I am loving the plains more than ever it seems—and the SKY—Anita you have never seen SKY—it is wonderful—
                              Pat.

In this letter, Georgia O'Keeffe is writing about herself. The main idea is a implied self-definition: *I am a lover of the plains.* She uses intimate personal language and she reveals an emotional response of becoming aware of how she is "loving the plains." She reveals an ongoing relationship when she says, "I wondered what you are doing." She assumes that what interests her, her emotional response to the plains and her aesthetic values, will also interest Anita Pollitzer.

COMBINATIONS

The different kinds of self-expression blend together rather easily. In a diary, elements of autobiography may appear. In friendly letters, the writer may communicate the kinds of minor details of life that we see in diaries and journals. "The Way" by John Graves, although primarily autobiographical, exhibits some characteristics of personal self-expression as well.

WRITING STRATEGIES

If your purpose is expressive, all you have to do is write whatever you want to write. Sometimes that's harder to do than you would think. To begin, write down whatever comes into your head. Get words down on paper in whatever order they come to you. You can arrange them later. Think of expressive writing as a sort of laboratory where you can experiment with language. You have the freedom to say whatever you want to say.

As you think about your topic, consider the following questions.

- How do you feel about the topic—what emotions does it arouse?
- How does it affect you?
- How does it make you feel when you think about it?
- What do you want to do when you think about it?
- What events in your life do you associate with your topic?
- Why do you think you feel the way you do?
- How does it relate to your value system?
- How does it affect your goals for the future?

Literary Writing

From the myths and songs in primal cultures to modern poetry and fiction, artists have created structures with language that please and delight their audiences. All literary works, no matter how different they may seem, have one thing in common: the writer has deliberately arranged the words so that the effect produced in the reader or audience is one of pleasure.

In this respect, literature is like other art forms. They all please us, or at least have as their purpose to please. One of the outcomes of the aesthetic pleasure that art gives us is this: a work of art will bear repetition. We listen to music we like over and over. We may go back to see again a movie we especially enjoyed. We hang paintings or posters on our walls and look at them, or at least see them, almost everyday. So it is with literary writing. We may reread a poem or a story many times and get just as much pleasure from it each time.

It is the arrangement of words in literary writing that appeals to our aesthetic sensibilities. The literary structures created by the various combinations of words and images please us when we read them. Even if the images themselves may not be appealing, as in the case of horror stories, the structuring of them in a dramatic form may produce enjoyment in many readers.

Literature is most commonly classified by genre: poetry, drama, the short story, and the novel. A major distinction is usually made between poetry and prose. Poetry is traditionally defined as a rhythmical use of language. Everyone is familiar with the rhythms and rhymes of traditional verse, a regular repetition of stresses and sounds. Prose, on the other hand, more closely resembles the patterns of ordinary, everyday speech and is the kind of language used in fiction. In modern literature, however, the distinction between prose and poetry has diminished. Modern poetry relies less on strict metrical rhythms and modern fiction has become increasingly poetic. Some nonfiction may be literary if its purpose is to entertain. Humorous essays are clearly literary.

No matter what form it takes, literary writing has as its purpose to create an aesthetically pleasing effect with language. To produce this effect a literary work will have theme, tension, verisimilitude, and aesthetic language.

GENERAL CHARACTERISTICS

- Theme and artistic unity are apparent.
- Tension is created.
- Verisimilitude is present.
- Language that creates an aesthetic response is used.

THEME AND ARTISTIC UNITY

In a work called *Poetics*, the Greek philosopher Aristotle said that a literary work must have a beginning, a middle, and an end. Although it may seem to be a statement of the obvious, it nevertheless describes an important feature of literary art. This statement means that a literary work is unified, that the ending of the work comes inevitably out of what has come before. Each part of the work is connected to every other part. The recognition of that interconnectedness of the events is called unity of plot. In addition to plot, time and place have also been traditionally regarded as unities, especially in drama.

In modern literature, we usually recognize other elements that unify a work, such as characterization, style, symbolism, and theme. When we talk about the *theme* of a literary work, we are recognizing the unity of the work that allows us to identify a theme. For instance, a theme commonly developed in Renaissance poetry is that art is timeless and immortal. A theme expresses in a single statement the combined effect that all elements in a literary work produce.

TENSION

The structure of literary writing creates tension. Some elements, such as dramatic action, create tension through conflict. A character in a story may be involved in either physical, social, or psychological conflict. A physical conflict is usually external, with one character pitted against another character or against the forces of nature. A social conflict occurs when a character is at odds with the conventions or mores of society. Psychological conflict is internal, caused by a dilemma in the mind of the character.

Tension is also created when two contrasting elements are juxtaposed, when two things that are different are put side by side. For instance, when two characters who are very different from each other are put into a plot together, they serve to create such a contrast. Even if no overt physical conflict is developed, the difference between the two characters creates tension.

VERISIMILITUDE

The author of a literary work presents events or scenes by using a variety of literary devices that shape the reader's perception of the experiences recorded in the work. Elements such as a setting, dialogue, and characterization are used to create a plot or a scene. These devices allow the reader to identify with the settings and events depicted in the work. A graphic description of the setting, a vivid portrayal of a character, or a conversation between characters will enable the reader to become a part of the imaginative world of the writer.

AESTHETIC LANGUAGE

A literary artist deliberately selects words that have an aesthetic effect on the reader. This is the hallmark of literary writing and is especially apparent in the author's use of imagery, symbolism, connotations, rhythm, and sound patterns.

Imagery

Imagery involves choosing a word or phrase that engages the senses. When we read an image in a work of literature, that image involves us in the work in a way that is different from our objective understanding of the meaning of the word or words used to create the image. Images are of two types: literal and figurative.

Literal Images

As the word implies, these images mean exactly what they say. In literary writing, however, the writer presents them to the reader in an unusual way. They are graphic and vivid and take advantage of the connotations of the words used to create them. Instead of saying, "I saw a beautiful sunset," the literary artist might say something like, "I saw a brilliant orange sunset streaked with clouds of rose and plum." Instead of saying, "I touched a tree," the literary artist might say, "I rubbed the rough bark of the tree, fingering the tiny bits of it that crumbled in my hand and inhaling its pungent aroma." Notice that even though the images are literal, the second wording is more concrete and vivid. The images of the second version in each case engage our senses with more specific detail and take advantage of the connotative meanings of the words.

Figurative Images

Figurative language is a prominent feature of much literary writing, although literary works certainly can be written without using any figures of speech at all. Still, the use of figurative language is one of those features that tells us that we may be looking at a work which is primarily literary. In contrast to literal images, figurative images can be thought of as non-literal images because the impressions they present to the reader are not intended to be realistic. The three most commonly used figurative images (figures of speech) are the simile, the metaphor, and personification.

A simile is a comparison between two different objects or concepts using the word *like* or *as*. Look at the following example:

The clouds look like fluffy balls of cotton.

The comparison is figurative, not literal. Clouds and cotton balls are not in the same class of things, but the comparison seems appropriate because it calls our attention to the similarity in the appearance of the two things and deepens our response by allowing us to associate the image of clouds with the sense of touch, the feel of cotton balls.

The comparison made in the metaphor is more direct, as in the following example:

Look at those fluffy balls of cotton floating in the sky.

The effect of the metaphor is more startling than the effect of the simile, but the comparison is the same.

Personification gives human characteristics to animals, plants, objects, or abstractions, as in the following example:

The clouds are smiling at us.

Clouds don't smile; people do. The comparison is figurative.

Symbolism

A symbol is an object, a person, a place, or an action that stands for something else in addition to its literal meaning in the literary work. In other words, the symbol suggests a meaning beyond itself. There are universal symbols and symbols that are particular to the literary work itself. A universal symbol has the same meaning in a number of different literary works because of some qualities inherent in the symbol itself. For instance, the ocean is often used as a symbol of time or eternity.

In literature almost anything can be a symbol, depending on how it is used in the work. John Keats, in his "Ode on a Grecian Urn," used the image of an urn with figures depicted on it to symbolize the timelessness of art.

Connotative Language

As we saw in Chapter 1, connotations are the associated, emotional meanings of words. (Denotations are the literal dictionary meanings.) Authors of literary works are very sensitive to the connotations of words and deliberately select language that will have an emotional effect on the reader.

Rhythm and Sound Patterns

Literary works, particularly poems, are characterized by the use of sound patterns and rhythms that help create mood and tone. The following excerpt from John Keats' "La Belle Dame sans Merci" illustrates how rhythm and rhyme help create a feeling of sadness and despondency.

> *O what can ail thee, knight at arms,*
> *Alone and palely loitering?*
> *The sedge has wither'd from the lake,*
> *And no birds sing.*

Although the regular pattern of stressed and unstressed syllables creates an even emotional tone throughout the stanza, the shortened last line makes the mood suddenly somber. Coupled with the words "alone," "palely," and "wither'd," this use of rhythm creates the impression of a plaintive, mournful scene.

The rhyme scheme follows the traditional structure of the ballad stanza, the second and fourth lines rhyming. The repetition of the sound -*ing* focuses our attention on the words "loitering" (suggesting passivity) and "sing" (suggesting activity). The last line, however, tells us that the activity of singing is absent and this reinforces the dominant impression of sadness.

AN EXAMPLE

The following excerpt from John Gardner's novel entitled *October Light* illustrates how the literary narrative creates tension and interest through conflict as well as through imagery, both literal and figurative.

AN INTERLUDE

JOHN GARDNER

While his great-aunt Estelle was thinking of Notre Dame, Terence Parks stood in the old man's sitting room-bedroom, turning the French horn around and around, emptying water from the tubing. He was as shy a boy as ever lived, as shy as the girl seated now on the sagging, old fashioned bed with her hands on the flute in her lap. She, Margie Phelps, gazed steadily at the floor, her silver-blonde hair falling straight past her shoulders, soft as flax. Her face was serious, though she was prepared to smile if he should wish her to. She wore a drab green dress that was long and (he could not know) expensive, striped kneesox, and fashionably clunky shoes. As for Terence, he had brown hair that curled below his ears, glasses without which he was utterly helpless, and a small chin. He had, at least in his own opinion, nothing to recommend him, not even a sense of humor. He therefore dressed, always, with the greatest care—dark blue shirts, never with a shirttail hanging out, black trousers, black shoes and belt. He fitted the mouthpiece back into the horn and glanced at Margie. He had had for some time a great, heart-slaughtering crush on her, though he hadn't told her that, or anyone else. In his secret distress, he was like the only Martian in the world. As if she'd known he would do it, Margie looked up for an instant at exactly the moment he glanced at her, and immediately—blushing—both of them looked down.

He set his horn down carefully on the chair and went over to the window at the foot of the bed to look out. A noisy, blustering wind had come up, pushing large clouds across the sky, a silver-toothed wolf pack moving against the moon, quickly consuming it, throwing the hickory tree, the barn and barnyard into darkness. He could hear what sounded like a gate creaking, metal against metal.

"Is it raining yet?" she asked, her voice almost inaudible.

As she came up timidly behind him, Terence moved over a little to give her room at the window.

Her hand on the windowsill was white, almost blue. He could easily reach over and touch it. In the living room behind them—the door was part way open—the grown-ups were laughing and talking, DeWitt Thomas still picking his guitar and singing. You couldn't hear the words. He looked again at her hand, then at the side of her face, then quickly back out at the night.

"Rain scares me," she said. Though her face turned only a little, he could feel her watching him.

The moon reappeared, the black clouds sweeping along like objects in a flood. Terence put his hand on the windowsill near hers, as if accidentally. He listened for the sound of someone coming into the room and realized only now that the door to his left went to the back entryway and, beyond that, the kitchen. He felt panic, thinking they might go out that door unmissed. Something white blew across the yard, moving slowly, like a form in a dream.

"What's that?" she asked, startled, and put her hand on his. Her head came slightly closer and, despite the violence of the storm in his chest, he smelled her hair.

"Fertilizer bag, I think," he said.

"What?" she said.

He said it again, this time loud enough to hear. She did not draw her hand away, though the touch was light, as if at the slightest sign she would quickly remove it. His mind raced almost as fast as his heart, and he pressed closer to the window, pretending to follow the white thing's ghostly flight. Again he smelled her hair, and now her breath—a warm scent of apple.

As for Dr. Phelps' granddaughter Margie, her heart thudded and her brain tingled; she half believed she might faint. Her friend Jennifer at school had told her weeks ago that Terry Parks had a crush on her, and she hadn't doubted it, though it seemed to her a miracle. When he played his French horn in the school orchestra or at the Sage City Symphony, his playing gave her goosebumps, and when they had answering parts in the woodwind quintet, she blushed. Finding him here at the Pages tonight had been a kind of confirmation of the miracle, and when the grown-ups had suggested that the two of them might play duets together, and had sent them here, so that the adults could talk . . .

Now another cloud, larger than those before it, was swallowing the moon. The noise of the wind half frightened, half thrilled her. The barn stood out stark, sharply outlined. The white thing—fertilizer bag, that was right—was snagged in a fence, gray as bone, suddenly inert.

He moved his hand a little, closing it on hers. She drew her breath in sharply. Was someone coming?

"You kids want baked apples?" Virginia Hicks called from the doorway behind them.

They parted hands quickly and whirled around, frightened and confused.

"I'll leave them here on the bedside table," Virginia said, smiling. She seemed to have seen nothing. "You two make beautiful music together," she said, and smiled again, with a wave of her cigarette.

Neither of them spoke, heads spinning, smiling at the floor. Virginia left them.

Something thudded hard against the house, a small limb, perhaps, but no window broke, the walls did not sway, and so they laughed, embarrassed by their momentary fear. As they laughed they walked toward the bedside table where the baked apples stood oozing juice.

"Mmm, baked apples," Margie said softly. She picked up her plate and seated herself primly on the bedside, eyes cast down. Terence came and sat beside her.

"Listen to that wind," he said. The night howled and thudded like an orchestra gone wrong, dissonant and senseless, dangerous, but Margie was happy, for once in her life utterly without fear, except of him. She laid her hand casually on the cover beside her, conscious of the laughter and talk in the next room and also now a sound like arguing, coming from upstairs. She glanced at Terence and smiled. Smiling back, secretive and careful, he put his hand over hers.

Even though this excerpt was taken from a longer work, it has a unity that allows us to think of it as complete. Indeed, within the structure of the novel, it is almost an aside that has little to do with the movement of the plot of the novel as a whole. This beautifully written little scene illustrates all the general characteristics of literary writing outlined above.

Gardner creates verisimilitude through the physical descriptions of the two characters, Terence and Margie, and through the description of the setting. With the characterizations and the creation of a realistic setting the author gives us the feeling that the characters are real and that the events depicted actually happened. We develop some sympathy for Terence and Margie. We willingly involve ourselves as readers in the fiction that the author has created and participate in the events along with the characters. The dialogue also helps us to feel the reality of the scene.

The tension developed in this narrative derives from the characters and the circumstances they find themselves in. Their shyness creates some tension since they are thrown together in a bedroom. Since neither one of them has ever expressed the feelings they have for the other, the internal conflict builds as the plot moves forward. Tension is also increased because the two of them feel isolated: the adults are in the other room and the storm is going on outside.

This episode has artistic unity. Each element—characterization, setting, dialogue, figurative language, and symbolism—moves the plot along towards its inevitable conclusion. Gardner's use of language that evokes an aesthetic response is particularly effective. The description of the clouds as "a silver-toothed wolf pack" is a threatening image that increases the tension of the plot. The symbolism of the storm is effective because it suggests not only turmoil and disorder outside the house, but also reflects the internal conflict, especially in Terence when we are made aware of "the violence of the storm in his chest. . . ."

FOUR KINDS OF LITERARY WRITING

We can divide literary writing into four categories, regardless of the genre. These categories reflect four different approaches to a literary work. These approaches embody the theoretical principles a writer uses to select and organize the content of the work. (Writers may or may not realize that they are using a particular approach.) Some writers consciously adhere to a theory, deliberately following its principles of construction; others simply follow the prevailing literary conventions or imitate what other writers have done without ever consciously adopting a unified, consistent theory. The four approaches to literary writing—expressive, imitative, objective, and pragmatic—address different aspects of the question, "What is literature?"

THE EXPRESSIVE APPROACH

As the name suggests, the expressive approach produces a highly personal kind of literature, similar in some ways to the expressive writing discussed in Chapter 1. The expressive approach became important in England in the nineteenth century when a group of writers that we now call Romantics began to emphasize the importance of recording their emotional responses in the poetry they wrote. The following characteristics are usually found in literature that has been written according to an expressive approach.

- Personal experiences are recorded.
- Personal images and/or symbols are used.
- First person pronouns are used.
- Emotional reactions are expressed.

Personal Experiences

The writer creates the literary work out of personal experiences. Those events that are most memorable to the writer are transformed into literary language.

Personal Images and/or Symbols

The imagery and/or symbolism found in a literary work using the expressive theory of art are based on the personal experience of the writer. These personal images and symbols have meaning to the writer even though they may be almost incomprehensible to the reader.

First Person Pronouns

Almost invariably, works using the expressive theory are written in the first person. The use of first person pronouns is the natural result of the personal focus of the expressive theory of art.

Emotional Reactions

The words the writer uses express emotional reactions to the experiences recorded. As a result, such writing may seem similar to expressive writing.

AN EXAMPLE

In this poem Lyman Grant explores a transformation of the self through an examination of his relationship with "things."

FOUND THINGS

LYMAN GRANT

I stumble from room to room
lost like a young wild boy
whose pockets once were stuffed
with marbles and frogs,
foreign coins and knotted string,
a pocket knife and a hollow
silver locket, but now has
discovered his clothing empty.

He searches under his bed, behind
bookcases, in the far back
reaches of his black closet
where he sometimes hides. Nothing.
Where could it all have gone?
Vanished as strangely and miraculously
as it all had come to him—
found things, gifts and thefts.

This has happened so often.
So this time before he takes
his papers and paints and throws
them to the floor, before he shouts
so that everyone in the distant
corners of his house come running,
this time he stops and imagines
a pile of lost things someone else

will find: unasked for treasures,
coins from places unheard of, string
from kites set free, an empty locket
once held close to a heart in love.
I wander the rooms of my house now,
not searching, not angry, not
even hopeful. I am merely ready
for the miracle of found things.

Grant uses free verse, a form characterized by its lack of constraints and its absence of any formal rhyme schemes to shed light on the wonder of discovering a found object. After establishing that the speaker is an adult, through the use of the simile "like a young wild boy," the poet evokes personal images in the form of common boyhood objects like "marbles . . . frogs, foreign coins and a hollow silver locket." These images hold meaning for the speaker, and seem to evoke in him a wonder of the past, something that he wants to reclaim. The poet seems to be in an agitated state and the reader senses his troubled emotional response in the use of the words "stumble," "angry," and "shouts." The personal pronouns switch between "I" and "he" indicating two selves: a current one that is searching for something and a past self that seems to have reveled in the easy marvel of finding items that evoked wonder. The poet's presence can be felt in the use of the pronouns, which also indicate a conflict he has with himself. Eventually, the anger fades and the sense of wonder returns when the speaker expresses an emotional response stating he is "merely ready for the miracle of found things." Here, the state of agitation that started the poem and sustained most of it has been replaced with a sense of calm acceptance and awe.

THE IMITATIVE APPROACH

The writer using an imitative approach attempts to imitate or mirror reality. A preponderance of the works of modern fiction use the conventions of realism and so reflect the imitative approach. The following characteristics are apparent.

- Real life situations are presented.
- Realistic language is used.
- Realistic, often ordinary, people are depicted.
- Realistic settings are described.

Real Life Situations

Situations that have the feel of reality are presented to the reader. The writer attempts to present the events of the plot in a way that seems to be consistent with similar events that take place in everyday life and so creates an impression of reality.

Realistic Language

Characters in a literary work that has an imitative approach will use language that seems appropriate to that character. In other words, the words used fit with the way we might expect the character to speak if we were to really meet him or her. Even though the dialogue in a literary work may not be exactly the way people say things, it does give the reader the *impression* that the characters are real.

Ordinary People

The characters are like those we might expect to meet in real life. The physical descriptions of the characters add to an overall impression of reality. Further, the writer may make the reader aware of the thoughts of the characters.

Realistic Settings

Settings are described in some detail with an eye toward accurately recreating the place where the action occurs. These descriptions reinforce the impression that the characters are like those we would expect to meet in our everyday existence and that the events narrated are probable.

AN EXAMPLE

Joseph Conrad could easily be considered one of the greatest stylists in the English language. Born in Poland, he only became fluent in English in his twenties while working in the merchant navy. His writing was representative of realism, a literary movement of the late nineteenth century that was concerned with recreating a sensory experience of the world, as well the modernist movement of the twentieth century that broke with established literary conventions and engaged in experimentation. The following passage is taken from his novel, *Lord Jim*, and describes the scene on the deck of the ship, the *Patna*, that is ferrying Muslim pilgrims to Mecca. The excerpt illustrates an imitative approach, writing that imitates life.

THE PASSAGE

JOSEPH CONRAD

A draught of air, fanned from forward by the speed of the ship, passed steadily through the long gloom between the high bulwarks, swept over the rows of prone bodies; a few dim flames in globe-lamps were hung short here and there under the ridge-poles, and in the blurred circles of light thrown down and trembling slightly to the unceasing vibration of the ship appeared a chin upturned, two closed eyelids, a dark hand with silver rings, a meagre limb draped in a torn covering, a head bent back, a naked foot, a throat bared and stretched as if offering itself to the knife. The well-to-do had made for their families shelters with heavy boxes and dusty mats; the poor reposed side by side with all they had on earth tied up in a rag under their heads; the lone old men slept, with drawn-up legs, upon their prayer-carpets, with their hands over their ears and one elbow on each side of the face; a father, his shoulders up and his knees under his forehead, dozed dejectedly by a boy who slept on his back with tousled hair and one arm commandingly extended; a woman covered from head to foot, like a corpse, with a piece of white sheeting, had a naked child in the hollow of each arm; the Arab's belongings, piled right aft, made a heavy mound of broken outlines, with a cargo-lamp swung above, and a great confusion of vague forms behind: gleams of paunchy brass pots, the foot-rest of a deck-chair, blades of spears, the straight scabbard of an old sword leaning against a heap of pillows, the spout of a tin coffee-pot. The patent log on the taffrail periodically rang a single tinkling stroke for every mile traversed on an errand of faith. Above the mass of sleepers a faint and patient sigh at times floated, the exhalation of a troubled dream; and short metallic clangs bursting out suddenly in the depths of the ship, the harsh scrape of a shovel, the violent slam of a furnace-door, exploded brutally, as if the men handling the mysterious things below had their breasts full of fierce anger: while the slim high hull of the steamer went on evenly ahead, without a sway of her bare masts, cleaving continuously the great calm of the waters under the inaccessible serenity of the sky.

Conrad's description is rife with details that paint a vivid picture of the ship and the travelers upon it. Conrad's engages each of the readers' senses in turn. The movement of the vessel is felt in the "draft of air" and the "unceasing vibration of the ship." We see the travelers in Conrad's exquisite use of visual details: "upturned, two closed eyelids, a dark hand with silver rings, a meagre limb draped in a torn covering, a head bent back, a naked foot, a throat bared and stretched." Conrad juxtaposes images to contrast the differences between the people on board. He describes the "well-to-do" having made "shelters with heavy boxes and dusty mats" and a poor "woman covered from head to foot, like a corpse, with a piece of white sheeting, had a naked child in the hollow of each arm." We hear the "short metallic clangs bursting out suddenly in the depths of the ship, the harsh scrape of a shovel, the violent slam of a furnace-door" while the "steamer . . . without a sway of her bare masts, cleav[es] continuously the great calm of the waters under the inaccessible serenity of the sky." This use of sensory details and images make the scene appear vivid and real.

THE OBJECTIVE APPROACH

A writer who is influenced by the objective approach sees literature as existing for its own sake. You may have heard the phrase "Art for Art's Sake" used to characterize this theory. Edgar Allan Poe made reference to it when he spoke of the dignity and nobility of a "poem per se—[a] poem which is a poem and nothing more—[a] poem written solely for the poem's sake." In England during the last part of the nineteenth century, Oscar Wilde reflected the influence of this aesthetic theory in his brilliantly witty dramas. In twentieth-century American poetry a group of poets called the Imagists are a notable example of the influence of this approach. The objective approach has four characteristics.

- The focus on the experience depicted is sharp and limited.
- Structural unity is emphasized.
- The sound and/or appearance of words is emphasized.
- Exact images are used.

Sharp and Limited Focus

The writer operating from the objective approach tends to focus on limited areas of experience or on a small part of a setting using sharp, precise images. There is a concentration of focus. Rather than offering complete explanations, the work may suggest or intimate.

Structural Unity

Everything in the work is unified. The writer strives to use words and images that contribute to the overall aesthetic effect of the work. Often the unity is created by the imagery used or by symbolism.

Emphasis on Sound and/or Appearance of Words

The writer pays special attention to each word, not only to its denotative and connotative meanings, but also to its sound and perhaps even its appearance on the page. Rhythms are often used to create a certain mood.

Exact Images

The writer using an objective approach strives for concreteness and exactness. All the images presented support the aesthetic whole.

AN EXAMPLE

Haiku is a traditional Japanese form of poetry having three lines and a set number of syllables—5, 7, 5. Many haiku incorporate references to a season of the year, and all haiku please the reader because they contain evocative imagery. Here are four examples.

FOUR HAIKU

I

Music from a flute
Asks me to stop and listen
To the soft spring rain.

II

Silver clouds touch earth—
My summer-tired feet and eyes
Must know more than dirt.

III

Rabbit disappears
Hiding among brittle weeds:
Small clouds drift away.

IV

A tree stands cold, still,
Reaches upward for the sky—
I know only now.

These four haiku illustrate how poetry can create a complex set of meanings through a compressed structure. The connotations of the images produce many connections with other images in each of the poems.

In the first haiku, for instance, the image of music is associated with the flute and also, by implication, with the sound of the rain. The music "asks" the poet to "stop and listen." We become aware of both action (listening) and inaction (stopping). In the same moment of realization we discover that the sound of "the soft spring rain" has an aesthetic quality and that is something to be appreciated as we would enjoy hearing the music "from a flute."

In the second poem "silver clouds" exist in contrast to the heat and the "dirt" of summer. And yet the contrast is overcome because the clouds "touch the earth" forming a kind of bond between clouds and earth. The poet is allowed to transcend the oppressiveness of the summer.

The third haiku presents us first with the image of a rabbit disappearing and "hiding among the brittle weeds." The disappearance of the rabbit is somehow connected to the drifting away of the small clouds. The image of "brittle weeds" reinforces the impression that the situation is transitory, and may suggest the coming of autumn, the season of transition from summer to winter.

In the last haiku the impression of yet a fourth season, winter, is suggested by the word "cold." The tension between earth and sky is emphasized by the image of the tree reaching "upward for the sky." Confronted by the stark reality of the barren tree, the poet is struck by the importance of being aware of the present moment.

THE PRAGMATIC APPROACH

The pragmatic approach (also known as the didactic theory) is generally discounted in modern literature; nonetheless, modern literary criticism recognizes its existence by acknowledging the tendency of literature to focus on theme. Certainly, the theory has been important in the history of literature. Aesop's fables are a notable example. Allegories, like John Bunyan's *The Pilgrim's Progress*, are frequently didactic. The characteristics of this approach are these.

- A lesson is taught or a theme is drawn from the experiences reported.
- The experience presented is related to the theme.
- A value system is adopted and/or rejected.
- Harmony is achieved.

A Lesson or Theme

The lesson in a pragmatic literary work may actually be appended to the story or poem in the form of a moral which confirms or rejects social mores. In *Paradise Lost* John Milton says that his purpose in writing the poem is to "justify the ways of God to man." Such a statement reflects the universal scope of the work and reinforces many of the religious tenets of Milton's society.

Relation of Experience to Theme

The theme is often presented by references to moral principles or codes of behavior. If characters are involved, it is through the action of the characters that the writer shapes our attitudes.

A Value System Is Adopted

The lesson or moral of a pragmatic work of literature reflects a referenced value system. Part of the intent of the work is to give support to the values expressed in the work. Satire, making fun of some set of values, is often used to debunk something, frequently some custom or social institution that the writer finds offensive or ridiculous.

Harmony

Harmony means that in the resolution of the narrative, order is restored or maintained. Even though harmony may be disrupted, the ultimate conclusion of works based on a pragmatic theory is a restoration or maintenance of a world consistent with the lesson being taught.

AN EXAMPLE

In this work W. Joe Hoppe expresses a familiar cultural value. By putting the ideas into poetic form, he allows us to see them in a new way.

IN THE PALM OF YOUR HAND

W. JOE HOPPE

There's a planet
There's a past life and a future
There's a question mark
if you follow the line of your thumb
up around your index finger
and trail off around the
remaining three digits
The palm of your hand
holds a light bulb
a bright idea of possibilities
Don't squeeze too tight
it could break and cut
or even burn
The palm of your hand
holds a bird's nest
blue speckled eggs
ready to hatch
two three four
birds in the hand
Everything you need
is within your grasp.

Hoppe's didactic approach is clear in the last two lines of the poem. Hoppe intends to provide a principle to the reader by proposing some type of value system. The attention to the reader is evident through the use of the second person pronoun, *you*, which addresses the reader directly and instructs the reader though the use of directives: "if you follow" and "don't." The poet offers up to the reader a certain philosophy with which to approach life, perhaps, engaging the reader with advice that appears to emphasize self-reliance and actualization. However, the poet also cautions the reader that this outcome can only be achieved through gentle, cautious, and introspective means. With this approach, the poet proposes and eventually embraces a certain value system.

COMBINATIONS

Finding a work of literature that embodies only one of the approaches is rare. For example, even a highly expressive work may reveal a realistic view of the world and draw our attention to concrete images.

WRITING STRATEGIES

If you plan to write a literary piece, there are some things to consider before you begin. Go through your memories, your childhood and adolescence, people you remember. Try to recall an outstanding event and think it through—when it began, what happened, how it ended. Or if you prefer, invent something entirely out of your imagination.

As you think about your literary project, consider these questions.

- What is your story about?
- What are the major events?
- Who are the characters in the story?
- What do the characters look like?
- What conflict is occurring?
- When does the moment of crisis occur?
- How is the conflict resolved?
- Where does the conflict take place?
- What are the physical details of the setting?
- Over what period of time does the story take place?

Persuasive Writing

We encounter persuasion every day. It would be difficult to imagine living in the modern world without coming into contact with attempts to persuade us. We see and hear communication intended to affect or to change our opinions everywhere we turn—on billboards by the side of the road, in magazines, in newspapers, and in conversations with friends, acquaintances, or even total strangers. We are exposed to persuasion probably more than to communications that have any of the other purposes. Someone always seems ready to sell us something or impose an opinion on us.

In persuasive writing, the writer attempts to change a reader's attitudes or beliefs and move the reader to some action based on that change in beliefs. The basis of that attempt is called an *issue*—a point of disagreement or dispute, a debatable proposition, a matter that is unsettled. Issues deal with attitudes, opinions, or questions of morality, ethics, and values.

The following issues address social and public policy debates:

> Whether abortion should be legal.
> Whether nuclear power plants ought to be built.
> Whether we should use drones against foreign terrorists.

Many questions like these are decided by the government or by other social institutions through a process that involves consideration of the arguments on all sides of the issue.

Issues like the following can be found in political and commercial advertising:

Whether you should vote for candidate X.
Whether you ought to buy product Y.
Whether you should donate to charity Z.

Of course, some issues like the following reflect purely personal values:

Whether you should go to Hawaii on vacation.
Whether you should ride your bicycle to work.
Whether you should plant a vegetable garden.

Since persuasion deals with attitudes and opinions, the issues addressed cannot be resolved by the application of scientific logic. Nevertheless, many of the issues considered in persuasive arguments are extremely important and deserve careful consideration. In fact, persuasion is usually the only tool, short of physical force, that we have available to influence and change people's behavior.

In persuasion the argument consists of a claim defending a position on some issue (a debatable proposition). The claim is supported by substantiating details and by appeals to the reader. The argument is authenticated by a warrant (a general belief that the reader will be likely to accept) and is presented with language appropriate to the reader, language the reader can relate to.

GENERAL CHARACTERISTICS

- A claim is made.
- Support for the claim is offered.
- A warrant (a general belief) is present.
- Reader-oriented language is used.

CLAIM

A claim is an assertion about the rightness of the writer's position on the issue. In effect, a claim (usually stated as a general statement and sometimes called a thesis statement) is what the writer wants the reader to accept. For example, a claim derived from the issue of whether or not nuclear power plants ought to be built would be either that *the building of nuclear power plants ought to be continued* or *the building of nuclear power plants ought to be stopped*. These two assertions represent opposing claims made about the issue.

SUPPORT AND GROUNDS

Direct support is an assertion that is made to convince the audience that the claim is a sound one. For instance, the claim that *the building of nuclear power plants ought to be stopped* could be supported by the assertion that *they are dangerous and represent a threat to the environment and to human beings.* Such assertions provide the reasons that directly support the argument.

In addition, the argument must have *grounds*, the underlying foundation for the argument. Depending on the claim and the kind of argument, the grounds may be such things as experimental data, common knowledge, observations, or statistics.

Other support comes in the form of personal experience, slogans, or other devices that appeal to the audience. These *motivational supports*, in the form of appeals, are discussed later.

WARRANT AND BACKING

Warrants are those beliefs that give authenticity to the support and make it relevant to the claim. A warrant is a general belief or principle that most people take for granted. Warrants are often expressed as cultural or social myths.

A social or cultural myth is a value system accepted by a majority of people in a society or culture. If a particular belief is not accepted in a culture, some arguments cannot be made. For instance, in some cultures, throughout history and even in modern times, an argument to support the claim "women should have an education" could not be made because the warrant "all people are created equal" is not part of the belief system of the culture.

A successful persuasive writer shows an understanding of the myths present in a culture. The advertising industry is very sensitive to these myths and uses them to sell products. Changes in public values are reflected almost immediately in advertising.

Warrants are not self-evident, so they may require additional backing to make them acceptable to the audience. Usually such backing establishes a broader context for the principles expressed by the warrant.

READER-ORIENTED LANGUAGE

The writer of persuasion usually has a specific audience in mind, so he or she uses language appropriate to that reader. By using language that the reader finds familiar, the writer has an easier time getting the reader to agree with the claim, so any kind of language that promotes that end is used. As a result, the writer may use everyday speech, slang, jargon, or Standard Edited American English, if that is what the reader expects and will accept. The language is also appropriate to the situational context, that is, the occasion for the writing. A situational context tells the writer what kind of audience is being addressed and, as a result, it influences the kind of language used.

The writer may also personalize the language by using second person pronouns (*you, your, yours*) or imperative sentences (commands) to draw the reader into the argument and gain identification with the reader. It is important for the writer to know who the reader is.

AN EXAMPLE

The following article by Anna Quindlen illustrates the characteristics of persuasive writing.

DEATH PENALTY'S FALSE PROMISE: AN EYE FOR AN EYE

ANNA QUINDLEN

Ted Bundy and I go back a long way, to a time when there was a series of unsolved murders in Washington State known only as the Ted murders. Like a lot of other reporters, I'm something of a crime buff. But the Washington Ted murders—and the ones that followed in Utah, Colorado and finally in Florida, where Ted Bundy was convicted and sentenced to die—fascinated me because I could see myself as one of the victims. I looked at the studio photographs of young women with long hair, pierced ears, easy smiles, and I read the descriptions: polite, friendly, quick to help, eager to please. I thought about being approached by a handsome young man asking for help, and I knew if I had been in the wrong place at the wrong time I would have been a goner.

By the time Ted finished up in Florida, law enforcement authorities suspected he had murdered dozens of young women. He and the death penalty seemed made for each other.

The death penalty and I, on the other hand, seem to have nothing in common. But Ted Bundy had made me think about it all over again, now that the outlines of my 60s liberalism have been filled in with a decade as a reporter covering some of the worst back alleys in New York City and three years a mother who, like most, would lay down her life for her kids.

Simply put, I am opposed to the death penalty. I would tell that to any judge or lawyer undertaking the voir dire of jury candidates in a state in which the death penalty can be imposed. That is why I would be excused from such a jury. In a rational, completely cerebral way, I think the killing of one human being as punishment for the killing of another makes no sense and is inherently immoral.

But whenever my response to an important subject is rational and completely cerebral, I know there is something wrong with it—and so it is here. I have always been governed by my gut, and my gut says I am hypocritical about the death penalty. That is, I do not in theory think that Ted Bundy, or others like him, should be put to death. But if my daughter had been the one clubbed to death as she slept in a Tallahassee sorority house, and if the bite mark left in her buttocks had been one of the prime pieces of evidence against the young man charged with her murder, I would with the greatest pleasure kill him myself.

The State of Florida will not permit the parents of Bundy's victims to do that, and in a way, that is the problem with an emotional response to capital punishment. The only reason for a death penalty is to exact retribution. Is there anyone who really thinks that it is a deterrent, that there are considerable numbers of criminals out there who think twice about committing crimes because of the sentence involved? The ones I have met in the course of my professional duties have either sneered at the justice system, where they can exchange one charge for another with more ease than they could return a shirt to a clothing store, or they have simply believed that it is the other guy who will get caught, get convicted, get the stiffest sentence. Of course, the death penalty would act as a deterrent by eliminating recidivism, but then so would life without parole, albeit at greater taxpayer expense.

I don't believe that deterrence is what most proponents seek from the death penalty anyhow. Our most profound emotional response is to want criminals to suffer as their victims did. When a man is accused of throwing a child from a high-rise terrace, my emotional—some might say hysterical—response is that he should be given an opportunity to see how endless the seconds are from the 31st story to the ground. In a civilized society that will never happen. And so what many people want from the death penalty, they will never get.

Death is death, you may say, and you would be right. But anyone who has seen someone die suddenly of a heart attack and someone else slip slowly into the clutches of cancer knows that there are gradations of dying.

I watched a television re-enactment one night of an execution by lethal injection. It was well done; it was horrible. The methodical approach, people standing around the gurney waiting, made it more awful. One moment there was a man in a prone position; the next moment that man was gone. On another night I watched a television movie about a little boy named Adam Walsh, who disappeared from a shopping center in Florida. There was a re-enactment of Adam's parents coming to New York, where they appeared on morning talk shows begging for their son's return, and in their hotel room, where they received a call from the police saying that Adam had been found: not all of Adam, actually, just his severed head, discovered in the waters of a Florida canal. There was nothing anyone could do that is bad enough for an adult who took a 6-year-old boy away from his parents, perhaps tortured, then murdered him and cut off his head. Nothing at all. Lethal injection? The electric chair? Bah.

And so I come back to the position that the death penalty is wrong, not only because it consists of stooping to the level of the killers, but also because it is not what it seems. Just before Ted Bundy's most recent execution date was postponed, pending further appeals, the father of his last known victim, a 12-year-old girl, said what almost every father in his situation must feel. "I wish they'd bring him back to Lake City," said Tom Leach of the town where Kimberly Leach had lived and died, "and let us all have at him." But the death penalty does not let us all have at him in the way Mr. Leach seems to mean. What he wants is for something as horrifying as what happened to his child to happen to Ted Bundy. And that is impossible.

In this essay Anna Quindlen defends the claim that we should not practice capital punishment. She states her argument explicitly at the beginning of the last paragraph: "the death penalty is wrong, not only because it consists of stooping to the level of the killers, but also because it is not what it seems." That argument is initially suggested to the reader by the title "Death Penalty's False Promise."

Throughout the work she cleverly supports the claim with examples and her own personal experiences. The warrant that makes her support credible is that our society is civilized and that a civilized society cannot exact the retribution that our emotions tell us that criminals who are convicted of horrible crimes deserve.

FOUR KINDS OF PERSUASIVE WRITING

The success of persuasive writing depends on whether or not the reader accepts the writer's position. As we have seen, the initial support for the claim comes in the form of direct support, an assertion that explains why the writer is making the claim. In addition, to gain that acceptance, the writer of persuasion may use any of four appeals. Each of these four appeals (personal, emotional, rational, and stylistic) focuses on a different aspect of the problem of persuasion.

THE PERSONAL APPEAL

Personal appeal focuses on the credibility of the writer. A positive image of the writer is put forth. If the writer can be presented in a favorable light, then the audience is more likely to accept the argument. The following characteristics can be found in writing using the personal appeal.

- The writer's identification with the reader is shown.
- The writer is presented as an expert on the issue.
- The writer's good intentions are revealed.
- The writer's honesty is asserted.

Reader Identification

The persuasive writer using a personal appeal appears to be part of the same group as the reader, using the same language and sharing the same values.

The writer may use slang and jargon that the audience would use or accept. If the writer is successful at establishing this identification with the reader, then the task of persuasion is much easier.

Expertness

The writer appears to know what he or she is talking about. If the writer is accepted as an expert, the reader is more likely to believe any statements the writer makes. Three ways of making the writer appear to be an expert are by referring to personal experience, by citing some authority, and by endorsements.

Sometimes writers tell us about *their own experiences* as evidence of their expertise. The writer says "I've been there; I know what it's like."

Other writers introduce themselves as *authorities*. They claim to have studied the issue and areas that relate to it.

In advertising we see products *endorsed* by celebrities who are probably not experts on anything. The fact that they are celebrities, nevertheless, gives credibility to the product they are promoting.

Good Intentions

The writer expresses the intention of helping the reader. In fact, the writer might say "I have your best interests at heart." If the audience believes that the writer is working for them, they are more likely to accept the writer's argument.

Honesty

The writer asserts that he or she is honest and might even say, "I'm being honest with you." That the reader sees the writer as truthful is important to the success of the persuasion. As readers, we aren't likely to accept the arguments of anyone we believe to be dishonest.

AN EXAMPLE

A representative to the US House from 1969-1983, Shirley Chisholm was a dedicated advocate of social justice. She was the first black representative to Congress and she was the first black woman to seek the nomination for the presidency. In this essay, written in 1970, she uses personal appeal to make a case for political activism.

I'D RATHER BE BLACK THAN FEMALE

SHIRLEY CHISHOLM

Being the first black woman elected to Congress has made me some kind of phenomenon. There are nine other blacks in Congress; there are ten other women. I was the first to overcome both handicaps at once. Of the two handicaps, being black is much less of a drawback than being female.

If I said that being black is a greater handicap than being a woman, probably no one would question me. Why? Because "we all know" there is prejudice against black people in America. That there is prejudice against women is an idea that still strikes nearly all men—and, I am afraid, most women—as bizarre.

Prejudice against blacks was invisible to most white Americans for many years. When blacks finally started to "mention" it, with sit-ins, boycotts, and freedom rides, Americans were incredulous. "Who, us?" they asked in injured tones. "We're prejudiced?" It was the start of a long, painful reeducation for white America. It will take years for whites—including those who think of themselves as liberals—to discover and eliminate the racist attitudes they all actually have.

How much harder will it be to eliminate the prejudice against women? I am sure it will be a longer struggle. Part of the problem is that women in America are much more brainwashed and content with their roles as second-class citizens than blacks ever were.

Let me explain. I have been active in politics for more than twenty years. For all but the last six, I have done the work—all the tedious details that make the difference between victory and defeat on election day—while men reaped the rewards, which is almost invariably the lot of women in politics.

It is still women—about three million volunteers—who do most of this work in the American political world. The best any of them can hope for is the honor of being district or county vice-chairman, a kind of separate-but-equal position with which a woman is rewarded for years of faithful envelope stuffing and card-party organizing. In such a job, she gets a number of free trips to state and sometimes national meetings and conventions, where her role is supposed to be to vote the way her male chairman votes.

When I tried to break out of that role in 1963 and run for the New York State Assembly seat from Brooklyn's Bedford-Stuyvesant, the resistance was bitter. From the start of that campaign, I faced undisguised hostility because of my sex.

But it was four years later, when I ran for Congress, that the question of my sex became a major issue. Among members of my own party, closed meetings were held to discuss ways of stopping me.

My opponent, the famous civil-rights leader James Farmer, tried to project a black, masculine image; he toured the neighborhood with sound trucks filled with young men wearing Afro haircuts, dashikis, and beards. While the television crews ignored me, they were not aware of a very important statistic, which both I and my campaign manager, Wesley MacD. Holder, knew. In my district there are 2.5 women for every man registered to vote. And those women are organized—in PTAs, church societies, card clubs, and other social and service groups. I went to them and asked their help. Mr. Farmer still doesn't quite know what hit him.

When a bright young woman graduate starts looking for a job, why is the first question always: "Can you type?" A history of prejudice lies behind that question. Why are women thought of as secretaries, not administrators? Librarians and teachers, but not doctors and lawyers? Because they are thought of as different and inferior. The happy homemaker and the contented darky are both stereotypes produced by prejudice.

Women have not even reached the level of tokenism that blacks are reaching. No women sit on the Supreme Court. Only two have held Cabinet rank, and none do at present. Only two women hold ambassadorial rank. But women predominate in the lower-paying, menial, unrewarding, dead-end jobs, and when they do reach better positions, they are invariably paid less than a man gets for the same job.

If that is not prejudice, what would you call it?

A few years ago, I was talking with a political leader about a promising young woman as a candidate. "Why invest time and effort to build the girl up?" he asked me. "You know she'll only drop out of the game to have a couple of kids just about the time we're ready to run her for mayor."

Plenty of people have said similar things about me. Plenty of others have advised me, every time I tried to take another upward step, that I should go back to teaching, a woman's vocation, and leave politics to the men. I love teaching, and I am ready to go back to it as soon as I am convinced that this country no longer needs a woman's contribution.

When there are no children going to bed hungry in this rich nation, I may be ready to go back to teaching. When there is a good school for every child, I may be ready. When we do not spend our wealth on hardware to murder people, when we no longer tolerate prejudice against minorities, and when the laws against unfair housing and unfair employment practices are enforced instead of evaded, then there may be nothing more for me to do in politics.

But until that happens—and we all know it will not be this year or next—what we need is more women in politics, because we have a very special contribution to make. I hope that the example of my success will convince other women to get into politics—and not just to stuff envelopes, but to run for office.

It is women who can bring empathy, tolerance, insight, patience, and persistence to government—the qualities we naturally have or have had to develop because of our suppression by men. The women of a nation mold its morals, its religion, and its politics by the lives they live. At present, our country needs women's idealism and determination, perhaps more in politics than anywhere else.

Chisholm's claim that "what we need is more women in politics" is supported by the impression that she is speaking as an expert, that she is honest, that she identifies with the reader, and that she has good intentions. She demonstrates her expertness when she chronicles her experiences in politics and tells about the resistance she faced when she tried to run for office. She shows us her honesty when she speaks truthfully about politics. She says, "It is still women who do most of the work in the American political world" and "women have not reached the level of tokenism that blacks are reaching." Her identification with the reader is apparent when she reveals how she has experienced what other women have experienced. She says, "Plenty of people have said similar things to me." She reveals her good intentions in saying that it is the women of a nation who "mold its morals, its religion, and its politics." She creates a positive image of herself, one that highlights her independence and fortitude and so supports her claim.

THE EMOTIONAL APPEAL

The emotional appeal is the most direct of the four appeals of persuasive writing. With it, the writer seeks to arouse the reader's emotions and thereby affect how the reader sees the issue in question. It is a very powerful appeal and so it is sometimes abused by unscrupulous writers. The following characteristics are apparent in persuasive writing with an emotional appeal.

- The reader's desires, needs, and/or fears are appealed to.
- The importance of the issue is shown.
- The benefit to be derived from accepting the writer's position on the issue is shown.
- The good intentions of the writer are supported.

Appeal to Desires, Needs, and Fears

By using the emotional appeal, the writer presents images that have a strong emotional context, appealing to desires, needs, or fears. For example, we all want to belong to some group and we fear being seen as an outcast. If the writer can make us feel that having a certain belief or owning a particular product will make us *belong*, we may be more likely to accept the argument that goes along with the appeal. Almost any emotion can be manipulated by the clever writer.

Importance of the Issue

The appeal to the emotions of the reader emphasizes the importance of the issue. Because emotions are engaged, the reader *feels* the urgency of the persuasive claim.

Explanation of the Benefits

The benefit to the reader of accepting the writer's position supposedly will be that the reader's fears won't become a reality or the reader's desires will come true. This offering of a benefit helps to reinforce the claim.

Support for Good Intentions

The emotions aroused in the reader may support the good intentions of the writer; that is, they provide evidence that the writer is trying to help. The writer is seen as an instrument for achieving the reader's desires or needs.

AN EXAMPLE

Jonathan Edwards was one of the most famous Puritan ministers in Colonial America. Noted for his effectiveness in the pulpit, he was a master of the use of emotional appeals. The following example is from "Sinners in the Hands of an Angry God," the best-known sermon in American history. It illustrates how a skilled writer and speaker can manipulate the emotions of an audience.

SINNERS IN THE HANDS OF AN ANGRY GOD

JONATHAN EDWARDS

Your wickedness makes you as it were heavy as lead, and to tend downwards with great weight and pressure towards hell; and if God should let you go, you would immediately sink and swiftly descend and plunge into the bottomless gulf, and your healthy constitution, and your own care and prudence, and best contrivance, and all your righteousness, would have no more influence to uphold you and keep you out of hell, than a spider's web would have to stop a falling rock. Were it not that so is the sovereign pleasure of God, the earth would not bear you one moment; for you are a burden to it; the creation groans with you; the creature is made the subject to the bondage of your corruption, not willingly; the sun does not willingly shine upon you to give you light to serve sin and Satan; the earth does not willingly yield her increase to satisfy your lusts; nor is it willingly a stage for your wickedness to be acted upon; the air does not willingly serve you for breath to maintain the flame of life in your vitals while you spend your life in the service of God's enemies. God's creatures are good, and were made for men to serve God with, and do not willingly subserve to any other purpose, and groan when they are abused to purposes so directly contrary to their nature and end. And the world would spew you out, were it not for the sovereign hand of Him who hath subjected your heads, full of the dreadful storm and big with thunder; and were it not for the restraining hand of God, it would immediately burst forth upon you. The sovereign pleasure of God, for the present, stays His rough wind; otherwise it would come with fury, and your destruction would come like a whirlwind, and you would be like the chaff of the summer threshing floor.

The wrath of God is like great waters that are dammed for the present; they increase more and more, and rise higher and higher, till an outlet is given; and the longer the stream is stopped, the more rapid and mighty is its course when once it is let loose. It is true that judgment against your evil works has not been executed hitherto; the floods of God's vengeance have been withheld; but your guilt in the meantime is constantly increasing, and you are every day treasuring up more wrath; the waters are continually rising and waxing more and more mighty; and there is nothing but the mere pleasure of God that holds the waters back that are unwilling to be stopped and press hard to go forward. If God should only withdraw His hand from the floodgate, it would immediately fly open, and the fiery floods of the fierceness and wrath of God would rush forth with inconceivable fury and would come upon you with omnipotent power; and if your strength were ten thousand times greater than it is, yea ten thousand times greater than the strength of the stoutest, sturdiest devil in hell, it would be nothing to withstand or endure it.

The bow of God's wrath is bent, and the arrow made ready on the string and justice bends the arrow at your heart and strains the bow, and it is nothing but the mere pleasure of God, and that of an angry God, without any promise or obligation at all, that keeps the arrow one moment from being made drunk with your blood. Thus are all you that never passed under a great change of heart, by the mighty power of the Spirit of God upon your souls; all that were never born again, and made new creatures, and raised from being dead in sin, to a state of new, and before altogether unexperienced light and life, are in the hands of an angry God. However you may have reformed your life in many things, and may have had religious affections, and keep up a form of religion in your families and closets, and in the house of God, it is nothing but His mere pleasure that keeps you from being this moment swallowed up in everlasting destruction. However unconvinced you may now be of the truth of what you hear, by and by you will be fully convinced of it. Those that are gone from being in the like circumstances with you see that it was so with them; for destruction came suddenly upon most of them; when they expected nothing of it and while they were saying, "peace and safety;" now they see that those things that they depended for peace and safety, were nothing but thin air and empty shadows.

The God that holds you over the pit of hell, much as one holds a spider or some loathsome insect over the fire, abhors you and is dreadfully provoked: His wrath towards you burns like fire; He looks upon you as worthy of nothing else but to be cast into the fire; He is of purer eyes than to bear to have you in His sight; you are ten thousand times more abominable in His eyes than the most hateful and venomous serpent is in ours. You have offended Him infinitely more than ever a stubborn rebel did his prince; and yet it is nothing but His hand that holds you from falling into the fire every moment. It is to be ascribed to nothing else, that you did not go to hell the last night; that you were suffered to awake against in this world, after you closed your eyes to sleep. And there is no other reason to be given why you have not dropped into hell, since you have sat here in the house of God, provoking His pure eyes by your sinful wicked manner of attending. His solemn worship. Yea, there is nothing else that is to be given as a reason why you do not this very moment drop down into hell.

O sinner! Consider the fearful danger you are in: it is a great furnace of wrath, a wide and bottomless pit, full of the fire of wrath, that you are held over in the hand of that God, whose wrath is provoked and incensed as much against you, as against many of the damned in hell. You hang by a slender thread, with the flames of divine wrath flashing about it and ready every moment to singe it, and burn it asunder; and you have no interest in any Mediator and nothing to lay hold of to save yourself, nothing to keep off the flames of wrath, nothing of your own, nothing that you ever have done, nothing that you can do to induce God to spare you one moment.

Edwards establishes the importance of the issue—eternal damnation. He tries to convince his audience—those who have "never passed under a great change of heart," those who have never been "born again, and made new creatures"—that they are in "fearful danger." To persuade them of this,

Edwards presents a frightening picture of eternal damnation and God's wrath. Such images as God holding the sinner over "the pit of hell . . . as one holds a spider or some loathsome insect over the fire" and the sinner hanging "by a slender thread with flames of divine wrath flashing around it" are calculated to arouse the emotions of fear and disgust. Those emotions may have had a powerful effect on Edwards' audiences, convincing them to examine their lives for evidence that they are one of God's elect.

THE RATIONAL APPEAL

Rational appeal is an attempt to persuade by using language structures that are associated with mental processes we call logical. The following characteristics appear in persuasive writing that uses rational appeal.

- Assertions are made and the opposing view may be refuted.
- The expertness of the writer is supported.
- Common sense is appealed to.
- Logical structures are used.

Assertions, Refutations, and Qualifiers

An assertion is a statement supporting the issue. The writer may make a direct assertion like, "My position is correct" or "My proposal will benefit you." Such unsupported assertions have a power of their own. In addition to making assertions, the writer may attack the opposing view and try to refute the arguments of the opposition. Furthermore, the argument may need qualifiers, words like *usually*, *for most people*, or *unless*, if the claim cannot be universally applied.

Expertise

The use of logic (or that which appears to be logical) supports the impression that the writer is an expert. Indeed, anyone's expertise depends on having facts and logical proofs at hand. The writer of persuasion may present facts without intending to use them in a logical way. The presentation of facts and statistics may have an effect on the undiscriminating reader, even if the information is not relevant to the issue.

Common Sense

The appeal to common sense is an effort to take advantage of what people may regard as native good judgment, those ideas that emphasize the common feelings of humanity. When people say, "It's just common sense," they mean that their assertions should be obvious to everybody and that anyone who doesn't see the obvious, doesn't have any common sense. Such assertions seem to stand on their own without needing any support.

Logical Structures

Using logical structures involves the application of the principles of deductive and inductive reasoning.

Deductive Reasoning

Deductive reasoning is the kind of logical process that draws particular truths from general truths. The structure of the deductive process can be seen most clearly in the syllogism.

A **syllogism** consists of three statements: a major premise, a minor premise, and a conclusion. If the major and minor premises are true, then the conclusion must be true. It cannot be otherwise. The following illustrates the structure of a syllogism.

> *Major Premise*: All men are foolish.
> *Minor Premise*: Harvey is a man.
> *Conclusion*: Therefore, Harvey is foolish.

An **enthymeme** is an abbreviated syllogism in which one of the premises is omitted. The enthymeme often appears in persuasive writing because the writer may not want the reader to be aware that one of the premises is missing. In addition, the reader may grow impatient with a full blown deductive argument. In the following enthymeme, derived from the syllogism above, the major premise is omitted.

> *Harvey is foolish because he is a man.*

Slogans, proverbs, aphorisms, and adages represent another abbreviated form of deduction. Such statements seem to ring true when we hear them, but the problem with them is obvious when we pair one with another one that contradicts it.

> *Absence makes the heart grow fonder.*
> but
> *Out of sight, out of mind.*
> *You're never too old to learn.*
> but

> *You can't teach an old dog new tricks.*
> *Never put off till tomorrow what you can do today.*
> but
> *All things come to those who wait.*

Inductive Reasoning

Inductive reasoning moves from particular to general. That is, a general truth (conclusion) is derived from particular instances (**evidence**).

Evidence is a compilation of facts, observations, and data that supports the inductive thesis. Reasoning from evidence is the kind of inductive reasoning we are concerned with in interpretive writing. (This kind of reasoning will be discussed more extensively in Chapter 4.) Although evidence may be presented in practically any form, facts are often given numerical values and used in the form of statistics.

Evidence may be used as a part of an inductive persuasive argument, but a relevant **example**, selected for its appropriateness to the claim, may be more convincing to the reader than a mass of facts and figures. Examples represent an abbreviation of evidence and typically appear in persuasive writing. Such an abbreviation would not be valid as evidence in interpretive referential writing using inductive reasoning, which would require more extensive evidence to constitute an inductive proof.

Used as a rational appeal, an **analogy** can be quite persuasive, but it can only be pushed to the limits the reader will accept. For instance, we might argue that the principles of law that govern the business world and professions like medicine and law ought to apply to education, that schools ought to be held accountable for negligence and failure to perform. Such an argument relies on an analogy. Whether or not that argument will be accepted depends, at least in part, on the audience being addressed.

AN EXAMPLE

When Barack Obama became president in January of 2009, he faced the Great Recession, the worst financial crisis since the Great Depression of the 1930s. In the following speech delivered as a radio address on January 29, 2009, he tried to convince his listeners, especially members of Congress, that immediate action was required. In the speech he makes extensive use of rational appeal.

FIRST PRESIDENTIAL WEEKLY ADDRESS

BARACK OBAMA

We begin this year and this Administration in the midst of an unprecedented crisis that calls for unprecedented action. Just this week, we saw more people file for unemployment than at any time in the last twenty-six years, and experts agree that if nothing is done, the unemployment rate could reach double digits. Our economy could fall $1 trillion short of its full capacity, which translates into more than $12,000 in lost income for a family of four. And we could lose a generation of potential, as more young Americans are forced to forgo college dreams or the chance to train for the jobs of the future.

In short, if we do not act boldly and swiftly, a bad situation could become dramatically worse.

That is why I have proposed an American Recovery and Reinvestment Plan to immediately jumpstart job creation as well as long-term economic growth. I am pleased to say that both parties in Congress are already hard at work on this plan, and I hope to sign it into law in less than a month.

It's a plan that will save or create three to four million jobs over the next few years, and one that recognizes both the paradox and the promise of this moment—the fact that there are millions of Americans trying to find work even as, all around the country, there's so much work to be done. That's why this is not just a short-term program to boost employment. It's one that will invest in our most important priorities like energy and education; health care and a new infrastructure that are necessary to keep us strong and competitive in the 21st century.

Today I'd like to talk specifically about the progress we expect to make in each of these areas.

To accelerate the creation of a clean energy economy, we will double our capacity to generate alternative sources of energy like wind, solar, and biofuels over the next three years. We'll begin to build a new electricity grid that lay down more than 3,000 miles of transmission lines to convey this new energy from coast to coast. We'll save taxpayers $2 billion a year by making 75% of federal buildings more energy efficient, and save the average working family $350 on their energy bills by weatherizing 2.5 million homes.

To lower health care cost, cut medical errors, and improve care, we'll computerize the nation's health record in five years, saving billions of dollars in health care costs and countless lives. And we'll protect health insurance for more than 8 million Americans who are in danger of losing their coverage during this economic downturn.

To ensure our children can compete and succeed in this new economy, we'll renovate and modernize 10,000 schools, building state-of-the-art classrooms, libraries, and labs to improve learning for over five million students. We'll invest more in Pell Grants to make college affordable for seven million more students, provide a $2,500 college tax credit to four million students, and triple the number of fellowships in science to help spur the next generation of innovation.

Finally, we will rebuild and retrofit America to meet the demands of the 21st century. That means repairing and modernizing thousands of miles of America's roadways and providing new mass transit options for millions of Americans. It means protecting America by securing 90 major ports and creating a better communications network for local law enforcement and public safety officials in the event of an emergency. And it means expanding broadband access to millions of Americans, so business can compete on a level-playing field, wherever they're located.

I know that some are skeptical about the size and scale of this recovery plan. I understand that skepticism, which is why this recovery plan must and will include unprecedented measures that will allow the American people to hold my Administration accountable for these results. We won't just throw money at our problems—we'll invest in what works. Instead of politicians doling out money behind a veil of secrecy, decisions about where we invest will be made public, and informed by independent experts whenever possible. We'll launch an unprecedented effort to root out waste, inefficiency, and unnecessary spending in our government, and every American will be able to see how and where we spend taxpayer dollars by going to a new website called recovery.gov.

No one policy or program will solve the challenges we face right now, nor will this crisis recede in a short period of time. But if we act now and act boldly; if we start rewarding hard work and responsibility once more; if we act as citizens and not partisans and begin again the work of remaking America, then I have faith that we will emerge from this trying time even stronger and more prosperous than we were before.

Thanks for listening.

In this speech Obama uses rational appeal to support his claim that America should take immediate action to prevent the recession from becoming worse. He identifies four areas of focus for the economic recovery package—energy, health care, education, and infrastructure—and gives examples of the kinds of things that will be done. Throughout the argument he uses statistics to clarify the examples. At the end of the speech, he refutes opposing positions and qualifies some of the assertions he has made.

THE STYLISTIC APPEAL

The stylistic appeal convinces by presenting pleasing images that entice the reader to accept the claim of the persuader. The following characteristics are usually present in a stylistic appeal.

- Aesthetically pleasing images and/or symbols are presented.
- Concrete, graphic imagery is used.
- Startling, unusual images and/or dramatic situations to get the attention of the reader are used.
- Images that are consistent with the social or cultural myths are used.

Imagery

Images in stylistic appeals are used to get the reader's attention and are often connected to emotional appeals. Images that are pleasing tend to make the reader accept the message being presented. Such images are frequently the kinds used in literary writing—similes, metaphors, and personification. In his famous speech, "I Have a Dream," Martin Luther King used figurative imagery, comparing the failure to end segregation and discrimination to an uncashed check, a promissory note.

Concrete, graphic imagery (that may also be startling) is used because it captures the reader's attention. If the reader is intrigued by and subsequently engaged in the images presented, then the persuasive argument is enhanced. King used the image of "chains" to identify the effects of segregation.

Images that are consistent with a current social and cultural myth will be readily accepted by the reader. The reader, more than likely, already has accepted any prevailing cultural belief. If the writer can show that his or her position is in line with the accepted myth, the reader will be more willing to accept the argument.

Rhyme and Rhythm

The cadence and rhythms of the writing can have a positive effect on the reader. Rhyme may also be used, especially if slogans are part of the message. For example, the following slogan takes advantage of a rhyme to make it more likely that the reader will remember the slogan. Prestige Motors: The best never rest.

Repetition

Repeating key words and phrases throughout the argument is not only an effective technique for achieving coherence, but it may also serve as an aesthetically pleasing device that underscores the claim. In "I Have a Dream" King repeated the sentence "I have a dream" nine times and "Let freedom ring" eleven times. Those two uses of repetition in his speech have a powerful effect on anyone who reads or hears the speech.

Dramatic Situations

Dramatic episodes that are similar to literary narratives are often used to get the reader's attention. They may also be part of the rational appeal.

CRISSCROSS CORD SHIRT

The Territory Ahead

If you're shy, this isn't the shirt for you. The fabric—a richly colored, crosshatched cotton corduroy— is so supremely soft and texturey, it has a tendency to attract unsolicited attention. In fact, when our V.P. of Merchandising wore it on a recent trip, an otherwise well-mannered young woman had to be gently dissuaded from stroking his sleeve long enough for him to board his plan home. Details include a spread collar; button-through patch pockets; handsome, wood-style buttons; and a box pleat in back. Imported in Olive; Barn Red; Amber; Blue-Gray; Plum.

Reg. Sizes: S–XXL.   143004 $59.50
Tall Sizes: MT–XXLT. 143181 $65.50

The descriptive detail "supremely soft and texturey," together with the intriguing narrative about "unsolicited attention," create a compelling stylistic appeal. The description is created to prompt the reader to imagine himself wearing one of the "richly coloured" shirts and having to "gently" discourage the attentions of a "young woman."

COMBINATIONS

Personal appeal and stylistic appeal rarely appear alone. They are most often used in combination with rational and emotional appeals. Some appeals inevitably appear with others. For instance, an example used as a rational appeal may have a strong emotional appeal as well. The use of all four appeals in the same piece of persuasive writing is not at all unusual.

WRITING STRATEGIES

The most important consideration in creating a persuasive argument is to know the audience. Remember that persuasion is the most pragmatic of the kinds of writing. The purpose of persuasion is the practical matter of convincing the reader of the rightness of your position and perhaps moving the reader to act on that conviction. The appropriateness of the appeals you use depends upon your understanding of the nature of the audience. As a result, an important part of the process of writing persuasion is to figure out the values and beliefs of the specific audience you are addressing.

Consider these questions as you begin drafting your persuasive paper.

- Who is your audience?
- How can you create interest in your topic?
- How can you establish your credibility as an authority?
- What values do your readers have that would predispose them to agree with your position?

- What issue are you addressing?
- What is your position on this issue?
- State your position as a thesis statement.
- What background will your audience need to understand your argument?
- What appeals could you use to support your thesis?
- What reasons support your argument?
- How would you answer objections to your position?
- What are the implications of your argument?
- What emotional appeal best supports your argument?

AN OUTLINE FOR PERSUASION

The persuasive structure reflected in the following outline has been used for thousands of years and is still an effective way to present a persuasive argument.

I.   Introduction
    A. Create interest in the topic.
    B. Show the importance of the issue.
    C. Establish your credibility as an authority.
    D. Establish common ground for both you and the reader.
    E. Show fair-mindedness.
    F. State the claim.

II. Background
    A. Explain the treatment of the issue in the past.
    B. Give relevant facts about the topic (may include statistics).

III. Lines of Argument
    A. Present rational and/or emotional appeals.
    B. Present reasons in order of importance.
    C. Show that your position is in the readers' best interest.

IV. Refutation of Any Opposing Arguments
    A. Consider any opposing views.
    B. Note advantages and disadvantages of opposing views.
    C. Refute the opposing positions.

V. Conclusion
   A. Summarize the argument.
   B. Elaborate on the implications of the argument.
   C. Make clear what you want readers to think and do.
   D. Make a final emotional appeal, but don't overdo it.

You can see how this outline is developed in practice by looking at Barack Obama's "First Presidential Weekly Address" in the section "The Rational Appeal" in this chapter and at the student paper titled "Beauty Becomes the Beast" in Chapter 14.

Referential Writing

R eferential writing overwhelms us in modern life. At no time in history has there been such a profusion of documents designed to explain our world. Business, industry, science, academia, government, and the news media all produce massive quantities of information. Libraries devote an enormous amount of space to the storage of reference works, research materials, scholarly journals, government publications, scientific treatises, news reports as well as other kinds of referential writing. The term *Information Age* refers in large part to this explosion in the production of referential writing.

In all its various forms, the purpose of referential writing is to explain a topic. The explanation will have four features: thesis, evidence, validity, and topic-oriented language.

GENERAL CHARACTERISTICS

- A thesis is present.
- Evidence consistent with the thesis is offered.
- The validity of the evidence is apparent.
- Topic-oriented language is used.

THESIS

A thesis is a generalization about the content of the work that tells the reader what the focus of the presentation will be. In other words, the thesis indicates how the topic will be explained. Although a thesis statement may appear anywhere in the work, it is usually included in the introduction where the scope of the discussion is set out. The nature of the thesis depends on the kind of subject matter presented.

The following are examples of referential thesis statements.

- A number of European countries have abandoned the use of nuclear reactors as a way to produce electricity.
- Dietary changes can improve health for many people.
- Many new immigrants to the United States still believe in the "American Dream."

Each of these statements is a generalization indicating the main idea to be addressed in a paper.

A thesis in referential writing differs from a claim in persuasion in that the referential thesis focuses on an examination of the subject matter rather than presenting a defense of one side of an issue. For example, the referential thesis that there is a high correlation between fast driving and accidents is different from the persuasive claim that people ought to slow down when they drive. Even though some of the same information might be included in a paper on each subject, the intent of the two would be different. One would be referential and the other would be persuasive.

EVIDENCE

Evidence included in referential writing will provide support for the thesis. Evidence may take the form of facts, questions, or other details to help explain the topic. The evidence needed in the paper is implicit in the thesis. A paper explaining the changes in the use of nuclear energy in Europe would include evidence giving specific examples of countries in Europe where the change had occurred. A paper about the connection between diet and health might have evidence consisting of empirical studies that show a correlation between the nutrition people had and the state of their health. A paper about immigrants' views of the "American Dream" would probably include reports of interviews with new American immigrants about their attitudes or the results of surveys designed to collect information about those attitudes.

VALIDITY

The evidence presented in referential writing has validity. The validity of that evidence is apparent to the reader, either because the facts themselves are indisputable or because the logic of the presentation is clear. Validity is ensured by an attention to data that can be supported in some way, either by some authority (the credibility of the writer) or by logic.

In most cases we assume that the information included in referential writing is accurate and that if false information is presented, it will be corrected. For instance, when a credible newspaper prints a story, we assume that the report is valid because of our previous dealings with that newspaper. When a scientist publishes research findings, we assume that the information reported is valid because of our knowledge of the nature of scientific investigation. And in both cases we assume that any distorted information or inaccurate data will be quickly corrected or explained.

In addition, if facts presented by the writer correspond to what we already know about the subject, that is, conform to common knowledge, then we have more confidence in the information presented. For example, if the writer refers to historical events that we already have some knowledge of, then the validity of the information will be reinforced.

TOPIC-ORIENTED LANGUAGE

The language used in referential writing will be appropriate to the topic; as a result the topic will control the kind of language used. The information presented will be accurate and concepts will be clearly stated. Third person pronouns are typically used. Conventions of standard usage are followed and unambiguous terms are used.

The degree of formality in referential writing will depend on how the topic is treated. Some kinds of referential writing are more formal than others. Articles in academic journals and scientific studies, for instance, usually demand a fairly formal presentation. News reports, though less formal than scholarly works, are more formal than feature articles, human interest stories, and speculative essays, which may allow some degree of subjectivity and authorial intrusion.

AN EXAMPLE

In the following example, the famed naturalist John Muir offers an explanation of a body of evidence to support his thesis. This example illustrates the general characteristics of referential writing.

WHERE THE SEQUOIA GROWS

John Muir

It is generally believed that this grand Sequoia was once far more widely distributed over the Sierra; but after long and careful study I have come to the conclusion that it never was, at least since the close of the glacial period, because a diligent search along the margins of the groves, and in the gaps between, fails to reveal a single trace of its previous existence beyond its present bounds. Notwithstanding, I feel confident that if every Sequoia in the range were to die today, numerous monuments of their existence would remain, of so imperishable a nature as to be available for the student more than ten thousand years hence.

In the first place we might notice that no species of coniferous tree in the range keeps its individuals so well together as Sequoia; a mile is perhaps the greatest distance of any straggler from the main body, and all of these stragglers that have come under my observation are young, instead of old monumental trees, relics of a more extended growth.

Again, Sequoia trunks frequently endure for centuries after they fall. I have a specimen block, cut from a fallen trunk, which is hardly distinguishable from specimens cut from living trees, although the old trunk-fragment from which it was derived has lain in the damp forest more than 380 years, probably twice as long. The time measure in the case is simply this: when the ponderous trunk to which the old vestige belonged fell, it sunk itself into the ground, thus making a long, straight ditch, and in the middle of this ditch a Silver Fir is growing that is now four feet in diameter and 380 years old, as determined by cutting it half through and counting the rings, thus demonstrating that the remnant of the trunk that made the ditch has lain on the ground *more* than 380 years. For it is evident that to find the whole time, we must add to the 380 years the time that the vanished portion of the trunk lay in the ditch before being burned out of the way, plus the time that passed before the seed from which the monumental fir sprang fell into the prepared soil and took root. Now, because Sequoia trunks are never wholly consumed in one forest fire, and those fires recur only at considerable intervals, and because Sequoia ditches after being cleared are often left unplanted for centuries, it becomes evident that the trunk remnant in question may probably have lain a thousand years or more. And this instance is by no means a rare one.

But admitting that upon those areas supposed to have been once covered with Sequoia every tree may have fallen, and every trunk may have been burned or buried, leaving not a remnant, many of the ditches made by the fall of the ponderous trunks, and the bowls made by their upturning roots, would remain patent for thousands of years after the last vestige of the trunks that made them had vanished. Much of this ditch-writing would no doubt be quickly effaced by the flood-action of overflowing streams and rain-washing; but no inconsiderable portion would remain enduringly engraved on the ridge-tops beyond such destructive action; for, where all the conditions are favorable, it is almost imperishable. Now these historic ditches and root bowls occur in all the present Sequoia groves and forests, but as far as I have observed, not the faintest vestige of one presents itself outside them.

We therefore conclude that the area covered by Sequoia has not been diminished during the last eight or ten thousand years, and probably not at all in post-glacial times.

In the first paragraph of this essay the author states the thesis—that the Sequoia were never more widely distributed over the Sierras than they are now. In this way the scope of the topic is defined and the kind of evidence needed to prove the thesis is suggested. Throughout the rest of the essay, the author presents evidence relevant to the thesis.

The evidence presented includes personal observations about the current range of the Sequoia groves, the existence of a trunk fragment that had been lying on the ground for over 380 years, and the absence of ditches and root bowls created by fallen trees outside the current range. All the evidence taken together proves the thesis and makes Muir's conclusion highly probable. The evidence is valid because it is logically connected to the thesis. The validity of Muir's factual observations is self-evident. The language used to present the information is formal and objective. There is no subjective bias in the presentation.

FOUR KINDS OF REFERENTIAL WRITING

Referential writing can be divided into four groups—informative, interpretive, exploratory, and reflective—each with a different focus for explaining the topic.

THE INFORMATIVE FOCUS

In referential writing with an informative focus, the writer presents the information, but does not do anything more with that information. The objective of such writing is simply to present the facts to the reader.

Referential writing with an informative focus has four characteristics.

- The thesis is a summative generalization of the content.
- Factual language is used.
- The evidence is comprehensive.
- Surprise value is maintained.

Summative Generalization

As with all referential thesis statements, an informative thesis will be a generalization. The informative thesis will present the most general information on the topic. For example, the following thesis statement would be the most general statement included in a report about a train wreck: *A train derailed after hitting a truck at a railway crossing in northern Illinois this weekend.* The statement would provide the basis for other evidence that would follow it. More specific evidence would be needed to fill in the details of the accident and provide a full explanation.

An informative thesis would not contain inferences or ask questions about the evidence, but instead would simply be a summation of the details of the written work.

Factuality

A fact is anything that is verifiable or that has real, demonstrable existence. If something is a fact, it can be verified. For instance, the Preface to *Webster's Third New International Dictionary* says that the volume contains 450,000 words. The fact, the number of words in the dictionary, is something that can be verified objectively (by counting them). Most people probably wouldn't actually count the number of words in the dictionary. They would simply accept the word of the publisher. That's how most of us deal with information. As readers, we don't usually set about trying to verify everything we read. If we read something in the newspaper, we probably accept the item as factual (assuming that we believe that the newspaper is a credible source of information and that the paper would print a correction if it had made an error). Our past experiences with publishing tell us which sources are credible and which are not. We are always aware that if a bit of information is a fact, it can be verified.

Attributions (telling where the information comes from) are not necessary if the facts are common knowledge. If the facts being presented are not common knowledge, identifying the source of the information is essential. Research papers exemplify this feature.

In research papers using the MLA style of documentation, complete information on the sources used is given on the last page of the paper under "Works Cited." In the body of the paper the only information that needs to be given is the exact page number from which the information is taken and any other information that is necessary (usually the name of the author) to enable the reader to find the source in the "Works Cited" list.

Comprehensiveness

A work is comprehensive if it contains all the information necessary to inform the reader about the topic. But just how much is enough? This is sometimes a difficult question to answer. Part of the answer depends on the pattern of organization used (see Chapters 5–8). For example, to be comprehensive, a physical description of a person, a place, or an object would need to include enough detail so that a reader would be able to visualize the thing being described. A narrative would need to include all events necessary so that the reader could understand the entire sequence. When writing news stories, journalists make sure that they answer the questions: who? what? when? where? why? and how? The answers to those questions ensure that the basic facts of an event are reported in the story. (See "Journalistic Questions" in Chapter 10.)

Comprehensiveness may also be determined by how the information is to be used. For instance, many dictionaries have far fewer than the 450,000 words contained in *Webster's Third New International Dictionary*, and yet they achieve comprehensiveness because their use is limited to looking up the most commonly used words.

Another consideration that determines whether or not a work is comprehensive is the audience for whom the work is intended. For example, although the *World Book Encyclopedia* contains much less information than the *Encyclopedia Britannica*, it does achieve comprehensiveness because it's aimed at a much younger audience that presumably would find it more difficult to use a work as comprehensive as the *Encyclopedia Britannica*.

Surprise Value

Surprise value is the extent to which reader interest is maintained. Information is *surprising* if the reader has an interest in the facts presented. Those facts are surprising if the reader's response to the information is "I didn't know that." Once the information is known, the surprise value diminishes for that particular reader. But another reader, unfamiliar with the same information, may find it surprising. Informative writing does not bear repetition in the way that literary writing does. We may read a news story again, but only because we want to see the information again, not because we find it aesthetically pleasing.

The arrangement of the facts in a news story usually reflects the emphasis on surprise value. The most important facts, those with the most surprise value, are given first. Less important facts follow and may be skipped over by the reader (or omitted by the editor before the story is printed).

AN EXAMPLE

In this informative excerpt from *Wild Heritage* (1965), Sally Carrighar presents facts about the field of ethology. By explaining what ethologists do, she develops an extended definition of the term *ethology*.

ETHOLOGY

Sally Carrighar

By . . . the 1920's and 1930's, there was a new generation of biologists and many were ready to listen. While some of them have preferred to do their work in laboratories, others have gone out of doors, to make a real science of animal observation. They call themselves, these co-operating indoor and outdoor men, ethologists, and it is largely due to their efforts that we now have a reliable body of knowledge about our animal forebears.

For laymen ethology is probably the most interesting of the biological sciences for the very reason that it concerns animals in their normal activities and therefore, if we wish, we can assess the possible dangers and advantages in our own behavioral roots. Ethology also is interesting methodologically because it combines in new ways very scrupulous field observations with experimentation in laboratories.

The field workers have had some handicaps in winning respect for themselves. For a long time they were considered as little better than amateur animal-watchers—certainly not scientists, since their facts were not gained by experimental procedures: they could not conform to the hard-and-fast rule that a problem set up and solved by one scientist must be tested by other scientists, under identical conditions and reaching identical results. Of course many situations in the lives of animals simply cannot be rehearsed and controlled in this way. The fall flocking of wild free birds can't be, or the homing of animals over long distances, or even details of spontaneous family relationships. Since these never can be reproduced in a laboratory, are they then not worth knowing about?

The ethologists who choose field work have got themselves out of this impasse by greatly refining the techniques of observing. At the start of a project all the animals to be studied are live-trapped, marked individually, and released. Motion pictures, often in color, provide permanent records of their subsequent activities. Recording of the animals' voices by electrical sound equipment is considered essential, and the most meticulous notes are kept of all that occurs. With this material other biologists, far from the scene, later can verify the reports. Moreover, two field observers often go out together, checking each other's observations right there in the field.

Ethology, the word, is derived from the Greek *ethos*, meaning the characteristic traits or features which distinguish a group—any particular group of people or, in biology, a group of animals such as a species. Ethologists have the intention, as William H. Thorpe explains, of studying "the whole sequence of acts which constitute an animal's behavior." In abridged dictionaries ethology is sometimes defined simply as "the objective study of animal behavior," and ethologists do emphasize their wish to eliminate myths.

Perhaps the most original aspect of ethology is the way that field observation is combined with experimentation in laboratories. Although the flocking of birds cannot be studied indoors, many other significant actions of animals that are seen only infrequently in the field, or seen only as hints, may be followed up later with indoor tests. Likewise investigations made first in laboratories can be checked by observations of animals ranging free in their normal environments.

Suppose that a field man, watching marked individuals, notes that an infant animal, *a*, is nursed by a female, *B*, known not to be its mother. Later he sees other instances of such maternal generosity. Is this willingness on the female's part a case of inherited behavior, or has it been picked up as one of the social customs of the species; that is, is it *learned*? Does it mean that all the adult females of this species feel some responsibility for the young, and if so, is such a tendency innate, or could behavior like that be acquired?

Elephant mothers are among those which give milk to offspring not their own. A group of elephants cannot very well be confined in a laboratory; but if the field worker is concerned with a species of smaller animals, he can bring newborn young into captivity, raise them and mate them there, and then note the behavior of the new mothers. Since they never have seen other females nursing young, their actions will be innate, inherited. And if it does turn out that one of these females will nurse any young that come to her, it will further have to be determined whether she recognizes her own. That question too can be answered in the laboratory; it is an easy problem for an experimental psychologist. By such techniques it has been found, for example, that in the species of small brown bats called *Myotis myotis* the mothers do know their own young and likewise will nurse any hungry infant regardless of blood relationship. This maternal behavior could have been observed in a colony of animals kept for generations indoors, but since the habitat there is artificial, the only way to know whether the behavior is normal to the species was to observe it first in animals living free in their natural world. Only by such a combination of laboratory and field work can instincts and acquired characteristics be distinguished. The value of knowledge like that is so great that the wonder is why such cooperation had not developed much earlier.

This work presents the reader with facts about the field of ethology, addressing both the derivation of the word itself and the processes used by ethologists in their study of animal behavior. The comprehensiveness of the topic is controlled by the limitations of her definitions. She develops the work by using examples of the work done by ethologists. These examples help give the work its validity. Her use of a specialized vocabulary also contributes to the validity of the work as well as to the objectivity of its tone.

THE INTERPRETIVE FOCUS

Referential writing with an interpretive focus is an attempt to explain the meaning of the evidence presented. The writer, through the use of logic, attempts to prove the validity of the interpretation. Scholarly works in all the academic disciplines usually have an interpretive focus. Biologists explain the laws governing life on Earth; literary critics interpret novels and poems; psychologists analyze the functioning of the human mind; physicists explore the forces controlling matter and energy. No matter where we look in the academic world, scholars and scientists are trying to offer logical explanations of the various subjects studied in their disciplines.

Four characteristics define referential writing with an interpretive focus.

- The thesis is an inference about the meaning of the evidence.
- Proof is provided by the evidence.
- Objective language is used.
- Explanatory reasoning is used.

Inference

The thesis is an inference that explains in general terms what the evidence means. For example, the thesis statement "Some industries are causing water pollution by discharging toxic chemicals" is an inference that would explain the meaning of evidence gathered through a scientific analysis of any affected bodies of water.

Proof

The evidence presented in interpretive writing provides the proof supporting the inference that is implicit in the thesis. All the evidence included is necessary so that the reader can understand the legitimacy of the thesis. For example, to prove that a particular industry was causing water pollution, a researcher would have to present evidence that toxic chemicals produced by the industry were present in the water in large amounts. The evidence would probably contain data derived from an analysis of the water in question.

Objectivity

The presentation of evidence in interpretive writing is objective. The writer uses denotative language. Language that is biased and slanted is excluded. Conventions of standard usage are followed and unambiguous terms are used.

Any specialized terms must be defined accurately because the definition of a term may affect the validity of the proof. In many academic disciplines certain words have very special meanings that are different from common definitions.

Explanatory Reasoning

Explanatory reasoning refers to three major types of logical thinking based on inference: deduction, induction, and abduction. We can think of these three types of reasoning in terms of certainty: deductive inference is *certainly* true; inductive inference is *probably* true; and abductive inference is *possibly* true. We have discussed deduction and induction to some degree already in Chapter 3, but in this chapter we will look at these concepts as they are used in proving the validity of a referential interpretive thesis.

Deductive Reasoning

Deductive reasoning is a purely logical process moving from the general to the specific. The syllogism reflects this aspect of deductive reasoning. Deduction draws particular truths from some general truth. The conclusion is implicit in the premises. The kind of syllogism examined in Chapter 3 is called a **categorical syllogism** because it sets up a category and shows that some individual case does or does not fit into the category.

Another kind of syllogism is called the **hypothetical syllogism**. This kind of syllogism sets up a hypothesis, an *if-then* statement. The logic of the syllogism is such that if part of the *if-then* statement is true, then the conclusion must follow. The following example from Charles Darwin's *Origin of Species* illustrates how both categorical and hypothetical syllogisms may appear in a deductive interpretation of a natural phenomenon.

> How will the struggle for existence . . . act in regard to variation? Can the principle of selection, which we have seen is so potent in the hands of man, apply in nature? I think we shall see that it can act most effectually. Let it be borne in mind in what an endless number of strange peculiarities our domestic productions, and, in a lesser degree, those under nature, vary; and how strong the hereditary tendency is. Under domestication, it may

be truly said that the whole organization becomes in some degree plastic. Let it be borne in mind how infinitely complex and close-fitting are the mutual relations of all organic beings to each other and to their physical conditions of life. Can it, then be thought improbable, seeing that variations useful to man have undoubtedly occurred, that other variations useful in some way to each being in the great and complex battle of life, should sometimes occur in the course of thousands of generations? If such do occur, can we doubt (remembering that many more individuals are born than can possibly survive) that individuals having any advantage, however slight, over others, would have the best chance of surviving and of procreating their kind? On the other hand, we may feel sure that any variation in the least degree injurious would be rigidly destroyed. This preservation of favorable variations and the rejection of injurious variations, I call Natural Selection. Variations neither useful nor injurious would not be affected by natural selection, and would be left a fluctuating element. . . .

In written prose the deductive argument may be more complex than a single syllogism. The essence of the deductive reasoning in Darwin's passage about natural selection can be seen in the following statements:

- Offspring vary endlessly.
- Beings have a close-fitting relationship to their environment.
- Variations useful to man occur.
- Variations useful to each being occur in nature.
- More individuals are born than can survive.
- Individuals with an advantage have the best chances of surviving and procreating.
- Individuals with variations that would be injurious would be destroyed.
- Favorable variations are preserved.
- Injurious variations are rejected.

A number of these assertions can be converted to syllogisms.

Hypothetical Syllogism

- *Major Premise*: If many variations are produced, then some will be useful.

- *Minor Premise*: Many variations are produced.
- *Conclusion*: Some are useful.

Categorical Syllogism

- *Major Premise*: Those individuals with any advantage have a better chance of surviving.
- *Minor Premise*: Individuals with favorable variations have an advantage.
- *Conclusion*: Individuals with favorable variations have a better chance of surviving.

Categorical Syllogism

- *Major Premise*: Variations passed to offspring are preserved.
- *Minor Premise*: Favorable variations are passed to offspring.
- *Conclusion*: Favorable variations are preserved.

Inductive Reasoning

Inductive reasoning moves from the specific to the general. It involves making inferences (generalizations) based on observations (specific statements). A general truth becomes known through particular, empirical observations.

The conclusions in inductive reasoning are not as certain as the conclusions arrived at by deductive reasoning. Inductive conclusions are at best highly probable. The advantage of induction is that it is self-correcting; that is, new evidence or additional evidence may alter the conclusions drawn previously.

Analogy is a simple form of induction, but its application is fairly limited. The two things being compared in an analogy have to be very similar for the inference to be valid. For example, if I bought a new pair of jeans, I could reason by analogy that since the new jeans were similar in style, price, and material to an old pair I had, then the new pair should wear about as well as the old ones did. (Analogy as a pattern of organization is also discussed in Chapters 3 & 5.)

The **inductive generalization** is more widely applicable than analogy. A valid inference can be made if observed events are in agreement. For instance, a field biologist might make observations about the conditions necessary for a particular species of animal to live in a given location. If the presence of certain conditions (say a limited temperature range) coincided with the presence of the animal, and the absence of those conditions coincided with the absence of the animal, then the biologist might logically conclude that the condition (temperature range) determined whether the animals would live in the habitat. Furthermore, the biologist would probably record the observations as statistics, i.e. numbers of animals, temperatures, and other variables that might affect the study.

For an inference to be valid, it must be generalizable. For instance, it would be a mistake to say that because some women between the ages of 25 and 30 leave their jobs to have children, all women between the ages of 25 and 30 will leave their jobs to have children. Such a generalization would not be very dependable.

The following example from Charles Darwin's *The Descent of Man* illustrates how interpretations are made by using an inductive reasoning process.

> Most of the more complex emotions are common to the higher animals and ourselves. Every one has seen how jealous a dog is of his master's affection, if lavished on any other creature; and I have observed the same fact with monkeys. This shows that animals not only love, but have desire to be loved. Animals manifestly feel emulation. They love approbation or praise; and a dog carrying a basket of his master exhibits in a high degree self-complacency or pride. There can, I think, be no doubt that a dog feels shame, as distinct from fear, and something very like modesty when begging too often for food. . . . Several observers have stated that monkeys certainly dislike being laughed at; and they sometimes invent imaginary offenses.

Reduced to the bare essentials of the evidence presented, Darwin's **inductive reasoning** would look something like this:

- Animals love and desire to be loved.
- Dogs show jealousy.
- Monkeys show jealousy.
- Animals feel emulation and pride.
- A dog carrying a basket shows self-complacency.
- Animals feel shame and modesty.
- Dogs show modesty when begging too often for food.
- Monkeys dislike being laughed at.
- *Conclusion*: Most of the more complex emotions are common to higher animals and ourselves.

Abductive Reasoning

Abductive reasoning, like inductive reasoning, depends on making an inference based on observation, yet it does not have as high a probability of truth as induction. An abductive inference offers the best explanation of an occurrence, given the available evidence. It is sometimes called "an educated guess," the "most likely explanation, "or simply "everyday reasoning."

Consider the following scenario. One morning you hear a commotion outside in the street in front of your house. When you look out the window, you see your neighbor standing beside the open door of his car yelling at his dog as it chases a raccoon up a tree. You then notice that your trashcan has been knocked over and trash is scattered in the street.

Abductive reasoning (your "best guess") tells you that the raccoon knocked over the trashcan and your neighbor's dog did what dogs do and decided to chase the raccoon. It certainly is the "most likely " explanation. It is *possible*, however, that your neighbor's dog knocked over the trashcan and, seeing the raccoon, decided to chase it. It is also *possible* that your neighbor ran into the trashcan with his car and that the dog escaped from the car when your neighbor got out to inspect the damage. It is even *possible* that your neighbor actually got out of his car and knocked over the trashcan himself, that the dog bolted through the open door, and that the raccoon was simply an innocent bystander. You can, no doubt, think of other *possible* explanations. Although it is not certain that any one of them is correct, that the raccoon knocked over the trashcan is the most likely explanation. The validity of abductive reasoning is that the simplest, most obvious explanation is often correct.

Despite its obvious limitation, abductive reasoning is a necessary method in a number of different academic and professional areas. For example, medical doctors use abductive reasoning when diagnosing a patient's illness and prescribing a treatment. Based on the patient's symptoms, the doctor makes an "educated guess" that gives a "best explanation" of the cause of the patient's condition. However, the initial examination may not reveal all the symptoms for several reasons: the patient may not provide all the information relevant to the case; the patient may be unconscious; or the results of tests may not be available immediately. Nevertheless, the doctor will prescribe a course of treatment that can be changed as more information becomes available. Abductive reasoning also plays a part in law enforcement. Police, when they are investigating a crime, initially make an "educated guess" about a "likely" suspect based on the evidence available to them. Later, a prosecutor will decide to indict and go to trial based on available evidence, even though a defendant's lawyer my call into question the inferences made by the prosecutor by suggesting other possible explanations for the same evidence. Further, a judge or a jury will decide whether the prosecutor's "likely explanation" is warranted. Paleontologists and archeologists use abductive reasoning when they are trying to understand the meaning of fossils of the remains of extinct species and artifacts from societies that longer exist. In each case these scientists gradually gather more evidence and with each new discovery make another educated guess about the significance of what they have uncovered. Eventually, some evidence may form a complete picture of the subject under study; many investigations, however, remain incomplete and fragmentary.

The Scientific Method

The Scientific Method, also called the **hypothetico-deductive** method, is a technique of investigation that uses a combination of all three types of explanatory reasoning. This method involves setting up a hypothesis to explain certain facts gathered by observation (abductive reasoning) and then deducing new conclusions from the hypothesis and testing those conclusions by experiment (deductive and inductive reasoning).

The development of the theory of gravitation, from Newton to Einstein, is an example of how this method has been used at various times to test a theory when new information has been discovered. The theory of gravitation has been modified several times to account for new discoveries. Variations of this basic method of observation and experimentation are used in all the physical sciences.

Statistics are often used as evidence to prove a thesis in writing that has an interpretive focus. Using statistical methods allows us to collect, organize, and interpret numerical information in a meaningful way. If, for instance, we were studying the problem of solid waste disposal, we might report the increase in the amount of waste disposed of in our society by converting the numbers to percentage increases per year, or to increases per person. Such a use of statistics would make the information more meaningful.

Statistics is usually divided into two classes: descriptive statistics and inferential statistics. Descriptive statistics refers to methods used to describe and summarize numerical information that has been collected. Writers often use tables, charts, and graphs to depict the summarized data. Inferential statistics (also known as inductive statistics and sampling statistics) refers to methods that allow us to make inferences about a larger group from the data collected on a smaller group. Opinion polls and experimental research studies make use of the techniques of inferential statistics.

When you use statistics to support interpretations, you should make sure that you have not misused statistical information. Errors of inference in the use of statistics are not always apparent because of the mathematical language used to present the information. Remember Disraeli's comment, "There are three kinds of lies: lies, damned lies, and statistics." However, you should also remember that when misuse of statistics occurs, the problem is neither with the statistics nor with statistical methods, but with their careless use.

The following excerpt from Charles Darwin's *Origin of Species* illustrates how a scientific interpretation made from a body of evidence uses the hypothetico-deductive method. Note that Darwin sets up an experiment and uses statistics to support the inductive generalization that there is a great interdependence among animals and plants in nature.

> I am tempted to give one more instance showing how plants and animals, remote in the scale of nature, are bound together by a web of complex relations. I shall hereafter have occasion to show that the exotic Lobelia filgens is never visited in my garden by insects, and consequently, from its peculiar structure, never sets a seed. Nearly all our orchidaceous plants absolutely require the visits of insects to remove their pollen-masses and thus to fertilize them. I find from experiments that humble-bees are almost indispensable to the fertilization of the heartsease (*Viola tricolor*), for other bees do not visit this flower. I have also found that the visits of bees are necessary for the fertilization of some kinds of clover; for instance, 20 heads of Dutch clover (*Trifolium repens*) yielded 2290 seeds, but 20 other heads protected from bees produced not one. Again, 100 heads of red clover (*T. pratense*) produced 2700 seeds, but the same number of protected heads produced not a single seed. Humble-bees alone visit red clover, as other bees cannot reach the nectar. It has been suggested that moths may fertilize the clovers; but I doubt whether they could do so in the case of the red clover, from their weight not being sufficient to depress the wind-petals. Hence we may infer as highly probable that, if the whole genus of humble-bees became extinct or very rare in England, the heartsease and red clover would become very rare, or wholly disappear. The number of

humble-bees in any district depends in a great measure on the number of field-mice, which destroy their combs and nests; and Col. Newman, who has long attended to the habits of humble-bees, believes that "more than two-thirds of them are thus destroyed all over England." Now the number of mice is largely dependent as everyone knows, on the number of cats; and Col. Newman says, "Near villages and small towns I have found the nests of humble-bees more numerous than elsewhere, which I attribute to the number of cats that destroy the mice." Hence it is quite credible that the presence of a feline animal in large numbers in a district might determine, through the intervention first of mice and then of bees, the frequency of certain flowers in that district!

AN EXAMPLE

René Dubos, a microbiologist by training, wrote on a wide range of topics, especially environmentalism. He often referred to these writings as his theology of life on earth. He is sometimes credited with originating the slogan, "Think globally, act locally." He won the Pulitzer Prize in 1969 for his book So *Human an Animal*. In the following analysis we can see the characteristics of the referential interpretive focus.

THE ROOTS OF ALTRUISM

RENÉ DUBOS

In view of the fact that human beings evolved as hunters, it is not surprising that they have inherited a biological propensity to kill, as have all animal predators. But it is remarkable that a very large percentage of human beings find killing an extremely distasteful and painful experience. Despite the most subtle forms of propaganda, it is difficult to convince them that war is desirable. In contrast, altruism has long been practiced, often going so far as self-sacrifice. Altruism certainly has deep roots in man's biological past for the simple reason that it presents advantages for the survival of the group. However, the really human aspect of altruism is not its biological origin or its evolutionary advantages but rather the fact that humankind has now made it a virtue regardless of practical advantages or disadvantages. Since earliest recorded history altruism has become one of the absolute values by which humanity transcends animality.

The existence of altruism was recognized as far back as Neanderthal times, among the very first people who can be regarded as truly human. In the Shanidar cave of Iraq, for example, there was found a skeleton of a Neanderthalian adult male, dating from approximately 50,000 years ago. He had probably been blind, and one of his arms had been amputated above the elbow early in life. He had been killed by a collapse of the cave wall. As he was 40 years old at the time of his death and must have been incapable of fending for himself during much of his lifetime, it seems reasonable to assume that he had been cared for by the members of his clan. Several similar cases that could be interpreted as examples of "charity" have been recognized in other prehistoric sites. In fact, one of the first Neanderthalian skeletons to be discovered in Europe was that of a man approximately 50 years old who had suffered from extensive arthritis. His disease was so severe that he must have been unable to hunt or to engage in other strenuous activities. He, also, must therefore have depended for his survival upon the care of his clan.

Many prehistoric finds suggest attitudes of affection. A Stone Age tomb contains the body of a woman holding a young child in her arms. Caves in North America that were occupied some 9,000 years ago have yielded numerous sandals of different sizes: those of children's sizes are lined with rabbit fur, as if to express a special kind of loving care for the youngest members of the community.

Whether or not the words of altruism and love had equivalents in the languages of the Stone Age, the social attitudes which they denote existed. The fact that the philosophy of nonviolence was clearly formulated at the time of Jesus and Buddha suggests that it had developed at a much earlier date. The Golden Rule, "Do unto others as you would have them do unto you," exists in all religious doctrines, even in those that have reached us through the very first written documents. It must therefore have an extremely ancient origin.

Dubos' interpretive analysis of the origins of altruism in humans addresses the thesis that altruism has "ancient origins." He offers as evidence, discoveries made in a number of prehistoric sites that suggest that Stone Age people were capable of charitable acts and "attitudes of affection." His use of objective language and his careful definition of the concept of altruism support the validity of his analysis. He uses explanatory reasoning to show that the condition of skeletal remains and kinds of artifacts found in burial sites are examples of charity for the disabled and affection for children. He also concludes that the codification of philosophies of nonviolence, like those in the teachings of Jesus and the Buddha, supports the inference that such ideas were much older.

THE EXPLORATORY FOCUS

Writing that has an exploratory focus is speculative. The writer engaging in exploration may go beyond the standard interpretations.

Four characteristics are found in exploratory writing.

- The thesis is presented as a question or questions.
- Alternative explanations are offered.
- Tentative solutions are suggested.
- Informal style is used.

Questions

Exploratory writing emphasizes discovery. This emphasis is reflected in the process of asking questions about the subject matter being considered. The problems presented cannot be explained by available theories. This kind of thinking is the first step in scientific investigation. Notice how the following statements of an exploratory thesis suggest a range of possible answers.

- What can human beings do to allow a polluted environment to regenerate itself?
- What can increase students' success in school?

Alternative Explanations

Alternative explanations are offered. Exploratory writing allows the writer to put forth possible explanations that may seem unusual or startling. An unusual alternative explanation or several possible explanations of the topic provide the evidence to support the exploratory thesis.

Tentative Solutions

Although solutions are suggested and conclusions are drawn, they are tentative. That is, they are subject to change. It is this tentativeness that gives the speculation in exploratory writing its validity.

Informal Style

Exploratory writing is more subjective than other forms of referential writing. This subjectivity is reflected in the language used. First person pronouns sometimes appear and the style is probably more informal than most interpretive writing.

Tentative language is used. Words like *it seems* and *perhaps* indicate that the writer is offering explanations that are based on speculation rather than incontrovertible logic.

AN EXAMPLE

The following article from *The Atlantic* illustrates the range of questions that can be addressed in referential writing with an exploratory focus.

HOW SELF-DRIVING CARS WILL THREATEN PRIVACY

Adrienne LaFrance

Allow me to join you, if I may, on your morning commute sometime in the indeterminate future.

Here we are, stepping off the curb and into the backseat of a vehicle. As you close the car door behind you, the address of your office—our destination—automatically appears on a screen embedded in the back of a leather panel in front of you. "Good morning," says the car's humanoid voice, greeting you by name before turning on NPR for you like it does each day.

You decide you'd like a cup of coffee, and you tell the vehicle so. "Peet's coffee, half-a-mile away," it confirms. Peet's, as it turns out, is a few doors down from Suds Cleaners. The car suggests you pick up your dry cleaning while you're in the neighborhood. "After work instead," you say. The car tweaks your evening travel itinerary accordingly.

As we run into Peet's to grab coffee, the car circles the block. Then, we're back in the vehicle, en route to your office once again. There's a lunch special coming up at the vegetarian place you like, the car tells you as we pass the restaurant. With your approval, it makes a reservation for Friday. We ride by a grocery store and a list of sale items appears on the screen. With a few taps, you've added them to your existing grocery list. The car is scheduled to pick up and deliver your order this evening.

We're less than a mile from your office now. Just like every morning, your schedule for the morning—a conference call at 10 a.m., a meeting at 11 a.m.—appears on the screen, along with a reminder that today is a colleague's birthday.

This is the age of self-driving cars, an era when much of the minutiae of daily life is relegated to a machine. Your commute was pleasant, relaxing, and efficient. Along with promising unprecedented safety on public roadways, driverless cars could make our lives a lot easier—freeing up people's time and attention to focus on other matters while they're moving from one place to the next.

But there's a darker side to all this, too. Let's rewind and take a closer look at your commute for a minute.

There we were. The car picked us up. We wanted coffee. It suggested Peet's. But if we'd stopped to look at the map on the screen when this happened, we might have noticed that Peet's wasn't actually the most efficient place to stop, nor was it on your list of preferred coffee shops, which the car's machine-learning algorithm developed over time. Peet's was, instead, a sponsored destination—not unlike a sponsored search result on Google. The car went ever-so-slightly out of the way to take you there.

Same goes for your dry cleaner's. The only reason you dropped off your clothes there in the first place was that the car suggested it. And the car suggested it because Suds paid Google, the maker of the self-driving car, to be a featured dry-cleaning destination in your area.

As for the lunch special, that really *is* a favorite restaurant of yours—but the car has never driven you there before. It knows your preferences because the vehicle has combed through your emails, identified key words, and assessed related messages for emotional tone. Similarly, the car knew which sale items to show you from the grocery store because it reviewed your past shopping activity. Plus, there was that one time you told a friend who was sitting in the car with you how much you liked a particular beer you'd tried the night before. The car heard your conversation, picked up on brand keywords, and knew to suggest the same beer for your shopping list when it went on sale.

In this near-future filled with self-driving cars, the price of convenience is surveillance.

This level of data collection is a natural extension of a driverless car's functionality. For self-driving cars to work, technologically speaking, an ocean of data has to flow into a lattice of sophisticated sensors. The car has to know where it is, where it's going, and be able to keep track of every other thing and creature on the road. Self-driving cars will rely on high-tech cameras and ultra-precise GPS data. Which means cars will collect reams of information about the people they drive around—like the data Uber has amassed about its customers's transportation habits, but down to a level of detail that's astonishing. The more personalized these vehicles get—or, the more conveniences they offer—the more individual data they'll incorporate into their services. The future I described might be a ways off, yet, but there's no reason to believe it's especially far-fetched.

The companies building self-vehicles have been cagey, so far, about how they're thinking about using individual data. At a Congressional hearing about driverless cars last week, Senator Ed Markey, a Democrat from Massachusetts, asked repeatedly whether driverless car manufacturers would undertake a minimum standard for consumer privacy protection. No one who was there to testify—including representatives from Google, GM, and the ride-sharing service Lyft—had a clear answer. "You need a minimal standard," Markey said at one point. "I'm not in a position to comment on that for Google," said Chris Urmson, the head of Google's self-driving car project.

Google has avoided this question before, too.

Last June, John M. Simpson, the director of the Privacy Project for the nonprofit advocacy group, Consumer Watchdog, attended Google's annual shareholder meeting. (Simpson bought two shares of Google stock, he told me, just so he could have the opportunity to question the company's executives.)

Simpson asked: "Would you be willing to protect driverless car users' privacy in the future, and commit today to using the information gathered by driverless cars only for operating the vehicle—and not for other purposes such as marketing?"

The executives on the stage glanced at each other for a moment, before David Drummond, a senior vice president and Google's chief legal counsel, spoke.

"I think it's pretty early in the game with driverless cars . . . to have a lot of rules saying, 'thou shalt not do X, Y, and Z, with the data,'" Drummond said. "I think once we get these operational, the value could be significant . . . it's a little early to be drawing conclusions which would, in a lot of ways, reduce innovation and our ability to deliver a great consumer product."

One approach to protecting privacy could be to anonymize all of the data that self-driving cars collect—making sure specific travel itineraries or details from a given trip aren't tied to an individual, for example.

But there's huge potential value to companies who mine individual data and use it for marketing and other services. Self-driving car makers could require an opt-in from consumers before collecting their data—but even that approach is often imperfect. For one thing, self-driving car manufacturers could choose to make opting in a requirement for using the technology at all. And even if individuals are given the choice to opt out of sharing their data—as anyone who has signed a tech platform's terms of service without reading it knows—terms of service agreements are often lengthy, full of legal jargon, and difficult to parse. Shashua is convinced that Google and its peers have enough incentive to be transparent about how it intends to use passenger data.

"For companies like Google and Uber, privacy issues are very important," said Amnon Shashua, a co-founder of MobileEye, which makes machine-vision technology for self-driving cars. "That could kill a business, if you don't handle privacy properly."

Simpson, from Consumer Watchdog, doesn't believe that privacy being important means tech giants will do the right thing. "Sometimes it's just that the people who are designing the gizmo don't even think in terms of privacy," he told me. "They just think: More data is always better. In their minds, it's just, 'We may not know what we're going to do with that data.'"

But that's not good enough, Simpson says. "It's inappropriate."

In this article, Adrienne LaFrance poses a problem that could result from our overreliance on technology to manage the mundane processes of our daily lives. She speculates about the potential outcomes and how something as innocent as one's daily route to and from work could potentially turn into a serious invasion of privacy. However, her conclusions are not certain because they cannot be proven and she herself admits that the future she describes is some time away. The author's exploration of this problem, though, raises questions about the potential impact of the adoption of technology into our daily lives and the ramifications this has on our privacy.

THE REFLECTIVE FOCUS

Any work that has a reflective focus, including the so-called *New Journalism* that appeared in the 1960s and 70s, tries to maintain reader interest almost to the point of losing its objectivity. Such writing usually focuses on stories about people and often appears in biographies. Many of its techniques are similar to those used by the writer of realistic fiction. But reflective writing focuses on real people. What keeps such writing from being literary is that the writer is making an effort to explain a subject. The entertainment we derive from reading reflective writing is secondary to our interest in the subject being revealed to us. Sometimes reflective writing is called parajournalistic writing because it can be distinguished from the typical informative patterns present in traditional journalism.

Reflective writing has four characteristics.

- The thesis addresses the significance of the topic.
- A dramatic structure is used to present the evidence.
- First person or omniscient point of view is used.
- Realistic detail is used.

Significance

The topic explained in reflective writing will have some significance. The thesis will address that significance. The thesis in reflective writing may not be stated explicitly because the initial interest in the work may be created by dramatic tension. If a thesis is stated, it will necessarily be limited by the scope of the facts in the work.

Dramatic Structure

The writer uses a scene by scene construction. Events are reported that cast some light on the characters or place being explained.

Point of View

The writer may intrude into the narrative through a first person point of view or may appear to know what is in the mind of the characters depicted in the work through an omniscient point of view.

Critics of this kind of writing say that such uses of point of view compromise the objectivity of the report. However, writers who have used omniscient point of view have defended the practice by saying that they research and interview people with just that in mind, to find out what the characters being written about are thinking.

Defenders of authorial intrusion argue that objectivity is a fiction anyway and that the writer, by revealing his or her own responses to the scene or events, is simply being honest.

Realistic Detail

The details the writer uses may reveal the status of the subject being investigated. For instance, a description of an item of jewelry or a mannerism may reveal quite a lot about the character. Details also help create a setting, as in literary writing. Dialogue may be used to allow the reader to better understand the characters involved. The kinds of things characters say give important clues to their personalities.

AN EXAMPLE

In *The Shadow of the Sun* (2001) Ryszard Kapuscinski records his travels in Africa as a foreign correspondent. In this excerpt, we can see how Kapuscinski uses the techniques of reflective writing to communicate his impressions of Africa as it emerged from colonialism.

THE LAZY RIVER

Ryszard Kapuscinski

Ngura is the parish of the missionary Stanislaw Stanislawek, whose car we are now following. Without him, we would never be able to find our way here. In Africa, if you leave the few main roads, you are lost. There are no guideposts, signs, markings. There are no detailed maps. Furthermore, the same roads run differently depending on the time of year, the weather, the level of the water, the reach of the constant fires.

Your only hope is some local, someone who knows the area intimately and can decipher the landscape, which for you is merely a baffling collection of signs and symbols, as unintelligible and bewildering as Chinese characters to a non-Chinese. 'What does this tree tell you?' 'Nothing!' 'Nothing? Why, it says that you must now turn left, or otherwise you will be lost. And this rock?' 'This rock? Also nothing!' 'Nothing? Don't you see that it is telling you to make a sharp right, at once, because straight ahead lies wilderness, a wasteland, death?'

In this way the native, that unprepossessing, barefoot expert on the writing of the landscape, the fluent reader of its inscrutable hieroglyphics, becomes your guide and your savior. Each one carries in his head a small geography, a private picture of the world that surrounds him, a most priceless knowledge and art, because in the worst tempest, in the deepest darkness, it enables him to find his way home and thus be saved, survive.

Father Stanislawek has lived here for years, and so guides us without effort through this remote region's intricate labyrinth. We arrive at his rectory. It is a poor, shabby barracks, once a country school but now closed for lack of a teacher. One classroom is now the priest's apartment: a bed and a table, a little stove, an oil lamp. The other classroom is the chapel. Next door stand the ruins of a little church, which collapsed. The missionary's task, his main occupation, is the construction of a new church. An unimaginable struggle, years of labour. There is no money, no workers, no materials, no effective means of transport. Everything depends on the priest's old car. What if it breaks down, falls apart, stops? Then everything will come to a standstill: the construction of the church, the teaching of the gospel, the saving of souls.

Later, we drove along the hill tops (below us stretched a plain covered in a thick green carpet of forest, enormous, endless, like the sea) to a settlement of gold diggers, who were searching for treasure in the bed of the winding and lazy Ngabadi River. It was afternoon already, and because there is no dusk here, and darkness can descend with sudden abruptness, we went first to where the diggers were working.

The river flows along the bottom of a deep gorge. Its bed is shallow, sandy, and gravelly. Its every centimeter has been ploughed, and you can see everywhere deep craters, pits, holes, ravines. Over this battlefield swarm crowds of half-naked, black-skinned people, streaming with sweat and water, all of them feverish, in a trance. For there is a peculiar climate here, one of excitement, desire, greed, risk, an atmosphere not unlike that of a darkly lit casino. It's as though an invisible roulette wheel were spinning somewhere near, capriciously whirling. But the dominant noises here are the hollow tapping of hoes digging through the gravel, the rustle of sand shaken through handheld sieves, and the monotonous utterances, neither calls not songs, made by the men working at the bottom of the gorge. It doesn't look as if these diggers are finding anything much, putting much aside. They shake the troughs, pour water into them, strain them, inspect the sand in the palm of their hand, hold it up to the light, throw everything back in the river.

And yet sometimes they do find something. If you gaze up to the top of the gorge, to the slopes of the hills that it intersects, you will see, in the shade of mango trees, under the thin umbrellas of acacias and tattered palms, the tents of Arabs. They are gold merchants from the Sahara, from neighbouring Niger, from Nidjamena and from Nubia. Dressed in white djellabas and snowy, gorgeously wound turbans, they sit idly in tent entrances drinking tea and smoking ornate water pipes. From time to time, one of the exhausted, sinewy black diggers climbs up to them from the bottom of the crowded gorge. He squats in front of an Arab, takes out and unrolls a piece of paper. In its crease lie several grains of gold sand. The Arab looks at them indifferently, deliberates, calculates, then names a figure. The grime-covered black Cameroonian, master of this land and of this river—it is, after all, his country and his gold—cannot contest the price, or argue for a higher one. Another Arab would give him the same measly sum. And the next one, too. There is only one price. This is a monopoly.

Darkness descends, the gorge empties and grows quiet, and one can no longer see its interior, now a black, undifferentiated chasm. We walk to the settlement, called Colomine. It is a hastily thrown together little town, so makeshift and scruffy that its inhabitants will have no qualms abandoning it once the gold in the river runs out. Shack leaning against shack, hovel against hovel, the streets of slums all emptying into the main one, which has bars and shops and where evening and nightlife take place. There is no electricity. Oil lamps, torches, fires and candles are burning everywhere. What their glow picks out from the darkness is flickering and wobbly. Here, some silhouettes slip by; over there, someone's face suddenly appears, an eye glitters, a hand emerges. That piece of tin, that's a roof. That flash you just saw, that's a knife. And that piece of plank—who knows what it's from and what purpose it serves. Nothing connects, arranges itself, can be composed into a whole. We know only that this darkness all around us is in motion, that it has shapes and emits sounds; that with the assistance of light we can bring bits of it up to the surface and momentarily observe them, but that as soon as the light goes out, everything will escape us and vanish. I saw hundreds of faces in Colomine, heard dozens of conversations, passed countless people walking, bustling about, sitting. But because of the way the images shimmered in the flickering flames of the lamps, because of their augmentation and the speed with which they followed one another, I am unable to connect a single face with a distinct individual or a single voice with some particular person that I met there.

In this excerpt Kapuscinski presents his observations of the search for gold in the Ngabadi River near Colomine, Cameroon. The first person narrative is presented in three dramatic scenes: the trip to Father Stanislawek's church, the gold diggers, and the description of Colomine. He uses dialogue to create tension in the narrative of the trip. He uses realistic detail to describe the landscape, the gold diggers at the river, and the settlement. Although there is not a stated thesis, we get the impression of the randomness and impermanence of the places he describes.

COMBINATIONS

Obviously, informative elements appear in other kinds of referential writing. It is what the writer does with the information presented that distinguishes one form of referential writing from another. Interpretive elements may appear in exploratory writing and exploration provides the basis of much scientific research.

WRITING STRATEGIES

All referential writing starts with facts. A referential purpose reflects an attempt on the part of the writer to explain some subject to the reader. Even though you may feel that you don't know enough to write an extended referential paper on anything, you know quite a lot about many subjects. Search your experiences. You can also gain information through reading and research.

Remember that accuracy and clarity are central to referential writing. Topics which, for you, are laden with emotion or which involve debatable issues that can't be proved with certainty will be developed in expressive and persuasive writing rather than in referential writing.

A clearly stated thesis is usually the key to a well-developed referential paper. Consider the following thesis: *Endangered species is a difficult problem to solve.* Such a statement is too vague to be a good starting point for a paper about endangered species. A better thesis statement would be this one: *Habitat destruction threatens many species of animals and plants with extinction.* This thesis provides more focus for the paper and suggests the kind of evidence that would be needed to support the thesis. A paper with such a thesis would probably include studies of the changes in the numbers of threatened species of animals and plants in areas where natural habitat had been destroyed.

Consider the following questions as you develop your ideas for a referential paper:

- Is your thesis clearly stated?
- What evidence relates to your thesis?
- Is all the evidence available to you?
- Can you draw any conclusions from the evidence you have?
- Do your conclusions account for all the evidence?
- Is the validity of the evidence apparent?
- Is the conclusion supported by most of the evidence?

AN OUTLINE

A commonly used organizational structure for writing in the sciences, both physical and behavioral, is the so-called IMRAD format. It is especially appropriate for reporting research based on experimentation but can also be used for reporting other kinds of information. A paper written in the IMRAD format usually conforms to the following outline.

   I. Introduction
      A. State the research question.
      B. Explain the significance of the topic.
      C. Discuss the background of the topic.
         1. Explain what is already known about the topic.
         2. Discuss the state of current research on the topic.

II. Method (Design and Procedure)
   A. Explain the design of the study.
   B. Discuss the procedure for collecting information.

III. Results
   A. Summarize the findings.
   B. Note the main trends in the data or any unexpected outcomes.

IV. Discussion
   A. Explain what the results show and how they answer the research question.
   B. Discuss the limitations of the results and/or the design.
   C. Discuss the implications of the study (what it suggests for further research).
   D. Include a conclusion*, a list of works cited and appendices.

*Although not a part of the IMRAD format, a formal conclusion may be appropriate for papers written for college courses.

PATTERN
Part 2

Classification
Description
Narration
Evaluation

Classification

We seem to use classification almost automatically to organize the enormous amount of information we deal with everyday. Examples of classification are all around us. For instance, we are able to find products in a supermarket because they are in a particular place along with other products of the same *kind*. Produce is in one place, meat in another, and dairy products in still another. This arrangement of products in a supermarket is based on a system of classification. We know where to look for a book in a library because it has been put in a place with other books of the same *type*. Psychology books are in one place; English books, in another; and books about automotive repair, in yet another. Again the principle of arrangement is based on a classification system, putting books of the same *category* together.

The tendency to classify seems to be a human preoccupation. Films are rated G, PG, PG-13, R, and NC-17. Vitamins are labeled A, B, C, etc. Singers are classified as sopranos, altos, tenors, and basses. Musical instruments are grouped into strings, woodwinds, brasses, and percussion.

We can call this use of classification formal classification. Two other variations of the use of classification are 1) comparison and contrast and 2) definition. Comparison and contrast involves two elements in a classification system while definition involves just one.

FORMAL CLASSIFICATION

When we classify, we arrange information into groups and then name the groups. These groups, or classes, are related to each other categorically. In other words, we put similar things into categories together. We are concerned with groups of things, rather than with individuals. We are interested in showing how groups are related to each other, how something is like others of its class, and what all members of the class have in common.

Using a system of classification to organize a paper is an effective method of explaining a topic clearly. Almost any topic can be organized by using a system of classification. All it takes is asking the question, "What kinds of _____ are there?" The answer to the question is a system of classification that tells us how to arrange the details of the topic. If we ask a question like, "What kinds of alternate energy sources are there?" the answer will suggest a system of classification, a way of organizing a paper about alternate energy sources. The classification system for alternate energy sources might look something like this:

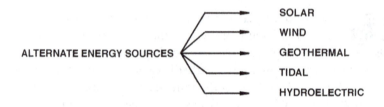

Alternative energy sources is the general category. It includes the sub-classes of solar, wind, geothermal, tidal, and hydroelectric. These sub-classes are related to each other categorically because they are members of the same class, alternative energy sources. You can develop almost any topic by using classification, but you will need to keep in mind three considerations: the scope of the topic, the basis of classification, and the hierarchical relationships.

As a general rule, for papers written in school, the number of categories will need to be limited. In the example above, kinds of alternative energy sources, we can see that the topic limited itself naturally to five categories. Not all topics, however, are quite so easy. For some topics, the structure of the system must be altered in order to get the kind of narrowing of the topic needed.

Classification systems, although they are logical, are arbitrary. For most topics, classification systems can be changed by changing the basis of the classification. For example, for the topic *household appliances*, we could create a classification system based on the manufacturer of the appliance. The following list illustrates this principle: Admiral, Amana, AMC, Brothers, Caloric, Emerson, Frigidaire, Gaffers/Sattler, Gibson,

GE/Hotpoint, Jenn-Air, Kelvinator, Kenmore, Kitchen-Aid, Litton, Magic Chef, Maytag, Modern Maid, Norse, Quasar, Roper, Scotsman, Sears, Speed Queen, Sub-Zero, Tappan, Thermador, U Line, Wards, Westinghouse, and Whirlpool. Obviously, a paper with that many categories would be unmanageable. The categories would have to be limited in some way, but selecting just three or four brands to discuss would not be adequate, especially if the purpose of the explanation was referential. A referential paper with an informative focus creates the expectation of comprehensiveness on the part of the reader.

Changing the *basis of classification* would create a new way of looking at the topic. If the basis of classification were changed to the location of the appliance in the house, the system would look like this.

This classification system has three categories. By selecting one of the locations, say the kitchen, another classification system could be created, as shown in the following tree diagram.

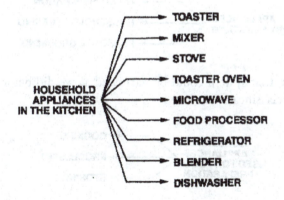

This system could be limited further by narrowing the scope of the category.

or

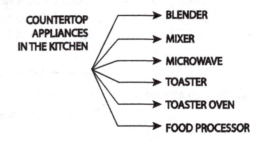

With a basis of classification other than manufacturer or location, such as the use or the function of the appliance, a classification system would look like this.

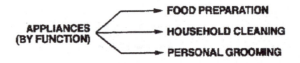

Of course, that system could be narrowed as we did before with the other bases of classification.

Classification involves not only the relationships among the categories of the system, but also a hierarchical relationship from general to specific. In the tree diagrams used to represent classification systems, each category is more specific than the one to the left of it. The following diagram illustrates this concept.

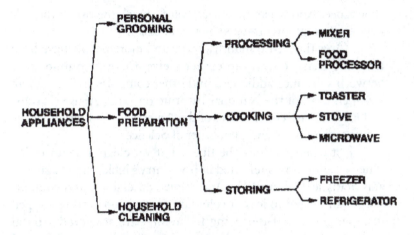

In the preceding diagram, the category *stove* is more specific than the category *cooking*, which is more specific than the category *food preparation*. The same kind of relationship between specific and general exists in all classification systems. The categories for personal grooming and household cleaning could be completed in a similar way.

AN EXAMPLE

In the following essay we discover how formal classification is used to explain a complex body of medical research on addiction.

'BEHAVIORAL' ADDICTIONS: DO THEY EXIST?

CONSTANCE HOLDEN

Aided by brain imaging advances, scientists are looking for evidence that compulsive nondrug behaviors lead to long-term changes in reward circuitry.

People toss around the term "addiction" to describe someone's relationship to a job, a boyfriend, or a computer. But scientists have traditionally confined their use of the term to substances—namely alcohol and other drugs—that clearly foster physical dependence in the user.

That's changing, however. New knowledge about the brain's reward system, much gained by superrefined brain scan technology, suggests that as far as the brain is concerned, a reward's a reward, regardless of whether it comes from a chemical or an experience. And where there's a reward, there's the risk of the vulnerable brain getting trapped in a compulsion.

"Over the past 6 months, more and more people have been thinking that, contrary to earlier views, there is commonality between substance addictions and other compulsions," says Alan Leshner, head of the National Institute on Drug Abuse (NIDA) and incoming executive officer of the American Association for the Advancement of Science, publisher of Science.

Just where to draw the line is not yet clear. The unsettled state of definitions is reflected in psychiatry's bible, the Diagnostic and Statistical Manual IV. Addictions, obsessions, and compulsions—all related to loss of voluntary control and getting trapped in repetitious, self-defeating behavior—are scattered around under "substance-related disorders," "eating disorders," "sexual and gender identity disorders," "anxiety disorders," and "impulse-control disorders not elsewhere classified." In that last grab-bag are compulsive gambling, kleptomania, fire-setting, hair-pulling, and "intermittent explosive disorder."

Addiction used to be defined as dependence on a drug as evidenced by craving, increased tolerance, and withdrawal. But even some seemingly classical addictions don't follow that pattern. Cocaine, for example, is highly addictive but causes little withdrawal. And a person who gets hooked on morphine while in the hospital may stop taking the drug without developing an obsession with it.

Now many researchers are moving toward a definition of addiction based more on behavior, and they are starting to look at whether brain activity and biochemistry are affected the same way in "behavioral" addictions as they are by substance abuse. One who endorses this perspective is psychologist Howard Shaffer, who heads the Division on Addictions at Harvard. "I had great difficulty with my own colleagues when I suggested that a lot of addiction is the result of experience . . . repetitive, high-emotion, high-frequency experience," he says. But it's become clear that neuroadaptation—that is, changes in neural circuitry that help perpetuate the behavior—occurs even in the absence of drug-taking, he says.

The experts are fond of saying that addiction occurs when a habit "hijacks" brain circuits that evolved to reward survival-enhancing behavior such as eating and sex. "It stands to reason if you can derange these circuits with pharmacology, you can do it with natural rewards too," observes Stanford University psychologist Brian Knutson. Thus, drugs are no longer at the heart of the matter. "What is coming up fast as being the central core issue . . . is continued engagement in self-destructive behavior despite adverse consequences," says Steven Grant of NIDA.

Not everybody is on board with this open-ended definition. For one thing, says longtime addiction researcher Roy Wise of NIDA, drugs are far more powerful than any "natural" pleasure when it comes to the amounts of dopamine released. Nonetheless, behavioral resemblances to addiction are getting increasing notice.

Gambling

In a class of its own as the disorder that most resembles drug addiction is pathological gambling. Compulsive gamblers live from fix to fix, throwing away the rest of their lives for another roll of the dice—and deluding themselves that luck will soon smile on them. Their subjective cravings can be as intense as those of drug abusers; they show tolerance through their need to increase betting; and they experience highs rivaling that of a drug high. Up to half of pathological gamblers "show withdrawal symptoms looking like a mild form of drug withdrawal," says Shaffer—including churning guts, sleep disturbance, sweating, irritability, and craving. And like drug addicts, they are at risk of sudden relapse even after many years of abstinence.

Furthermore, what's going on inside gamblers' heads looks like what goes on in addicts' heads. Yale psychiatrist Marc Potenza finds that when pathological gamblers are exposed to videos of people gambling and talking about gambling, they show activity changes in some of the same frontal and limbic brain regions as do cocaine addicts exposed to images that stir up drug craving, as assessed by functional magnetic resonance imaging (fMRI). And a positron emission tomography study of pathological gamblers playing blackjack, conducted by psychiatrist Eric Hollander of Mount Sinai School of Medicine in New York City, showed significant changes in cortical arousal depending on whether they were just playing cards or betting with a $100 stake. He says it resembles another study showing alcoholics' brain reactions to looking at a bottle of Coke versus a bottle of whiskey.

Like addicts, gamblers also respond to drugs that block drug highs. Suck Won Kim, a psychiatrist at the University of Minnesota Medical School in Minneapolis, has tried naltrexone, an opiate antagonist, on a variety of compulsive behaviors including gambling. In an 11-week trial on 45 gamblers, naltrexone inhibited both the urge to gamble and the high from it in 75% of the group—compared with 24% of a comparable group on placebo—suggesting that drugs and gambling stimulate some of the same biochemical pathways.

And finally, there's cognitive evidence: Gamblers, like drug addicts, do badly at a "gambling task," success at which requires the ability to perceive that delayed gains will be larger than immediate ones.

Food

Can food be said to be an addiction? Overeaters Anonymous—which, like Gamblers Anonymous, is patterned on Alcoholics Anonymous—says yes. The experts, however, say it depends on the disorder.

Compulsive overeating certainly has the look of an addiction that can dominate a person's life. There's also biochemical evidence suggesting a kinship. Psychiatrist Nora Volkow of Brookhaven National Laboratory in Upton, New York, and colleagues found that in a group of compulsive overeaters, dopamine receptor availability was lower, an anomaly also seen in drug addicts. "Dopamine deficiency in obese individuals may perpetuate pathological eating as a means to compensate for decreased activation of these circuits," Volkow's team suggests.

Bulimia, which is characterized by bingeing and vomiting, also looks a lot like an addiction, Hollander notes. Unlike anorexia, which involves rigidly controlled behavior and no high, "bulimia and binge eating have an impulsive component—pleasure and arousal followed by guilt and remorse."

Patricia Faris, a gastrointestinal physiologist at the University of Minnesota, Minneapolis, believes that as with drug addictions, bulimic behavior is initially voluntary but is transformed into a compulsion because of changes that it wreaks on the nervous system. Bulimia clearly affects reward centers: Faris says patients become increasingly depressed and anxious before episodes; immediately following, they uniformly report a pleasant "afterglow."

Faris has come up with a novel hypothesis: that bulimia disregulates the vagal nerve, which regulates heart and lungs as well as the vomiting impulse. She suspects that a binge-purge episode then brings the vagal nerve back to its normal role. This retraining of the vagal nerve also has long-term effects on the brain's reward circuitry, she believes, as suggested by the fact that bulimics have a high relapse rate and are very hard to help once they've been at it for a few years. Kim says that although the theory is speculative, he believes Faris is on the right track in approaching the problem "from neural system concepts" as opposed to a more traditional emphasis on biochemistry.

Sex

There's not much research on sex as an addiction, and some researchers are dubious about whether such a basic function can have that distinction. Sex is really a distinct subject because it's "wired separately," in the opinion of Kim of Minnesota. He notes, for example, that the opioid antagonist naltrexone "really doesn't affect sexual desire that much," so it doesn't follow the same pathways as, say, gambling.

Yet so-called sex addicts do display behaviors characteristic of addiction: They obsess about whatever their favorite practice is, never get enough, feel out of control, and experience serious disruption of their lives because of it. That leads Shaffer to conclude that some behaviors qualify as sex addictions: "I think those things that are robust and reliable shifters of subjective experience all hold the potential for addiction." To be sure, he adds, sex trails behind drugs or gambling, being "relatively robust but unreliable" in delivering satisfaction.

Anna Rose Childress, who does brain imaging studies at the University of Pennsylvania in Philadelphia, says sex addicts resemble cocaine addicts and probably share with them a defect in "inhibitory circuitry." In both instances, "people say when they're in this big 'go' state they feel as though there is override [of inhibition] . . . a feeling of being unable to stop," says Childress.

Scientists are just beginning to use imaging to try to determine whether there's a tangible basis to these feelings. Childress has been comparing the circuits activated by cocaine in addicts and sexual desire in normal subjects in hope of identifying the "stop!" circuitry. And psychiatrist Peter Martin at Vanderbilt University in Nashville, Tennessee, says a preliminary study with normal subjects indicates that brain activity associated with sexual arousal looks like that accompanying drug consumption. He plans to do further comparisons using self-described sex addicts.

Shopping, running, clicking . . .

Although there is no shortage of therapies for every imaginable addiction, there is little or no published research on other disorders. One problem that afflicts a great many women, in particular, is compulsive shopping, says Kim. Compulsive shoppers typically end up with huge debts and their houses stuffed with unused merchandise. Shopping binges are very often precipitated by feelings of depression and anxiety, Shaffer says; the shopping itself can generate temporary druglike highs before the shopper—like a cocaine addict—crashes into depression, guilt, anxiety, and fatigue.

Some have no doubt this is an addiction. "In my clinical experience, [compulsive shoppers] have a similar kind of withdrawal," says Shaffer. Kim agrees: "These people can't control it. We think it's essentially the same thing as gambling." Kim thinks compulsive shoplifting (kleptomania) is also closely related and, in fact, has published the first formal study trying doses of naltrexone with kleptomania; 9 of 10 patients, he says, were much improved after 11 weeks of treatment.

Then there's Internet abuse, the country's fastest growing "addiction." But whether any such phenomenon exists is something about which scientists—if not therapists—are cautious. There are indeed people who neglect the rest of their lives as they spend every waking moment at the monitor. But is it the technology or the behavior that the technology enables that people are really hooked on? The things people are addicted to on the Net are the same things people get hooked on without it: gambling (including day trading), pornography, and shopping, notes Marc Pratarelli of the University of Southern Colorado in Pueblo. His group is doing factor analysis of questionnaire responses by computer users to get at the "core issues" and to determine "if it is in fact just one more fancy tool" to enable a primary habit.

And what about "positive addictions"? Some years ago jogging was touted as one that raised endorphin levels (which in turn stoke up the dopamine) and resulted in a "natural high." Although human behavioral addictions are difficult if not impossible to model in animals, Stefan Brené of the Karolinska Institute in Stockholm, Sweden, thinks he has done it with running. He says rats that have been bred to be addiction-prone spend much more time on the running wheel than other rats do. Furthermore, biochemical tests indicate the impulses both to run and to consume cocaine are governed by "similar biochemical adaptations." He also says the work—most of it as yet unpublished—shows that in an addiction-prone rat, running can increase preference for ethanol—"indicating that a natural, nontoxic . . . addiction can under some instances potentiate the preference for a drug."

The above by no means exhausts the list of behaviors that some scientists see as addictive. And it seems to be true across the board that having one addiction lowers the threshold for developing another, says Walter Kaye, who does research on eating disorders at the University of Pittsburgh Medical Center. Just what form addictions take has a lot to do with one's sex, says Pratarelli. Men are overwhelmingly represented among sex "addicts" and outnumber women by about 2 to 1 in gambling and substance abuse; women are prone to what psychiatrist Susan McElroy of the University of Cincinnati College of Medicine calls the "mall disorders"—eating, shopping, and kleptomania. (Kim says the ratio of females to males in kleptomania is 2 or 3 to 1; perhaps 90% of compulsive shoppers are women.)

To cast more light on the mechanisms of addiction, scientists have taken a growing interest in behavior of the brain's reward circuitry in normal subjects. In a much-cited paper in last May's issue of Neuron, Hans Breiter of Massachusetts General Hospital in Boston and his colleagues used fMRI to map the responses of normal males in a roulette-type game of chance. Blood flow in dopamine-rich areas, the scientists found, indicated that "the same neural circuitry is involved in the highs and lows of winning money, abusing drugs, or anticipating a gastronomical treat." Other research has been showing that many types of rewards besides money—including chocolate, music, and beauty—affects those reward circuits.

Shaffer and others in his camp believe that if such a reward is powerful enough, it can retrain those circuits in a vulnerable person. Not everyone, however, buys the idea that nondrug stimuli really can be potent enough to generate what has been traditionally thought of as addiction. "Many people believe that [only] addictive drugs alter the circuitry in some critical way," says Wise of NIDA. And, he says, drugs are far more powerful than "natural" rewards, increasing dopamine "two to five times more strongly." Kaye also warns that the fact that certain disorders share the same pathways does not necessarily prove they're closely linked. After all, he notes, "stroke and Parkinson's also involve the same pathway."

> Despite the uncertainties, addiction research is "going beyond the earlier conceptual framework," says neuroscientist Read Montague of Baylor College of Medicine in Houston. "Historically, these definitions have come out of animal behavior literature," and addiction has been defined in terms of rats frenziedly pressing levers for cocaine. Now, he says, "we need a better theory of how the brain processes rewarding events," one that involves discovering the "algorithms" people follow that lead them into and then keep them trapped in their disastrous behaviors.

In this work we can see clearly how classification enables the writer to present information clearly and coherently. Each category is addressed in sequence. This arrangement allows the reader to see the relationships that exist within the classification system.

VARIATIONS IN FORMAL CLASSIFICATION

The discussion of classification so far has focused on its use in referential writing. When classification is used as a pattern of organization for one of the other kinds of writing (expressive, literary, or persuasive), the structure explained above may change in some ways. For instance, the need for comprehensiveness is associated with informative writing. However, expressive, literary, and persuasive classifications don't necessarily require that the writer include all possible categories for a topic. In addition, in nonreferential writing, categories may overlap and different bases of classifition may appear in the system.

EXPRESSIVE CLASSIFICATION

Although formal classification with an expressive purpose is not very common, sometimes it does appear. When it is used in expressive writing, formal classification will appear more frequently in works that have either an autobiographical or a ritual perspective because those forms of expressive writing are less spontaneous than either personal or interpersonal forms are.

AN EXAMPLE

The following example from *The Autobiography of Bertrand Russell* illustrates how classification can be used to reveal the identity of the writer.

THREE PASSIONS

BERTRAND RUSSELL

Three passions, simple but overwhelmingly strong, have governed my life: the longing for love, the search for knowledge, and unbearable pity for the suffering of mankind. These passions, like great winds, have blown me hither and thither, in a wayward course, over a deep ocean of anguish, reaching to the very verge of despair.

I have sought love, first, because it brings ecstasy—ecstasy so great that I would often have sacrificed all the rest of life for a few hours of this joy. I have sought it, next because it relieves loneliness—that terrible loneliness in which one shivering consciousness looks over the rim of the world into the cold unfathomable lifeless abyss. I have sought it, finally, because in the union of love I have seen, in a mystic miniature, the prefiguring vision of the heaven that saints and poets have imagined. This is what I sought, and though it might seem too good for human life, this is what—at last—I have found.

With equal passion I have sought knowledge. I have wished to understand the hearts of men. I have wished to know why the stars shine. And I have tried to apprehend the Pythagorean power by which number holds sway above the flux. A little of this, but not much, I have achieved.

Love and knowledge, so far as they were possible, led upward toward the heavens. But always pity brought me back to earth. Echoes of cries of pain reverberate in my heart. Children in famine, victims tortured by oppressors, helpless old people a hated burden to their sons, and the whole world of loneliness, poverty, and pain make a mockery of what human life should be. I long to alleviate the evil, but I cannot, and I too suffer.

This has been my life. I have found it worth living, and would gladly live it again if the chance were offered me.

Bertrand Russell, a distinguished philosopher, reveals his analytical mind in this excerpt. In his carefully considered analysis of his own inner emotional responses and his values, he defines himself and allows us to share in his vision of himself.

He organizes the writing by putting his passions into three categories: love, knowledge, and pity. Each category is then developed by adding details, examples, and, in the case of knowledge, further classification.

LITERARY CLASSIFICATION

Formal classification, when it appears as an organizing principle for writing with a literary purpose, is usually not a work of fiction because fiction, both long and short, is typically organized by a combination of narration and description. Consequently, literary works that organize with classification will usually be non-fiction.

AN EXAMPLE

The following example is taken from an article in the eighteenth-century periodical entitled the *Spectator*, an influential paper written by Joseph Addison and Sir Richard Steele. This excerpt is from an article written by Addison for the *Spectator* on Monday, March 12, 1711. In it Addison identifies the different kinds of audiences he intends the *Spectator* to affect.

THE AIMS OF THE SPECTATOR

JOSEPH ADDISON

It is with much satisfaction that I hear this great city inquiring day by day after my papers, and receiving my morning lectures with a becoming seriousness and attention. My publisher tells me that there are already three thousand of them distributed every day. So that if I allow twenty readers to every paper, which I look upon as a modest computation, I may reckon about three-score thousand disciples in London and Westminster, who I hope will take care to distinguish themselves from the thoughtless herd of their ignorant and unattentive brethren. Since I have raised myself so great an audience, I shall spare no pains to make their instruction agreeable, and their diversion useful. For which reasons I shall endeavor to enliven morality with wit, and to temper wit with morality, that my readers may, if possible, both ways find their account in the speculation of the day. And to the end that their virtue and discretion may not be short, transient, intermitting starts of thought, I have resolved to refresh their memories from day to day, till I have recovered them out of that desperate state of vice and folly into which the age is fallen. The mind that lies fallow but a single day sprouts up in follies that are only to be killed by a constant and assiduous culture. It was said of Socrates that he brought philosophy down from heaven, to inhabit among men; and I shall be ambitious to have it said of me that I have brought philosophy out of closets and libraries, schools and colleges, to dwell in clubs and assemblies, at tea tables and in coffeehouses.

I would therefore in a very particular manner recommend these my speculations to all well-regulated families that set apart an hour in every morning for tea and bread and butter; and would earnestly advise them for their good to order this paper to be punctually served up, and to be looked upon as part of the tea equipage.

Sir Francis Bacon observes that a well-written book, compared with its rivals and antagonists, is like Moses' serpent, that immediately swallowed up and devoured those of the Egyptians. I shall not be so vain as to think that where *The Spectator* appears the other public prints will vanish; but shall leave it to my reader's consideration whether is it not much better to be let into the knowledge of one's self, than to hear what passes in Muscovy or Poland; and to amuse ourselves with such writings as tend to the wearing out of ignorance, passion, and prejudice, than such as naturally conduce to inflame hatreds, and make enmities irreconcilable?

In the next place, I would recommend this paper to the daily perusal of those gentlemen whom I cannot but consider as my good brothers and allies, I mean the fraternity of spectators, who live in the world without having anything to do in it; and either by the affluence of their fortunes or laziness of their dispositions have no other business with the rest of mankind but to look upon them. Under this class of men are comprehended all contemplative tradesmen, titular physicians, fellows of the Royal Society, Templars that are not given to be contentious, and statesmen that are out of business; in short, everyone that considers the world as a theater, and desires to form a right judgment of those who are the actors on it.

There is another set of men that I must likewise lay a claim to, whom I have lately called the blanks of society, as being altogether unfurnished with ideas, till the business and conversation of the day has supplied them. I have often considered these poor souls with an eye of great commiseration, when I have heard them asking the first man they have met with, whether there was any news stirring? and by that means gathering together materials for thinking. These needy persons do not know what to talk of till about twelve o'clock in the morning; for by that time they are pretty good judges of the weather, know which way the wind sits, and whether the Dutch mail be come in. As they lie at the mercy of the first man they meet, and are grave or impertinent all the day long, according to the notions which they have imbibed in the morning, I would earnestly entreat them not to stir out of their chambers till they have read this paper, and do promise them that I will daily instil into them such sound and wholesome sentiments as shall have a good effect on their conversation for the ensuing twelve hours.

In this excerpt we are made aware of three groups of readers: well-regulated families, the fraternity of spectators, and blanks of society. As you can see, the literary purpose of the essay is especially apparent in Addison's humorous characterization of the "blanks of society."

PERSUASIVE CLASSIFICATION

The categories developed in persuasive classifications can be used to create an appeal to the audience.

AN EXAMPLE

John F. Kennedy, the charismatic thirty-fifth President of the United States, illustrates in his "Inaugural Address" how classification can be used to persuade an audience.

INAUGURAL ADDRESS

John F. Kennedy

We observe today not a victory of party but a celebration of freedom, symbolizing an end as well as a beginning, signifying renewal as well as change. For I have sworn before you and Almighty God the same solemn oath our forebears prescribed nearly a century and three-quarters ago.

The world is very different now. For man holds in his mortal hands the power to abolish all forms of human poverty and all forms of human life. And yet the same revolutionary belief for which our forebears fought is still at issue around the globe, the belief that the rights of man come not from generosity of the state but from the hand of God.

We dare not forget today that we are the heirs of the first revolution. Let the word go forth from this time and place, to friend and foe alike, that the torch has been passed to a new generation of Americans, born in this century, tempered by war, disciplined by a hard and bitter peace, proud of our ancient heritage, and unwilling to witness or permit the slow undoing of those human rights to which this nation has always been committed, and to which we are committed today at home and around the world.

Let every nation know, whether it wishes us well or ill, that we shall pay any price, bear any burden, meet any hardship, support any friend, oppose any foe to assure the survival and the success of liberty.

This much we pledge—and more.

To those allies whose cultural and spiritual origins we share, we pledge the loyalty of faithful friends. United, there is little we cannot do in a host of co-operative ventures. Divided, there is little we can do, for we dare not meet a powerful challenge at odds and split asunder.

To those new states whom we welcome to the ranks of the free, we pledge our word that one form of colonial control shall not have passed away merely to be replaced by a far more iron tyranny. We shall not always hope to find them strongly supporting their own freedom, and to remember that, in the past, those who foolishly sought power by riding the back of the tiger ended up inside.

To those people in the huts and villages of half the globe struggling to break the bonds of mass misery, we pledge our best efforts to help them help themselves, for whatever period is required, not because the communists may be doing it, not because we seek their votes, but because it is right. If a free society cannot help the many who are poor, it cannot save the few who are rich.

To our sister republics south of the border, we offer a special pledge: to convert our good words into good deeds, in a new alliance for progress, to assist free men and free governments in casting off the chains of poverty. But this peaceful revolution of hope cannot become the prey of hostile powers. Let all our neighbors know that we shall join with them to oppose aggression or subversion anywhere in the Americas. And let every other power know that this hemisphere intends to remain the master of its own house.

To that world assembly of sovereign states, the United Nations, our last best hope in an age where the instruments of war have far outpaced the instruments of peace, we renew our pledge of support: to prevent it from becoming merely a forum for invective, to strengthen its shield of the new and the weak, and to enlarge the area in which its writ may run.

Finally, to those nations who would make themselves our adversary, we offer not a pledge but a request: that both sides begin anew the quest for peace, before the dark powers of destruction unleashed by science engulf all humanity in planned or accidental self-destruction.

We dare not tempt them with weakness. For only when our arms are sufficient beyond doubt can we be certain beyond doubt that they will never be employed.

But neither can two great and powerful groups of nations take comfort from our present course—both sides over-burdened by the cost of modern weapons, both rightly alarmed by the steady spread of the deadly atom, yet both racing to alter that uncertain balance of terror that stays the hand of mankind's final war.

So let us begin anew, remembering on both sides that civility is not a sign of weakness, and sincerity is always subject to proof. Let us never negotiate out of fear, but let us never fear to negotiate.

Let both sides explore what problems unite us instead of belaboring those problems which divide us.

Let both sides seek to invoke the wonders of science instead of its terrors. Together let us explore the stars, conquer the deserts, eradicate disease, tap the ocean depths and encourage the arts and commerce.

Let both sides unite to heed in all corners of the earth the commands of Isaiah to "undo the heavy burdens . . . [and] let the oppressed go free."

And if a beachhead of co-operation may push back the jungle of suspicion, let both sides join in creating a new endeavor, not a new balance of power, but a new world of law, where the strong are just and the weak secure and the peace preserved.

All this will not be finished in the first one hundred days. Nor will it be finished in the first one thousand days, nor in the life of this Administration, nor even perhaps in our lifetime on this planet. But let us begin.

In your hands, my fellow citizens, more than mine, will rest the final success or failure of our course. Since this country was founded, each generation of Americans has been summoned to give testimony to its national loyalty. The graves of young Americans who answered the call to service surround the globe.

Now the trumpet summons us again—not as a call to bear arms, though arms we need; not as a call to battle, though embattled we are; but a call to bear the burden of a long twilight struggle, year in and year out, "rejoicing in hope, patient in tribulation," a struggle against the common enemies of men: tyranny, poverty, disease and war itself.

Can we forge against these enemies a grand and global alliance, North and South, East and West, that can assure a more fruitful life for all mankind? Will you join in that historic effort?

In the long history of the world, only a few generations have been granted the role of defending freedom in its hour of maximum danger. I do not shrink from this responsibility; I welcome it. I do not believe that any of us would exchange places with any other people or any other generation. The energy, the faith, the devotion which we bring to this endeavor will light our country and all who serve it, and the glow from that fire can truly light the world.

And so, my fellow Americans, ask not what your country can do for you; ask what you can do for your country.

My fellow citizens of the world, ask not what America will do for you, but what together we can do for the freedom of man.

Finally, whether you are citizens of America or citizens of the world, ask of us here the same high standards of strength and sacrifice which we ask of you. With a good conscience our only sure reward, with history the final judge of our deeds, let us go forth to lead the land we love, asking His blessing and His help, but knowing that here on earth God's work must truly be our own.

Kennedy's speech uses classification to identify the various kinds of audiences he is addressing. Since the speech is persuasive rather than referential, the categories are arranged for rhetorical effect rather than for logical coherence. Some categories overlap and some are not parallel to the others. For example, the categories "allies," "new states," "sister republics south of the border," and "nations that would make themselves our adversary" are all included in the category "world assembly of sovereign states." The category "people in the huts and villages of half the globe struggling to break the bonds of mass misery" is not parallel to the other categories.

REFERENTIAL CLASSIFICATION

Classification is used frequently to organize information in referential writing. It has the advantage of allowing the writer to organize a large amount of information and present it to the reader in a meaningful way.

AN EXAMPLE

In his book *The Wealth of Nation* (1776), Adam Smith gives his famous defense of capitalism. In this excerpt from Chapter 5, he uses classification to explain the four employments of capital.

THE FOUR EMPLOYMENTS FOR CAPITAL

ADAM SMITH

A capital may be employed in four different ways; either, first, in procuring the rude produce annually required for the use and consumption of the society; or, secondly, in manufacturing and preparing that rude produce for immediate use and consumption; or, thirdly in transporting either the rude or manufactured produce from the places where they abound to those where they are wanted; or, lastly, in dividing particular portions of either into such small parcels as suit the occasional demands of those who want them. In the first way are employed the capitals of all those who undertake improvement or cultivation of lands, mines, or fisheries; in the second, those of all master manufacturers; in the third, those of all wholesale merchants; and in the fourth, those of all retailers. It is difficult to conceive that a capital should be employed in any way which may not be classed under some one or other of those four.

Smith creates four categories. He then goes back and gives examples of occupations that fit into each of the four categories.

WRITING STRATEGIES

If you are using classification to organize your paper, consider the following questions.

- What "kinds" of your topic are there? (List them)
- What principle of classification accounts for how you generated your categories?
- If you have generated more than five categories, how can you limit the number?
- What details will you include in each category?
- What other patterns of organization will you use to develop the categories?

COMPARISON AND CONTRAST

Comparison and contrast is a method of organization derived from classification that shows how two closely related things are similar and/or different. For example, we can compare and contrast two people, two cars, two cats, or two of just about anything. But we can make meaningful comparisons and contrasts only if there is a categorical relationship between the two things being compared and contrasted. Although a comparison and contrast between an oak tree and house is possible, it probably would not be very meaningful. (The discussion of *analogy* in the next section of this chapter shows that there are circumstances when the comparison of an oak tree and a house could be made.) In most cases, the similarities and differences are meaningful only if they are derived from a classification system. We recognize similarities and differences when we create a classification system. For example, a marine biologist might classify whales, which are members of the same species, by noting the differences in the kind of food they eat. The potential for comparison and contrast is always present in a classification system.

PATTERNS OF COMPARISON AND CONTRAST

There are two types of organization used in comparison and contrast. Comparison and contrast can be structured by presenting the similarities and then the differences, a pattern called *separation of detail*, or by alternating between the similarities and differences of each aspect of the subject, a pattern called *alternation of detail*.

As with other decisions about the appropriate organizational pattern, whether to use alternation or separation of detail depends on the purpose, the audience, and the situational context. The length of the work may be a factor as well.

SEPARATION OF DETAIL

Separation of detail can be used effectively if there are only a few points to be considered. If the two things being compared and contrasted are complicated with a great many details to consider, the reader may be overburdened in trying to make the connections between them. The conclusion is especially important when separation of detail is used.

AN EXAMPLE

In this classic study of culture in *Patterns of Culture* (1934), anthropologist Ruth Benedict compares two kinds of Native American culture.

THE PUEBLOS OF NEW MEXICO
Ruth Benedict

The Pueblos are a ceremonious people. But that is not the essential fashion in which they are set off from the other peoples of North America and Mexico. It goes much deeper than any difference in degree in the amount of ritual that is current among them. The Aztec civilization of Mexico was as ritualistic as the Pueblo, and even the Plains Indians with their sun dance and their men's societies, their tobacco orders and their war rituals, had a rich ceremonialism.

The basic contrast between the Pueblos and the other cultures of North America is the contrast that is named and described by Nietzsche in his studies of Greek tragedy. He discusses two diametrically opposed ways of arriving at the value of existence. The Dionysian pursues them through 'the annihilation of the ordinary bounds and limits of existence'; he seeks to attain in his most valued moments escape from the boundaries imposed upon him by his five senses, to break through into another order of experience. The desire of the Dionysian, in personal experience or in ritual, is to press through it toward a certain psychological state, to achieve excess. The closest analogy to the emotions he seeks is drunkenness, and he values the illuminations of frenzy. With Blake, he believes 'the path of excess leads to the palace of wisdom.' The Apollonian distrusts all this, and has often little idea of the nature of such experiences. He finds means to outlaw them from his conscious life. He 'knows but one law, measure in the Hellenic sense.' He keeps the middle of the road, stays within the known map, does not meddle with disruptive psychological states. In Nietzsche's fine phrase, even in the exaltation of the dance he 'remains what he is, and retains his civic name.'

The Southwest Pueblos are Apollonian. Not all of Nietzsche's discussion of the contrast between Apollonian and Dionysian applies to the contrast between the Pueblos and the surrounding peoples. The fragments I have quoted are faithful descriptions, but there were refinements of the types in Greece that do not occur among the Indians of the Southwest, and among these latter, again, there are refinements that did not occur in Greece. It is with no thought of equating the civilization of Greece with that of aboriginal America that I use, in describing the cultural configurations of the latter, terms borrowed from the culture of Greece. I use them because they are categories that bring clearly to the fore the major qualities that differentiate Pueblo culture from those of other American Indians, not because all the attitudes that are found in Greece are found also in aboriginal America.

Apollonian institutions have been carried much further in the pueblos than in Greece. Greece was by no means single-minded. In particular, Greece did not carry out as the Pueblos have the distrust of individualism that the Apollonian way of life implies, but which in Greece was scanted because of forces with which it came in conflict. Zuñi ideals and institutions on the other hand are rigorous on this point. The known map, the middle of the road, to any Apollonian is embodied in the common tradition of his people. To stay always within it is to commit himself to precedent, to tradition. Therefore those influences that are powerful against tradition are uncongenial and minimized in their institutions, and the greatest of these is individualism. It is disruptive, according to Apollonian philosophy in the Southwest, even when it refines upon and enlarges the tradition itself. That is not to say that the Pueblos prevent this. No culture can protect itself from additions and changes. But the process by which these come is suspect and cloaked, and institutions that would give individuals a free hand are outlawed.

It is not possible to understand Pueblo attitudes toward life without some knowledge of the culture from which they have detached themselves: that of the rest of North America. It is by the force of the contrast that we can calculate the strength of their opposite drive and the resistances that have kept out of the Pueblos the most characteristic traits of the American aborigines. For the American Indians as a whole, and including those of Mexico, were passionately Dionysian. They valued all violent experience, all means by which human beings may break through the usual sensory routine, and to all such experiences they attributed the highest value.

The Indians of North America outside the Pueblos have, of course, anything but uniform culture. They contrast violently at almost every point, and there are eight of them that it is convenient to differentiate as separate culture areas. But throughout them all, in one or another guise, there run certain fundamental Dionysian practices. The most conspicuous of these is probably their practice of obtaining supernatural power in a dream or vision, of which we have already spoken. On the western plains men sought these visions with hideous tortures. They cut strips from the skin of their arms, they struck off fingers, they swung themselves from tall poles by straps inserted under the muscles of their shoulders. They went without food and water for extreme periods. They sought in every way to achieve an order of experience set apart from daily living. It was grown men, on the plains, who went out after visions. Sometimes they stood motionless, their hands tied behind them, or they staked out a tiny spot from which they could not move till they had received their blessing. Sometimes, in other tribes, they wandered over distant regions, far out into dangerous country. Some tribes chose precipices and places especially associated with danger. At all events a man went alone, or, if he was seeking his vision by torture and some had to go out with him to tie him to the pole from which he was to swing till he had his supernatural experience, his helper did his part and left him alone for his ordeal.

Benedict's comparison of two cultures is organized by separation of detail. She contrasts Pueblo cultures to other North American cultures by using the categories described by Nietzsche in his study of Greek tragedy.

ALTERNATION OF DETAIL

Alternation of detail makes it easier to maintain a balanced treatment of the topic and allows the reader to follow the comparison and contrast without confusion. However, if there are a great number of points to compare or contrast, alternation of detail can become somewhat tedious.

AN EXAMPLE

Mathew Arnold gives a point by point comparison and contrast of two major influences on Western culture.

HEBRAISM AND HELLENISM

MATTHEW ARNOLD

Hebraism and Hellenism,—between these two points of influence moves our world. At one time it feels more powerfully the attraction of one of them, at another time of the other; and it ought to be, though it never is, evenly and happily balanced between them.

The final aim of both Hellenism and Hebraism, as of all great spiritual disciplines, is no doubt the same: man's perfection or salvation. The very language which they both of them use in schooling us to reach this aim is often identical. Even when their language indicates by variation,—sometimes a broad variation, often a but slight and subtle variation,—the different courses of thought which are uppermost in each discipline, even then the unity of the final end and aim is still apparent. To employ the actual words of that discipline with which we ourselves are all of us most familiar, and the words of which, therefore, come most home to us, that final end and aim is "that we might be partakers of the divine nature." These are the words of a Hebrew apostle, but of Hellenism and Hebraism alike this is, I say, the aim. When the two are confronted, as they very often are confronted, it is nearly always with what I may call a rhetorical purpose; the speaker's whole design is to exalt and enthrone one of the two, and he uses the other only as a foil and to enable him the better to give effect to his purpose. Obviously, with us, it is usually Hellenism which is thus reduced to minister to the triumph of Hebraism. There is a sermon on Greece and the Greek spirit by a man never to be mentioned without interest and respect, Frederick Robertson, in which this rhetorical use of Greece and the Greek spirit, and the inadequate exhibition of them necessarily consequent upon this, is almost ludicrous, and would be censurable if it were not to be explained by the exigencies of a sermon. On the other hand, Heinrich Heine, and other writers of his sort, give us the spectacle of the table completely turned, and of Hebraism brought in just as a foil and contrast to Hellenism, and to make the superiority of Hellenism more manifest. In both these cases there is injustice and misrepresentation. The aim and end of both Hebraism and Hellenism is, as I have said, one and the same, and this aim and end is august and admirable.

Still, they purse this aim by very different courses. The uppermost idea with Hellenism is to see things as they really are; the uppermost idea with Hebraism is conduct and obedience. Nothing can do away with this ineffaceable difference. The Greek quarrel with the body and its desires is, that they hinder right thinking; the Hebrew quarrel with them is, that they hinder right acting. "He that keepeth the law, happy is he"; "Blessed is the man that feareth the Eternal, that delighteth greatly in his commandments"; that is the Hebrew notion of felicity; and, pursued with passion and tenacity, this notion would not let the Hebrew rest till, as is well known, he had at last got out of the law a network of prescriptions to enwrap his whole life, to govern every moment of it, every impulse, every action. The Greek notion of felicity, on the other hand, is perfectly conveyed in these words of a great French moralist: *"C'est le bonheur des hommes,"*—when? when they abhor that which is evil?—no; when they exercise themselves in the law of the Lord day and night?—no; when they die daily?—no; when they walk about the New Jerusalem with palms in their hand?—no; but when they think aright, when their thought hits: *"quand ils pensent juste."* At the bottom of both the Greek and the Hebrew notion is the desire, native in man, for reason and the will of God, the feeling after the universal order,—in a word, the love of God. But, while Hebraism seizes upon certain plain, capital intimations of the universal order, and rivets itself, one may say, with unequalled grandeur of earnestness and intensity on the study and observance of them, the bent of Hellenism is to follow, with flexible activity, the whole play of the universal order, to be apprehensive of missing any part of it, of sacrificing one part to another, to slip away from resting in this or that intimation of it, however capital. An unclouded clearness of mind, an unimpeded play of thought, is what this bent drives at. The governing idea of Hellenism is *spontaneity of consciousness*; that of Hebraism, *strictness of conscience.*

1869

Arnold's comparison and contrast of Hebraism and Hellenism is organized by alternation of detail. He moves from detail to detail on each aspect of the comparison. Throughout the essay, within each paragraph Arnold treats first one concept and then the other, explaining different aspects of each.

ANALOGY

An analogy is a comparison between two things that may be similar in some ways, but come from different classification systems. Similes and metaphors (discussed in Chapter 2) are analogies. When we use the term analogy, however, we usually associate it with a comparison more elaborate than a simile or a metaphor. An analogy could be thought of as an *extended* metaphor. In referential writing and persuasion, an analogy is used to explain something that is unfamiliar by comparing it with something that is familiar. For instance, the structure of the human eye, something unfamiliar to most of us, can be explained by comparing it to a camera; or the human circulatory system can be explained by comparing it to a plumbing system.

AN EXAMPLE

In his book *On Human Nature* (1978), Edward O. Wilson explains the difference between nature and nurture by using an analogy.

THE DEVELOPMENT OF HUMAN BEHAVIOR

EDWARD O. WILSON

Thus even in the relatively simple categories of behavior we inherit a *capacity* for certain traits, and a bias to learn one or another of those available. Scientists as diverse in their philosophies as Konrad Lorenz, Robert A. Hinde, and B. F. Skinner have often stressed that no sharp boundary exists between the inherited and the acquired. It has become apparent that we need new descriptive techniques to replace the archaic distinction between nature and nurture. One of the most promising is based on the imagery invented by Conrad H. Waddington, the great geneticist who died in 1975. Waddington said that development is something like a landscape that descends from highlands to the shore. Development of a trait—eye color, handedness, schizophrenia, or whatever—resembles the rolling of a ball down the slopes. Each trait traverses a different part of the landscape, each is guided by a different pattern of ridges and valleys. In the case of eye color, given a starting set of genes for blue or some other iris pigment, the topography is a single, deep channel. The ball rolls inexorably to one destination: once the egg has been joined by a sperm, only one eye color is possible. The developmental landscape of the mosquito can be similarly envisioned as a parallel series of deep, unbranching valleys, one leading to the sexual attraction of the wingbeat's sound, another to automatic bloodsucking, and so on through a repertory of ten or so discrete responses. The valleys form a precise, unyielding series of biochemical steps that proceed from the DNA in the fertilized egg to the neuromuscular actions mediated by the mosquito's brain.

The developmental topography of human behavior is enormously broader and more complicated, but it is still a topography. In some cases the valleys divide once or twice. An individual can end up either right- or left-handed. If he starts with the genes or other early physiological influences that predispose him to the left hand, that branch of the developmental channel can be viewed as cutting the more deeply. If no social pressure is exerted the ball will in most cases roll on down into the channel for left-handedness. But if parents train the child to use the right hand, the ball can be nudged into the shallower channel for right-handedness. The landscape for schizophrenia is a broader network of anastomosing channels, more difficult to trace, and the ball's course is only statistically predictable.

The landscape is just a metaphor, and it is certainly inadequate for the most complex phenomena, but it focuses on a critical truth about human social behavior. If we are to gain full understanding of its determination, each behavior must be treated separately and traced to some extent, as a developmental process leading from the genes to the final product.

Wilson compares the interaction between genetic and environmental influences on the development of human behavior to a ball rolling through a landscape from highlands to the shore. The analogy does not prove the validity of Wilson's account of the development of human behavior. It simply explains a difficult scientific process in terms that most readers would understand.

VARIATIONS IN COMPARISON AND CONTRAST

The structure of the comparison/contrast will be affected by what the purpose of the paper is. For instance, more emphasis may be given to one of the two things being compared if the argument involves an issue and the purpose of the argument is to convince the audience of the rightness of the writer's position. On the other hand, in a referential comparison/contrast, the writer would try to maintain a balanced treatment of the two topics.

EXPRESSIVE COMPARISON AND CONTRAST

Expressive comparisons are controlled by the values and emotional responses of the writer. One of the two things being compared and contrasted may be preferred over the other.

AN EXAMPLE

Mark Twain is the pseudonym of Samuel Langhorne Clemens, an American writer who is perhaps best known for his novel *Huckleberry Finn* (1884), which many critics regard as the most influential novel ever written. Some have called it the first Great American Novel. This excerpt is from Life on the *Mississippi* (1885), an autobiographical travel book about the time Twain spent as a steamboat pilot on the Mississippi River. In this expressive contrast he reveals how his views of the river change as he became more familiar with it.

TWO WAYS OF VIEWING THE RIVER

MARK TWAIN

Now when I had mastered the language of this water, and had come to know every trifling feature that bordered the great river as familiarly as I knew the letters of the alphabet, I had made a valuable acquisition. But I had lost something, too. I had lost something which could never be restored to me while I lived. All the grace, the beauty, the poetry, had gone out of the majestic river! I still keep in mind a certain wonderful sunset which I witnessed when steamboating was new to me. A broad expanse of the river was turned to blood; in the middle distance the red hue brightened into gold, through which a solitary log came floating black and conspicuous; in one place a long, slanting mark lay sparkling upon the water; in another the surface was broken by boiling, tumbling rings, that were as many-tinted as an opal; where the ruddy flush was faintest, was a smooth spot that was covered with graceful circles and radiating lines, ever so delicately traced; the shore on our left was densely wooded, and the somber shadow that fell from this forest was broken in one place by a long, ruffled trail that shone like silver; and high above the forest wall a clean-stemmed dead tree waved a single leafy bough that glowed like a flame in the unobstructed splendor that was flowing from the sun. There were graceful curves, reflected images, woody heights, soft distances; and over the whole scene, far and near, the dissolving lights drifted steadily, enriching it every passing moment with new marvels of coloring.

I stood like one bewitched. I drank it in, in a speechless rapture. The world was new to me, and I had never seen anything like this at home. But as I have said, a day came when I began to cease from noting the glories and the charms which the moon and the sun and the twilight wrought upon the river's face; another day came when I ceased altogether to note them. Then, if that sunset scene had been repeated, I should have looked upon it without rapture, and should have commented upon it, inwardly, after this fashion: "This sun means that we are going to have wind to-morrow; that floating log means that the river is rising, small thanks to it; that slanting mark on the water refers to a bluff reef which is going to kill somebody's steamboat one of these nights, if it keeps on stretching out like that; those tumbling 'boils' show a dissolving bar and a changing channel there; the lines and circles in the slick water over yonder are a warning that that troublesome place is shoaling up dangerously; that silver streak in the shadow of the forest is the 'break' from a new snag, and he has located himself in the very best place he could have found to fish for steamboats; that tall dead tree, with a single living branch, is not going to last long, and then how is a body ever going to get through this blind place at night without the friendly old landmark?"

No, the romance and beauty were all gone from the river. All the value any feature of it had for me now was the amount of usefulness it could furnish toward compassing the safe piloting of a steamboat. Since those days, I have pitied doctors from my heart. What does the lovely flush in a beauty's cheek mean to a doctor but a "break" that ripples above some deadly disease? Are not all her visible charms sown thick with what are to him the signs and symbols of hidden decay? Does he ever see her beauty at all, or doesn't he simply view her professionally, and comment upon her unwholesome condition all to himself? And doesn't he sometimes wonder whether he has gained most or lost most by learning his trade?

Mark Twain's use of comparison and contrast reveals his changing perceptions. He makes emotional responses when he reflects on the beauty of his initial contact with the river. He says that he "stood like one bewitched." Twain reveals his value system when he expresses regret about his loss of the sense of "romance and beauty" he first felt.

LITERARY COMPARISON AND CONTRAST

Literary comparisons are often analogies. They may use many of the devices of language characteristic of literature: graphic images, figurative images, and personification.

AN EXAMPLE

Samuel Johnson uses analogy to present Shakespeare to us. He makes use of a great many graphic images and figures of speech to express his admiration for Shakespeare's abilities as a writer.

ON SHAKESPEARE

SAMUEL JOHNSON

The work of a correct and regular writer is a garden accurately formed and diligently planted, varied with shades, and scented with flowers; the composition of Shakespeare is a forest, in which oaks extend their branches, and pines tower in the air, interspersed sometimes with weeds and brambles, and sometimes giving shelter to myrtles and to roses; filling the eye with awful pomp and gratifying the mind with endless diversity. Other poets display cabinets of precious rarities, minutely finished, wrought into shape, and polished into brightness. Shakespeare opens a mine which contains gold and diamonds in unexhaustible plenty, though clouded by incrustations, debased by impurities, and mingled with a mass of meaner minerals.

Johnson uses four analogies in this brief commentary on Shakespeare's work. He compares the work of regular writers to a garden "accurately formed" and "diligently planted." He compares Shakespeare's writing to a forest that, although it sometimes has "weeds and brambles," also offers majesty and "endless diversity." The work of other poets he compares to carefully wrought jewelry in "display cabinets." On the other hand, he compares Shakespeare's work to a mine that, even though mixed with impurities, is an inexhaustible source of "gold and diamonds." The vivid, graphic images Johnson uses create an appealing picture of Shakespeare's work.

PERSUASIVE COMPARISON AND CONTRAST

A writer may use comparison and contrast to convince us to favor one thing over another. Presenting one topic in relation to another allows for the selection of details that favor the preferred position and cast the other in a less favorable light.

AN EXAMPLE

In this selection the noted feminist Gloria Steinem uses comparison and contrast to support a persuasive claim.

EROTICA AND PORNOGRAPHY

GLORIA STEINEM

Human beings are the only animals that experience the same sex drive at times when we can—and cannot—conceive.

Just as we developed uniquely human capacities for language, planning, memory, and invention along our evolutionary path, we also developed sexuality as a form of expression; a way of communicating that is separable from our need for sex as a way of perpetuating ourselves. For humans alone, sexuality can be and often is primarily a way of bonding, of giving and receiving pleasure, bridging differentness, discovering sameness, and communicating emotion.

We developed this and other human gifts through our ability to change our environment, adapt physically, and in the long run, to affect our own evolution. But as an emotional result of this spiraling path away from other animals, we seem to alternate between periods of exploring our unique abilities to change new boundaries, and feelings of loneliness in the unknown that we ourselves have created; a fear that sometimes sends us back to the comfort of the animal world by encouraging us to exaggerate our sameness.

The separation of "play" from "work," for instance, is a problem only in the human world. So is the difference between art and nature, or an intellectual accomplishment and a physical one. As a result, we celebrate play, art, and invention as leaps into the unknown; but any imbalance can send us back to nostalgia for our primate past and the conviction that the basics of work, nature, and physical labor are somehow more worthwhile or even moral.

In the same way, we have explored our sexuality as separable from conception: a pleasurable, empathetic bridge to strangers of the same species. We have even invented contraception—a skill that has probably existed in some form since our ancestors figured out the process of birth—in order to extend this uniquely human difference. Yet we also have times of atavistic suspicion that sex is not complete—or even legal or intended-by-god—if it cannot end in conception.

No wonder the concepts of "erotica" and "pornography" can be so crucially different, and yet so confused. Both assume that sexuality can beseparated from conception, and therefore can be used to carry a personal message. That's a major reason why, even in our current culture, both may be called equally "shocking" or legally "obscene," a word whose Latin derivative means "dirty, containing filth." This gross condemnation of all sexuality that isn't harnessed to childbirth and marriage has been increased by the current backlash against women's progress. Out of fear that the whole patriarchal structure might be upset if women really had the autonomous power to decide our reproductive futures (that is, if we controlled the most basic means of production), right-wing groups are not only denouncing prochoice abortion literature as "pornographic," but are trying to stop the sending of all contraceptive information through the mails by invoking obscenity laws. In fact, Phyllis Schlafly recently denounced the entire Women's Movement as "obscene."

Not surprisingly, this religious, visceral backlash has a secular, intellectual counterpart that relies heavily on applying the "natural" behavior of the animal world to humans. That is questionable in itself, but these Lionel Tigerish studies make their political purpose even more clear in the particular animals they select and the habits they choose to emphasize. The message is that females should accept their "destiny" of being sexually dependent and devote themselves to bearing and rearing their young.

Defending against such reaction in turn leads to another temptation: to merely reverse the terms, and declare that *all* non-procreative sex is good. In fact, however, this human activity can be as constructive as destructive, moral or immoral, as any other. Sex as communication can send messages as different as life and death; even the origins of "erotica" and "pornography" reflect that fact. After all, "erotica" is rooted in *eros* or passionate love, and thus in the idea of positive choice, free will, the yearning for a particular person. (Interestingly, the definition of erotica leaves open the question of gender.) "Pornography" begins with a root meaning "prostitution" or "female captives," thus letting us know that the subject is not mutual love, or love at all, but domination and violence against women. (Though, of course, homosexual pornography may imitate this violence by putting a man in the "feminine" role of victim.) It ends with a root meaning "writing about" or "description of" which puts still more distance between subject and object, and replaces a spontaneous yearning for closeness with objectification and a voyeur.

The difference is clear in the words. It becomes even more so by example.

Look at any photo or film of people making love; really making love. The images may be diverse, but there is usually a sensuality and touch and warmth, an acceptance of bodies and nerve endings. There is always a spontaneous sense of people who are there because they *want* to be, out of shared pleasure.

Now look at any depiction of sex in which there is clear force, or an unequal power that spells coercion. It may be very blatant, with weapons of torture or bondage, wounds and bruises, some clear humiliation, or an adult's sexual power being used over a child. It may be much more subtle: a physical attitude of conqueror and victim, the use of race or class difference to imply the same thing, perhaps a very unequal nudity, with one person exposed and vulnerable while the other is clothed. In either case, there no sense of equal choice or equal power.

The first is erotic: a mutually pleasurable, sexual expression between people who have enough power to be there by positive choice. It may or may not strike a sense-memory in the viewer, or be creative enough to make the unknown seem real; but it doesn't require us to identify with a conqueror or a victim. It is truly sensuous, and may give us a contagion of pleasure.

The second is pornographic: its message is violence, dominance, and conquest. It is sex being used to reinforce some inequality, or to create one, or to tell us the lie that pain and humiliation (ours or someone else's) are really the same as pleasure. If we are to feel anything, we must identify with conqueror or victim. That means we can only experience pleasure through the adoption of some degree of sadism or masochism. It also means that we may feel diminished by the role of conqueror, or enraged, humiliated, and vengeful by sharing identity with the victim.

Perhaps one could simply say that erotica is about sexuality, but pornography is about power and sex-as-weapon—in the same way we have come to understand that rape is about violence, and not really about sexuality at all.

Yes, it's true that there are women who have been forced by violent families and dominating men to confuse love with pain; so much so that they have become masochists. (A fact that in no way excuses those who administer such pain.) But the truth is that, for most women—and or men with enough humanity to imagine themselves into the predicament of women—true pornography could serve as aversion therapy for sex.

Of course, there will always be personal differences about what is and is not erotic, and there may be cultural differences for a long time to come. Many women feel that sex makes them vulnerable and therefore may continue to need more sense of personal connection and safety before allowing any erotic feelings. We now find competence and expertise erotic in men, but that may pass as we develop those qualities in ourselves. Men, on the other hand, may continue to feel less vulnerable, and therefore more open to such potential danger as sex with strangers. As some men replace the need for submission from childlike women with the pleasure of cooperation from equals, they may find a partner's competence to be erotic, too.

Such group changes plus individual differences will continue to be reflected in sexual love between people of the same gender, as well as between women and men. The point is not to dictate sameness, but to discover ourselves and each other through sexuality that is an exploring, pleasurable, empathetic part of our lives; a human sexuality that is unchained both from unwanted pregnancies and from violence.

But that is a hope, not a reality. At the moment, fear of change is increasing both the indiscriminate repression of all nonprocreative sex in the religious and "conservative" male world, and the pornographic vengeance against women's sexuality in the secular world of "liberal" and "radical" men. It's almost futuristic to debate what is and is not truly erotic, when many women are again being forced into compulsory motherhood, and the number of pornographic murders, tortures, and woman-hating images are on the increase in both popular culture and real life.

It's a familiar division: wife or whore, "good" woman who is constantly vulnerable to pregnancy or "bad" woman who is unprotected from violence. *Both* roles would be upset if we were to control our own sexuality. And that's exactly what we must do.

In spite of all our atavistic suspicions and training for the "natural" role of motherhood, we took up the complicated battle for reproductive freedom. Our bodies had borne that health burden of endless births and poor abortions, and we had a greater motive for separating sexuality and conception.

Now we have to take up the equally complex burden of explaining that all nonprocreative sex is *not* alike. We have a motive: our right to a uniquely human sexuality, and sometimes even to survival. As it is, our bodies have too rarely been enough our own to develop erotica in our own lives, much less in art and literature. And our bodies have too often been the objects of pornography and the woman-hating, violent practice that it preaches. Consider also our spirits that break a little each time we see ourselves in chains or full labial display for the conquering male viewer, bruised or on our knees, screaming a real or pretended pain to delight the sadist, pretending to enjoy what we don't enjoy, to be blind to the images of our sisters that really haunt us—humiliated often enough ourselves by the truly obscene idea that sex and the domination of women must be combined.

Sexuality *is* human, free, separate—and so are we.

But until we untangle the lethal confusion of sex with violence, there will be more pornography and less erotica. There will be little murders in our beds—and very little love.

Steinem's claim that women should control their own sexuality is supported by her comparison and contrast of erotica and pornography. Through this comparison and contrast, she argues further that pornography results from the confusion of sex with violence and presents women as objects to be dominated.

REFERENTIAL COMPARISON AND CONTRAST

Referential comparison and contrast gives an accurate and clear explanation of the two things. The author makes an effort to balance the presentation and present an unbiased view.

AN EXAMPLE

In the following example John Dryden compares two of the most famous playwrights in English literature. It is taken from "An Essay of Dramatic Poesy," written in 1666 during the closure of the London theaters because of the plague.

SHAKESPEARE AND JONSON

JOHN DRYDEN

To begin then with Shakespeare; he was the man who of all Modern, and perhaps Ancient Poets, had the largest and most comprehensive soul. All the Images of Nature were still present to him, and he drew them not laboriously, but luckily: when he describes any thing, you more than see it, you feel it too. Those who accuse him to have wanted learning, give him the greater commendation: he was naturally learned; he needed not the spectacles of Books to read Nature; he looked inwards, and found her there. I cannot say he is every where alike; were he so, I should do him injury to compare him with the greatest of Mankind. He is many times flat, insipid; his Comic wit degenerating into clenches; his serious swelling into Bombast. But he is always great when some great occasion is presented to him: no man can say he ever had a fit subject for his wit, and did not then raise himself as high above the rest of the Poets. . . .

As for Jonson, to whose Character I am now arrived, if we look upon him while he was himself, (for his last Plays were but his dotages) I think him the most learned and judicious Writer which any Theater ever had. He was a most severe Judge of himself as well as others. One cannot say he wanted wit, but rather that he was frugal of it. In his works you find little to retrench or alter. Wit and Language, and Humor also in some measure we had before him; but something of Art was wanting to the Drama till he came. He managed his strength to more advantage than any who preceded him. You seldom find him making Love in any of his Scenes, or endeavoring to move the Passions; his genius was too sullen and saturnine to do it gracefully, especially when he knew he came after those who had performed both to such an height. Humor was his proper Sphere, and in that he delighted most to represent Mechanic people. He was deeply conversant in the Ancients, both Greek and Latin, and he borrowed boldly from them: there is scarce a Poet or Historian among the Roman Authors of those times whom he has not translated. . . . If I would compare him with Shakespeare, I must acknowledge him the more correct Poet, but Shakespeare the greater wit. Shakespeare was the Homer, or Father of our Dramatick Poets; Jonson was the Virgil, the pattern of elaborate writing; I admire him, but I love Shakespeare. To conclude of him, as he has given us the most correct Plays, so in the precepts which he has laid down in his Discoveries, we have as many and profitable Rules for perfecting the Stage as any wherewith the French can furnish us.

Dryden's comparison of the two playwrights gives the reader a better understanding of the work of each one. He characterizes the work of each writer and in his conclusion sums up his analysis.

WRITING STRATEGIES

If you are using comparison and contrast to organize your work, consider the following questions:

- How are the two subjects similar?
- How are the two subjects different?
- What details should be included?
- How should those details be arranged?

DEFINITION

A definition is a statement of the meaning of a word, a phrase, or a term. When we define, we typically use the principles of classification. Instead of presenting an entire classification system, however, we consider only a single category.

KINDS OF DEFINITIONS

Definitions can be either simple or extended. A simple definition will give a concise meaning of the term. An extended definition will give an elaborated explanation of a complicated concept.

Simple Definitions

Three commonly used methods of giving simple definitions are to put the term we are defining in its class, to give a synonym for it, or to give an example of it. If we defined a desk as a piece of furniture, we would be putting it in a general category or class. Defining it as a writing table would be defining by synonym. Saying that an example of a desk is the oak roll-top in the library would be defining the term by example.

Simple definitions are used not to develop an entire essay, but rather to clarify and explain terms that the reader may not understand. This function of definition is often important in interpretive writing when technical language is used.

Extended Definitions

As the term implies, an extended definition is an elaborate explanation of a concept. Such a definition will go into some detail and will structure an entire essay or even an entire book. Extended definitions usually make use of other patterns of organization to explain the term or concept being defined.

AN EXAMPLE

Rybczynski gives an extended definition of comfort. Note that he makes extensive use of examples to develop his definition.

A DEFINITION OF "COMFORT"

Witold Rybczynski

What is comfort? Perhaps the question should have been asked earlier, but without a review of the long evolution of this complex and profound subject the answer would almost certainly have been wrong, or at least incomplete. The simplest response would be that comfort concerns only human physiology—feeling good. Nothing mysterious about that. But this would not explain why, although the human body has not changed, our idea of what is comfortable differs from that of a hundred years ago. Nor is the answer that comfort is a subjective experience of satisfaction. If comfort were subjective, one would expect a greater variety of attitudes toward it; instead, at any particular historical period there has always been a demonstrable consensus about what is comfortable and what is not. Although comfort is experienced personally, the individual judges comfort according to broader norms, indicating that comfort may be an objective experience.

If comfort is objective, it should be possible to measure it. This is more difficult than it sounds. It is easier to know when we are comfortable than why, or to what degree. It would be possible to identify comfort by recording the personal reactions of large numbers of people, but this would be more like a marketing or opinion survey than a scientific study; a scientist prefers to study things one at a time, and especially to measure them. It turns out that in practice it is much easier to measure *dis*comfort than comfort. To establish a thermal "comfort zone," for example, one ascertains at which temperatures most people are either too cold or too hot, and whatever is in between automatically becomes "comfortable." Or if one is trying to identify the appropriate angle for the back of a chair, one can subject people to angles that are too steep and too flat, and between the points where they express discomfort lies the "correct" angle. Similar experiments have been carried out concerning the intensity of lighting and noise, the size of room dimensions, the hardness and softness of sitting and lying furniture, and so on. In all these cases, the range of comfort is discovered by measuring the limits at which people begin to experience discomfort. When the interior of the Space Shuttle was being designed, a cardboard mock-up of the cabin was built. The astronauts were required to move around in this full-size model, miming their daily activities, and every time they knocked against a corner or a projection, a technician would cut away the offending piece. At the end of the process, when there were no more obstructions left, the cabin was judged to be "comfortable." The scientific definition of comfort would be something like "Comfort is that condition in which discomfort has been avoided."

Most of the scientific research that has been carried out on terrestrial comfort has concerned the workplace, since it has been found that comfortable surroundings will affect the morale, and hence the productivity, of workers. Just how much comfort can affect economic performance is indicated by a recent estimate that backaches—the result of poor working posture—account for over ninety-three million lost workdays, a loss of nine billion dollars to the American economy. The modern office interior reflects the scientific definition of comfort. Lighting levels have been carefully controlled to fall within an acceptable level for optimal reading convenience. The finishes of walls and floors are restful; there are no garish or gaudy colors. Desks and chairs are planned to avoid fatigue.

But how comfortable do the people feel who work in such surroundings? As part of an effort to improve its facilities, one large pharmaceutical corporation, Merck & Company, surveyed two thousand of its office staff regarding their attitudes to their place of work—an attractive modern commercial interior. The survey team prepared a questionnaire that listed various aspects of the workplace. These included factors affecting appearance, safety, work efficiency, convenience, comfort, and so on. Employees were asked to express their satisfaction, or dissatisfaction, with different aspects, and also to indicate those aspects that they personally considered to be the most important. The majority distinguished between the visual qualities of their surroundings—decoration, color scheme, carpeting, wall covering, desk appearance—and the physical aspects—lighting, ventilation, privacy, and chair comfort. The latter group were all included in a list of the ten most important factors, together with size of work area, safety, and personal storage space. Interestingly, none of the purely visual factors was felt to be of major importance, indicating just how mistaken is the notion that comfort is solely a function of appearance or style.

What is most revealing is that the Merck employees expressed some degree of dissatisfaction with *two-thirds* of the almost thirty different aspects of the workplace. Among those about which there was the strongest negative feelings were the lack of conversational privacy, the air quality, the lack of visual privacy, and the level of lighting. When they were asked what aspects of the office interior they would like to have individual control over, most people identified room temperature, degree of privacy, choice of chair and desk, and lighting intensity. Control over decor was accorded the lowest priority. This would seem to indicate that although there is wide agreement about the importance of lighting or temperature, there is a good deal of difference of opinion about exactly how much light or heat feels comfortable to different individuals; comfort is obviously both objective and subjective.

The Merck offices had been designed to eliminate discomfort, yet the survey showed that many of the employees did not experience well-being in their workplace—an inability to concentrate was the common complaint. Despite the restful colors and the attractive furnishings (which everyone appreciated), something was missing. The scientific approach assumes that if background noises are muffled and direct view controlled, the office worker will feel comfortable. But working comfort depends on many more factors than these. There must also be a sense of intimacy and privacy, which is produced by a balance between isolation and publicness; too much of one or the other will produce discomfort. A group of architects in California recently identified as many as nine different aspects of workplace enclosure that must be met in order to create this feeling. These included the presence of walls behind and beside the worker, the amount of open space in front of the desk, the area of the workspace, the amount of enclosure, a view to the outside, the distance to the nearest person, the number of people in the immediate vicinity, and the level and type of noise. Since most office layouts do not address these concerns directly, it is not surprising that people have difficulty concentrating on their work.

The fallacy of the scientific definition of comfort is that it considers only those aspects of comfort that are measurable, and with not untypical arrogance denies the existence of the rest—many behavioral scientists have concluded that because people experience only discomfort, comfort as a physical phenomenon does not really exist at all. It is hardly surprising that genuine intimacy, which is impossible to measure, is absent in most planned office environments. Intimacy in the office, or in the home, is not unusual in this respect; there are many complicated experiences that resist measurement. It is impossible, for example, to describe scientifically what distinguishes a great wine from a mediocre one, although a group of wine experts would have no difficulty establishing which was which. The wine industry, like manufacturers of tea and coffee, continues to rely on nontechnical testing—the "nose" of an experienced taster—rather than on objective standards alone. It might be possible to measure a threshold below which wine would taste "bad"—acidity, alcohol content, sweetness, and so on—but no one would suggest that simply avoiding these deficiencies would result in a good wine. A room may feel uncomfortable—it may be too bright for intimate conversations, or too dark for reading—but avoiding such irritations will not automatically produce a feeling of well-being. Dullness is not annoying enough to be disturbing, but it is not stimulating either. On the other hand, when we open a door and think, "What a comfortable room," we are reacting positively to something special, or rather to a series of special things.

Here are two descriptions of comfort. The first is by a well-known interior decorator, Billy Baldwin: "Comfort to me is a room that works for you and your guests. It's deep upholstered furniture. It's having a table handy to put down a drink or a book. It's also knowing that if someone pulls up a chair for a talk, the whole room doesn't fall apart. I'm tired of contrived decorating." The second is by an architect, Christopher Alexander: "Imagine yourself on a winter afternoon with a pot of tea, a book, a reading light, and two or three huge pillows to lean back against. Now make yourself comfortable. Not in some way which you can show to other people, and say how much you like it. I mean so that you *really* like it, for yourself. You put the tea where you can reach it: but in a place where you can't possibly knock it over. You pull the light down, to shine on the book, but not too brightly, and so that you can't see the naked bulb. You put the cushions behind you, and place them, carefully, one by one, just where you want them, to support your back, your neck, your arm: so that you are supported just comfortably, just as you want to sip your tea, and read, and dream." Baldwin's description was the result of sixty years of decorating fashionable homes; Alexander's was based on the observation of ordinary people and ordinary places. Yet they both seem to have converged in the depiction of a domestic atmosphere that is instantly recognizable for its ordinary, human qualities.

These qualities are something that science has failed to come to grips with, although to the layman a picture, or a written description, is evidence enough. "Comfort is simply a verbal invention," writes one engineer despairingly. Of course, that is precisely what comfort is. It is an invention—a cultural artifice. Like all cultural ideas—childhood, family, gender—it has a past, and it cannot be understood without reference to its specific history. One-dimensional, technical definitions of comfort, which ignore history, are bound to be unsatisfactory. How rich, by comparison, are Baldwin's and Alexander's descriptions of comfort. They include convenience (a handy table), efficiency (a modulated light source), domesticity (a cup of tea), physical ease (deep chairs and cushions), and privacy (reading a book, having a talk). Intimacy is also present in these descriptions. All these characteristics together contribute to the atmosphere of interior calm that is a part of comfort.

This is the problem with understanding comfort and with finding a simple definition. It is like trying to describe an onion. It appears simple on the outside, just a spheroidal shape. But this is deceptive, for an onion also has many layers. If we cut it apart, we are left with a pile of onion skins, but the original form has disappeared; if we describe each layer separately, we lose sight of the whole. To complicate matters further, the layers are transparent, so that when we look at the whole onion we see not just the surface but also something of the interior. Similarly, comfort is both something simple and complicated. It incorporates many transparent layers of meaning—privacy, ease, convenience—some of which are buried deeper than others.

The onion simile suggests not only that comfort has several layers of meaning, but also that the idea of comfort has developed historically. It is an idea that has meant different things at different times. In the seventeenth century, comfort meant privacy, which lead to intimacy and, in turn, to domesticity. The eighteenth century shifted the emphasis to leisure and ease, the nineteenth to mechanically aided comforts—light, heat, and ventilation. The twentieth-century domestic engineers stressed efficiency and convenience. At various times, and in response to various outside forces—social, economic, and technological—the idea of comfort has changed, sometimes drastically. There was nothing foreordained or inevitable about the changes. If seventeenth-century Holland had been less egalitarian and its women less independent, domesticity would have arrived later than it did. If eighteenth-century England had been aristocratic rather than bourgeois, comfort would have taken a different turn. If servants had not been scarce in our century, it is unlikely that anyone would have listened to Beecher and Frederick. But what is striking is that the idea of comfort, even as it has changed, has preserved most of its earlier meanings. The evolution of comfort should not be confused with the evolution of technology. New technical devices usually—not always—rendered older ones obsolete. The electric lamp replaced the gasolier, which replaced the oil lamp, which replaced candles, and so on. But new ideas about how to achieve comfort did not displace fundamental notions of domestic well-being. Each new meaning added a layer to the previous meanings, which were preserved beneath. At any particular time, comfort consists of *all* the layers, not only the most recent.

So there it is, the Onion Theory of Comfort—hardly a definition at all, but a more precise explanation may be unnecesary. It may be enough to realize that domestic comfort involves a range of attributes—convenience, efficiency, leisure, ease, pleasure, domesticity, intimacy, and privacy—all of which contribute to the experience; common sense will do the rest. Most people—"I may not know why I like it, but I know what I like"—recognize comfort when they experience it. This recognition involves a combination of sensations—many of them subconscious—and not only physical, but also emotional as well as intellectual, which makes comfort difficult to explain and impossible to measure. But it does not make it any less real. We should resist the inadequate definitions that engineers and architects have offered us. Domestic well-being is too important to be left to experts; it is, as it has always been, the business of the family and the individual. We must rediscover for ourselves the mystery of comfort, for without it, our dwellings will indeed be machines instead of homes.

Rybczynski explores the complexities of defining a simple term. He uses narration and analogy to develop the definition.

WRITING STRATEGIES

If your work involves the use of definition, consider the following questions:

- What general class is your subject a member of?
- What is a synonym for the thing being defined?
- What are its characteristics?
- What details should be included in the definition?
- What is an example of the thing being defined?

Description

When we organize with description, we attempt to give the reader an impression of a person, a place, a thing, or a concept. Description focuses on the uniqueness of the thing depicted, how it is different from those that may be in the same class. Instead of looking at general features that would be found in other members of its class, as we do when we organize by classification, we look at specific features that differentiate that one thing from all others. We ask what makes the thing we are describing unique. For instance, if you wanted to describe a particular building, you would focus on those characteristics that make it different from all other buildings.

There are three different ways of using description: to depict a physical appearance, to divide a subject into its component parts, and to analyze a concept. In all three of these variations of description we are dealing with an organizing principle based on a relationship between the whole and its parts. With description, we show how the various parts of the thing we are depicting fit together to form the whole. If you were describing a building, you would tell where the doors and windows were, what the roof was like, what the walls were made of, and what other significant design features were apparent. You would show how each part was related to the other parts and situated in relation to the whole.

PHYSICAL DESCRIPTION

When we try to give an impression of what a person, place, or thing is like, we are creating physical descriptions. These descriptions reveal the physical characteristics of whatever it is we are describing. We may start by giving an overall impression (the whole) and then include relevant details (the parts). The selection and ordering of the details of the description reflect the point of view the writer has in relation to the thing being described.

DESCRIBING A PERSON

The problem we face when we describe people is how much detail to include in the description. We don't have to include some details because everybody knows in general what a person looks like. We assume that the reader will know that the person has the same physical characteristics as other people—a head, hair, a nose, and hands. Only if some physical characteristic is different, will we make note of it and indicate that "he is tall" or that "she has purple hair."

Frequently in descriptions of people we include other details besides physical characteristics. Such descriptions are called character sketches. In addition to recording observations about physical characteristics, the character sketch will give impressions of personality traits and mannerisms.

AN EXAMPLE

In the following example, Thomas Carlyle, an English essayist, gives us an impression of what the English poet Alfred, Lord Tennyson was like at the age of thirty-four. This excerpt is from a letter to the American philosopher Ralph Waldo Emerson, August 5, 1844.

TENNYSON

Thomas Carlyle

Alfred is one of the few British or Foreign Figures (a not increasing number I think!) who are and remain beautiful to me;—a true human soul, or some authentic approximation thereto, to whom your own soul can say, Brother!—However, I doubt he will not come; he often skips me, in these brief visits to Town; skips everybody indeed; being a man solitary and sad, as certain men are dwelling in an element of gloom,—carrying a bit of Chaos about him, in short, which he is manufacturing into Cosmos!

Alfred is the son of a Lincolnshire Gentleman Farmer, I think; indeed, you see in his verses that he is a native of "moated granges," and green, fat pastures, not of mountains and their torrents and storms. He had his breeding at Cambridge, as if for the Law or Church; being master of a small annuity on his Father's decease, he preferred clubbing with his Mother and some Sisters, to live unpromoted and write Poems. In this way he lives still, now here, now there; the family always within reach of London, never in it; he himself making rare and brief visits, lodging in some old comrade's rooms. I think he must be under forty, not much under it. One of the finest-looking men in the world. A great shock of rough dusty-dark hair; bright-laughing hazel eyes; massive aquiline face, most massive yet delicate; of sallow-brown complexion, almost Indian-looking; clothes cynically loose, free-and-easy;—smokes infinite tobacco. His voice is musical metallic,—fit for loud laughter and piercing wail, and all that may lie between; speech and speculation free and plenteous: I do not meet, in these late decades, such company over a pipe!—We shall see what he will grow to. He is often unwell; very chaotic,— his way is through Chaos and the Bottomless and Pathless; not handy for making out many miles upon.

Carlyle describes Tennyson in terms of both his physical appearance and his behavior. Notice that Carlyle focuses on Tennyson's outstanding physical characteristics: his "great shock of rough dusty-dark hair," his "hazel eyes," his "massive aquiline face," and his "sallow-brown complexion." These distinguishing physical features make Tennyson unique. Carlyle also includes a description of his voice—"musical metallic"—his clothing—"cynically loose"—and his characteristic behavior—"smokes infinite tobacco." Taken together these details give us a memorable portrait of Tennyson.

DESCRIBING A PLACE

As with the description of people, it is impossible to include every single detail in a description of a place. The point of view of the observer is especially important in descriptions of places.

AN EXAMPLE

Peter Matthiessen, in *The Tree Where Man Was Born* (1972), records his travels through East Africa in 1969. The following excerpt gives us a striking description of a river valley.

THE TREE WHERE MAN WAS BORN

Peter Matthiessen

Winds of the southeast monsoon blew up from the hot nyika, and a haze of desert dust obscured the mountains. But the Uaso Nyiro flows all year, and along its green banks the seasons are the same. A dark lioness with a shining coat lay on a rise, intent on the place where game came down to water. At a shady bend, on sunlit sandbars, baboon and elephant consorted, and a small crocodile, gray-green and gleaming at the edge of the thick river, evoked a childhood dream of darkest Africa. Alone on the plain, waiting for his time to come full circle, stood an ancient elephant, tusks broken and worn, hairs fallen from his tail; over his monumental brow, poised for the insects started up by the great trunk, a lilac-breasted roller hung suspended, spinning turquoise lights in the dry air.

On a plateau that climbs in steps from the south bank of the river, three stone pools in a grove of doum palms form an oasis in the elephant-twisted thorn scrub and dry stone. The lower spring, where the water spreads into a swampy stream, has a margin of high reeds and sedge; here the birds and animals come to water. One afternoon I swam in the steep-sided middle pool, which had been, in winter, as clear as the desert wind; now the huge gangs building the road north to Ethiopia were washing here with detergent soaps that bred a heavy film, and I soon got out, letting the sun dry me. A turtle's shadow vanished between ledges of the pool, and dragonflies, one fire-colored and the other cobalt blue, zipped dry-winged through the heat. Despite the wind, there was stillness in the air, expectancy: at the lower spring a pair of spurwing plover stood immobile, watching man grow older.

In the dusty flat west of the spring, ears alert, oryx and zebra waited. Perhaps one had been killed the night before, for jackals came and went in their hangdog way east of the springs and vultures sat like huge galls in the trees. With a shift in the wind, a cloud across the sun, the rush of fronds in the dry palms took on an imminence. Beyond the springs oryx were moving at full run, kicking up dust as they streamed onto the upper plateau. Nagged by the wind, I put my clothes on and set off for camp.

Matthiessen begins his description of the Kenyan landscape by creating an overall impression of the scene—the wind, the haze of desert dust, and the green banks of a river. He adds details showing the specific features of the place and including references to various animals: "a dark lioness" lying on a rise, "baboon and elephant" on sand bars, and "a small crocodile, gray-green and gleaming at the edge of the thick river." Intertwined with the description is a narrative of Matthiessen swimming in a pool, drying in the sun, returning to camp. Other images, like references to dragonflies, "one fire-colored and the other cobalt blue," add depth to the description.

DESCRIBING A THING

Describing a thing often begins by putting it into a class. Then the various individual features of the thing are identified and elaborated on.

AN EXAMPLE

In the following example, written in 1901, John Muir describes the Sequoias. He examines the features of those gigantic redwood trees in some detail.

THE SEQUOIA

JOHN MUIR

The Big Tree (Sequoia gigantea) is Nature's forest masterpiece, and, so far as I know, the greatest of living things. It belongs to an ancient stock, as its remains in old rocks show, and has a strange air of other days about it, a thoroughbred look inherited from the long ago—the auld lang syne of trees. Once the genus was common, and with many species flourished in the now desolate Arctic regions, in the interior of North America, and in Europe, but in long, eventful wanderings from climate to climate only two species have survived the hardships they had to encounter, the gigantea and sempervirens, the former now restricted to the western slopes of the Sierra, the other to the Coast Mountains, and both to California, excepting a few groves of Redwood which extend into Oregon.

The Pacific Coast in general is the paradise of conifers. Here nearly all of them are giants, and display a beauty and magnificence unknown elsewhere. The climate is mild, the ground never freezes, and moisture and sunshine abound all the year. Nevertheless it is not easy to account for the colossal size of the Sequoias. The largest are about three hundred feet high and thirty feet in diameter. Who of all the dwellers of the plains and prairies and fertile home forests of round-headed oak and maple, hickory and elm, ever dreamed that earth could bear such growths—trees that the familiar pines and firs seem to know nothing about, lonely, silent, serene, with a physiognomy almost godlike; and so old, thousands of them still living had already counted their years by tens of centuries when Columbus set sail from Spain and were in the vigor of youth or middle age when the star led the Chaldean sages to the infant Saviour's cradle! As far as man is concerned they are the same yesterday, to-day, and forever, emblems of permanence.

No description can give any adequate idea of their singular majesty, much less their beauty. Excepting the sugar-pine, most of their neighbors with pointed tops seem to be forever shouting Excelsior, while the Big Tree, though soaring above them all, seems satisfied, its rounded head, poised lightly as a cloud, giving no impression of trying to go higher. Only in youth does it show like other conifers a heavenward yearning, keenly aspiring with a long quick-growing top. Indeed the whole tree for the first century or two, or until a hundred to a hundred and fifty feet high, is arrowhead in form, and, compared with the solemn" rigidity of age, is as sensitive to the wind as a squirrel tail. The lower branches are gradually dropped as it grows older, and the upper ones thinned out until comparatively few are left. These, however, are developed to great size, divide again and again, and terminate in bossy rounded masses of leafy branchlets, while the head becomes dome-shaped. Then poised in fullness of strength and beauty, stern and solemn in mien, it glows with eager, enthusiastic life, quivering to the tip of every leaf and branch and far-reaching root, calm as a granite dome, the first to feel the touch of the rosy beams of the morning, the last to bid the sun good-night.

Perfect specimens, unhurt by running fires or lightning, are singularly regular and symmetrical in general form, though not at all conventional, showing infinite variety in sure unity and harmony of plan. The immensely strong, stately shafts, with rich purplish brown bark, are free of limbs for a hundred and fifty feet or so, though dense tufts of sprays occur here and there, producing an ornamental effect, while long parallel furrows give a fluted columnar appearance. It shoots forth its limbs with equal boldness in every direction, showing no weather side. On the old trees the main branches are crooked and rugged, and strike rigidly outward mostly at right angles from the trunk, but there is always a certain measured restraint in their reach which keeps them within bounds. No other Sierra tree has foliage so densely massed or outline so finely, firmly drawn and so obediently subordinate to an ideal type. A particularly knotty, angular, ungovernable-looking branch, five to eight feet in diameter and perhaps a thousand years old, may occasionally be seen pushing out from the trunk as if determined to break across the bounds of the regular curve, but like all the others, as soon as the general outline is approached the huge limb dissolves into massy bosses of branchlets and sprays, as if the tree were growing beneath an invisible bell glass against the sides of which the branches were moulded, while many small, varied departures from the ideal form give the impression of freedom to grow as they like.

Except in picturesque old age, after being struck by lightning and broken by a thousand snowstorms, this regularity of form is one of the Big Tree's most distinguishing characteristics. Another is the simple sculptural beauty of the trunk and its great thickness as compared with its height and the width of the branches, many of them being from eight to ten feet in diameter at a height or two hundred feet from the ground, and seeming more like finely modeled and sculptured architectural columns than the stems of trees, while the great strong limbs are like rafters supporting the magnificent dome head.

The root system corresponds in magnitude with the other dimensions of the tree, forming a flat far-reaching spongy network two hundred feet or more in width without any taproot, and the instep is so grand and fine, so suggestive of endless strength, it is long ere the eye is released to look above it. The natural swell of the roots, though at first sight excessive, gives rise to buttresses no greater than are required for beauty as well as strength, as at once appears when you stand back far enough to see the whole tree in its true proportions. The fineness of the taper of the trunk is shown by its thickness at great heights—a diameter of ten feet at a height of two hundred being, as we have seen, not uncommon. Indeed the boles of but few trees hold their thickness as well as Sequoia. Resolute, consummate, determined in form, always beheld with wondering admiration, the Big Tree always seems unfamiliar, standing alone, unrelated, with peculiar physiognomy, awfully solemn and earnest. Nevertheless, there is nothing alien in its looks. . . .

The bark of full grown trees is from one to two feet thick, rich cinnamon brown, purplish on young trees and shady parts of the old, forming magnificent masses of color with the underbrush and beds of flowers. Toward the end of winter the trees themselves bloom while the snow is still eight or ten feet deep. The pistillate flowers are about three eighths of an inch long, pale green, and grow in countless thousands on the ends of the sprays. The staminate are still more abundant, pale yellow, a fourth of an inch long; and when the golden pollen is ripe they color the whole tree and dust the air and the ground far and near.

The cones are bright grass-green in color, about two and a half inches long, one and a half wide, and are made up of thirty or forty strong, closely packed, rhomboidal scales with four to eight seeds at the base of each. The seeds are extremely small and light, being only from an eighth to a fourth of an inch long and wide, including a filmy surrounding wing, which causes them to glint and waver in falling and enables the wind to carry them considerable distances from the tree.

The faint lisp of snowflakes as they alight is one of the smallest sounds mortal can hear. The sound of falling Sequoia seeds, even when they happen to strike on flat leaves or flakes of bark, is about as faint. Very different is the bumping and thudding of the falling cones. Most of them are cut off by the Douglas squirrel and stored for the sake of the seeds, small as they are. In the calm Indian summer these busy harvesters with ivory sickles go to work early in the morning, as soon as breakfast is over, and nearly all day the ripe cones fall in a steady pattering, bumping shower. Unless harvested in this way they discharge their seeds and remain on the trees for many years. In fruitful seasons the trees are fairly laden. On two small specimen branches one and a half and two inches in diameter I counted four hundred and eighty cones. No other California conifer produces nearly so many seeds, excepting perhaps its relative, the Redwood of the Coast Mountains. Millions are ripened annually by a single tree, and the product of one of the main groves in a fruitful year would suffice to plant all the mountain ranges of the world.

The dense tufted sprays make snug nesting places for birds, and in some of the loftiest, leafiest towers of verdure thousands of generations have been reared, the great solemn trees shedding off flocks of merry singers every year from nests, like the flocks of winged seeds from the cones.

The Big Trees keeps its youth far longer than any of its neighbors. Most silver firs are old in their second or third century, pines in their fourth or fifth, while the Big Tree growing beside them is still in the bloom of its youth, juvenile in every feature at the age of old pines, and cannot be said to attain anything like prime size and beauty before its fifteen hundredth year, or under favorable circumstances become old before its three thousandth. Many, no doubt, are much older than this. On one of the Kings River giants, thirty-five feet and eight inches in diameter exclusive of bark, I counted upwards of four thousand annual wood-rings, in which there was no trace of decay after all these centuries of mountain weather.

There is no absolute limit to the existence of any tree. Their death is due to accidents, not, as of animals, to the wearing out of organs. Only the leaves die of old age, their fall is foretold in their structure; but the leaves are renewed every year and so also are the other essential organs—wood, roots, bark, buds. Most of the Sierra trees die of disease. Thus the magnificent silver firs are devoured by fungi, and comparatively few of them live to see their three hundredth birth year. But nothing hurts the Big Tree. I never saw one that was sick or showed the slightest sign of decay. It lives on through indefinite thousands of years until burned, blown down, undermined, or shattered by some tremendous lightning stroke. No ordinary bolt ever seriously hurts Sequoia. In all my walks I have seen only one that was thus killed outright. Lightning, though rare in the California lowlands, is common on the Sierra. Almost every day in June and July small thunderstorms refresh the main forest belt. Clouds like snowy mountains of marvelous beauty grow rapidly in the calm sky about midday and cast cooling shadows and showers that seldom last more than an hour. Nevertheless these brief, kind storms wound or kill a good many trees.

I have seen silver firs two hundred feet high split into long peeled rails and slivers down to the roots, leaving not even a stump, the rails radiating like the spokes of a wheel from a hole in the ground where the tree stood. But the Sequoia, instead of being split and slivered, usually has forty or fifty feet of its brash knotty top smashed off in short chunks about the size of cord-wood, the beautiful rosy red ruins covering the ground in a circle a hundred feet wide or more. I never saw any that had been cut down to the ground or even to below the branches except one in the Stanislaus Grove, about twelve feet in diameter, the greater part of which was smashed to fragments, leaving only a leafless stump about seventy-five feet high. It is a curious fact that all the very old Sequoias have lost their heads by lightning. "All things come to him who waits." But of all living things Sequoia is perhaps the only one able to wait long enough to make sure of being struck by lightning. Thousands of years it stands ready and waiting, offering its head to every passing cloud as if inviting its fate, praying for heaven's fire as a blessing; and when at last the old head is off, another of the same shape immediately begins to grow on. Every bud and branch seems excited, like bees that have lost their queen, and tries hard to repair the damage. Branches that for many centuries have been growing out horizontally at once turn upward and all their branch-lets arrange themselves with reference to a new top of the same peculiar curve as the old one. Even the small subordinate branches halfway down the trunk do their best to push up to the top and help in this curious head-making.

The great age of these noble trees is even more wonderful than their huge size, standing bravely up, millennium in, millennium out, to all that fortune may bring them, triumphant over tempest and fire and time, fruitful and beautiful, giving food and shelter to multi-tudes of small fleeting creatures dependent on their bounty.

Muir's description gives us an idea of what Sequoias look like. He includes descriptions of their shape, the bark, the leaves, the root system, and their cones. By including such detail in his description, Muir creates a picture for us that is so accurate, we could doubtless identify the tree easily.

VARIATIONS IN PHYSICAL DESCRIPTION

A change of purpose will alter the nature of a physical description. The way the details are presented, which details are selected, and what pattern of presentation is used will be determined by the purpose.

EXPRESSIVE DESCRIPTION

Expressive descriptions may be disjointed and fragmented. They may also be layered with emotional responses.

AN EXAMPLE

Two days after the death of his six-year-old son Waldo, Ralph Waldo
Emerson made the following entry in his journal dated January 30, 1842.
In this entry we find various descriptions that reflect his feelings about the
death of his son.

JOURNAL

Ralph Waldo Emerson

What he looked upon is better, what he looked not upon is
insignificant. The morning of Friday I woke at 3 oclock, & every
cock in every barnyard was shrilling with the most unnecessary
noise. The sun went up the morning sky with all his light, but
the landscape was dishonored by this loss. For this boy in whose
remembrance I have both slept & awaked so oft, decorated for me
the morning star, & the evening cloud, how much more all the
particulars of daily economy; for he had touched with his lively
curiosity every trivial fact & circumstance in the household, the
hard coal & the soft coal which I put into my stove; the wood of
which he brought his little quota for grandmother's fire, the ham-
mer, the pincers, & file, he was so eager to use; the microscope,
the magnet, the little globe, & every trinket and instrument in the
study; the loads of gravel on the meadow, the nests in the henhouse
and many & many a little visit to the doghouse and to the barn—
For every thing he had his own name & way of thinking, his own
pronunciation & manner. And every word came mended from that
tongue. A boy of early wisdom, of a grave & even majestic deport-
ment, of a perfect gentleness.

Every tramper that ever tramped is abroad but the little feet
are still.

He gave up his little innocent breath like a bird.

He dictated a letter to his cousin Willie on Monday night to
thank him for the Magic Lantern which he had sent him, and said
I wish you would tell Cousin Willie that I have so many presents
that I do not need that he should send me any more unless he
wishes to very much.

The boy had his full swing in this world. Never I think did a
child enjoy more. He had been thoroughly respected by his parents

& those around him & not interfered with; and he had been the most fortunate in respect to the influences near him for his Aunt Elizabeth had adopted him from his infancy & treated him ever with that plain & wise love which belongs to her and, as she boasted, had never given him sugar plums. So he was won to her & always signalized her arrival as a visit to him & left playmates playthings & all to go to her. Then Mary Russell had been his friend & teacher for two summers with true love & wisdom. Then Henry Thoreau had been one of the family for the last year, & charmed Waldo by the variety of toys whistles boats popguns & all kinds of instruments which he could make & mend; & possessed his love & respect by the gentle firmness with which he always treated him. Margaret Fuller & Caroline had also marked the boy & caressed & conversed with him whenever they were here. Meantime every day his Grandmother gave him his reading lesson & had by patience taught him to read & spell; by patience & love for she loved him dearly.

   Sorrow makes us all children again, destroys all differences of intellect. The wisest knows nothing.

   The places Emerson describes in this entry take on new meaning in light of his son's death. The details he selects are controlled by his emotional responses to that event. He includes many things that were important to Waldo.

LITERARY DESCRIPTION

Literary descriptions must fit into the design for an overall aesthetic effect. Graphic, vivid images enhance the aesthetic appeal of such descriptions for the reader.

AN EXAMPLE

   Charles Dickens was a British author who wrote such memorable works as *David Copperfield*, *Oliver Twist*, and "A Christmas Carol." In this excerpt from his satirical novel *Hard Times* we find a description of Coketown, a fictional industrial town. With this description Dickens reveals the harsh working conditions prevalent in mill towns during the Victorian Age.

COKETOWN

Charles Dickens

It was a town of red brick, or of brick that would have been red if the smoke and ashes had allowed it; but as matters stood, it was a town of unnatural red and black like the painted face of a savage. It was a town of machinery and tall chimneys, out which interminable serpents of smoke trailed themselves for ever and ever and never got uncoiled. It had a black canal in it, and a river that ran purple with ill-smelling dye, and vast piles of building full of windows where there was a rattling and a trembling all day long, and where the piston of the steam-engine worked monotonously up and down, like the head of an elephant in a state of melancholy madness. It contained several large streets all very like one another, and many small streets still more like one another, inhabited by people equally like one another, who all went in and out at the same hours, with the same sound upon the same pavements, to do the same work, and whom every day was the same as yesterday and to-morrow, and every year the counterpart of the last and the next.

In this descriptive passage Dickens creates an impression of discomfort by using literal images that engage the senses, such as "unnatural red and black," "a black canal," "a river that ran purple with ill-smelling dye," and "a rattling and trembling." His use of a simile to compare the red and black bricks to "the painted face of a savage" creates impression of hostility. The metaphorical description of the smoke as "interminable serpents" that "trailed themselves for ever and ever and never got uncoiled" creates a feeling of anxiety. He underscores the monotony of factory work in the repetitious description of the streets and the people. With all these images, Dickens reinforces the impression of the unpleasantness of life in a factory town.

PERSUASIVE DESCRIPTION

A persuasive description will portray the person, place, or thing being described in a way that supports the claim the writer is defending. Notice the description of Coketown in the previous example. It presents a rather grim picture of mill towns in Victorian England. It is part of a novel, but it could have been used as part of a persuasive argument urging that the working conditions in mill towns should be improved. In fact, Dickens' novel has a secondary persuasive purpose since it is satirical and satires, although primarily literary, also have a persuasive intent.

AN EXAMPLE

This description, taken from *The Territory Ahead* catalogue, is designed to motivate the reader to buy the product. Notice how the detail included is intended to make the reader associate the product with a notable cultural icon from film history.

WOMEN'S EUROPA JACKET

THE TERRITORY AHEAD

You must remember this. Ingrid Bergman in Casablanca, creating a gallery of iconic moments. The dramatic entry at Rick's Café. The romantic interlude in war-torn Paris. The electric tension of the final farewell. No matter what the mood, she captured it perfectly. Likewise, our beautifully detailed Europa Jacket adapts seamlessly to any occasion. It's crafted of rich, supple cowhide, tumbled for a comfortably broken-in look and feel. Features include a mandarin collar with contrast piping; princess seaming for a feminine, slightly shaped silhouette. Finished with topstitching and brass rivets on the sleeves; on-seam pockets with rivets; and antiqued brass snaps at collar and cuffs. Zip front with inner weather flap. Low-hip length. Imported in Black.

Regular: XS–XL	320181	$299.00
Petites: P–XP	320204	$299.00

The writer's selection of detail is controlled by the persuasive purpose. Notice that the details such as "broken in look and feel" and "feminine, slightly shaped silhouette" suggest a kind of worldly femininity. The ad is obviously designed to persuade the reader that wearing the leather jacket will make her as alluring and mysterious as the character created by Ingrid Bergman in *Casablanca*.

REFERENTIAL DESCRIPTION

Referential descriptions focus on accuracy. They support the clear explanation of a topic by adding details that allow the reader to picture the thing described as it really is (or at least a close approximation).

AN EXAMPLE

The famous novelist Henry James offers this rather objective description of Chartres Cathedral.

CHARTRES CATHEDRAL

HENRY JAMES

I spent a long time looking at Chartres Cathedral. I revolved around it, like a moth around a candle; I went away and I came back; I chose twenty different standpoints; I observed it during the different hours of the day, and saw it in the moonlight as well as the sunshine. I gained, in a word, a certain sense of familiarity with it; and yet I despair of giving any coherent account of it. Like most French Cathedrals, it rises straight out of the street, and is without that setting of turf and trees and deaneries and canonries which contribute so largely to the impressiveness of the great English churches. Thirty years ago a row of old houses was glued to its base and made their back walls of its sculptured sides. These have been plucked away, and, relatively speaking, the church is fairly isolated. But the little square that surrounds it is regretfully narrow, and you flatten your back against the opposite houses in the vain attempt to stand off and survey the towers. The proper way to look at the towers would be to go up in a balloon and hang poised, face to face with them, in the blue air. There is, however, perhaps an advantage in being forced to stand so directly under them, for this position gives you an overwhelming impression of their height. I have seen, I suppose, churches as beautiful as this one, but I do not remember ever to have been so touched and fascinated by architectural beauty. The endless upward reach of the great west front, the clear, silvery tone of its surface, the way a few magnificent features are made to occupy its vast serene expanse, its simplicity, majesty, and dignity—these things crowd upon one's sense with a force that makes the act of vision seem for the moment almost all of life. The impressions produced by architecture lend themselves as little to interpretation by another medium as those produced by music. Certainly there is something of the beauty of music in the sublime proportions of the facade of Chartres.

The doors are rather low, as those of the English cathedral are apt to be, but (standing three together) are set in a deep framework of sculpture—rows of arching grooves, filled with admirable little images, standing with their heels on each other's heads. The church, as it now exists, except the northern tower, are full of the grotesqueness of the period. Above the triple portals is a vast round-topped window, in three divisions, of the grandest dimensions and the stateliest effect. Above the window is a circular aperture, of huge circumference, with a double row of sculptured spokes radiating from its centre and looking on its lofty field of stone as expansive and symbolic as if it were the wheel of Time itself. Higher still is a little gallery with a delicate balustrade, supported on a beautiful cornice and stretching across the front from tower to tower; and above this is a range of niched statues of kings—fifteen, I believe, in number. Above the statues is a gable, with an image of the Virgin and Child on its front, and another of Christ on its apex. In the relation of all these parts there is such a spaciousness and harmony that while on the one side the eye rests on a great many broad stretches of naked stone there is no approach on the other to over profusion of detail.

The arrangement of detail is from the perspective of a tourist. Notice how James places one detail in relation to others with such words as "above," "centre," and "across the front." This placement allows the observer to picture how the details are situated in the whole structure.

WRITING STRATEGIES

When you write descriptions, you will go through a process of selecting which details should be included in the description and then arranging them into an effective pattern. Consider these questions to help you get started when you are writing a physical description.

- What are you describing?
- What is its shape?
- What color is it?
- What does it taste like?
- What does it smell like?
- What does it feel like when you touch it?
- What does it sound like?
- What are its unique characteristics?
- What does it remind you of?
- What is its overall appearance?

DIVISION

Like physical descriptions, organization by division shows the relationship between the various parts that make up a whole. Although division has some features similar to classification, it deals not with classes, but with parts. Division answers the question, what are its component parts? Classification answers the questions, what kinds of the topic are there? If we wanted to explain the parts of a school building, we could list and define the parts that make up the whole: classrooms, offices, hallways, rest rooms, auditoriums, and laboratories. This division details the parts of a school building. If we discussed *kinds* of buildings—like office buildings, schools, factories, shopping centers—we would be classifying buildings by categories, and thereby arranging into groups.

THE STRUCTURE OF DIVISION

With division we are interested not so much in the overall impression of the thing being considered as we are in the individual parts that make up the whole. The parts of the whole are separated and examined in some detail

AN EXAMPLE

In the following exerpt from Benjamin Franklin's *Autobiography* (1784), we find an explanation of the various parts of what he calls a "project" for achieving "moral perfection."

THE ARDUOUS PROJECT OF ARRIVING AT MORAL PERFECTION

BENJAMIN FRANKLIN

It was about this time that I conceiv'd the bold and arduous Project of arriving at moral Perfection. I wish'd to live without committing any Fault at any time; I would conquer all that either Natural Inclination, Custom, or Company might lead me into. As I knew, or thought I knew, what was right and wrong, I did not see why I might not always do the one and avoid the other. But I soon found I had undertaken a Task of more Difficulty than I had imagined. While my *Attention was taken up* in guarding against one Fault, I was often surpriz'd by another. Habit took the Advantage of Inattention. Inclination was sometimes too strong for Reason. I concluded at length, that the mere speculative Conviction that it was our Interest to be compleatlyvirtuous, was not sufficient to prevent our Slipping, and that the contrary Habits must be broken and good ones acquired and established, before we can have any Dependance on a steady uniform Rectitude of Conduct. For this purpose I therefore contriv'd the following Method.

In the various Enumerations of the moral Virtues I had met with in my Reading, I found the Catalogue more or less numerous, as different Writers included more or fewer Ideas under the same Name. Temperance, for Example, was by some confin'd to Eating and Drinking, while by others it was extended to mean the moderating every other Pleasure, Appetite, Inclination or Passion, bodily or mental, even to our Avarice and Ambition. I propos'd to myself, for the sake of Clearness, to use rather more Names with fewer Ideas annex'd to each, than a few Names with more Ideas; and I included under Thirteen Names of Virtues all that at that time occurr'd to me as necessary or desirable, and annex'd to each a short Precept, which fully express'd the Extent I gave to its Meaning.

These Names of Virtues with their Precepts were

1. TEMPERANCE.

Eat not to Dullness.
Drink not to Elevation.

2. SILENCE.

Speak not but what may benefit others or yourself. Avoid trifling Conversation.

3. ORDER.

Let all your Things have their Places. Let each Part of your Business have its Time.

4. RESOLUTION.

Resolve to perform what you ought. Perform without fail what you resolve.

5. FRUGALITY.

Make no Expence but to do good to others or yourself: i.e., Waste nothing.

6. INDUSTRY.

Lose no Time. Be always employ'd in something useful. Cut off all unnecessary Actions.

7. SINCERITY.

Use no hurtful Deceit.
Think innocently and justly; and, if you speak, speak accordingly.

8. JUSTICE.

Wrong none, by doing Injuries or omitting the Benefits that are your Duty.

9. MODERATION.
Avoid Extreams. Forbear resenting Injuries so much as you think they deserve.

10. CLEANLINESS.
Tolerate no Uncleanness in Body, Cloaths or Habitation.

11. TRANQUILITY.
Be not disturbed at Trifles, or at Accidents common or unavoidable.

12. CHASTITY.
Rarely use Venery but for Health or Offspring: Never to Dulness, Weakness, or the Injury of your own or another's Peace or Reputation.

13. HUMILITY.
Imitate Jesus and Socrates.

My Intention being to acquire the *Habitude* of all these Virtues, I judg'd it would be well not to distract my Attention by attempting the whole at once, but to fix it on one of them at a time, and when I should be Master of that, then to proceed to another, and so on till I should have gone thro' the thirteen. And as the previous Acquisition of some might facilitate the Acquisition of certain others, I arrang'd them with that View as they stand above. *Temperance* first, as it tends to produce that Coolness and Clearness of Head, which is so necessary where constant Vigilance was to be kept up, and Guard maintained, against the unremitting Attraction of ancient Habits, and the Force of perpetual Temptations. This being acquir'd and establish'd, Silence would be more easy, and my Desire being to gain Knowledge at the same time that I improv'd in Virtue, and considering that in Conversation it was obtain'd rather by use of the Ears than of the Tongue, and therefore wishing to break a Habit I was getting into of Prattling, Punning and Joking, which only made me acceptable to trifling Company, I gave Silence the second Place. This, and the next, *Order*, I expected would allow me more Time for attending to my Project and my Studies; RESOLUTION, once become habitual, would keep me firm in my Endeavours to obtain all the subsequent Virtues; *Frugality* and Industry, by freeing me from my remaining Debt, and producing Affluence and Independance, would make more easy the Practice of *Sincerity* and *Justice*, &c. &c. Conceiving then that agreable to the Advice of Pythagoras in his Golden Verses daily Examination would be necessary, I contriv'd the following Method for conducting that Examination.

I made a little Book in which I allotted a Page for each of the Virtues. I rul'd each Page with red Ink, so as to have seven Columns, one for each Day of the Week, marking each Column with a Letter for the Day. I cross'd these Columns with thirteen red Lines, marking the Beginning of each Line with the first Letter of one of the Virtues, on which Line and in its proper Column I might mark by a little black Spot every Fault I found upon Examination to have been committed respecting that Virtue upon that Day.

This reading answers the question, "What are the parts of moral perfection?" Franklin divides his topic into its component parts, the virtues he wants to achieve.

WRITING STRATEGIES

Consider the following questions when you are using division to organize your writing.

- What are the parts?
- What is each part like?
- How are the parts arranged?

ANALYSIS

Like division, analysis divides a subject into its component parts, but it goes beyond simple division. Analytical organization allows us to examine a concept in some detail and so come to understand not only how the parts are interrelated, but also why they exist.

THE STRUCTURE OF ANALYSIS

An analysis will have a structure that allows the writer to make clear to the reader complex concepts and subjects. The parts are identified and defined. The relationships among the various parts are explained. Finally the interactions among the parts are described.

AN EXAMPLE

Alan M. Dershowitz is a lawyer who taught at Harvard Law School from 1967 until 2013. Throughout his career he was involved in a number of high profile legal cases: Claus von Bulow's appeal of a murder conviction (later made into the movie *Reversal of Fortune* in 1990); the 1995 O. J. Simpson murder trial; and most recently, the impeachment trial of President Trump. In this essay, Dershowitz analyzes a famous 1919 Supreme Court case.

SHOUTING "FIRE!"

ALAN M. DERSHOWITZ

When the Reverend Jerry Falwell learned the Supreme Court had reversed his $200,000 judgment against *Hustler* magazine for the emotional distress that he had suffered from an outrageous parody, his response was typical of those who seek to censor speech: "Just as no person may scream 'Fire!' in a crowded theater when there is no fire, and find cover under the First Amendment, likewise, no sleazy merchant like Larry Flynt should be able to use the First Amendment as an excuse for maliciously and dishonestly attacking public figures, as he has so often done."

Justice Oliver Wendell Holmes's classic example of unprotected speech—falsely shouting "Fire!" in a crowded theater—has been invoked so often, by so many people, in such diverse contexts, that it has become part of our national folk language. It has even appeared—most appropriately—in the theater: in Tom Stoppard's play *Rosencrantz and Guildenstern Are Dead* a character shouts "Fire!" He then quickly explains: "It's all right--I'm demonstrating the misuse of free speech." Shouting "Fire!" in the theater may well be the only jurisprudential analogy that has assumed the status of a folk argument. A prominent historian recently characterized it as "the most brilliantly persuasive expression that ever came from

Holmes' pen." But in spite of its hallowed position in both the jurisprudence of the First Amendment and the arsenal of political discourse, it is and was an inapt analogy, even in the context in which it was originally offered. It has lately become—despite, perhaps even because of, the frequency and promiscuousness of its invocation—little more than a caricature of logical argumentation.

The case that gave rise to the "Fire!"-in-a-crowded-theater analogy—Schenck v. United States—involved the prosecution of Charles Schenck, who was the general secretary of the Socialist Party in Philadelphia, and Elizabeth Baer, who was its recording secretary. In 1917 a jury found Schenck and Baer guilty of attempting to cause insubordination among soldiers who had been drafted to fight in the First World War. They and other party members had circulated leaflets urging draftees not to "submit to intimidation" by fighting in a war being conducted on behalf of "Wall Street's chosen few." Schenck admitted, and the Court found, that the intent of the pamphlets' "impassioned language" was to "influence" draftees to resist the draft. Interestingly, however, Justice Holmes noted that nothing in the pamphlet suggested that the draftees should use unlawful means to oppose conscription: "In form at least [the pamphlet] confined itself to peaceful measures, such as petition for the repeal of the act" and an exhortation to exercise "your right to assert your opposition to the draft." Many of its most impassioned words were quoted directly from the Constitution.

Justice Holmes acknowledged that "in many places and in ordinary times the defendants, in saying all that was said in the circular, would have been within their constitutional rights." "But," he added, "the character of every act depends upon the circumstances in which it done." And to illustrate that truism he went on to say,

> The most stringent protection of free speech would not protect a man in falsely shouting fire in a theater, and causing a panic. It does not even protect a man from an injunction against uttering words that may have all the effect of force.

Justice Holmes then upheld the convictions in the context of a wartime draft, holding that the pamphlet created "a clear and present danger" of hindering the war effort while our soldiers were fighting for their lives and our liberty.

The example of shouting "Fire!" obviously bore little relationship to the facts of the Schenck case. The Schenck pamphlet contained a substantive political message. It urged its draftee readers to think about the message and then—if they so chose—to act on it in a lawful and nonviolent way. The man who shouts "Fire!" in a crowded theater is neither sending a political message nor inviting his listener to think about what he has said and decide what to do in a rational, calculated manner. On the contrary, the message is designed to force action without contemplation. The message "Fire!" is directed not to the mind and the conscience of the listener but, rather, to his adrenaline and his feet. It is a stimulus to immediate action, not thoughtful reflection. It is—as Justice Holmes recognized in his follow-up sentence—the functional equivalent of "uttering words that may have all the effect of force."

Indeed, in that respect the shout of "Fire!" is not even speech, in any meaningful sense of that term. It is a *clang sound*—the equivalent of setting off a nonverbal alarm. Had Justice Holmes been more honest about his example, he would have said that freedom of speech does not protect a kid who pulls a fire alarm in the absence of a fire. But that obviously would have been irrelevant to the case at hand. The proposition that pulling an alarm is not protected speech certainly leads to the conclusion that shouting the word fire is also not protected. But the core analogy is the nonverbal alarm, and the derivative example is the verbal shout. By cleverly substituting the derivative shout for the core alarm, Holmes made it possible to analogize one set of words to another—as he could not have done if he had begun with the selfevident proposition that setting off an alarm bell is not free speech.

The analogy is thus not only inapt but also insulting. Most Americans do not respond to political rhetoric with the same kind of automatic acceptance expected of schoolchildren responding to a fire drill. Not a single recipient of the Schenck pamphlet is known to have changed his mind after reading it. Indeed, one draftee, who appeared as a prosecution witness, was asked whether reading a pamphlet asserting that the draft law was unjust would make him "immediately decide that you must erase that law." Not surprisingly, he replied, "I do my own thinking." A theatergoer would probably not respond similarly if asked how he would react to a shout of "Fire!"

Another important reason why the analogy is inapt is that Holmes emphasizes the factual falsity of the shout of "Fire!" The Schenck pamphlet, however, was not factually false. It contained political opinions and ideas about the causes of the war and about appropriate and lawful responses to the draft. As the Supreme Court recently reaffirmed (in *Falwell v. Hustler*), "The First Amendment recognizes no such thing as a false idea." Nor does it recognize false opinions about the causes of or cures for war.

A closer analogy to the facts of the Schenck case might have been provided by a person's standing outside a theater advising them that in his opinion the theater was structurally unsafe, and urging them not to enter but to complain to the building inspectors. That analogy, however, would not have served Holmes's argument for punishing Schenck. Holmes needed an analogy that would appear relevant to Schenck's political speech but that would invite the conclusion that censorship was appropriate.

Unsurprisingly, a war-weary nation—in the throes of a know-nothing hysteria over immigrant anarchists and socialists—welcomed the comparision between what was regarded as a seditious political pamphlet and a malicious shout of "Fire!" Ironically, the "Fire!" analogy is nearly all that survives of the Schenck case; the ruling itself is almost certainly not good law. Pamphlets of the kind that resulted in Schenck's imprisonment have been circulated with impunity during subsequent wars.

Over the past several years I have assembled a collection of instances—cases, speeches, arguments—in which proponents of censorship have maintained that the expression at issue is "just like" or "equivalent to" falsely shouting "Fire!" in a crowded theater and ought to be banned, "just as" shouting "Fire!" ought to be banned. The analogy is generally invoked, often with self-satisfaction, as an absolute argument-stopper. It does, after all, claim the high authority of the great Justice Oliver Wendell Holmes. I have rarely heard it invoked in a convincing, or even particularly relevant, way. But that, too, can claim lineage from the great Holmes.

Not unlike Falwell, with his silly comparison between shouting "Fire!" and publishing an offensive parody, courts and commentators have frequently invoked "Fire!" as an analogy to expression that is not an automatic stimulus to panic. A state supreme court held that "Holmes' aphorism . . . applies with equal force to pornography"—in particular to the exhibition of the movie *Carmen Baby* in a drive-in theater in close proximity to highways and homes. Another court analogized "picketing . . . in support of a secondary boycott" to shouting "Fire!" because in both instances "speech and conduct are brigaded." In the famous Skokie case one of the judges argued that allowing Nazis to march through a city where a large number of Holocaust survivors live "just might fall into the same category as one's 'right' to cry fire in a crowded theater."

Outside court the analogies become even more badly stretched. A spokesperson for the New Jersey Sports and Exposition Authority complained that newspaper reports to the effect that a large number of football players had contracted cancer after playing in the Meadowlands—a stadium atop a landfill— were the "journalistic equivalent of shouting fire in a crowded theater." The philosopher Sydney Hook, in a letter to The *New York Times* bemoaning a Supreme Court decision that required a plain- tiff in a defamation action to prove that the offending statement was actually false, argued that the First Amendment does not give the press carte blanche to accuse innocent persons "any more than the First Amendment protects the right of someone falsely to shout fire in a crowded theater."

Some close analogies to shouting "Fire!" or setting off an alarm are, or course, available: calling in a false bomb threat; dialing 911 and falsely describing an emergency; making a loud, gunlike sound in the presence of the President; setting off a voice- activated sprinkler system by falsely shouting "Fire!" In one case in which the "Fire!" analogy was directly to the point, a creative defen- dant tried to get around it. The case involved a man who calmly advised an airline clerk that he was "only here to hijack the plane." He was charged, in effect, with shouting "Fire!" in a crowded the- ater, and his rejected defense—as quoted by the court—was as fol- lows: "If we built fire-proof theaters and let people know about this, then the shouting of "Fire!" would not cause panic."

Here are some more-distant but still related examples: the recent incident of the police slaying in which some members of an onlooking crowd urged a mentally ill vagrant who had taken an officer's gun to shoot the officer; the screaming of racial epithets during a tense confrontation; shouting down a speaker and pre- venting him form continuing his speech.

Analogies are, by their nature, matters of degree. Some are closer to the core example than others. But any attempt to analogize political ideas in a pamphlet, ugly parody in a magazine, offensive movies in a theater, controversial newspaper articles, or any of the other expressions and actions catalogued above to the very different act of shouting "Fire!" in a crowded theater is either self-deceptive or self-serving.

The government does, of course, have some arguably legitimate bases for suppressing speech which bear no relationship to shouting "Fire!" It may ban the publication of nuclear-weapon codes, of information about troop movements, and of the identity of undercover agents. It may criminalize extortion threats and conspiratorial agreements. These expressions may lead directly to serious harm, but the mechanisms of causation are very different from that at work when an alarm is sounded. One may also argue—less persuasively, in my view—against protecting certain forms of public obscenity and defamatory statements. Here, too, the mechanisms of causation are very different. None of these exceptions to the First Amendment's exhortation that the government "shall make no law . . . abridging the freedom of speech, or of the press" is anything like falsely shouting "Fire!" in a crowded theater; they all must be justified on other grounds.

A comedian once told his audience, during a stand-up routine, about the time he was standing around a fire with a crowd of people and got in trouble for yelling "Theater, theater!" That, I think, is about as clever and productive a use as anyone has ever made of Holmes's flawed analogy.

In his analysis Dershowitz looks at three interrelated concepts: freedom of speech, the details of a court case, and the use of an analogy in that case. He argues that, although there are limits to the constitutional protection of free speech, the often-used example of someone falsely shouting "fire" in a crowded theater, when there is in fact no fire, does not an accurately depict that limitation. He examines the most famous example of the concept when it was used in support of a Supreme Court decision that upheld the criminal conviction of Charles Schenck in 1917 for handing out pamphlets opposing America's involvement in World War I. In the Supreme Court ruling reached in 1919, Justice Oliver Wendell Holmes wrote that handing out the antiwar pamphlets represented a "clear and present danger" to

American society and he further compared the effect of the statements written in the pamphlets to someone falsely shouting "fire" in a crowded theater. Analogies are frequently used in legal reasoning when there is no precedent that is entirely on point for a case the court is considering. Although the analogy seems to make sense, Dershowitz's analysis shows that shouting "fire" in a crowded theater is not really speech at all; rather it raises an alarm. Further, he breaks down the parts of the legal argument in the Schenck case and concludes that handing out a pamphlet did not cause an immediate panic among its readers nor did it endanger American troops fighting in the war. Consequently, Schenck's action is not analogous to creating a panic among people in a public place. His analysis shows that Holmes' opinion is flawed and that the comparison of shouting "fire" to handing out a pamphlet is an inapt analogy. Finally, Dershowitz cites a number of legitimate reasons the government might have for abridging the right to free speech, but he notes that none of them is analogous to shouting "fire" in a crowded theater. In this complex analysis Dershowitz examines the first amendment protection of free speech as well as its limitations, the details of the Schenck case, and the applicability of the analogy of shouting '"fire" when there is no fire.

CRITICAL ANALYSIS OF WRITING

We have looked at the basic structure of analysis and have seen that an analysis of a subject works on the assumption that the whole is composed of parts. With an analysis the writer not only presents elements that make up the concept being analyzed, but also explains the interrelations among the elements. In this section we briefly look at critical analysis of writing, a kind of analysis used in a great many areas of academic work. The ability to read and analyze a written work is an essential requirement in most college courses. Although the method of analysis in each academic discipline may be slightly different, they all involve an examination of the parts of a written text. Which aspects of a document are analyzed will be determined in part by its purpose. An analysis of expressive writing like memoirs and diaries will focus on the values and emotional responses of the writer. An analysis of literary writing will look at literary uses of language. An analysis of persuasive writing will focus on the various appeals to the audience. Finally, an analysis of referential writing will examine the validity of the evidence presented in the work. Analysis of any kind of writing demands a critical examination of the material presented in a document.

In history courses you may be asked to analyze personal documents such as personal letters and journals written by historical figures. The analysis of these primary sources is an important part of historical research. Historians rely on such documents, not only for information that explains the actions and motivations of the writer, but also for clues about the cultural values prevalent in the society during the period being investigated. In addition, these primary sources may add additional information about well-known historical figures and events that are discussed in history textbooks.

In literature courses you will certainly be asked to write papers analyzing literary texts. The analysis of literature (also called critical analysis) involves an understanding of literary devices and literary terminology. You will remember from the discussion of literary writing in Chapter 2 that we referred to a number of elements associated with literature. These elements include (but are not limited to) character, dialogue, setting, plot, conflict, imagery, and symbolism. An analysis of a work of literature may involve one or several of these elements. A literary critic might analyze the dominant symbolism of a poem or explain the types of conflict in a work of fiction. The analysis following John Gardner's "An Interlude" in Chapter 2 illustrates how some of those elements can be incorporated into a written analysis of a literary work. (See also Lauriat Lane, Jr.'s "Why 'Huckleberry Finn' Is a Great World Novel" in Chapter 8 as an example of a critical analysis of a novel.)

In courses in composition, communications, business, and marketing/ advertising you may need to write papers analyzing methods of persuasion. The analysis of persuasion (also called rhetorical analysis) requires a recognition and understanding of rhetorical techniques and strategies of argumentation including the various appeals discussed in Chapter 3 (personal, emotional, rational and stylistic). In addition, you should be able to identify and explain statements that contain logical fallacies. Logical fallacies appear in arguments of all kinds. At first glance such statements may seem to be valid, but a closer inspection will reveal their logical inconsistencies.

Statements like "My opponent is an immoral con man" (an example of name calling) or "He is a notorious liar; you can't believe a word he says" (an example of poisoning the well) are fairly obvious. Both are illustrations of an ad *hominem* fallacy (Latin for "against the man"). The statement "Young people nowadays don't respect their elders" is an obvious example of a sweeping generalization. It is easily refuted by simply finding one young person who respects his or her elders. The use of qualifying language like "many" or "some" or even "most" would make the statement more defensible. A little reflection tells us that the statement "The police would not abuse a suspect because the job of the police department is to protect and serve" is a problematic because it assumes in the premise what it is trying to prove, a fallacy called circular reasoning.

The logical inconsistencies may be a little more difficult to spot in an argument like this: "Scientific studies show that chickadees raised in captivity lose the ability to find food on their own, so we should not fund nutritional programs or provide other forms of government assistance because people will lose all initiative to provide for themselves." The statement is a false analogy because people are not birds and the behavior of birds is not analogous to the behavior of people. As we discovered in Chapter 4 under "Inductive Reasoning," for an analogy to be used as proof, the two things being compared must be closely related to each other. (See Alan Dershowitz's "Shouting 'Fire!'" in this chapter for a detailed analysis of the use of an "inapt analogy" in a legal case.)

Statements that purport to explain causes can also lead to fallacies. Superstitions are a prime example of this kind of fallacy. Consider the following statement: "A black cat crossed the street in front of me and then I ran into a tree, so black cats are bad luck." It illustrates the fallacy called *post hoc ergo propter hoc* (Latin for "After this therefore because of this"). Canadian humorist Stephen Leacock in *Sunshine Sketches in a Little Town* (1912) created a memorable example of the post hoc fallacy when he wrote "When I state that my lectures were followed almost immediately by the union of South Africa, the banana riots in Trinidad, and the Turco-Italian war, I think the reader can form some opinion of their importance." Just because one event precedes another does not mean that the former caused the latter. Consider this statement: "There has been a rise in the number of single-parent homes at the same time that there has been a rise in violent crime; therefore, the rise in single-parent homes has caused the increase in violent crime." Causal reasoning is usually more complicated than that. A correlation does not necessarily imply causation. The rise in single-parent homes may have nothing to do with the increase in violent crime, and even if it is a contributing factor, it is certainly not the only cause. At the very least, the statement is an oversimplification of a complex social phenomenon. Another fallacy in causal reasoning occurs in the following: "If you drop out of school, you will not get a good job, and if you don't get a good job, you will not make enough money for a place to live and will be forced to live on the streets." This fallacy is appropriately named the slippery slope fallacy, an obvious exaggeration of a possible series of unfortunate events. We cannot be sure that each event in a chain of events will cause the next one to occur. Slippery slope arguments are typically used as a fear tactic.

We have identified only a few of the many logical fallacies. A number of websites offer further explanations and examples. The website logicallyfalacious.com, for example, identifies over 300 logical fallacies.

In courses in the behavioral and physical sciences you may be asked to write papers analyzing research studies. In the sciences these studies in are typically reported as referential documents in which the researchers attempt to interpret a body of evidence according to the conventions of explanatory reasoning. (See Chapter 4 for a discussion of explanatory reasoning.) Such reports, published in scientific and professional journals, may be highly technical and involve complicated methodologies and statistical analyses. Reading reports of scientific studies requires an understanding of the scope and the limitation of the methodologies used. Sometimes, when these studies are reported in mainstream media, some of the nuance of the original research is lost. Reports in the media may fail to call attention to the limitations and qualifications that research studies point out. Such discrepancies may lead to a misunderstanding of the meaning and significance of a given study. For example, biomedical and health related studies are often widely reported in news sources. The original studies usually carefully qualify the significance of the study, limiting what can and cannot be inferred from the results, what advice about health can be given, what conclusions about causation can be drawn, and how applicable the study is to humans. Journalistic reporting, however, may oversimplify some aspects of what should be a more complex interpretation of the evidence presented. Advice may be exaggerated, causal statements may be made from correlational results, and conclusions about the effects of a treatment on humans may be drawn from studies of animals. If a research study does not give specific advice, make statements about cause, or say conclusively that animal studies can be generalized to humans, then those kinds of inferences are unwarranted.

In all academic disciplines you will be required to employ critical thinking in order to analyze documents relevant to the body of knowledge in those disciplines. Critical thinking and analysis are essential, not only to your study in college courses, but also to your progress in professional areas after college.

WRITING STRATEGIES

FOR ANALYSIS

- How are the parts related to each other?
- How do the parts affect each other?

FOR CRITICAL ANALYSIS

Since critical analysis involves distinguishing and explaining the various parts of a written text, you must begin the process of critical analysis by reading the text. As you are reading, you may find it helpful to identify words and phrases that you think might be important to your analysis of the work you are analyzing. These words and phrases can be used to support the interpretation you give to what you have read.

The following questions may help you organize your work on a critical analysis:

- What features does the selection have that identify it as expressive, literary, persuasive, or referential?
- What organizational patterns are used?
- What examples from the selection support your interpretation?
- How do all the features you have found work together help the writer achieve the purpose?

Narration

When we create details that take place in time, we organize them by narration. The organizing principle of narration is the relationship between events in time. We present one event or occurrence after another so that they create a coherent sequence. Each event is connected causally to each event that precedes it and each event that follows it. Narrations of all kinds are dynamic; that is, they change over time. The story is the most familiar form of narration, but narration can also be used to explain a process or to examine causes and effects.

NARRATION OF EVENT

A narration of an event is a record of a sequence of actions that has occurred only once. Those events have never happened before and they will never happen again. A historian, for instance, writing about what happened at the Battle of Little Bighorn when the Sioux defeated Custer would be narrating a series of events that obviously took place only once.

NARRATIVE CUES

Narratives always have cues that tell us we are reading a narrative. These narrative cues are words that refer to time or action. Notice the underlined words in the following narrative.

> *As* I *hiked* down the hillside, the clouds *tumbled* across the darkening sky. *Earlier* in the day, the sky had been clear and the air, still. *Now* the *gusty* wind *blew* through the trees, *whistling*

and *moaning*, *shaking* the limbs and *bending* the trunks. *Soon* the rain *would start*. I *hurried*, *trying to find* shelter *before* the storm *engulfed* me.

The words *hiked, tumbled, blew, whistling, moaning, shaking, bending, would start, hurried, trying to find*, and *engulfed* create the ongoing action of the narrative. They tell us what is happening. The words *as, earlier, now, soon*, and *before* help us understand how the events being recounted are sequenced and so help us orient ourselves in relation to the action as we read.

THE STAGES OF A NARRATION OF EVENT

A complete narration of an event has a number of specific stages. First a potential for action must exist. Then something, an inciting event, creates a disturbance that causes the action to move forward and become complicated. This complication, produced by conflict and an interaction of forces, moves the action to a crisis that must be resolved. When the resolution occurs, the narration ends. Imagine the surface of a pond, clear and unmoving. If a stone were thrown into it, ripples would form and move out until they dissipated at the bank. That is the way a narration of an event works. The surface of the pond represents the potential for action. The stone being thrown into the water corresponds to the inciting event that causes an interaction of forces to create the ripples, just as conflict moves the action of a plot to crisis and eventual resolution.

The stages of a narration of an event can be seen in the following diagram.

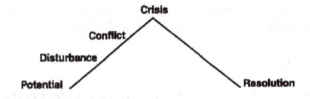

PARTIAL NARRATIVES

Not all narrations of event are complete. Some narratives, like epic poems, begin in the middle of the action. The earlier events are filled in by flashback to previous events, or they may already be known if the plot of the narrative is based on some well-known myth or legend. A number of Classical Greek dramas were based on myths that would have been known by the contemporary audiences that attended the performances. Many of Shakespeare's history plays were adaptations of actual historical events that his audiences would have been well acquainted with. Some narrations end before the resolution occurs. These narratives are said to have indeterminate endings. Modern short story writers often end their stories before the resolution to suggest a universal human condition and to allow the audience to participate in the action of the plot. Because we know the stages of the complete narrative intuitively, we tend to want to fill in the beginning or the end with our imaginations.

It is possible to have a narrative devoted to each one of the stages of narration. A narration devoted to the potential for action is called a *field narrative*. It involves quite a lot of description and only suggests that action may be possible. A *disturbance narrative* focuses on the moment of transition when potential becomes action. A *conflict narrative* centers on those events leading to crisis. A *crisis narrative* looks only at the action associated with the crisis and does not dwell on events building up to that crisis or on the events leading to its resolution. A *resolution narrative* would focus on the conclusion of the action.

THE NARRATOR

The narrator is the person who is telling the story. That person can be a first-person narrator who is actually involved in the events of the narration and who uses first-person personal pronouns (*I, me, my, mine*). The narrator may also be a third-person narrator who is telling the story from a vantage point outside the action of the narrative and who uses third-person pronouns (*he, she, it, they, them*).

AN EXAMPLE

In this excerpt from Owen Wister's novel *The Virginian* we see an episode that, although brief, does illustrate the different stages of the narration of event as told by a first-person narrator.

THE VIRGINIAN DOES SOME ROPING

OWEN WISTER

Some notable sight was drawing the passengers, both men and women to the window; and therefore I rose and crossed the car to see what it was. I saw near the track an enclosure, and round it some laughing men, and inside it some whirling dust, and amid the dust some horses, plunging, huddling, and dodging. There were cow ponies in a corral, and one of them would not be caught, no matter who threw the rope. We had plenty of time to watch this sport, for our train had stopped that the engine might take water at the tank before it pulled us up beside the station platform of Medicine Bow. We were also six hours late, and starving for entertainment. The pony in the corral was wise, and rapid of limb. Have you seen a skillful boxer watch his antagonist with a quiet, incessant eye? Such an eye as this did the pony keep upon whatever man took the rope. The man might pretend to look at the weather, which was fine; or he might affect earnest conversation with a bystander; it was bootless. The pony saw through it. No feint hoodwinked him. This animal was thoroughly a man of the world. His undistracted eye stayed fixed upon the dissembling foe, and the gravity of his horse expression made the matter one of high comedy. The rope would sail out at him, but he was already elsewhere; and if horses laugh, gayety must have abounded in that corral. Sometimes the pony took a turn alone; next he had slid in a flash among his brothers, and the whole of them like a school of playful fish whipped round the corral, kicking up the fine dust, and (I take it) roaring with laughter. Through the window-glass of our Pullman the thud of their mischievous hoofs reached us, and the strong, humorous curses of the cowboys. Then for the first time I noticed a man who sat on the high gate of the corral, looking on. For he now climbed down with lithe undulations of a tiger, smooth and easy, as if his muscles flowed beneath his skin. The others had all visibly whirled the rope, some of them even shoulder high. I did not see his arm lift or move. He appeared to hold the rope down, low, by his leg. But like a sudden snake I saw the noose go out its length and fall true; and the thing was done. As the captured pony walked in with a sweet, church-door expression, our train moved slowly on to the station, and a passenger remarked, "That man knows his business."

In this narrative the potential for action is the corral full of horses. The inciting event is the horse evading the rope. The complication and conflict increases between the frustrated ropers and the cagey pony. When the Virginian moves onto the scene, the narration approaches crisis which is resolved when the Virginian ultimately ropes the horse.

VARIATIONS IN NARRATION OF EVENT

The presentation of the events in the narrative will be altered depending on the writer's purpose. For example, some writers may alter the simple chronological sequence of presentation and tell some of the earlier events in flashback sequences (after the plot has already begun). This technique creates a dramatic effect and is frequently used in literary and expressive narratives.

EXPRESSIVE NARRATION OF EVENT

An expressive narrative will be episodic. The events of the narrative may be broken up and told in smaller units (episodes) that are all connected by the associations in the mind of the writer. Sometimes the reader can understand the associative connections and sometimes not.

AN EXAMPLE

The following excerpt from Chapter 7 of Frederick Douglass' autobiography, *Narrative of the Life of Frederick Douglass, an American Slave*, published in 1845, illustrates how the subjective nature of expressive writing affects the narrative.

HOW I LEARNED TO WRITE

FREDERICK DOUGLASS

I lived in Master Hugh's family about seven years. During this time, I succeeded in learning to read and write. In accomplishing this, I was compelled to resort to various stratagems. I had no regular teacher. My mistress, who had kindly commenced to instruct me, had, in compliance with the advice and direction of her husband, not only ceased to instruct, but had set her face against my being instructed by any one else. It is due, however, to my mistress to say of her, that she did not adopt this course of treatment immediately. She at first lacked the depravity indispensable to shutting me up in mental darkness. It was at least necessary for her to have some training in the exercise of irresponsible power, to make her equal to the task of treating me as though I were a brute.

My mistress was, as I have said, a kind and tender-hearted woman; and in the simplicity of her soul she commenced, when I first went to live with her, to treat me as she supposed one human being ought to treat another. In entering upon the duties of a slaveholder, she did not seem to perceive that I sustained to her the relation of a mere chattel, and that for her to treat me as a human being was not only wrong, but dangerously so. Slavery proved as injurious to her as it did to me. When I went there, she was a pious, warm, and tender-hearted woman. There was no sorrow or suffering for which she had not a tear. She had bread for the hungry, clothes for the naked, and comfort for every mourner that came within her reach. Slavery soon proved its ability to divest her of these heavenly qualities. Under its influence, the tender heart became stone, and the lamblike disposition gave way to one of tiger-like fierceness. The first step in her downward course was in her ceasing to instruct me. She now commenced to practise her husband's precepts. She finally became even more violent in her opposition than her husband himself. She was not satisfied with simply doing as well as he had commanded; she seemed anxious to do better. Nothing seemed to make her more angry than to see me with a newspaper. She seemed to think that here lay the danger. I have had her rush at me with a face made all up of fury, and snatch from me a newspaper, in a manner that fully revealed her apprehension. She was an apt woman; and a little experience soon demonstrated, to her satisfaction, that education and slavery were incompatible with each other.

From this time I was most narrowly watched. If I was in a separate room any considerable length of time, I was sure to be suspected of having a book, and was at once called to give an account of myself. All this, however, was too late. The first step had been taken. Mistress, in teaching me the alphabet, had given me the *inch*, and no precaution could prevent me from taking the *ell*.

The plan which I adopted, and the one by which I was most successful, was that of making friends of all the little white boys whom I met in the street. As many of these as I could, I converted into teachers. With their kindly aid, obtained at different times and in different places, I finally succeeded in learning to read. When I was sent of errands, I always took my book with me, and by going one part of my errand quickly, I found time to get a lesson before my return. I used also to carry bread with me, enough of which was always in the house, and to which I was always welcome; for I was much better off in this regard than many of the poor white children in our neighborhood. This bread I used to bestow upon the hungry little urchins, who, in return, would give me that more valuable bread of knowledge. I am strongly tempted to give the names of two or three of those little boys, as a testimonial of the gratitude and affection I bear them; but prudence forbids;—not that it would injure me, but it might embarrass them; for it is almost an unpardonable offence to teach slaves to read in this Christian country. It is enough to say of the dear little fellows, that they lived on Philpot Street, very near Durgin and Bailey's ship-yard. I used to talk this matter of slavery over with them. I would sometimes say to them, I wished I could be as free as they would be when they got to be men. "You will be free as soon as you are twenty-one, *but I am a slave for life*! Have not I as good a right to be free as you have?" These words used to trouble them; they would express for me the liveliest sympathy, and console me with the hope that something would occur by which I might be free.

I was now about twelve years old, and the thought of being *a slave for life* began to bear heavily upon my heart. Just about this time, I got hold of a book entitled "The Columbian Orator." Every opportunity I got, I used to read this book. Among much of other interesting matter, I found in it a dialogue between a master and his slave. The slave was represented as having run away from his master three times. The dialogue represented the conversation which took place between them, when the slave was retaken the third time. In this dialogue, the whole argument in behalf of slavery was brought forward by the master, all of which was disposed of by the slave. The slave was made to say some very smart as well as impressive things in reply to his master—things which had the desired though unexpected effect; for the conversation resulted in the voluntary emancipation of the slave on the part of the master.

In the same book, I met with one of Sheridan's mighty speeches on and in behalf of Catholic emancipation. These were choice documents to me. I read them over and over again with unabated interest. They gave tongue to interesting thoughts of my own soul, which had frequently flashed through my mind, and died away for want of utterance. The moral which I gained from the dialogue was the power of truth over the conscience of even a slaveholder. What I got from Sheridan was a bold denunciation of slavery, and a powerful vindication of human rights. The reading of these documents enabled me to utter my thoughts, and to meet the arguments brought forward to sustain slavery; but while they relieved me of one difficulty, they brought on another even more painful than the one of which I was relieved. The more I read, the more I was led to abhor and detest my enslavers. I could regard them in no other light than a band of successful robbers, who had left their homes, and gone to Africa, and stolen us from our homes, and in a strange land reduced us to slavery. I loathed them as being the meanest as well as the most wicked of men. As I read and contemplated the subject, behold! that very discontentment which Master Hugh had predicted would follow my learning to read had already come, to torment and sting my soul to unutterable anguish. As I writhed under it, I would at times feel that learning to read had been a curse rather than a blessing. It had given me a view of my wretched condition, without the remedy. It opened my eyes to the horrible pit, but to no ladder upon which to get out. In moments of agony, I envied my fellow-slaves for their stupidity. I have often wished myself a beast. I preferred the condition of the meanest reptile to my own. Any thing, no matter what, to get rid of thinking! It was this everlasting thinking of my condition that tormented me. There was no getting rid of it. It was pressed upon me by every object within sight or hearing, animate or inanimate. The silver trump of freedom had roused my soul to eternal wakeful-ness. Freedom now appeared, to disappear no more forever. It was heard in every sound, and seen in every thing. It was ever present to torment me with a sense of my wretched condition. I saw nothing without seeing it, I heard nothing without hearing it, and felt noth-ing without feeling it. It looked from every star, it smiled in every calm, breathed in every wind, and moved in every storm.

I often found myself regretting my own existence, and wish-ing myself dead; and but for the hope of being free, I have no doubt but that I should have killed myself, or done something for which I should have been killed. While in this state of mind, I was eager to hear any one speak of slavery. I was a ready listener. Every little while, I could hear something about the abolitionists. It was some time before I found what the word meant. It was always used in such connections as to make it an interesting word to me. If a slave ran away and succeeded in getting clear, or if a slave killed his master, set fire to a barn, or did any thing very wrong in the mind of a slaveholder, it was spoken of as the fruit of *abolition*. Hearing the word in this connection very often, I set about learning what it meant. The dictionary afforded me little or no help. I found it was "the act of abolishing;" but then I did not know what was to be abolished. Here I was perplexed. I did not dare to ask any one about its meaning, for I was satisfied that it was something they wanted me to know very little about. After a patient waiting, I got one of our city papers, containing an account of the number of petitions from the north, praying for the abolition of slavery in the District of Columbia, and of the slave trade between the States. From this time I understood the words *abolition* and *abolitionist*, and always drew near when that word was spoken, expecting to hear something of importance to myself and fellow-slaves. The light broke in upon me by degrees. I went one day down on the wharf of Mr. Waters; and seeing two Irishmen unloading a scow of stone, I went, unasked, and helped them. When we had finished, one of them came to me and asked me if I were a slave. I told him I was. He asked, "Are ye a slave for life?" I told him that I was. The good Irishman seemed to be deeply affected by the statement. He said to the other that it was a pity so fine a little fellow as myself should be a slave for life. He said it was a shame to hold me. They both advised me to run away to the north; that I should find friends there, and that I should be free. I pretended not to be interested in what they said, and treated them as if I did not understand them; for I feared they might be treacherous. White men have been known to encourage slaves to escape, and then, to get the reward, catch them and return them to their masters. I was afraid that these seemingly good men might use me so; but I nevertheless remembered their advice, and from that time I resolved to run away. I looked forward to a time at which it would be safe for me to escape. I was too young to think of doing so immediately; besides, I wished to learn how to write, as I might have occasion to write my own pass. I consoled myself with the hope that I should one day find a good chance. Meanwhile, I would learn to write.

The idea as to how I might learn to write was suggested to me by being in Durgin and Bailey's ship-yard, and frequently seeing the ship carpenters, after hewing, and getting a piece of timber ready for use, write on the timber the name of that part of the ship for which it was intended. When a piece of timber was intended for the larboard side, it would be marked thus—"L." When a piece was for the starboard side, it would be marked thus—"S." A piece for the larboard side forward, would be marked thus—"L. F." When a piece was for starboard side forward, it would be marked thus—"S. F." For larboard aft, it would be marked thus—"L. A." For starboard aft, it would be marked thus—"S. A." I soon learned the names of these letters, and for what they were intended when placed upon a piece of timber in the ship-yard. I immediately commenced copying them, and in a short time was able to make the four letters named. After that, when I met with any boy who I knew could write, I would tell him I could write as well as he. The next word would be, "I don't believe you. Let me see you try it." I would then make the letters which I had been so fortunate as to learn, and ask him to beat that. In this way I got a good many lessons in writing, which it is quite possible I should never have gotten in any other way. During this time, my copy-book was the board fence, brick wall, and pavement; my pen and ink was a lump of chalk. With these, I learned mainly how to write. I then commenced and continued copying the Italics in Webster's Spelling Book, until I could make them all without looking on the book. By this time, my little Master Thomas had gone to school, and learned how to write, and had written over a number of copy-books. These had been brought home, and shown to some of our near neighbors, and then laid aside. My mistress used to go to class meeting at the Wilk Street meetinghouse every Monday afternoon, and leave me to take care of the house. When left thus, I used to spend the time in writing in the spaces left in Master Thomas's copy-book, copying what he had written. I continued to do this until I could write a hand very similar to that of Master Thomas. Thus, after a long, tedious effort for years, I finally succeeded in learning how to write.

Douglass uses the technique of episodic linking in his writing. He narrates a sequence of different events and short anecdotes that are linked together to convey his larger point: the struggle he had to go through and the strategies that he had to adopt in order to learn how to read and write.

LITERARY NARRATION OF EVENT

The narrative is perhaps the most frequently used pattern for literary works. Literary narratives focus on the conflict and crisis inherent in the narrative structure. They also typically include descriptions that present the setting and characters to the reader.

AN EXAMPLE

The following story was written by Saki (the pseudonym of H. H. Munro), an early twentieth-century Scottish writer, known for his cleverly plotted short stories, often with surprise endings. In this short story, "The Open Window," we find a narrative with a conflict that develops very gradually.

THE OPEN WINDOW

SAKI

"My aunt will be down presently, Mr. Nuttel," said a very self-possessed young lady of fifteen; "in the meantime you must try and put up with me."

Framton Nuttel endeavoured to say the correct something which should duly flatter the niece of the moment without unduly discounting the aunt that was to come. Privately he doubted more than ever whether these formal visits on a succession of total strangers would do much towards helping the nerve cure which he was supposed to be undergoing.

"I know how it will be," his sister had said when he was preparing to migrate to this rural retreat; "you will bury yourself down there and not speak to a living soul, and your nerves will be worse than ever from moping. I shall just give you letters of introduction to all the people I know there. Some of them, as far as I can remember, were quite nice."

Framton wondered whether Mrs. Sappleton, the lady to whom he was presenting one of the letters of introduction came into the nice division.

"Do you know many of the people round here?" asked the niece, when she judged that they had had sufficient silent communion.

"Hardly a soul," said Framton. "My sister was staying here, at the rectory, you know, some four years ago, and she gave me letters of introduction to some of the people here."

He made the last statement in a tone of distinct regret.

"Then you know practically nothing about my aunt?" pursued the self-possessed young lady.

"Only her name and address," admitted the caller. He was wondering whether Mrs. Sappleton was in the married or widowed state. An undefinable something about the room seemed to suggest masculine habitation.

"Her great tragedy happened just three years ago," said the child; "that would be since your sister's time."

"Her tragedy?" asked Framton; somehow in this restful country spot tragedies seemed out of place.

"You may wonder why we keep that window wide open on an October afternoon," said the niece, indicating a large French window that opened on to a lawn.

"It is quite warm for the time of the year," said Framton; "but has that window got anything to do with the tragedy?"

"Out through that window, three years ago to a day, her husband and her two young brothers went off for their day's shooting. They never came back. In crossing the moor to their favourite snipe-shooting ground they were all three engulfed in a treacherous piece of bog. It had been that dreadful wet summer, you know, and places that were safe in other years gave way suddenly without warning. Their bodies were never recovered. That was the dreadful part of it." Here the child's voice lost its self-possessed note and became falteringly human. "Poor aunt always thinks that they will come back someday, they and the little brown spaniel that was lost with them, and walk in at that window just as they used to do. That is why the window is kept open every evening till it is quite dusk. Poor dear aunt, she has often told me how they went out, her husband with his white waterproof coat over his arm, and Ronnie, her youngest brother, singing 'Bertie, why do you bound?' as he always did to tease her, because she said it got on her nerves. Do you know, sometimes on still, quiet evenings like this, I almost get a creepy feeling that they will all walk in through that window—"

She broke off with a little shudder. It was a relief to Framton when the aunt bustled into the room with a whirl of apologies for being late in making her appearance.

"I hope Vera has been amusing you?" she said.

"She has been very interesting," said Framton.

"I hope you don't mind the open window," said Mrs. Sappleton briskly; "my husband and brothers will be home directly from shooting, and they always come in this way. They've been out for snipe in the marshes today, so they'll make a fine mess over my poor carpets. So like you menfolk, isn't it?"

She rattled on cheerfully about the shooting and the scarcity of birds, and the prospects for duck in the winter. To Framton it was all purely horrible. He made a desperate but only partially successful effort to turn the talk on to a less ghastly topic, he was conscious that his hostess was giving him only a fragment of her attention, and her eyes were constantly straying past him to the open window and the lawn beyond. It was certainly an unfortunate coincidence that he should have paid his visit on this tragic anniversary.

"The doctors agree in ordering me complete rest, an absence of mental excitement, and avoidance of anything in the nature of violent physical exercise," announced Framton, who laboured under the tolerably widespread delusion that total strangers and chance acquaintances are hungry for the least detail of one's ailments and infirmities, their cause and cure. "On the matter of diet they are not so much in agreement," he continued.

"No?" said Mrs. Sappleton, in a voice which only replaced a yawn at the last moment. Then she suddenly brightened into alert attention—but not to what Framton was saying.

"Here they are at last!" she cried. "Just in time for tea, and don't they look as if they were muddy up to the eyes!"

Framton shivered slightly and turned towards the niece with a look intended to convey sympathetic comprehension. The child was staring out through the open window with a dazed horror in her eyes. In a chill shock of nameless fear Framton swung round in his seat and looked in the same direction.

In the deepening twilight three figures were walking across the lawn towards the window, they all carried guns under their arms, and one of them was additionally burdened with a white coat hung over his shoulders. A tired brown spaniel kept close at their heels. Noiselessly they neared the house, and then a hoarse young voice chanted out of the dusk: "I said, Bertie, why do you bound?"

Framton grabbed wildly at his stick and hat; the hall door, the gravel drive, and the front gate were dimly noted stages in his headlong retreat. A cyclist coming along the road had to run into the hedge to avoid imminent collision.

"Here we are, my dear," said the bearer of the white mackintosh, coming in through the window, "fairly muddy, but most of it's dry. Who was that who bolted out as we came up?"

"A most extraordinary man, a Mr. Nuttel," said Mrs. Sappleton; "could only talk about his illnesses, and dashed off without a word of goodby or apology when you arrived. One would think he had seen a ghost."

"I expect it was the spaniel," said the niece calmly; "he told me he had a horror of dogs. He was once hunted into a cemetery somewhere on the banks of the Ganges by a pack of pariah dogs, and had to spend the night in a newly dug grave with the creatures snarling and grinning and foaming just above him. Enough to make anyone lose their nerve."

Romance at short notice was her speciality.

As readers we are drawn into the narrative because we have accepted a reality that we share with Framton Nuttel. The narrator withholds the critical information about Vera's motives until the very end of the story. With the last sentence the conflict is resolved and the mystery is solved.

PERSUASIVE NARRATION OF EVENT

A narrative in persuasion will likely function as an example, which is a commonly used type of rational appeal. If the narrative is in the first person and reflects the experiences of the narrator, then the example would be a personal appeal included in an effort to enhance the credibility of the author.

AN EXAMPLE

This first-person narrative of a personal experience by Benjamin Franklin addresses the issue of what kind of approach should be used to defeat an opponent, in this case a political opponent. Franklin presents a surprising claim.

SEDUCING AN ENEMY

Benjamin Franklin

I therefore did not like the opposition of this new member, who was a gentleman of fortune and education with talents that were likely to give him in time great influence in the House, which indeed, afterwards happened. I did not, however, aim at gaining his favour by paying any servile respect to him, but after some time took this other method. Having heard that he had in his library a certain scarce and curious book, I wrote a note to him expressing my desire of perusing that book and requesting he would do me the favour of lending it to me for a few days. He sent it immediately; and I returned it in about a week with another note expressing strongly my sense of the favour. When we next met in the House, he spoke to me (which he had never done before), and with great civility. And he ever afterwards manifested a readiness to serve me on all occasions, so that we became great friends, and our friendship continued to his death. This is another instance of the truth of an old maxim I had learned, which says, "He that has once done you a kindness will be more ready to do you another than he whom you yourself have obliged." And it shows how much more profitable it is prudently to remove, than to resent, return and continue inimical proceedings.

Franklin addresses the issue of what kind of behavior is best in confronting an adversary. His claim is that instead of trying to curry favor from an opponent by doing that person favors, you should rather ask the opponent to do you a favor. In addition to telling his personal experience (both a personal and a rational appeal), Franklin quotes a maxim, which is another rational appeal.

REFERENTIAL NARRATION OF EVENT

Referential narratives give an orderly, clear presentation of the events. They present evidence to support a thesis.

AN EXAMPLE

This report of the earthquake that occurred on April 18, 1906 in San Francisco was originally published in *Collier's* magazine. Jack London, noted for his novels and short stories depicting life in harsh environments, records his impressions of the devastating events surrounding the earthquake. He selects events that reveal the extent of the destruction.

THE SAN FRANCISCO EARTHQUAKE

Jack London

The earthquake shook down in San Francisco hundreds of thousands of dollars' worth of walls and chimneys. But the conflagration that followed burned up hundreds of millions of dollars worth of property. There is no estimating within hundreds of millions the actual damage wrought. Not in history has a modern imperial city been so completely destroyed. San Francisco is gone. Nothing remains of it but memories and a fringe of dwelling-houses on its outskirts. Its industrial section is wiped out. Its business section is wiped out. The factories and warehouses, the great stores and newspaper buildings, the hotels and the palaces of the nabobs, are all gone. Remains only the fringe of dwelling-houses on the outskirts of what was once San Francisco.

Within an hour after the earthquake shock the smoke of San Francisco's burning was a lurid tower visible a hundred miles away. And for three days and nights this lurid tower swayed in the sky, reddening the sun, darkening the day, and filling the land with smoke.

On Wednesday morning at a quarter past five came the earthquake. A minute later the flames were leaping upward. In a dozen different quarters south of Market Street, in the working-class ghetto, and in the factories, fires started. There was no opposing the flames. There was no organization, no communication. All the cunning adjustments of a twentieth century city had been smashed by the earthquake. The streets were humped into ridges and depressions, and piled with the debris of fallen walls. The steel rails were twisted into perpendicular and horizontal angles. The telephone and telegraph systems were disrupted. And the great water-mains had burst. All the shrewd contrivances and safe-guards of man had been thrown out of gear by thirty seconds' twitching of the earth-crust.

The Fire Made Its Own Draft

By Wednesday afternoon, inside of twelve hours, half the heart of the city was gone. At that time I watched the vast conflagration from out on the bay. It was dead calm. Not a flicker of wind stirred. Yet from every side wind was pouring in upon the city. East, west, north, and south, strong winds were blowing upon the doomed city. The heated air rising made an enormous suck. Thus did the fire of itself build its own colossal chimney through the atmosphere. Day and night this dead calm continued, and yet, near to the flames, the wind was often half a gale, so mighty was the suck.

Wednesday night saw the destruction of the very heart of the city. Dynamite was lavishly used, and many of San Francisco's proudest structures were crumbled by man himself into ruins, but there was no withstanding the onrush of the flames. Time and again successful stands were made by the fire-fighters, and every time the flames flanked around on either side, or came up from the rear, and turned to defeat the hard-won victory.

An enumeration of the buildings destroyed would be a directory of San Francisco. An enumeration of the buildings undestroyed would be a line and several addresses. An enumeration of the deeds of heroism would stock a library and bankrupt the Carnegie Medal fund. An enumeration of the dead will never be made. All vestiges of them were destroyed by the flames. The number of victims of the earthquake will never be known. South of Market Street, where the loss of life was particularly heavy, was the first to catch fire.

Remarkable as it may seem, Wednesday night, while the whole city crashed and roared into ruin, was a quiet night. There were no crowds. There was no shouting and yelling. There was no hysteria, no disorder. I passed Wednesday night in the path of the advancing flames, and in all those terrible hours I saw not one woman who wept, not one man who was excited, not one person who was in the slightest degree panic-stricken.

Before the flames, throughout the night, fled tens of thousands of homeless ones. Some were wrapped in blankets. Others carried bundles of bedding and dear household treasures. Sometimes a whole family was harnessed to a carriage or delivery wagon that was weighted down with their possessions. Baby buggies, toy wagons, and go-carts were used as trucks, while every other person was dragging a trunk. Yet everybody was gracious. The most perfect courtesy obtained. Never, in all San Francisco's history, were her people so kind and courteous as on this night of terror.

A Caravan of Trunks

All night these tens of thousands fled before the flames. Many of them, the poor people from the labor ghetto, had fled all day as well. They had left their homes burdened with possessions. Now and again they lightened up, flinging out upon the street clothing and treasures they had dragged for miles.

They held on longest to their trunks, and over these trunks many a strong man broke his heart that night. The hills of San Francisco are steep, and up these hills, mile after mile, were the trunks dragged. Everywhere were trunks, with across them lying their exhausted owners, men and women. Before the march of the flames were flung picket lines of soldiers. And a block at a time, as the flames advanced, these pickets retreated. One of their tasks was to keep the trunk-pullers moving. The exhausted creatures, stirred on by the menace of bayonets, would arise and struggle up the steep pavements, pausing from weakness every five or ten feet.

Often, after surmounting a heart-breaking hill, they would find another wall of flame advancing upon them at right angles and be compelled to change anew the line of their retreat. In the end, completely played out, after toiling for a dozen hours like giants, thousands of them were compelled to abandon their trunks. Here the shopkeepers and soft members of the middle class were at a disadvantage. But the working men dug holes in vacant lots and backyards and buried their trunks.

The Doomed City

At nine o'clock Wednesday evening I walked down through the very heart of the city. I walked through miles and miles of magnificent buildings and towering skyscrapers. Here was no fire. All was in perfect order. The police patrolled the streets. Every building had its watchman at the door. And yet it was doomed, all of it. There was no water. The dynamite was giving out. And at right angles two different conflagrations were sweeping down upon it.

At one o'clock in the morning I walked down through the same section. Everything still stood intact. There was no fire. And yet there was a change. A rain of ashes was falling. The watchmen at the doors were gone. The police had been withdrawn. There were no firemen, no fire engines, no men fighting with dynamite. The district had been absolutely abandoned. I stood at the corner of Kearney and Market, in the very innermost heart of San Francisco. Kearney Street was deserted. Half a dozen blocks away it was burning on both sides. The street was a wall of flame, and against this wall of flame, silhouetted sharply, were two United States cavalrymen sitting their horses, calmly watching. That was all. Not another person was in sight. In the intact heart of the city two troopers sat their horses and watched.

Spread of the Conflagration

Surrender was complete. There was no water. The sewers had long since been pumped dry. There was no dynamite. Another fire had broken out further uptown, and now from three sides conflagrations were sweeping down. The fourth side had been burned earlier in the day. In that direction stood the tottering walls of the Examiner building, the burned-out Call building, the smoldering ruins of the Grand Hotel, and the gutted, devastated, dynamited Palace Hotel.

The following will illustrate the sweep of the flames and the inability of men to calculate their spread. At eight o'clock Wednesday evening I passed through Union Square. It was packed with refugees. Thousands of them had gone to bed on the grass. Government tents had been set up, supper was being cooked, and the refugees were lining up for free meals.

At half-past one in the morning three sides of Union Square were in flames. The fourth side, where stood the great St. Francis Hotel, was still holding out. An hour later, ignited from top and sides, the St. Francis was flaming heavenward. Union Square, heaped high with mountains of trunks, was deserted. Troops, refugees, and all had retreated.

A Fortune for a Horse!

It was at Union Square that I saw a man offering a thousand dollars for a team of horses. He was in charge of a truck piled high with trunks for some hotel. It had been hauled here into what was considered safety, and the horses had been taken out. The flames were on three sides of the Square, and there were no horses.

Also, at this time, standing beside the truck, I urged a man to seek safety in flight. He was all but hemmed in by several conflagrations. He was an old man and he was on crutches. Said he, "Today is my birthday. Last night I was worth thirty thousand dollars. I bought five bottles of wine, some delicate fish, and other things for my birthday dinner. I have had no dinner, and all I own are these crutches."

I convinced him of his danger and started him limping on his way. An hour later, from a distance, I saw the truckload of trunks burning merrily in the middle of the street.

On Thursday morning, at a quarter past five, just twenty-four hours after the earthquake, I sat on the steps of a small residence on Nob Hill. With me sat Japanese, Italians, Chinese, and Negroes—a bit of the cosmopolitan flotsam of the wreck of the city. All about were the palaces of the nabob pioneers of Forty-nine. To the east and south, at right angles, were advancing two mighty walls of flame.

I went inside with the owner of the house on the steps of which I sat. He was cool and cheerful and hospitable. "Yesterday morning," he said, "I was worth six hundred thousand dollars. This morning this house is all I have left. It will go in fifteen minutes." He pointed to a large cabinet "That is my wife's collection of china. This rug upon which we stand is a present. It cost fifteen hundred dollars. Try that piano. Listen to its tone. There are few like it. There are no horses. The flames will be here in fifteen minutes."

Outside, the old Mark Hopkins residence, a palace, was just catching fire. The troops were falling back and driving the refugees before them. From every side came the roaring of flames, the crashing of walls, and the detonations of dynamite.

The Dawn of the Second Day

I passed out of the house. Day was trying to dawn through the smoke-pall. A sickly light was creeping over the face of things. Once only the sun broke through the smoke-pall, blood-red, and showing quarter its usual size. The smoke-pall itself, viewed from beneath, was a rose color that pulsed and fluttered with lavender shades. Then it turned to mauve and yellow and dun. There was no sun. And so dawned the second day on stricken San Francisco.

An hour later I was creeping past the shattered dome of the City Hall. Than it there was no better exhibit of the destructive forces of the earthquake. Most of the stone had been shaken from the great dome, leaving standing the naked frame-work of steel. Market Street was piled high with wreckage, and across the wreckage lay the overthrown pillars of the City Hall shattered into short crosswise sections.

This section of the city, with the exception of the Mint and the Post-Office, was already a waste of smoking ruins. Here and there through the smoke, creeping warily under the shadows of tottering walls, emerged occasional men and women. It was like the meeting of the handful of survivors after the day of the end of the world.

Beeves Slaughtered and Roasted

On Mission Street lay a dozen steers, in a neat row stretching across the street, just as they had been struck down by the flying ruins of the earthquake. The fire had passed through afterward and roasted them. The human dead had been carried away before the fire came. At another place on Mission Street I saw a milk wagon. A steel telegraph pole had smashed down sheer through the driver's seat and crushed the front wheels. The milkcans lay scattered around.

All day Thursday and all Thursday night, all day Friday and Friday night, the flames still raged.

Friday night saw the flames finally conquered, though not until Russian Hill and Telegraph Hill had been swept and three-quarters of a mile of wharves and docks had been licked up.

The Last Stand

The great stand of the fire-fighters was made Thursday night on Van Ness Avenue. Had they failed here, the comparatively few remaining houses of the city would have been swept. Here were the magnificent residences of the second generation of San Francisco nabobs, and these, in a solid zone, were dynamited down across the path of the fire. Here and there the flames leaped the zone, but these fires were beaten out, principally by the use of wet blankets and rugs.

San Francisco, at the present time, is like the crater of a volcano, around which are camped tens of thousands of refugees. At the Presidio alone are at least twenty thousand. All the surrounding cities and towns are jammed with the homeless ones, where they are being cared for by the relief committees. The refugees were carried free by the railroads to any point they wished to go, and it is estimated that over one hundred thousand people have left the peninsula on which San Francisco stood. The Government has the situation in hand, and, thanks to the immediate relief given by the whole United States, there is not the slightest possibility of a famine. The bankers and business men have already set about making preparations to rebuild San Francisco.

This report covers a specific time frame, Wednesday through Friday. Note that the introductory and concluding paragraphs provide a context for the events. Along with the major events of the narrative, London also includes descriptions that help the reader visualize the events he is recounting.

WRITING STRATEGIES

When you begin writing a narrative, think about the events as an interconnected series. You may find the following questions to be helpful.

- What are the events in your narrative?
- How do the forces interact?
- What is the crisis?
- How is the conflict resolved?
- Where does the narrative take place?
- Who is the narrator?

NARRATION OF PROCESS

A narration of process does not have the five stages that a narration of event has. All events in a narration of process are of equal importance. There is no point of crisis. The resolution is simply the last event. As a result, tension is not increased as the series of events is presented to the reader.

Most narrations of process are written in the present tense. This feature gives the presentation a sense of immediacy and reinforces the reader's impression that the process can be repeated over and over.

INSTRUCTIONAL PROCESS

Some narrations of process tell "how to" do something. They are written in the second person (you) and the imperative mood (commands). A set of instructions is an instructional process. It gives steps that must be completed to perform the activity.

AN EXAMPLE

In his book *The Relaxation Response* (1975), Herbert Benson, a medical doctor and an Associate Professor at The Harvard Medical School, explains how to elicit the Relaxation Response.

THE RELAXATION RESPONSE

HERBERT BENSON

It is important to remember that there is not a single method that is unique in eliciting the Relaxation Response. For example, Transcendental Meditation is one of the many techniques that incorporate these components. However, we believe it is not necessary to use the specific method and specific *secret*, personal sound taught by Transcendental Meditation. *Tests at the Thorndike Memorial Laboratory of Harvard have shown that a similar technique used with any sound or phrase or prayer or mantra brings forth the same physiologic changes noted during Transcendental Meditation:* decreased oxygen consumption; decreased carbon-dioxide elimination; decreased rate of breathing. In other words using the basic necessary components, any one of the age-old or the newly derived techniques produces the same physiological results regardless of the mental device used. The following set of instructions, used to elicit the Relaxation Response, was developed by our group at Harvard's Thorndike Memorial Laboratory and was found to produce the same physiologic changes we had observed during the practice of Transcendental Meditation. This technique is now being used to lower blood pressure in certain patients. A noncultic technique, it is drawn with little embellishment from the four basic components found in the myriad of historical methods. We claim no innovation but simply a scientific validation of age-old wisdom. The technique is our current method of eliciting the Relaxation Response in our continuing studies at the Beth Israel Hospital of Boston.

1. *Sit quietly in a comfortable position.*
2. *Close your eyes.*
3. *Deeply relax all your muscles, beginning at your feet and progressing up to your face. Keep them relaxed.*
4. *Breathe through your nose. Become aware of your breathing. As you breathe out, say the word, "ONE," silently to yourself. For example, breathe IN...OUT, "ONE"; IN...OUT, "ONE"; etc. Breathe easily and naturally.*
5. *Continue for 10 to 20 minutes. You may open your eyes to check the time, but do not use an alarm. When you finish, sit quietly for several minutes, at first with your eyes closed and later with your eyes opened. Do not stand up for a few minutes.*
6. *Do not worry about whether you are successful in achieving a deep level of relaxation. Maintain a passive attitude and permit relaxation to occur at its own pace. When distracting thoughts occur, try to ignore them by not dwelling upon them and return to repeating "ONE." With practice, the response should come with little effort. Practice the technique once or twice daily, but not within two hours after any meal, since the digestive processes seem to interfere with the elicitation of the Relaxation Response.*

The subjective feelings that accompany the elicitation of the Relaxation Response vary among individuals. The majority of people feel a sense of calm and feel very relaxed. A small percentage of people immediately experience ecstatic feelings. Other descriptions that have been related to us involve feelings of pleasure, refreshment, and well-being. Still others have noted relatively little change on a subjective level. Regardless of the subjective feelings described by our subjects, we have found that the physiologic changes such as decreased oxygen consumption are taking place.

There is no educational requirement or aptitude necessary to experience the Relaxation Response. Just as each of us experiences anger, contentment, and excitement, each has the capacity to experience the Relaxation Response. It is an innate response within us. Again, there are many ways in which people bring forth the Relaxation Response, and your own individual considerations may be applied to the four components involved. You may wish to use the technique we have presented but with a different mental device. You may use a syllable or phrase that may be easily repeated and sounds natural to you.

Another technique you may wish to use is a prayer from your religious tradition. Choose a prayer that incorporates the four elements necessary to bring forth the Relaxation Response. As we have shown in Chapter 5, we believe every religion has such prayers. We would reemphasize that we do not view religion in a mechanistic fashion simply because a religious prayer brings forth this desired physiologic response. Rather, we believe, as did William James, that these age-old prayers are one way to remedy an inner incompleteness and to reduce inner discord. Obviously, there are many other aspects to religious beliefs and practices which have little to do with the Relaxation Response. However, there is little reason not to make use of an appropriate prayer within the framework of your own beliefs if you are most comfortable with it.

Your individual considerations of a particular technique may place different emphasis upon the components necessary to elicit the Relaxation Response and also may incorporate various practices into the use of the technique. For example, for some a quiet environment with little distraction is crucial. However, others prefer to practice the Relaxation Response in subways or trains. Some people choose always to practice the Relaxation Response in the same place and at a regular time.

This instructional process tells the reader how to experience the relaxation response. Obviously, following the directions will enable the reader to reproduce the effects explained by Benson.

INFORMATIONAL PROCESS

An informational process is written in the third person. It tells how something is done, not how to do something.

AN EXAMPLE

In his book *The Relaxation Response* (1975), Herbert Benson explains physiological response called "the fight-or-flight response."

THE FIGHT-OR-FLIGHT RESPONSE

HERBERT BENSON

The stressful consequences of living in our modern, Western society—constant insecurity in a job, inability to make deadlines because of the sheer weight of obligations, or the shift in social rules once binding and now inappropriate—will be described here in a manner that clearly explains how they lead to the ravaging diseases such as hypertension which are prevalent today and which are likely to become more widespread in the years ahead. We are all too familiar with the stresses we encounter. However, we are less knowledgeable about the consequences of these stresses, not only psychological but physiologic. Humans, like other animals, react in a predictable way to acute and chronic stressful situations, which trigger an inborn response that has been part of our physiologic makeup for perhaps millions of years. This has been popularly labeled the "fight-or-flight" response. When we are faced with situations that require adjustment of our behavior, an involuntary response increases our blood pressure, heart rate, rate of breathing, blood flow to the muscles, and metabolism, preparing us for conflict or escape.

This innate fight-or-flight reaction is well recognized in animals. A frightened cat standing with arched back and hair on end, ready to run or fight; an enraged dog with dilated pupils, snarling at its adversary; an African gazelle running from a predator; all are responding by activation of the fight-or-flight response. Because we tend to think of man in Cartesian terms, as essentially a rational being, we have lost sight of his origins and of his Darwinian struggle for survival where the successful use of the fight-or-flight response was a matter of life or death.

Man's ancestors with the most highly developed fight-or-flight reactions had an increased chance of surviving long enough to reproduce. Natural selection favored the continuation of the response. As progeny of ancestors who developed the response over millions of years, modern man almost certainly still possesses it.

In fact, the fight-or-flight response, with its bodily changes of increased blood pressure, rate of breathing, muscle blood flow, metabolism, and heart rate, has been measured in man. Situations that demand that we adjust our behavior elicit this response. It is observed, for example, among athletes prior to a competitive event. But the response is not used as it was intended—that is, in preparation for running or fighting with an enemy. Today, it is often brought on by situations that require behavioral adjustments, and *when not used appropriately, which is most of the time, the fight-or-flight response repeatedly elicited may ultimately lead to the dire diseases of heart attack and stroke.*

Benson's informational process outlines the processes associated with the inborn fight-or-flight response. He explains the physiological mechanisms involved.

VARIATIONS IN NARRATION OF PROCESS

When the purpose of a narration of process changes, elements consistent with that purpose are introduced. In general, although the events recorded in all kinds of narration of process will receive equal emphasis, the number of events included will vary when the purpose is different.

EXPRESSIVE NARRATION OF PROCESS

Obviously, expressive narration of process will be in the first person. The writer is explaining how he or she usually completes some task. As a result, the events in the process will be unique to that person and will probably be different from the way other people might complete the same task.

AN EXAMPLE

Henry David Thoreau, in an excerpt from his journal in 1852, tells how he keeps a journal.

ON KEEPING A JOURNAL

HENRY DAVID THOREAU

To set down such choice experiences that my own writings may inspire me and at last I may make wholes of parts. Certainly it is a distinct profession to rescue from oblivion and to fix the sentiments and thoughts which visit all men more or less generally, that the contemplation of the unfinished picture may suggest its harmonious completion. Associate reverently and as much as you can with your loftiest thoughts. Each thought that is welcomed and recorded is a nest egg, by the side of which more will be laid. Thoughts accidentally thrown together become a frame in which more may be developed and exhibited. Perhaps this is the main value of a habit of writing, of keeping a journal—that so we remember our best hours and stimulate ourselves. My thoughts are my company. They have a certain individuality and separate existence, aye, personality. Having by chance recorded a few disconnected thoughts and then brought them into juxtaposition, they suggest a whole new field in which it was possible to labor and to think. Thought begat thought.

Thoreau's journal entry illustrates how an expressive purpose can affect a narration of process. He tells how he keeps a journal, but the presentation shifts from first person to third person to second person. The explanation is not an orderly account; rather it touches on those features of journal writing that Thoreau sees as most important and most valuable.

LITERARY NARRATION OF PROCESS

A narration of process with a literary purpose will include elements that are intended to entertain the reader. In fact, the process itself may be an imaginary creation with little or no correspondence to anything anybody would ever actually do.

AN EXAMPLE

In the following excerpt, the humorist Robert Benchley offers a delightful account of how he goes about writing a novel.

HOW I CREATE

Robert Benchley

In an article on How Authors Create, in which the writing methods of various masters of English prose like Conrad, Shaw, and Barrie are explained (with photographs of them in knickerbockers plaguing dogs and pushing against sundials), I discover that I have been doing the whole thing wrong all these years. The interviewer in this case hasn't got around to asking me yet—doubtless because I have been up in my room with the door shut and not answering the bell—but I am going to take a chance anyway and tell him how I do my creative work and just how much comes from inspiration and how much from hashish and other perfumes. I may even loosen up and tell him what my favorite hot weather dishes are.

When I am writing a novel I must actually live the lives of my characters. If, for instance, my hero is a gambler on the French Riviera, I make myself pack up and go to Cannes or Nice, willy-nilly, and there throw myself into the gay life of the gambling set until I really feel that I *am* Paul De Lacroix, or Ed Whelan, or whatever my hero's name is. Of course this runs into money, and I am quite likely to have to change my ideas about my hero entirely and make him a bum on a tramp steamer working his way back to America, or a young college boy out of funds who lives by his wits until his friends at home send him a hundred and ten dollars.

One of my heroes (Dick Markwell in "Love's How-do-you-do"), after starting out as a man-about-town in New York who "never showed his liquor" and was "an apparently indestructible machine devoted to pleasure," had to be changed into a patient in the Trembly Ward of a local institution, whose old friends didn't recognize him and furthermore didn't want to.

But, as you doubtless remember, it was a corking yarn.

This actually living the lives of my characters takes up quite a lot of time and makes it a little difficult to write anything. It was not until I decided to tell stories about old men who just sit in their rooms and shell walnuts that I ever got around to doing any work. It doesn't make for very interesting novels, but at any rate the wordage is there and there is something to show the publishers for their advance royalties. (Publishers are crotchety that way. They want copy, copy, copy all the time, just because they happen to have advanced a measly three hundred dollars a couple of years before. You would think that printing words on paper was their business.)

And now you ask me how I do my work, how my inspiration comes? I will tell you, Little Father. Draw up your chair and let me put my feet on it. Ah, that's better! Now you may go out and play!

Very often I must wait weeks and weeks for what you call "inspiration." In the meantime I must sit with my quill pen poised in air over a sheet of foolscap, in case the divine spark should come like a lightning bolt and knock me off my chair on to my head. (This has happened more than once.) While I am waiting I mull over in my mind what I am going to do with my characters.

Shall I have Mildred marry Lester, or shall Lester marry Evelyn? ("Who is Evelyn?" I often say to myself, never having heard of her before.) Should the French proletariat win the Revolution, or should Louis XVI come back suddenly and establish a Coalition Cabinet? Can I afford to let Etta clean up those dishes in the sink and get them biscuits baked, or would it be better to keep her there for another year, standing first on one foot and then on the other?

You have no idea how many problems an author has to face during those feverish days when he is building a novel, and you have no idea how he solves them. Neither has he.

Sometimes, while in the throes of creative work, I get out of bed in the morning, look at my writing desk piled high with old bills, odd gloves, and empty gingerale bottles, and go right back to bed again. The next thing I know it is night once more, and time for the Sand Man to come around. (We have a Sand Man who comes twice a day, which makes it very convenient. We give him five dollars at Christmas.)

Even if I do get up and put on a part of my clothes—I do all my work in a Hawaiian straw skirt and a bow tie of some neutral shade—I often can think of nothing to do but pile the books which are on one end of my desk very neatly on the other end and then kick them one by one off on to the floor with my free foot.

But all the while my brain is work, work, working, and my plot is taking shape. Sometimes it is the shape of a honeydew melon and sometimes a shape which I have never been quite able to figure out. It is a sort of amorphous thing with two heads but no face. When this shape presents itself, I get right back in bed again. I'm no fool.

I find that, while working, a pipe is a great source of inspiration. A pipe can be placed diagonally across the keys of a typewriter so that they will not function, or it can be made to give out such a cloud of smoke that I cannot see the paper. Then, there is the process of lighting it. I can make lighting a pipe a ritual which has not been equaled for elaborateness since the five-day festival to the God of the Harvest. (See my book on Rituals: the Man.)

In the first place, owing to twenty-six years of constant smoking without once calling in a plumber, the space left for tobacco in the bowl of my pipe is now the size of a medium body pore. Once the match has been applied to the tobacco therein, the smoke is over. This necessitates refilling, relighting, and reknocking. The knocking out of a pipe can be made almost as important as the smoking of it, especially if there are nervous people in the room. A good, smart knock of a pipe against a tin wastebasket and you will have a neurasthenic out of his chair and into the window sash in no time.

The matches, too, have their place in the construction of modern literature. With a pipe like mine, the supply of burnt matches in one day could be floated down the St. Lawrence River with two men jumping them . . .

When the novel is finished, it is shipped to the Cutting and Binding Room, where native girls roll it into large sheets and stamp on it with their bare feet. This accounts for the funny look of some of my novels. It is then taken back to the Drying Room, where it is rewritten by a boy whom I engage for the purpose, and sent to the publishers. It is then sent back to me.

And so you see now how we creative artists work. It really isn't like any other kind of work, for it must come from a great emotional upheaval in the soul of the writer himself; and if that emotional upheaval is not present, it must come from the works of any other writers which happen to be handy and easily imitated.

Benchley, in this humorous narration of process, exaggerates most of the events he includes in the essay. His creation of absurd situations is designed to make light of a process most people think of as a very serious activity. He distorts some actions, like the account of his ritual of smoking a pipe, in order to entertain. The events included in the process are selected for the humorous effect they have, rather than for their accuracy and comprehensiveness.

PERSUASIVE NARRATION OF PROCESS

A persuasive narration of process will support a claim advising the reader that an action should be performed in a certain way. In essence, the process is a set of rules for right behavior.

AN EXAMPLE

Ben Jonson (1572–1637), a contemporary of William Shakespeare, gives sound advice about writing well.

ON STYLE

BEN JONSON

For a man to write well there are required three necessities: to read the best authors, observe the best speakers, and much exercise of his own style. In style, to consider what ought to be written, and after what manner, he must first think and excogitate his matter, then choose his words, and examine the weight of either. Then take care, in placing and ranking both matter and words, that the composition be comely, and to do this with diligence and often. No matter how slow the style be at first, so it be labored and accurate; seek the best, and be not glad of the forward conceits, or first words, that offer themselves to us; but judge of what we invent, and order what we approve. Repeat often what we have formerly written; which beside that it helps the consequence and make the juncture better, it quickens the heat of the imagination, that often cools in the time of setting down, and gives new strength, as if it grew lustier by the going back. As we see in the contention of leaping, they jump farthest that fetch their race largest; or, as in throwing a dart or javelin, we force back our arms to make our loose the stronger. Yet if we have a fair gale of wind, I forbid not the steering out of our sail, so the favor of the gale deceive us not. For all that we invent does please us in the conception or birth, else we would never set it down. But the safest is to return to our judgment and handle over again those things the easiness of which might make them justly suspected. So did the best writers in their beginnings; they imposed upon themselves care and industry; they did nothing rashly: they obtained first to write well, and then custom made it easy and a habit. By little and little their matter showed itself to them more plentifully; their words answered; their composition followed; and all, as in a well-ordered family, presented itself in the place. So that the sum of all is, ready writing makes not good writing; but good writing brings on ready writing: yet, when we think we have got the faculty, it is even then good to resist it; as to give a horse a check sometimes with a bit, which doth not so much stop his course, as stirs his mettle. Again, whither a man's genius is best able to reach thither, it should more and more contend, lift, and dilate itself, as men of low stature raise themselves on their toes, and so ofttimes get even, if not eminent. Besides, as it is fit for grown and able writers to stand of themselves and work with their own strength, to trust and endeavor by their faculties: so it is fit for the beginner and learner to study others and the best. For the mind and memory are more sharply exercised in comprehending another man's things than our own; and such as accustom themselves, and are familiar with the best authors, shall never and anon find somewhat of them in themselves, and in the expression of their minds, even when they feel it not, be able to utter something like theirs, which hath an authority above their own. Nay, sometimes it is the reward of a man's study, the praise of quoting another man fitly: and though a man be more prone and able for one kind of writing than another, yet he must exercise all. For as in an instrument, so in style, there must be a harmony and consent of parts.

Jonson gives a number of steps that someone wanting to write well should follow. He especially addresses the matter of style and supports an implied claim that those wanting to improve their ability should practice writing and follow his advice. The elaboration of the process supports the claim. He addresses the reader directly using the imperative mood. His also uses analogy as rational and stylistic appeal.

REFERENTIAL NARRATION OF PROCESS

As we have seen previously, referential narration of process will include all the steps in the process so that the reader can either perform the process (instructional process) or understand it completely (informational).

AN EXAMPLE

This work explains the complex process of counting populations of animals.

HOW DO THEY COUNT POPULATIONS OF ANIMALS?

CAROLINE SUTTON

Humans are the only beasts who use telephones or permanent addresses, or fill out census forms. How are the other animals counted? How can anyone tell that the timber wolf and the California condor are rare and "endangered"? How do we know how many robins chirp every spring? The task of taking a census of wild animals is one of the most difficult in biology.

The methods of enumeration scientists use vary with the species; its size, behavior, and habitat make certain ways more practical than others. The best way to count ducks, whistling swans, elephants, antelope, caribou, and timber wolves is to fly over them in a helicopter or bush plane and count them one by one, taking photographs to verify the number. This is obviously not a good method for counting field mice; they are too small to be seen from the air, are too well camouflaged by the color of their fur, and spend too much time in their burrows. The only way to determine the number of mice living in a field is by "saturation trapping"—catching every single mouse until no more are left and counting them.

Lizards are counted by the "capture, recapture" method. To find the population in a certain area, a herpetologist (one who studies reptiles and amphibians) might catch 50 lizards, mark them all with a harmless paint or metal tag, and set them free again. After a few weeks, the marked lizards have dispersed back into the general population. The scientist then captures another 50 lizards and finds that some of this batch are creatures he marked in his first catch, and some are unmarked—meaning they were *not* in the first batch. The herpetologist's next step is to make assumptions for the purpose of his census. He assumes that the new batch of 50 marked and unmarked lizards is a representative sample—a microcosm—of the population as a whole. He assumes that after he marked the first 50 lizards and released them, they distributed themselves at random throughout the population. Thus, when he catches the second 50 and finds that he earlier marked, say, 10 of them—or 20 percent—he assumes that 20 percent of the entire *lizard population* is marked. He knows that he originally marked 50 lizards; concluding from the second sample that 20 percent were marked, he assumes that 50 is 20 percent of the total population. Since $5 \times 20\% = 100\%$, 5 times 50 lizards is the whole population: 250 lizards.

Fish are counted a similar way. Experimenters put a knock-out solution in the water, which does the fish no permanent harm but makes them float to the surface belly-up. They then collect the fish, count them, mark them with dye or tags, and revive and release them. The same number are later recaptured, the marked ones counted, and the total figured as for lizards.

How about animals that are harder to grab, such as songbirds? Ornithologists often use a grid system in a wooded area to get an approximate number. They mark evenly spaced, parallel straight trails through the region that interests them. People carrying pads and pens walk down the trails in a phalanx, each member keeping another in sight to the left and right, counting every bird they see or hear. Each member only counts birds observed a certain distance to either side of him, so that two people don't count the same bird. This ritual is performed several times and the results averaged.

How does one count things as small as the microscopic plankton that live in the ocean? A sample of ocean water is whipped around in a centrifuge, so that all the solids collect at one end, including the tiny plankton. This residue is slid under a microscope bit by bit and the plankton counted. That gives the plankton per unit volume of ocean water.

As you can see, different methods are needed to keep track of animals living in different niches or habitats. To get an idea of the total number of a species in an entire region or country (or planet), scientists determine the size of the habitat available to the species, instead of counting individuals, and multiply by the number of individuals that usually live in a given area of habitat. It is in the nature of living things that they fill any habitat with as many individuals as the food and space in the area will allow.

Knowing the number of acres of woodland, mountain, prairie, and city in the United States, we can arrive at a ballpark estimate of 6 billion land birds of all kinds in the country. By contrast, some water birds such as the whooping crane are not nearly so adaptable; whoopers can live only in certain areas of Texas marshland, where about 100 nest each year.

Other forms of life build on a minuscule scale and fit vast numbers of individuals into their ecological niches. Insects have adapted through evolution to live in an incredible variety of conditions. The world population of insects in their many habitats is estimated to total a *billion billion*, or 10 to the 18th power (10^{18})—the number 1 followed by 18 zeroes. That's roughly a billion times the world's human population; if the world insect population were represented by a bucketful of sand, the human population would be a single grain of sand in that bucket. More amazing still, if we look closely at the bodies of those insects, we find as many as a hundred thousand one-celled animals called protozoa living in the digestive tract of *each insect*, eating what the insect is unable to digest. There are therefore about 10^{23} of these digestive protozoa living in the world's insects. That number is greater than the number of stars in the universe.

As Jonathan Swift wrote after the invention of the microscope, which revealed for the first time the existence of protozoa, animals smaller than the naked eye could see:

> *Big fleas have little fleas*
> *Upon their backs to bite'em;*
> *And little fleas have lesser fleas,*
> *And so* ad infinitum.

This narration of process is in fact an explanation of a series of processes. Each one of the explanations is complete in itself, but taken together they reveal the complexity of counting animals.

WRITING STRATEGIES

Consider the following questions as you write a narration of process.

- What type of process are you narrating?
- What are the steps?
- Are they in the proper sequence?

- What is the goal of the process?
- Have you given the audience enough information?

CAUSE AND EFFECT

As with narration of event and narration of process when we organize with cause and effect, we arrange events as they occur in time. When organizing with cause and effect, however, we are interested in telling not only what happened, but also *why* it happened.

Causes and effects are implicit in all narrations. When we organize with cause and effect, we make them explicit. For example, a story about an automobile accident (that a car going through an intersection failed to stop and hit another car, critically injuring both drivers) would be a narration of an event. An explanation of why the accident happened (because the driver's brakes failed) and what the results of the accident were (the cars were totaled and the drivers were taken to the hospital) would have a cause and effect organization.

THE STRUCTURE

The structure of cause and effect narratives reflects not only the time order that all narratives have, but also two levels of causation—immediate and ultimate. In the previous example, attributing the immediate cause of the accident (that the driver's brakes failed) to the driver's failure to perform preventive maintenance on the car would be giving an ultimate cause. Similarly, going beyond the immediate effect (the drivers' being hospitalized) to explain some long-term disability (that they were confined to wheelchairs) would be explaining an ultimate effect.

Extensive analyses of both immediate and ultimate causes and effects are frequently used in historical writing. Explaining causes and effects allows scholars to support interpretations of events studied in their disciplines.

AN EXAMPLE

In the following essay, which first appeared in *The Immense Journey* (1957), Loren Eisley explains the causal relationship between the emergence of flowers and the development of mammals and birds.

HOW FLOWERS CHANGED THE WORLD

Loren Eiseley

If it had been possible to observe the Earth from the far side of the solar system over the long course of geological epochs, the watchers might have been able to discern a subtle change in the light emanating from our planet. That world of long ago would, like the red deserts of Mars, have reflected light from vast drifts of stone and gravel, the sands of wandering wastes, the blackness of naked basalt, the yellow of dust of endlessly moving storms. Only the ceaseless marching of the clouds and the intermittent flashes from the restless surface of the sea would have told a different story, but still essentially a barren one. Then, as the millennia rolled away and age followed age, a new and greener light would, by degrees, have come to twinkle across those endless miles.

This is the only difference those far watchers, by use of subtle instruments, might have perceived in the whole history of the planet Earth, Yet that slowly growing green twinkle would have contained the epic march of life from the tidal oozes upward across the raw and unclothed continents. Out of the vast chemical bath of the sea—not from the deeps, but from the element-rich, light-exposed platforms of the continental shelves—wandering fingers of green had crept upward along the meanderings of river systems and fringed the gravels of forgotten lakes.

In those first ages plants clung of necessity to swamps and watercourses. Their reproductive processes demanded direct access to water. Beyond the primitive ferns and mosses that enclosed the borders of swamps and streams the rocks still lay vast and bare, the winds still swirled the dust of a naked planet. The grass cover that holds our world secure in place was still millions of years in the future. The green marchers had gained a soggy foothold upon the land but that was all. They did not reproduce by seeds but by microscopic swimming sperm that had to wriggle their way through water to fertilize the female cell. Such plants in their higher forms had clever adaptations for the use of rain water in their sexual phases, and survived with increasing success in a wet land environment. They now seem part of man's normal environment. The truth is, however, that there is nothing very "normal" about nature. Once upon a time there were no flowers at all.

A little while ago—about one hundred million years, as the geologist estimates time in the history of our four-billion-year-old planet—flowers were not to be found anywhere on the five continents. Wherever one might have looked, from the poles to the equator, one would have seen only the cold dark monotonous green of a world whose plant life possessed no other color.

Somewhere, just a short time before the close of the Age of Reptiles, there occurred a soundless, violent explosion. It lasted millions of years, but it was an explosion, nevertheless. It marked the emergence of the angiosperms—the flowering plants. Even the great evolutionist, Charles Darwin, called them "an abominable mystery," because they appeared so suddenly and spread so fast.

Flowers changed the face of the planet. Without them, the world we know—even man himself—would never have existed. Francis Thompson, the English poet, once wrote that one could not pluck a flower without troubling a star. Intuitively he had sensed like a naturalist the enormous interlinked complexity of life. Today we know that the appearance of the flowers contained also the equally mystifying emergence of man.

If we were to go back into the Age of Reptiles, its drowned swamps and birdless forest would reveal to us a warmer but, on the whole, a sleepier world than that of today. Here and there, it is true, the serpent heads of bottom-feeding dinosaurs might be upreared in suspicion of their huge flesh-eating compatriots. Tyrannosaurs, enormous bipedal caricatures of men, would stalk mindlessly across the sites of future cities and go their slow way down into the dark of geologic time.

In all that world of living things nothing saw save with the intense concentration of the hunt, nothing moved except with the grave sleepwalking intentness of the instinct-driven brain. Judged by modern standards, it as a world in slow motion, a cold-blooded world whose occupants were most active at noonday but torpid on chill nights, their brains damped by a slower metabolism than any known to even the most primitive of warm-blooded animals today.

A high metabolic rate and the maintenance of a constant body temperature are supreme achievements in the evolution of life. They enable an animal to escape, within broad limits, from the overheating or the chilling of its immediate surroundings, and at the same time to maintain a peak mental efficiency. Creatures without a high metabolic rate are slaves to weather. Insects in the first frosts of autumn all run down like little clocks. Yet if you pick one up and breathe warmly upon it, it will begin to move about once more.

In a sheltered spot such creatures may sleep away the winter, but they are hopelessly immobilized. Though a few warm-blooded mammals, such as the woodchuck of our day, have evolved a way of reducing their metabolic rate in order to undergo winter hibernation, it is a survival mechanism with drawbacks, for it leaves the animal helplessly exposed if enemies discover him during his period of suspended animation. Thus bear or woodchuck, big animal or small, must seek, in this time of descending sleep, a safe refuge in some hidden den or burrow. Hibernation is, therefore, primarily a winter refuge of small, easily concealed animals rather than of large ones.

A high metabolic rate, however, means a heavy intake of energy in order to sustain body warmth and efficiency. It is for this reason that even some of these later warm-blooded mammals existing in our day have learned to descend into a slower, unconscious rate of living during the winter months when food may be difficult to obtain. On a slightly higher plane they are following the procedure of the cold-blooded frog sleeping in the mud at the bottom of a frozen pond.

The agile brain of the warm-blooded birds and mammals demands a high oxygen consumption and food in concentrated forms, or the creatures cannot long sustain themselves. It was the rise of flowering plants that provided that energy and changed the nature of the living world. Their appearance parallels in a quite surprising manner the rise of the birds and mammals.

Slowly, toward the dawn of the Age of Reptiles, something over two hundred and fifty million years ago, the little naked sperm cells wriggling their way through dew and raindrops had given way to a kind of pollen carried by the wind. Our present-day pine forests represent plants of a pollen-disseminating variety. Once fertilization was no longer dependent on exterior water, the march over drier regions could be extended. Instead of spores simple primitive seeds carrying some nourishment for the young plants had developed, but true flowers were still scores of millions of years away. After a long period of hesitant evolutionary groping, they exploded upon the world with truly revolutionary violence.

The event occurred in Cretaceous times in the close of the Age of Reptiles. Before the coming of the flowering plants our own ancestral stock, the warm-blooded mammals, consisted of a few mousy little creatures hidden in trees and underbrush. A few lizard-like birds with carnivorous teeth flapped awkwardly on ill-aimed flights among archiac shubbery. None of these insignificant creatures gave evidence of any remarkable talents. The mammals in particular had been around for some millions of years, but had remained well lost in the shadow of the mighty reptiles. Truth to tell, man was still, like the genie in the bottle, encased in the body of a creature about the size of a rat.

As for the birds, their reptilian cousins the Pterodactyls, flew farther and better. There was just one thing about the birds that paralleled the physiology of the mammals. They, too, had evolved warm blood and its accompanying temperature control. Nevertheless, if one had been seen stripped of its feathers, he would still have seemed a slightly uncanny and unsightly lizard.

Neither the birds nor the mammals, however, were quite what they seemed. They were waiting for the Age of Flowers. They were waiting for what flowers, and with them the true encased seed, would bring. Fish-eating, gigantic leather-winged reptiles, twenty-eight feet from wing tip to wing tip, hovered over the coasts that one day would be swarming with gulls.

Inland the monotonous green of the pine and spruce forests with their primitive wooden cone flowers stretched everywhere. No grass hindered the fall of the naked seeds to earth. Great sequoias towered to the skies. The world of that time has a certain appeal but it is a giant's world, a world moving slowly like the reptiles who stalked magnificently among the boles of its trees.

The trees themselves are ancient, slow-growing, and immense, like the redwood groves that have survived to our day on the California coast. All is stiff, formal, upright and green, monotonously green. There is no grass as yet; there are no wide plains rolling in the sun, no tiny daisies dotting the meadows underfoot. There is little versatility about this scene; it is, in truth, a giant's world.

A few nights ago it was brought home vividly to me that the world has changed since that far epoch. I was awakened out of a sleep by an unknown sound in my living room. Not a small sound—not a creaking timber or a mouse's scurry—but a sharp, rending explosion as though an unwary foot had been put down upon a wine glass. I had come instantly out of sleep and lay tense, unbreathing. I listened for another step. There was none.

Unable to stand the suspense any longer, I turned on the light and passed from room to room glancing uneasily behind chairs and into closets. Nothing seemed disturbed, and I stood puzzled in the center of the living room floor. Then a small button-shaped object upon the rug caught my eye. It was hard and polished and glistening. Scattered over the length of the room were several more shining up at me like wary little eyes. A pine cone that had been lying in a dish had been blown the length of the coffee table. The dish itself could hardly have been the source of the explosion. Beside it I found two ribbon-like strips of velvety-green. I tried to place the two strips together to make a pod. They twisted resolutely away from each other and would no longer fit.

I relaxed in a chair, then, for I had reached a solution of the midnight disturbance. The twisted strips were wisteria pods that I had brought in a day or two previously and placed in the dish. They had chosen midnight to explode and distribute their multiplying fund of life down the length of the room. A plant, a fixed, rooted thing, immobolized in a single pod, had devised a way of propelling its offspring across open space. Immediately there passed before my eyes the million airy troopers of the milkweed pod and the clutching hooks of the sandburs. Seeds on the coyote's tail, seeds on the hunter's coat, thistledown mounting on the winds—all were somehow triumphing over life's limitations. Yet the ability to do this had not been with them at the beginning. It was the product of endless effort and experiment.

The seeds on my carpet were not going to lie stiffly where they had dropped like their antiquated cousins, the naked seeds on the pine-cone scales. They were travelers. Struck by the thought, I went out the next day and collected several other varieties. I line them up now in a row on my desk—so many little capsules of life, winged, hooked or spiked. Every one is an angiosperm, a product of the true flowering plants. Contained in these little boxes is the secret of that far-off Cretaceous explosion of a hundred million years ago that changed the face of the planet. And somewhere in here, I think, as I spoke seriously at one particularly resistant seed-case of a wild grass, was once man himself.

Eisley explains the series of causes that began with the development the angiosperms at the end of the Age of Reptiles. He shows how the explosion of flowering plants created an environment where mammals and birds could thrive. At the end of the essay, his example of the explosion of some seedpods he had left in his living room graphically illustrates the power of flowering plants.

VARIATIONS IN CAUSE AND EFFECT

When the purpose of the writing changes, the author will alter the use of cause and effect accordingly. Both causes and effects will be treated in light of the demands of the purpose.

EXPRESSIVE CAUSE AND EFFECT

In expressive cause and effect writers will often look at events that have shaped identity and values and have had an impact on subsequent events.

AN EXAMPLE

Soul on Ice, published in 1968, is Eldridge Cleaver's shocking memoir recounting his experiences as a black man in America in the turbulent 1960s. In this excerpt he explains why he rejected American society.

HIGHER UNEDUCATION

ELDRIDGE CLEAVER

I'm perfectly aware that I'm in prison, that I'm, a Negro, that I've been a rapist, and that I have a Higher Uneducation. I never know what significance I'm supposed to attach to these factors. But I have a suspicion that, because of these aspects of my character, "free-normal-educated" people rather expect me to be more reserved, penitent, remorseful, and not too quick to shoot off my mouth on certain subjects. But I let them down, disappoint them, make them gape at me in a sort of stupor, as if they're thinking; "You've got your nerve! Don't you realize that you owe a debt to society?" My answer to all such thoughts lurking in their split-level heads, crouching behind their squinting bombardier eyes, is that the blood of Vietnamese peasants has paid off all my debts; that the Vietnamese people, afflicted with a rampant disease called Yankees, through their sufferings—as opposed to the "frustration" of fatassed American geeks safe at home worrying over whether to have bacon, ham, or sausage with their grade—A eggs in the morning, while Vietnamese worry each morning whether the Yankees will gas them, burn them up, or blow away their humble pads in a hail of bombs—have canceled all my IOUs.

In beginning this letter I could just as easily have mentioned other aspects of my situation; I could have said: "I'm perfectly aware that I'm tall, that I'm skinny, that I need a shave, that I'm hard-up enough to suck my grandmother's old withered tits, and that I would dig (deeper then deeply) getting clean once more—not only in the steam-bath sense, but in getting sharp as an Esquire square with a Harlem touch—or that I would like to put on a pair of bib overalls and become a Snicker, or that I'd like to leap the whole last mile and grow a beard and don whatever threads the local nationalism might require and comrade with Che Guevara, and share his fate, blazing a new pathfinder's trail through the stymied upbeat brain of the New Left, or how I'd just love to be in Berkeley right now, to roll in that mud, to frolic in that sty of funky revolution, to breathe in its heady fumes, and look with roving eyes for a new John Brown, Eugene Debs, a blacker-meaner-keener Malcolm X, a Robert Franklin Williams with less rabbit in his hot blood, an American Lenin, Fidel, a Mao-Mao, A MAO MAO, A MAO MAO, A MAO MAO, A MAO MAO, A MAO MAO, A MAO MAO...All of which is true.

In this passage, we can see the operation of cause and effect in an expressive work. Cleaver identifies the Vietnam War as a major cause of his rejection of American values. His decision to adopt a different set of values that are antithetical to what he sees as the values of white American society causes him to embrace a new identity. The effects of that new identity are expressed as goals for the future when he explains how would like to dress, where he would like to go, and what he would like to experience.

LITERARY CAUSE AND EFFECT

In literary works, we are usually more interested in the narrative itself than we are in the causes and effects that are embedded in the structure of the plots. But causes and effects are sometimes explored by writers who are influenced by a theory of naturalism. In stories by such writers, we become aware of the underlying causes that motivate and control characters.

AN EXAMPLE

Katherine Anne Porter, an American writer who won critical acclaim for her short stories and short novels, is perhaps best known for *Ship of Fools* (1962), her only full-length novel. In this literary essay, published in 1948, Porter explores the causes that motivate her fictitious character.

THE NECESSARY ENEMY

KATHERINE ANNE PORTER

She is a frank, charming, fresh-hearted young woman who married for love. She and her husband are one of those gay, good-looking young pairs who ornament this modern scene rather more in profusion perhaps than ever before in our history. They are handsome, with a talent for finding their way in their world, they work at things that interest them, their tastes agree and their hopes. They intend in all good faith to spend their lives together, to have children and do well by them and each other—to be happy, in fact, which for them is the whole point of their marriage. And all in stride, keeping their wits about them. Nothing romantic, mind you; their feet are on the ground.

Unless they were this sort of person, there would be not much point to what I wish to say; for they would seem to be an example of the high-spirited, right-minded young whom the critics are always invoking to come forth and do their duty and practice all those sterling old-fashioned virtues which in every generation seem to be falling into disrepair. As for virtues, these young people are more or less on their own, like most of their kind; they get very little moral or other aid from their society; but after three years of marriage this very contemporary young woman finds herself facing the oldest and ugliest dilemma of marriage.

She is dismayed, horrified, full of guilt and forebodings because she is finding out little by little that she is capable of hating her husband, whom she loves faithfully. She can hate him at times as fiercely and mysteriously, indeed in terribly much the same way, as often she hated her parents, her brothers and sisters, whom she loves, when she was a child. Even then it had seemed to her a kind of black treacherousness in her, her private wickedness that, just the same, gave her her only private life. That was one thing her parents never knew about her, never seemed to suspect. For it was never given a name. They did and said hateful things to her and to each other as if by right, as if in them it was a kind of virtue. But when they said to her, "Control your feelings," it was never when she was amiable and obedient, only in the black times of her hate. So it was her secret, a shameful one. When they punished her, sometimes for the strangest reasons, it was, they said, only because they loved her—it was for her good. She did not believe this, but she thought herself guilty of something worse than ever they had punished her for. None of this really frightened her: the real fright came when she discovered that at times her father and mother hated each other; this was like standing on the doorsill of a familiar room and seeing in a lightning flash that the floor was gone, you were on the edge of a bottomless pit. Sometimes she felt that both of them hated her, but that passed, it was simply not a thing to be thought of, much less believed. She thought she had outgrown all this, but here it was again, an element in her own nature she could not control, or feared she could not. She would have to hide from her husband, if she could, the same spot in her feelings she had hidden from her parents, and for the same no doubt disreputable, selfish reason: she wants to keep his love.

Above all, she wants him to be absolutely confident that she loves him, for that is the real truth, no matter how unreasonable it sounds, and no matter how her own feelings betray them both at times. She depends recklessly on his love; yet while she is hating him, he might very well be hating her as much or even more, and it would serve her right. But she does not want to be served right, she wants to be loved and forgiven—that is, to be sure he would forgive her anything, if he had any notion of what she had done. But best of all she would like not to have anything in her love that should ask forgiveness. She doesn't mean about their quarrels—they are not so bad. Her feelings are out of proportion, perhaps. She knows it is perfectly natural for people to disagree, have fits of temper, fight it out; they learn quite a lot about each other that way, and not all of it disappointing either. When it passes, her hatred seems quite unreal. It always did.

Love. We are early taught to say it. I love you. We are trained to the thought of it as if there were nothing else, or nothing else worth having without it, or nothing worth having which it could not bring with it. Love is taught, always by precept, sometimes by example. Then hate, which no one meant to teach us, comes of itself. It is true that if we say I love you, it may be received with doubt, for there are times when it is hard to believe. Say I hate you, and the one spoken to believes it instantly once for all.

Say I love you a thousand times to that person afterward and mean it every time, and still it does not change the fact that once we said I hate you, and meant that too. It leaves a mark on that surface love had worn so smooth with its eternal caresses. Love must be learned, and learned again and again; there is no end to it. Hate needs no instruction, but waits only to be provoked . . . hate, the unspoken word, the unacknowledged presence in the house, that faint smell of brimstone among the roses, that invisible tongue-tripper, that unkempt finger in every pie, that sudden oh-so-curiously chilling look—could it be boredom?—on your dear one's features, making them quite ugly. Be careful: love, perfect love, is in danger.

If it is not perfect, it is not love, and if it is not love, it is bound to be hate sooner or later. This is perhaps a not too exaggerated statement of the extreme position of Romantic Love, more especially in America, where we are all brought up on it, whether we know it or not. Romantic Love is changeless, faithful, passionate, and its sole end is to render the two lovers happy. It has no obstacles save those provided by the hazards of fate (that is to say, society), and such sufferings as the lovers may cause each other are only another word for delight: exciting jealousies, thrilling uncertainties, the ritual dance of courtship within the charmed closed circle of their secret alliance; all real troubles come from without, they face them unitedly in perfect confidence. Marriage is not the end but only the beginning of true happiness, cloudless, changeless to the end. That the candidates for this blissful condition have never seen an example of it, nor ever knew anyone who had, makes no difference. That is the ideal and they will achieve it.

How did Romantic Love manage to get into marriage at last, where it was most certainly never intended to be? At its highest it was tragic: the love of Héloise and Abélard. At its most graceful, it was the homage of the trouvere for his lady. In its most popular form, the adulterous strayings of solidly married couples who meant to stray for their own good reasons, but at the same time do nothing to upset the property settlements or the line of legitimacy; at its most trivial, the pretty trifling of shepherd and shepherdess.

This was generally condemned by church and state and a

word of fear to honest wives whose mortal enemy it was. Love within the sober, sacred realities of marriage was a matter of personal luck, but in any case, private feelings were strictly a private affair having, at least in theory, no bearing whatever on the fixed practice of the rules of an institution never intended as a recreation ground for either sex. If the couple discharged their religious and social obligations, furnished forth a copious progeny, kept their troubles to themselves, maintained public civility and died under the same roof, even if not always on speaking terms, it was rightly regarded as a successful marriage. Apparently this testing ground was too severe for all but the stoutest spirits; it too was based on an ideal, as impossible in its way as the ideal Romantic Love. One good thing to be said for it is that society took responsibility for the conditions of marriage, and the sufferers within its bounds could always blame the system, not themselves. But Romantic Love crept into the marriage bed, very stealthily, by centuries, bringing its absurd notions about love as eternal springtime and marriage as a personal adventure meant to provide personal happiness. To a Western romantic such as I, though my views have been much modified by painful experience, it still seems to me a charming work of the human imagination, and it is a pity its central notion has been taken too literally and has hardened into a convention as cramping and enslaving as the older one. The refusal to acknowledge the evils in ourselves which therefore are implicit in any human situation is as extreme and unworkable a proposition as the doctrine of total depravity; but somewhere between them, or maybe beyond them, there does exist a possibility for reconciliation between our desires for impossible satisfactions and the simple unalterable fact that we also desire to be unhappy and that we create our own suffering; and out of these sufferings we salvage our fragments of happiness.

Our young woman who has been taught that an important part of her human nature is not real because it makes trouble and interferes with her peace of mind and shakes her self-love, has been very badly taught; but she has arrived at a most important stage of her re-education. She is afraid her marriage is going to fail because she has not love enough to face its difficulties; and this because at times she feels a painful hostility toward her husband, and cannot admit its reality because such an admission would damage in her own eyes her view of what love should be, an absurd view, based on her vanity of power. Her hatred is real as her love is real, but her hatred has the advantage at present because it works on a blind instinctual level, it is lawless; and her love is subjected to a code of ideal conditions, impossible by their very nature of fulfillment, which prevents its free growth and deprives it of its right to recognize its human limitations and come to grips with them. Hatred is natural in a sense that love, as she conceives it, a young person brought up in the tradition of Romantic Love, is not natural at all. Yet it did not come by hazard, it is the very imperfect expression of the need of the human imagination to create beauty and harmony out of chaos, no matter how mistaken its notion of these things may be, nor how clumsy its methods. It has conjured love out of the air, and seeks to preserve it by incantations; when she spoke a vow to love and honor her husband until death, she did a very reckless thing, for it is not possible by an act of the will to fulfill such an engagement. But it was the necessary act of faith performed in defense of a mode of feelings, the statement of honorable intention to practice as well as she is able the noble, acquired faculty of love, that very mysterious overtone to sex which is the best thing in it. Her hatred is part of it, the necessary enemy and ally.

Porter explores the effects of Romantic Love on a young woman in a marriage. She also reveals how the attitudes of the characters in her narrative are shaped by social and culture forces.

PERSUASIVE CAUSE AND EFFECT

Cause and effect can provide a powerful argument for a persuasive claim. If a writer is able to convince the reader that a disaster will occur because of a certain cause, then an argument will have some force.

AN EXAMPLE

Joseph Wood Krutch taught English at Columbia University from 1937 to 1952. In 1955 he won the National Book Award for *The Measure of Man* (1954). Many of Krutch's writings focused on nature and the environment. In this excerpt from *The Voice of the Desert* (1954), he argues that humans must learn to share the earth with other creatures.

CONSERVATION IS NOT ENOUGH

Joseph Wood Krutch

Moralists often blame races and nations because they have never learned how to live and let live. In our time we seem to have been increasingly aware how persistently and brutally groups of men undertake to eliminate one another. But it is not only the members of his own kind that man seems to want to push off the earth. When he moves in, nearly everything else suffers from his intrusion—sometimes because he wants the space they occupy and the food they eat, but often simply because when he sees a creature not of his kind or a man not of his race his first impulse is "kill it."

Hence it is that even in the desert, where space is cheaper than in most places, the wild life grows scarcer and more secretive as the human population grows. The coyote howls further and further off. The deer seek closer and closer cover. To almost everything except man the smell of humanity is the most repulsive of all odors, the sight of man the most terrifying of all sights. Biologists call some animals "cryptozoic," that is to say "leading hidden lives." But as the human population increases most animals develop, as the deer has been developing, cryptozoic habits. Even now there are more of them around than we realize. They see us when we do not see them—because they have seen us first. Albert Schweitzer remarks somewhere that we owe kindness even to an insect when we can afford to show it, just because we ought to do something to make up for all the cruelties, necessary as well as unnecessary, which we have inflicted upon almost the whole of animate creation.

Probably not one man in ten is capable of understanding such moral and aesthetic considerations, much less of permitting his conduct to be guided by them. But perhaps twice as many, though still far from a majority, are beginning to realize that the reckless laying waste of the earth has practical consequences. They are at least beginning to hear about "conservation," though they are not even dimly aware of any connection between it and a large morality and are very unlikely to suppose that "conservation" does or could mean anything more than looking after their own welfare.

Hardly more than two generations ago Americans first woke up to the fact that their land was not inexhaustible. Every year since then more and more has been said, and at least a little more has been done about "conserving resources," about "rational use" and about such reconstruction as seemed possible. Scientists have studied the problem, public works have been undertaken, laws passed. Yet everybody knows that the using up still goes on, perhaps not so fast nor so recklessly as once it did, but unmistakably nevertheless. And there is nowhere that it goes on more nakedly, more persistently or with a fuller realization of what is happening than in the desert regions where the margin to be used up is narrower.

First, more and more cattle were set to grazing and overgrazing the land from which the scanty rainfall now ran off even more rapidly than before. More outrageously still, large areas of desert shrub were rooted up to make way for cotton and other crops watered by wells tapping underground pools of water which are demonstrably shrinking fast. These pools represent years of accumulation not now being replenished and are exhaustible exactly as an oil well is exhaustible. Everyone knows that they will give out before long, very soon, in fact, if the number of wells continues to increase as it has been increasing. Soon dust bowls will be where was once a sparse but healthy desert, and man, having uprooted, slaughtered or driven away everything which lived healthily and normally there, will himself either abandon the country or die. There are places where the creosote bush is a more useful plant than cotton.

To the question why men will do or are permitted to do such things there are many answers. Some speak of population pressures, some more brutally of unconquerable human greed. Some despair; some hope that more education and more public works will, in the long run, prove effective. But is there, perhaps, something more, something different, which is indispensable? Is there some missing link in the chain of education, law and public works? Is there not something lacking without which none of these is sufficient?

After a lifetime spent in forestry, wild-life management and conservation of one kind or another, after such a lifetime during which he nevertheless saw his country slip two steps backward for every one it took forward, the late Aldo Leopold pondered the question and came up with an unusual answer which many people would dismiss as "sentimental" and be surprised to hear from a "practical" scientific man. He published his article originally in the *Journal of Forestry* and it was reprinted in the posthumous volume, *A Sand County Almanac*, where it was given the seemingly neutral but actually very significant title "The Land Ethic."

This is a subtle and original essay full of ideas never so clearly expressed before and seminal in the sense that each might easily grow into a separate treatise. Yet the conclusion reached can be simply stated. Something *is* lacking and because of that lack education, law and public works fail to accomplish what they hope to accomplish. Without that something, the high-minded impulse to educate, to legislate and to manage become as sounding brass and tinkling cymbals. And the thing which is missing is love, some feeling for, as well as some understanding of, the inclusive community of rocks and soils, plants and animals, of which we are a part.

It is not, to put Mr. Leopold's thoughts in different words, enough to be enlightenedly selfish in our dealings with the land. That means, of course, that it is not enough for the farmer to want to get the most out of his farm and the lumberer to get the most out of his forest without considering agriculture and wood production as a whole both now and in the future. But it also means more than that. In the first place enlightened selfishness cannot be enough because enlightened selfishness cannot possibly be extended to include remote posterity. It may include the children, perhaps, and grandchildren, possibly, but it cannot be extended much beyond that because the very idea of "self" cannot be stretched much further. Some purely ethical considerations must operate, if anything does. Yet even that is not all. The wisest, the most enlightened, the most remotely long-seeing exploitation of resources is not enough, for the simple reason that the whole concept of exploitation is so false and so limited that in the end it will defeat itself and the earth will have been plundered no matter how scientifically and farseeingly the plundering has been done.

To live healthily and successfully on the land we must also live with it. We must be part not only of the human community, but of the whole community; we must acknowledge some sort of oneness not only with our neighbors, our countrymen and our civilization but also some respect for the natural as well as for the man-made community. Ours is not only "one world" in the sense usually implied by that term. It is also "one earth." Without some acknowledgment of that fact, men can no more live successfully than they can if they refuse to admit the political and economic interdependency of the various sections of the civilized world. It is not a sentimental but a grimly literal fact that unless we share this terrestrial globe with creatures other than ourselves, we shall not be able to live on it for long.

You may, if you like, think of this as a moral law. But if you are skeptical about moral laws, you cannot escape the fact that it has its factual, scientific aspect. Every day the science of ecology is making clearer the factual aspect as it demonstrates those more and more remote interdependencies which, no matter how remote they are, are crucial even for us.

Before even the most obvious aspects of the balance of nature had been recognized, a greedy, self-centered mankind naïvely divided plants into the useful and the useless. In the same way it divided animals into those which were either domestic on the one hand or "game" on the other, and the "vermin" which ought to be destroyed. That was the day when extermination of whole species was taken as a matter of course and random introductions which usually proved to be either complete failures or all too successful were everywhere being made. Soon, however, it became evident enough that to rid the world of vermin and to stock it with nothing but useful organisms was at least not a simple task—if you assume that "useful" means simply "immediately useful to man."

Yet even to this day the *ideal* remains the same for most people. They may know, or at least they may have been told, that what looks like the useless is often remotely but demonstrably essential. Out in this desert country they may see the land being rendered useless by overuse. They may even have heard how, when the mountain lion is killed off, the deer multiply; how, when the deer multiply, the new growth of trees and shrubs is eaten away; and how, when the hills are denuded, a farm or a section of grazing land many miles away is washed into gulleys and made incapable of supporting either man or any other of the large animals. They may even have heard how the wonderful new insecticides proved so effective that fish and birds died of starvation; how on at least one Pacific island insects had to be reintroduced to pollinate the crops; how when you kill off almost completely a destructive pest, you run the risk of starving out everything which preys upon it and thus run the risk that the pest itself will stage an overwhelming comeback because its natural enemies are no more. Yet, knowing all this and much more, their dream is still the dream that an earth for man's use only can be created if only we learn more and scheme more effectively. They still hope that nature's scheme of checks and balances which provides for a varied population, which stubbornly refuses to scheme only from man's point of view and cherishes the weeds and "vermin" as persistently as she cherishes him, can be replaced by a scheme of his own devising. Ultimately they hope they can beat the game. But the more the ecologist learns, the less likely it seems that man can in the long run do anything of the sort.

Krutch uses cause and effect to suggest that the actions of human beings are having a disastrous effect on the earth and that we should change our behavior and learn to live with the land.

REFERENTIAL CAUSE AND EFFECT

In many academic disciplines, but especially in the social sciences and the natural sciences, analysis of cause and effect is fundamental. To understand ourselves and our world, we rely on studies that tell us why phenomena of all kinds occur.

AN EXAMPLE

This short version of an essay published in *The Frontier in American History* (1920) was delivered at the meeting of the American Historical Society meeting in 1894. It illustrates an objective treatment of historical causes and effects.

AMERICAN INTELLECTUAL TRAITS FROM THE FRONTIER

FREDERICK JACKSON TURNER

From the conditions of frontier life came intellectual traits of profound importance. The works of travelers along each frontier from colonial days onward describe certain common traits, and these traits have, while softening down, still persisted as survivals in the place of their origin, even when a higher social organization succeeded. The result is that to the frontier the American intellect owes its striking characteristics. That coarseness and strength combined with acuteness and inquisitiveness; that practical, inventive turn of mind, quick to find expedients; that masterful grasp of material things, lacking in the artistic but powerful to effect great ends; that restless, nervous energy; that dominant individualism, working for good and for evil, and withal that buoyancy and exuberance which comes with freedom—these are traits of the frontier, or traits called out elsewhere because of the existence of the frontier. Since the days when the fleet of Columbus sailed into the waters of the New World, America has been another name for opportunity, and the people of the United States have taken their tone from the incessant expansion which has not only been open but has even been forced upon them. He would be a rash prophet who should assert that the expansive character of American life has now entirely ceased. Movement has been its dominant fact, and, unless this training has no effect upon a people, the American energy will continually demand a wider field for its exercise. But never again will such gifts of free land offer themselves. For a moment, at the frontier, the bonds of custom are broken and unrestraint is triumphant. There is not tabula rasa. The stubborn American environment is there with its imperious summons to accept its conditions; the inherited ways of doing things are also there; and yet, in spite of environment, and in spite of custom, each frontier did indeed furnish a new field of opportunity, a gate of escape from the bondage of the past; and freshness, and confidence, and scorn of older society, impatience of its restraints and its ideas, and indifference to its lessons, have accompanied the frontier. What the Mediterranean Sea was to the Greeks, breaking the bond of custom, offering new experiences, calling out new institutions and activities, that, and more, the ever retreating frontier has been to the United States directly, and to the nations of Europe more remotely. And now, four centuries from the discovery of America, at the end of a hundred years of life under the Constitution, the frontier has gone, and with its going has closed the first period of American history.

Turner explains the effects (American intellectual traits) that were caused by the conditions of the American frontier. The frontier is the cause; the intellectual traits are the effects.

WRITING STRATEGIES

You may want to consider the following questions if you are writing about causes and effects.

- What important events occurred?
- What are the immediate causes of each event?
- What are the ultimate causes?

Evaluation

When we organize with evaluation, we show a relationship between values and judgments. Evaluation involves saying whether the subject of evaluation is good or bad or something in between. The words *good* and *bad* or synonyms of relative degrees of goodness and badness appear in evaluations. Most of us make evaluations every day. Someone who said that a meal was *delicious* or that a movie was *terrible* would be making an evaluation.

VALUES

Values are those principles that tell us that something is worthwhile and desirable. Values tell us what we want and what we need. For instance, those possessions that we acquire and keep are usually what we consider to be valuable. Those possessions that we throw away or reject are what we consider to be worthless, without value.

THE STRUCTURE OF EVALUATION

Evaluation when used to organize any piece of writing will have a structure controlled by three elements: the presentation of the subject to be evaluated, the judgment, and the criteria.

THE SUBJECT PRESENTED

Whatever we are evaluating must be presented to the reader in some way. That presentation will depend on another pattern of organization: narration, description, or classification. What details we use to present the subject (narrative, descriptive, or classificatory) will affect how the audience perceives the evaluation and, to a certain extent, how we apply the criteria we are using.

THE JUDGMENT

The judgment is the outcome of our evaluation of the subject. The judgment may be positive, negative, or mixed depending on how the subject is viewed in relation to the criteria. Whatever the judgment is, it will reflect the connections we have made between the subject and the values that are controlling the evaluation.

THE CRITERIA

Criteria are the standards by which we make judgments. They are derived from the system of values relevant to the evaluation. These standards may be stated or unstated in the evaluation. But regardless, they are essential to making a judgment. A judgment cannot be made without criteria.

These standards are stated in such a way that they could be applied to other things that are in the same category as the subject being evaluated. In evaluating a particular community college, Austin Community College for instance, we might generate the criteria that a community college is good if it has

> qualified teachers,
>
> convenient locations,
>
> adequate library resources,
>
> low tuition, and
>
> a broad curriculum.

(Of course, other criteria are possible, but these illustrate the kinds of standards that would be considered in an evaluation.) Notice that these criteria could be used to evaluate another community college, that is, any member of the group that Austin Community College belongs to.

THE EVALUATION POSTULATE

Evaluation can be reduced to a single statement called an evaluation postulate. That statement is a kind of formula that includes those elements essential for any evaluation. Evaluations are usually not reduced to such brief terms, but the evaluation postulate does allow us to see clearly the essential elements of an evaluation. Sometimes it can be helpful to think about an evaluation in terms of its basic structure.

The following pattern can be used to create an evaluation postulate of any evaluation.

If something (the subject) has certain characteristics (the criteria), then it is good or bad (the judgment).

AN EXAMPLE

In 1862 Nathaniel Hawthorne, the author of *The Scarlet Letter*, wrote this evaluation of Abraham Lincoln.

LINCOLN
NATHANIEL HAWTHORNE

Of course, there was one other personage, in the class of statesmen, whom I should have been truly mortified to leave Washington without seeing; since (temporarily, at least, and by force of circumstances) he was the man of men. But a private grief had built up a barrier about him, impeding the customary free intercourse of Americans with their chief magistrate; so that I might have come away without a glimpse of his very remarkable physiognomy, save for a semi-official opportunity of which I was glad to take advantage. The fact is, we were invited to annex ourselves, as supernumeraries, to a deputation that was about to wait upon the President, from a Massachusetts whip factory, with a present of a splendid whip.

Our immediate party consisted only of four or five (including Major Ben Perley Poore, with his note-book and pencil), but we were joined by several other persons, who seemed to have been lounging about the precincts of the White House, under the spacious porch, or within the hall, and who swarmed in with us to take the chances of a presentation. Nine o'clock had been appointed as the time for receiving the deputation, and we were punctual to the moment; but not so the President, who sent us word that he was eating breakfast, and would come as soon as he could. His appetite, we were glad to think, must have been a pretty fair one; for we waited about half an hour in one of the antechambers, and then were ushered into a reception-room, in one corner of which sat the Secretaries of War and the Treasury, expecting, like ourselves, the termination of the Presidential breakfast. During this interval there were several new additions to our group, one or two of whom were in a working-garb, so that we formed a very miscellaneous collection of people, mostly unknown to each other, and without any common sponsor, but all with an equal right to look our head servant in the face.

By and by there was a little stir on the staircase and in the passageway, and in lounged a tall, loose-jointed figure, of an exaggerated Yankee port and de-meanor, whom (as being about the homeliest man I ever saw, yet by no means repulsive or disagreeable) it was impossible not to recognize as Uncle Abe.

Unquestionably, Western man though he be, and Kentuckian by birth, President Lincoln is the essential representative of all Yankees, and the veritable specimen, physically, of what the world seems determined to regard as our characteristic qualities. It is the strangest and yet the fittest thing in the jumble of human vicissitudes, that he, out of so many millions, unlooked for, unselected by any intelligible process that could be based upon his genuine qualities, unknown to those who chose him, unsuspected of what endowments may adapt him for his tremendous responsibility, should have found the way open for him to fling his lank personality into the chair of state—where, I presume, it was his first impulse to throw his legs on the council-table, and tell the Cabinet Ministers a story. There is no describing his lengthy awkwardness, nor the uncouthness of his movement; and yet it seemed as if I had been in the habit of seeing him daily, and had shaken hands with him a thousand times in some village street; so true was he to the aspect of the pattern American, though with a certain extravagance which, possibly, I exaggerated still further by the delighted eagerness with which I took it in. If put to guess his calling and livelihood, I should have taken him for a country school-master as soon as anything else. He was dressed in a rusty black frock coat and pantaloons, unbrushed, and worn so faithfully that the suit had adapted itself to the curves and angularities of his figure, and had grown to be an outer skin of the man. His hair was black, still unmixed with gray, stiff, somewhat bushy, and had apparently been acquainted with neither brush nor comb that morning, after the disarrangement of the pillow; and as to a nightcap, Uncle Abe probably knows nothing of such effeminacies. His complexion is dark and sallow, betokening, I fear, an insalubrious atmosphere around the White House; he has thick black eyebrows and an impending brow; his nose is large, and the lines around his mouth are very strongly defined.

The whole physiognomy is as coarse a one as you would meet anywhere in the length and breadth of the States; but, withal, it is redeemed, illuminated, softened, and brightened by a kindly though serious look out of his eyes, and an expression of homely sagacity, that seems weighted with rich results of village experience. A great deal of native sense; no bookish cultivation, no refinement; honest at heart, and thoroughly so, and yet, in some sort, sly—at least, endowed with a sort of tact and wisdom that are akin to craft, and would impel him, I think, to take an antagonist in flank, rather than to make a bull-run at him right in front. But, on the whole, I like this sallow, queer, sagacious visage, with the homely human sympathies that warmed it; and, for my small share in the matter, would as lief have Uncle Abe for a ruler as any man whom it would have been practicable to put in his place.

Immediately on his entrance the President accosted our member of Congress, who had us in charge, and, with a comical twist of his face made some jocular remark about the length of his breakfast. He then greeted us all round, not waiting for an introduction, but shaking and squeezing everybody's hand with the utmost cordiality, whether the individual's name was announced to him or not. His manner towards us was wholly without pretence, but yet had a kind of natural dignity, quite sufficient to keep the forwardest of us from clapping him on the shoulder and asking him for a story. A mutual acquaintance being established, our leader took the whip out of its case, and began to read the address of presentation. The whip was an exceedingly long one, its handle wrought in ivory (by some artist in the Massachusetts State Prison, I believe), and ornamented with a medallion of the President, and other equally beautiful devices; and along its whole length there was a succession of golden bands and ferrules. The address was shorter than the whip, but equally well made, consisting chiefly of an explanatory description of these artistic designs, and closing with a hint that the gift was a suggestive and emblematic one, and that the President would recognize the use to which such an instrument should be put.

This suggestion gave Uncle Abe rather a delicate task in his reply, because, slight as the matter seemed, it apparently called for some declaration, or intimation, or faint foreshadowing of policy in reference to the conduct of the war, and the final treatment of the Rebels. But the President's Yankee aptness and not-to-be-caughtness stood him in good stead, and he jerked or wiggled himself out of the dilemma with an uncouth dexterity that was entirely in character; although, without his gesticulation of eyeand mouth—and especially the flourish of the whip, with which he imagined himself touching a pair of fat horses—I doubt whether his words would be worth recording, even if I could remember them. The gist of the reply was, that he accepted the whip as an emblem of peace, not punishment; and, this great affair over, we retired out of the presence in high good humor, only regretting that we could not have seen the President sit down and fold up his legs (which is said to be a most extraordinary spectacle), or have heard him tell one of those delectable stories for which he is so celebrated. A good many of them are afloat upon the common talk of Washington, and are certainly the aptest, pithiest, and funniest little things imaginable; though, to be sure, they smack of the frontier freedom, and would not always bear repetition in a drawing-room, or on the immaculate page of the *Atlantic*.

Good Heavens! what liberties have I been taking with one of the potentates of the earth, and the man on whose conduct more important consequences depend than on that of any other historical personage of the century! But with whom is an American citizen entitled to take a liberty, if not with his own chief magistrate? However, lest the above allusions to President Lincoln's little peculiarities (already well known to the country and to the world) should be misinterpreted, I deem it proper to say a word or two in regard to him, of unfeigned respect and measurable confidence. He is evidently a man of keen faculties, and, what is still more to the purpose, of powerful character. As to his integrity, the people have that intuition of it which is never deceived. Before he actually entered upon his great office, and for a considerable time

afterwards, there is no reason to suppose that he adequately estimated the gigantic task about to be imposed on him, or, at least,
had any distinct idea how it was to be managed; and I presume
there may have been more than one veteran politician who proposed to himself to take the power out of President Lincoln's hands
into his own, leaving our honest friend only the public responsibility for the good or ill success of the career. The extremely imperfect
development of his statesmanly qualities, at that period, may have
justified such designs. But the President is teachable by events, and
has now spent a year in a very arduous course of education; he has a
flexible mind, capable of much expansion, and convertible towards
far loftier studies and activities than those of his early life; and if he
came to Washington a backwoods humorist, he has already transformed himself into as good a statesman (to speak moderately) as
his prime minister.

Hawthorne's evaluation presents his subject Abraham Lincoln in
several different ways, using several different patterns of organization. He
describes Lincoln as "a tall, loose-jointed figure" and as "the homeliest
man" he as ever seen. He talks further about his "awkwardness" and "the
uncouthness of his movement." Finally Hawthorne makes the physical
description even more detailed when he refers to Lincoln's hair, "black, still
unmixed with gray, stiff, somewhat bushy," to his "thick black eyebrows,"
and to his large nose. Overall he regards Lincoln's appearance as "coarse."
In contrast to those rather negative features, Hawthorne says that he has a
"serious look," "an expression of homely sagacity," and a "great deal of native
sense." In addition, to the physical descriptions, Hawthorne narrates the
events surrounding his meeting the president. When Lincoln is presented
with the gift of a whip from a Massachusetts whip factory, we discover that
he is quick witted and diplomatic.

Toward the end of the evaluation, Hawthorne makes his judgment
of Lincoln and reveals his "unfeigned respect" for and "confidence" in the
president, remarking on Lincoln's "powerful character" and "his integrity."
Finally, he observes that the president had become a "good statesman."
These judgments are based on criteria that most people would agree are
valid for measuring the performance of a political leader.

VARIATIONS IN EVALUATION

A change of purpose will create a different evaluation. As we saw in Chapter 1, expressive writing involves an articulation of a value system, so the potential for evaluation is always there. Persuasion, too, often involves using social and cultural values to convince the reader of the validity of a claim.

EXPRESSIVE EVALUATION

In expressive evaluations the criteria are often unstated. Because the writer of self-expression is defining the self at least partially in terms of a value system, the statement of values is usually inextricably intertwined with the identity of the writer.

AN EXAMPLE

After surrendering to U.S. troops in 1832, Black Hawk, chief of the Sauk tribe in the Midwest, delivered this speech. He evaluates himself, the Indians, and white men.

BLACK HAWK'S FAREWELL ADDRESS

BLACK HAWK

You have taken me prisoner with all my warriors. I am much grieved, for I expected, if I did not defeat you, to hold out much longer, and give you more trouble before I surrendered. I tried hard to bring you into ambush, but your last general understands Indian fighting. The first one was not so wise. When I saw that I could not beat you by Indian fighting, I determined to rush on you, and fight you face to face. I fought hard. But your guns were well aimed. The bullets flew like birds in the air, and whizzed by our ears like the wind through the trees in the winter. My warriors fell around me; it began to look dismal. I saw my evil day at hand. The sun rose dim on us in the morning, and at night it sunk in a dark cloud, and looked like a ball of fire. That was the last sun that shone on Black Hawk. His heart is dead, and no longer beats quick in his bosom. He is now a prisoner to the white men; they will do with him as they wish. But he can stand torture, and is not afraid of death. He is no coward. Black Hawk is an Indian.

He has done nothing for which an Indian ought to be ashamed. He has fought for his countrymen, the squaws and papooses, against white men, who came, year after year, to cheat them and take away their lands. You know the cause of our making war. It is known to all white men. They ought to be ashamed of it. The white men despise the Indians, and drive them from their homes. But the Indians are not deceitful. The white men speak bad of the Indian, and look at him spitefully. But the Indian does not tell lies; Indians do not steal.

An Indian who is as bad as the white men could not live in our nation; he would be put to death, and eaten up by the wolves. The white men are bad schoolmasters; they carry false looks, and deal in false actions; they smile in the face of the poor Indian to cheat him; they shake them by the hand to gain their confidence, to make them drunk, to deceive them, and to ruin our wives. We told them to let us alone, and keep away from us; but they followed on, and beset our paths, and they coiled themselves among us, like the snake. They poisoned us by their touch. We were not safe. We lived in danger. We were becoming like them, hypocrites and liars, adulterers, lazy drones, all talkers, and no workers.

We looked up to the Great Spirit. We went to our great father. We were encouraged. His great council gave us fair words and big promises; but we got no satisfaction. Things were growing worse. There were no deer in the forest. The opossum and beaver were fled; the springs were drying up, and our squaws and papooses without victuals to keep them from starving; we called a great council, and built a large fire. The spirit of our fathers arose and spoke to us to avenge our wrongs and die. We all spoke before the council fire. It was warm and pleasant. We set up the war-whoop, and dug up the tomahawk; our knives were ready, and the heart of Black Hawk swelled high in his bosom when he led his warriors to his duty. His father will meet him there, and commend him.

Black Hawk is a true Indian, and disdains to cry like a woman. He feels for his wife, his children, and his friends. But he does not care for himself. The white men do not scalp the head; but they do worse—they poison the heart; it is not pure with them. His countrymen will not be scalped, but they will, in a few years, become like the white men, so that you can't trust them, and there must be, as in the white settlements, nearly as many officers as men, to take care of them and keep them in order.

Farewell, my nation! Black Hawk tried to save you, and avenge your wrongs. He drank the blood of some of the whites. He has been taken prisoner, and his plans stopped. He can do no more. He is near his end. His sun is setting, and he will rise no more. Farewell to Black Hawk.

This speech illustrates what evaluation looks like with an expressive purpose. Based on the criteria that people are good if they are honest, brave, and hard working, Black Hawk makes judgments about white men and Indians. He says that "the Indian does not tell lies; Indians do not steal," and that any "Indian who is as bad as the white men could not live in our nation. . . ." Further he calls white men "bad schoolmasters" who "carry false looks," "deal in false actions," and "cheat" the Indian. He evaluates himself and gives a self-definition when he says, "Black Hawk is a true Indian. . . ." In this speech the self-expression is achieved through an evaluation of white and Indian culture.

LITERARY EVALUATION

The writer of literary evaluation tends to engage in satire and humor and often has a persuasive intent as well.

AN EXAMPLE

Mark Twain creates a humorous parody of the advice adults frequently offer to young people.

ADVICE TO YOUTH

Mark Twain

Being told I would be expected to talk here, I inquired what sort of a talk I ought to make. They said it should be something suitable to youth—something didactic, instructive, or something in the nature of good advice. Very well. I have a few things in my mind which I have often longed to say for the instruction of the young, for it is in one's tender early years that such things will best take root and be most enduring and most valuable. First, then, I will say to you, my young friends—and I say it beseechingly, urgingly—

Always obey your parents, when they are present. This is the best policy in the long run, because if you don't they will make you. Most parents think they know better than you do, and you can generally make more by humoring that superstition than you can by acting on your own better judgment.

Be respectful to your superiors, if you have any, also to strangers, and sometimes to others. If a person offend you, and you are in doubt as to whether it was intentional or not, do not resort to extreme measures; simply watch your chance and hit him with a brick. That will be sufficient. If you shall find that he had not intended any offense, come out frankly and confess yourself in the wrong when you struck him; acknowledge it like a man and say you didn't mean to. Yes, always avoid violence; in this age of charity and kindliness, the time has gone by for such things. Leave dynamite to the low unrefined.

Go to bed early, get up early—this is wise. Some authorities say get up with the sun; some others say get up with one thing, some with another. But a lark is really the best thing to get up with. It gives you a splendid reputation with everybody to know that you get up with the lark; and if you get the right kind of a lark, and work at him right, you easily train him to get up at half past nine, every time—it is no trick at all.

Now as to the matter of lying. You want to be very careful about lying; otherwise you are nearly sure to get caught. Once caught, you can never again be, in the eyes of the good and the pure, what you were before. Many a young person has injured himself permanently through a single clumsy and illfinished lie, the result of carelessness born of incomplete training. Some authorities hold that the young ought not to lie at all. That, of course, is putting it rather stronger than necessary; still, while I cannot go quite so far as that, I do maintain, and I believe I am right, that the young ought to be temperate in the use of this great art until practice and experience shall give them that confidence, elegance, and precision which alone can make the accomplishment graceful and profitable. Patience, diligence, painstaking attention to detail—these are the requirements; these, in time, will make the student perfect; upon these, and upon these only, may he rely as the sure foundation for future eminence. Think what tedious years of study, thought, practice, experience, went to the equipment of that peerless old master who was able to impose upon the whole world the lofty and sounding maxim that "truth is mighty and will prevail"—the most majestic compound fracture of fact which any of woman born has yet achieved. For the history of our race, and each individual's experience, are sown thick with evidence that a truth is not hard to kill and that a lie told well is immortal. There is in Boston a monument of the man who discovered anaesthesia; many people are aware, in these latter days, that that man didn't discover it at all, but stole the discovery from another man. Is this truth mighty, and will it prevail? Ah no, my hearers, the monument is made of hardy material, but the lie it tells will outlast it a million years. An awkward, feeble, leaky lie is a thing which you ought to make it your unceasing study to avoid; such a lie as that has no more real permanence than an average truth. Why, you might as well tell the truth at once and be done with it. A feeble, stupid, preposterous lie will not live two years—except it be a slander upon somebody. It is indestructible, then, of course, but that is no merit of yours. A final word: begin your practice of this gracious and beautiful art early—begin it now. If I had begun earlier, I could have learned how.

Never handle firearms carelessly. The sorrow and suffering that have been caused through the innocent but heedless handling of firearms by the young! Only four days ago, right in the next farmhouse to the one where I am spending the summer, a grandmother, old and gray and sweet, one of the loveliest spirits in the land, was sitting at her work, when her young grandson crept in and got down an old, battered, rusty gun which had not been touched for many years and was supposed not to be loaded, and pointed it at her, laughing and threatening to shoot. In her fright she ran screaming and pleading toward the door on the other side of the room; but as she passed him he placed the gun almost against her very breast and pulled the trigger! He had supposed it was not loaded. And he was right—it wasn't. So there wasn't any harm done. It is the only case of that kind I ever heard of. Therefore, just the same, don't you meddle with old unloaded firearms; they are the most deadly and unerring things that have ever been created by man. You don't have to take any pains at all with them; you don't have to have a rest, you don't have to have any sights on the gun, you don't have to take aim, even. No, you just pick out a relative and bang away, and you are sure to get him. A youth who can't hit a cathedral at thirty yards with a Gatling gun in three-quarters of an hour, can take up on old empty musket and bag his grandmother every time, at a hundred. Think what Waterloo would have been if one of the armies had been boys armed with old muskets supposed not to be loaded, and the other army had been composed of their female relations. The very thought of it makes one shudder.

There are many sorts of books; but good ones are the sort for the young to read. Remember that. They are a great, an inestimable, an unspeakable means of improvement. Therefore be careful in your selection, my young friends; be very careful; confine yourselves exclusively to Robertson's Sermons, Baxter's *Saint's Rest, The Innocents Abroad*, and works of that kind.

But I have said enough. I hope you will treasure up the instructions which I have given you, and make them a guide to your feet and a light to your understanding. Build your character thoughtfully and painstakingly upon these precepts, and by and by, when you have got it built, you will be surprised and gratified to see how nicely and sharply it resembles everybody else's.

Mark Twain, in this literary evaluation, entertains the reader by offering unexpected bits of advice. The style of the writing is didactic and at first seems to contain the kind of advice we might expect an adult to give to a young person. But as we read, we discover that every moral truism we anticipate is contradicted. In this way Twain delights us with humorous, outlandish twists on the expected. He reveals the true subject of the evaluation at the end of the essay. Rather than evaluating the behavior of young people, as he maintains at the beginning, he is really evaluating the behavior of everyone else. He makes this clear in the last sentence when he suggests that if young people will follow his contradictory advice, then they will "be surprised and gratified to see how nicely and sharply" their behavior "resembles everybody else's." At this point we become aware of a secondary persuasive purpose at work, a satire on human behavior.

PERSUASIVE EVALUATION

Evaluations tend toward persuasion, so persuasion is often a part of an evaluation no matter what other purpose the writer has. Any evaluation will become persuasive if an imperative is added, as in the following statement: this thing (subject) is good (judgment), so you should try it (persuasive assertion).

AN EXAMPLE

In the following essay Robert Lane Greene presents a persuasive argument supported by evaluation.

WHICH IS THE BEST LANGUAGE TO LEARN?

ROBERT LANE GREENE

For language lovers, the facts are grim: Anglophones simply aren't learning them any more. In Britain, despite four decades in the European Union, the number of A-levels taken in French and German has fallen by half in the past 20 years, while what was a growing trend of Spanish-learning has stalled. In America, the numbers are equally sorry. One factor behind the 9/11 attacks was the fact that the CIA lacked the Arabic-speakers who might have translated available intelligence. But ten years on, "English only" campaigns appeal more successfully to American patriotism than campaigns that try to promote language-learning, as if the most successful language in history were threatened.

Why learn a foreign language? After all, the one you already speak if you read this magazine is the world's most useful and important language. English is not only the first language of the obvious countries, it is now the rest of the world's second language: a Japanese tourist in Sweden or a Turk landing a plane in Spain will almost always speak English.

Nonetheless, compelling reasons remain for learning other languages. They range from the intellectual to the economical to the practical. First of all, learning any foreign language helps you understand all language better—many Anglophones first encounter the words "past participle" not in an English class, but in French. Second, there is the cultural broadening. Literature is always best read in the original.

Poetry and lyrics suffer particularly badly in translation. And learning another tongue helps the student grasp another way of thinking. Though the notion that speakers of different languages think differently has been vastly exaggerated and misunderstood, there is a great deal to be learned from discovering what the different cultures call this, that or *das oder.*

The practical reasons are just as compelling. In business, if the team on the other side of the table knows your language but you don't know theirs, they almost certainly know more about you and your company than you do about them and theirs—a bad position to negotiate from. Many investors in China have made fatally stupid decisions about companies they could not understand. Diplomacy, war-waging and intelligence work are all weakened by a lack of capable linguists. Virtually any career, public or private, is given a boost with knowledge of a foreign language.

So which one should you, or your children, learn? If you take a glance at advertisements in New York or A-level options in Britain, an answer seems to leap out: Mandarin. China's economy continues to grow at a pace that will make it bigger than America's within two decades at most. China's political clout is growing accordingly. Its businessmen are buying up everything from American brands to African minerals to Russian oil rights. If China is the country of the future, is Chinese the language of the future?

Probably not. Remember Japan's rise? Just as spectacular as China's, if on a smaller scale, Japan's economic growth led many to think it would take over the world. It was the world's second-largest economy for decades (before falling to third, recently, behind China). So is Japanese the world's third-most useful language? Not even close. If you were to learn ten languages ranked by general usefulness, Japanese would probably not make the list. And the key reason for Japanese's limited spread will also put the brakes on Chinese.

This factor is the Chinese writing system (which Japan borrowed and adapted centuries ago). The learner needs to know at least 3,000–4,000 characters to make sense of written Chinese, and thousands more to have a real feel for it. Chinese, with all its tones, is hard enough to speak. But the mammoth feat of memory required to be literate in Mandarin is harder still. It deters most foreigners from ever mastering the system—and increasingly trips up Chinese natives.

A recent survey reported in the *People's Daily* found 84% of respondents agreeing that skill in Chinese is declining. If such gripes are common to most languages, there is something more to it in Chinese. Fewer and fewer native speakers learn to produce characters in traditional calligraphy. Instead, they write their language the same way we do—with a computer. And not only that, but they use the Roman alphabet to produce Chinese characters: type in wo and Chinese language-support software will offer a menu of characters pronounced wo; the user selects the one desired. (Or if the user types in wo shi zhongguo ren, "I am Chinese", the software detects the meaning and picks the right characters.) With less and less need to recall the characters cold, the Chinese are forgetting them. David Moser, a Sinologist, recalls asking three native Chinese graduate students at Peking University how to write "sneeze":

> To my surprise, all three of them simply shrugged in sheepish embarrassment. Not one of them could correctly produce the character. Now, Peking University is usually considered the "Harvard of China". Can you imagine three PhD students in English at Harvard forgetting how to write the English word "sneeze"? Yet this state of affairs is by no means uncommon in China.

As long as China keeps the character-based system—which will probably be a long time, thanks to cultural attachment and practical concerns alike—Chinese is very unlikely to become a true world language, an auxiliary language like English, the language a Brazilian chemist will publish papers in, hoping that they will be read in Finland and Canada. By all means, if China is your main interest, for business or pleasure, learn Chinese. It is fascinating, and learnable—though Moser's online essay, "Why Chinese is so damn hard," might discourage the faint of heart and the short of time.

But if I was asked what foreign language is the most useful, and given no more parameters (where? for what purpose?), my answer would be French. Whatever you think of France, the language is much less limited than many people realise.

As their empire spun off and they became a medium-sized power after the second world war, the French, hoping to maintain some distance from America and to make the most of their former possessions, established La Francophonie. This club, bringing together all the countries with a French-speaking heritage, has 56 members, almost a third of the world's countries. Hardly any of them are places where French is everyone's native language. Instead, they include countries with Francophone minorities

(Switzerland, Belgium); those where French is official and wide-spread among elites (much of western Africa); those where it is not official but still spoken by nearly all educated people (Morocco, Lebanon); and those where French ties remain despite the fading of the language (Vietnam, Cambodia). It even has members with few ties to French or France, like Egypt, that simply want to asso-ciate themselves with the prestige of the French-speaking world. Another 19 countries are observer members.

French ranks only 16th on the list of languages ranked by native speakers. But ranked above it are languages like Telegu and Javanese that no one would call world languages. Hindi does not even unite India. Also in the top 15 are Arabic, Spanish and Portuguese, major languages to be sure, but regionally con-centrated. If your interest is the Middle East or Islam, by all means learn Arabic. If your interest is Latin America, Spanish or Portuguese is the way to go. Or both; learning one makes the second quite easy.

If your interests span the globe, and you've read this far, you already know the most useful global language. But if you want another truly global language, there are surprisingly few candi-dates, and for me French is unquestionably top of the list. It can enhance your enjoyment of art, history, literature and food, while giving you an important tool in business and a useful one in diplo-macy. It has native speakers in every region on earth. And lest we forget its heartland itself, France attracts more tourists than any other country—76.8m in 2010, according to the World Tourism Organisation, leaving America a distant second with 59.7m. Any visit there is greatly enhanced by some grasp of the language. The French are nothing but welcoming when you show them and their country respect, and the occasional frost that can greet visitors melts when they come out with their first fully formed sentence. So although there are other great languages out there, don't forget an easy, common one, with far fewer words to learn than English, that is almost certainly taught in your town. With French, *vous ne regretterez rien*.

Greene's essay has two persuasive arguments, one, that speakers of English should learn a second language and, two, that that language should be French. He supports the first claim, that you as an English speaker should learn another language, by saying that learning a foreign language will help you understand all language better, will broaden your cultural understanding, and will help you if you plan a career in business or government.

In order to determine which language you should learn, Greene establishes three criteria to be applied to any language: it should be of global importance; it should be useful; and it should be comparatively easy to learn. He then applies those criteria to Chinese and determines that although it is obvious that it has global importance and would be useful for business, it is difficult to learn. He describes the Chinese writing system where the "learner needs to know at least 3,000–4,000 characters to make sense of written Chinese," and comes to the conclusion that "as long as "China keeps the character-based system. . . Chinese is very unlikely to become a true world language."

Greene states a personal preference for French and evaluates it using the same criteria he used for Chinese. He says that "the language is much less limited than many people realize" and that learning French would "enhance your enjoyment of art, history, literature and food, while giving you an important tool in business and a useful one in diplomacy." He also notes that French speakers span the globe and that France also attracts the most tourists, so learning the language would keep you in good standing with the locals when visiting. Finally, Greene observes that unlike some other languages, French has "far fewer words to learn than English."

Greene's persuasive argument that French is the best foreign language for an English speaker to learn depends on the criteria he establishes to evaluate languages.

REFERENTIAL EVALUATION

Criteria in referential evaluations are derived by objective means. Writers of referential evaluations will need to consider the necessity of validating the criteria they use or at least making sure that there is a general agreement about the validity of the criteria used.

AN EXAMPLE

This essay evaluates one of the classic novels in American literature.

WHY "HUCKLEBERRY FINN" IS A GREAT WORLD NOVEL

LAURIAT LANE, JR.

Of all forms of literature, the novel is in many ways the hardest to describe with any precision. Its relative newness as a form and its varied and complex nature combine to make this so. Whenever we try to view such a full and living book as *The Adventures of Huckleberry Finn*, some of it always escapes our gaze. In fact, apart from its mere physical presence, paper, ink, glue, covers, and so forth, it is often easiest to assume that the novel does not exist at all, but only the experience of reading it. Each time we read *Huckleberry Finn* we read a certain book, and each time we read it we read a different book. No one of these books is the real *Huckleberry Finn*; in a sense, they all are.

At the heart of *Huckleberry Finn* lies a story about real human figures with genuine moral and ethical problems and decisions, figures placed in a society which we recognize as having everywhere in it the flavor of authenticity—the whole combination treated, for the most part, as directly and realistically as possible. I would like to move beyond this primary description or definition of *Huckleberry Finn*, however, and suggest that the novel may contain other elements equally important to a full appreciation. I would like to extend the novel in three directions, in space, in time, and in degree: in space, by considering some of the ways in which the book extends beyond its position as one of the masterworks of American fiction and becomes, if the term be allowed, a world novel; in time, by considering how much *Huckleberry Finn* resembles a literary form much older than the novel, the epic poem; and in degree, by considering just how much *Huckleberry Finn* transcends its position as a realistic novel and takes on the forms and qualities of allegory.

I

A world novel may be defined as that kind of novel whose importance in its own literature is so great, and whose impact on its readers is so profound and far-reaching, that it has achieved world-wide distinction. In the total picture of world literature, such a novel stands out as a work always to be reckoned with. The world novel, however, achieves its position not only through its importance but also because of its essential nature. And in discussing *Huckleberry Finn* as a world novel I shall deal not so much with this importance, as measured by permanent popularity and influence, as with the special qualities *Huckleberry Finn* has in common with certain other world novels.

The first real novel and the first world novel is, by almost universal consent, Cervantes' *The Adventures of Don Quixote*. The most important thing which *Don Quixote* has bequeathed to the novels after it (apart of course from the all-important fact of there being such a thing as a novel at all) is the theme which is central to *Don Quixote* and to almost every great novel since, the theme of appearance versus reality. This theme is also central to *Huckleberry Finn*.

Even on the simplest plot level the world of *Huckleberry Finn* is one of deception. The very existence of Huck at all is a continual deception—he is supposed to be dead. This falseness in his relations with the world at large merely reflects the difference between his standards and those of the outside world. Huck's truth and the truth of the world are diametrically opposed. Throughout the novel his truth is always cutting through the surfaces of the world's appearance and learning the contrary reality beneath. At the climax Huck tells himself, "You can't pray a lie—I found that out." That is to say, the lie of appearance is always far different from the truth of reality, and to the truly heroic and individual conscience no amount of self-delusion can ever bridge the gap lying between.

In the final section of the book, the theme of appearance versus reality reaches almost philosophical proportions. Both because of the way in which Jim's escape is carried out and because of the underlying fact of there being no need for him to escape at all, the situation is one of total dramatic and moral irony. At the end, however, Twain relaxes the tone, straightens out the plot complications, and lets the moral issue fade away. He avoids, in fact, the logical conclusion to the kind of disorder he has introduced into his world-in-fiction, a world in which the distinction between appearance and reality has, from the reader's point of view, been lost forever. For if we cannot tell appearance from reality, if the two do become totally confused and impossible to distinguish, the only answer can be the one Twain eventually came to in his most pessimistic work, *The Mysterious Stranger*; that all is illusion, and nothing really exists.

In *Huckleberry Finn*, Twain does not yet reach this point of despair. By centering his action within the essentially balanced mind of the boy, Huck, he keeps his hold on reality and manages to convey his hold to the reader. But the main issue of the novel, between the way things seem and the way they are, is nevertheless one that trembles in the balance almost up to the final page.

Huckleberry Finn also gains its place as a world novel by its treatment of one of the most important events of life, the passage from youth into maturity. The novel is a novel of education. Its school is the school of life rather than of books, but Huck's education is all the more complete for that reason. Huck, like so many other great heroes of fiction—Candide, Tom Jones, Stephen Dedalus, to mention only a few—goes forth into life that he may learn. One of the central patterns of the novel is the progress of his learning.

Yet another theme which *Huckleberry Finn* shares with most of the world's great novels is that of man's obsession with the symbols of material wealth. The book opens with an account of the six thousand dollars Huck got from the robber's hoard and ends on the same note. Throughout the intervening pages gold is shown to be not only the mainspring of most human action, but usually the only remedy mankind can offer to atone for the many hurts they are forever inflicting on one another. And as Mr. Lionel Trilling has remarked, in a certain sense all fiction is ultimately about money.

The world novel may also convey a total vision of the nation or people from which it takes its origin. It not only addresses the world in a language which is uniquely the language of that nation or people, but it brings before the view of the world at large many character types which are especially national. In *Huckleberry Finn* we recognize in Jim, in the Duke and the Dauphin, in Aunt Sally, and in Huck himself, typically American figures whom Twain has presented for inspection by the world's eye. *Huckleberry Finn* gains much of its justification as a world novel from the fact that it is an intensely American novel as well.

II

In his essay on "The Poetic Principle" Poe remarks that "no very long poem will ever be popular again." In part, no doubt, Poe bases this remark on his own special definition of poetry. But he is also recognizing that during the eighteenth and nineteenth centuries the epic poem was gradually dying out as a literary form. Or, to be more precise, it was gradually merging with another form, the novel. Much of the poetic form of the epic came from the requirements of oral rendition; with the invention of printing, these requirements vanished. More and more writers gradually turned to prose fiction as the appropriate form to accomplish what had once been accomplished in the epic poem. Some novelists, such as Fielding or Scott, drew quite consciously on epic tradition; other novelists and novels, by a more indirect drawing on tradition, took over some of the qualities originally associated with epic poetry.

One quality of the epic poem is simply scope. Some novels confine themselves to treating exhaustively and analytically a limited segment of life. But others seem to be constantly trying to gather all life into their pages and to say, within a single story, all the important things that need to be said. Such novels derive much of their strength from the epic tradition, and *Huckleberry Finn* is such a novel. It has geographical scope. It ranges down the length of the great river and cuts through the center of a whole nation. As it does so, it gains further scope by embracing all levels of society, from the lowest to the highest. And it has the added scope of its own varying qualities, ranging from high comedy to low farce, from the poetic tranquility of life on the raft to the mob violence and human depravity always waiting on the shore.

Epic poetry gives literary form to the national destiny of the people for whom it is written. *Huckleberry Finn* gives literary form to many aspects of the national destiny of the American people. The theme of travel and adventure is characteristically American, and in Twain's day it was still a reality of everyday life. The country was still very much on the move, and during the novel Huck is moving with it. Huck's movements also embody a desire to escape from the constrictions of civilized society. Such a desire is of course not uniquely American, but during the nineteenth century Americans took it and made it their own. The American of that time could always say, as did Huck at the very end of the story, "I reckon I got to light out for the territory ahead of the rest, because Aunt Sally she's going to adopt me and sivilize me, and I can't stand it. I been there before."

The epic hero is usually an embodiment of some virtue or virtues valued highly by the society from which he has sprung. Huck has many such virtues. He holds a vast store of practical knowledge which makes itself felt everywhere in the story. He knows the river and how to deal with it; and he knows mankind and how to deal with it. And he has the supreme American virtue of never being at a loss for words. In fact Huck, though he still keeps some of the innocence and naiveté of youth, has much in common with one of the greatest epic heroes, Odysseus, the practical man. Jim also has some of the qualities of an epic hero. He has strength and courage, and he possesses the supreme virtue of epic poetry, loyalty. It is part of Twain's irony that in Huck and Jim we have, in one sense, the two halves of an epic hero. In Huck, the skill and canniness; in Jim, the strength and simple loyalty.

In the society along the shore we see traces of other epic values, values which have survived from a more primitive world. The Grangerford-Shepherdson feud strikes the modern reader as a senseless mess, but as Huck says, "There ain't a coward amongst them Shepherdsons—not a one. And there ain't no cowards amongst the Grangerfords either." Huck sees the essential folly behind this courage, but the reader, one degree further removed from the harsh reality, is allowed the luxury of a double vision. Similarly, Colonel Sherburn, destroying a lynching mob merely by the courage of his presence, illustrates another epic theme, the bravery of one against many.

One final quality which *Huckleberry Finn* derives from its epic ancestry is its poetry. The novel is full of poetry. Not just the passages of lyric description, which mark a pause between the main actions and give a heightened and more literary tone just as they often did in the traditional epic, but also the many similes and turns of speech Huck uses, which, if they are not quite Homeric, are certainly unforgettable. And much of the exaggerated language of the frontier world, one not far removed in kind from that of the primitive migrations, is also a natural part of the epic style.

III

Allegory may be defined simply as the representation of one thing in the form of another. A second definition, more germane to literature, is that allegory is a process by which the spiritual is embodied in the physical. To go one step further, the main purpose of allegory is somehow to embody a spiritual action in a physical action. By making a suitable physical object stand for some metaphysical one, or at least for one which cannot be contained in the terms of normal, everyday life, the writer carries out one of the main purposes of all art, which is to bring to its audience, through the representation of real objects, an awareness and knowledge which transcend the limitations of such reality. Allegory, that is, deals primarily with matters of the spirit.

This assumption helps to explain why the great allegories deal either with a physical journey or a physical conflict or both. For a spiritual change, when embodied allegorically, will take the form of a meaningful physical journey through symbolic space. And a spiritual conflict, when embodied allegorically, will take the form of a real physical conflict between significant forces, each of them representing some metaphysical quality.

Although all novels are in a certain sense descended from *Don Quixote*, it is also true that in another sense all novels, and especially English ones, are descended from Bunyan's *Pilgrim's Progress*. The main difference between the allegorical novel as we know it today and Bunyan's narrative of the human soul is that whereas *Pilgrim's Progress* we have an allegory that tends to turn into a novel, in most modern instances we have a novel that tends to turn into an allegory. As the author, whether he be Melville or Mann or Twain, develops and elaborates his original materials, he may become aware of certain meaningful connections which are tending to establish themselves between the physical objects and the physical narrative he is describing and the related spiritual values and conflicts. Drawing on a tradition which has existed for a long time in literature and which is a natural part of the artistic process in any form, the author finds himself writing allegory. And this is what happened to Mark Twain. Writing as he was a great novel, his masterpiece in fact, he organized and related certain physical materials to certain metaphysical conditions so that their relationship became meaningful in a special way—became, in short, allegory.

Huckleberry Finn is the story of a journey, a real journey. If we are to find any meaning in Huck's journey beyond the literal level, we must seek it first in the medium through which Huck journeys, in the great river down which he drifts during much of the story. And Huck's movements take on at least the external form of a basic symbolic pattern, one seen in such poems as Shelley's *Alastor*, Arnold's *The Future*, and Rimbaud's *Bateau Ivre*, a pattern stated most directly in *Prometheus Unbound*, "My soul is an enchanted boat." Implicit in this pattern is the suggestion that the river journey can have a distinctly metaphysical quality, that it can be, in fact, a journey of the soul as well as of the body. This suggestion is not at all arbitrary. Of all forms of physical progression, that of drifting downstream in a boat, or on a raft, is the most passive one possible. The mind under such conditions is lulled, as Huck's mind is, into the illusion that it has lost all contact with reality and is drifting bodilessly through a world of sleep and of dreams. Thus the nakedness of Huck and Jim when they are alone on the raft becomes a symbol of how they have shucked off the excrescences of the real world, their clothes, and have come as close as possible to the world of the spirit.

All journeys, even allegorical ones, must have a goal. What is the goal of Huck's journey? We find the answer in what happens while Huck and Jim float down the river. The pattern is, very simply, one of an ever-increasing engagement of the world of the raft, of the spirit, with the world of the shore, of reality. As the book progresses, more and more Huck tells about events that take place on the banks, and less and less he tells about those that take place out on the river. No matter how hard Huck and Jim try to escape, the real world is always drawing them back into it. Finally, in the Duke and the Dauphin, themselves fleeing for the moment from the harsh reality of the river's shores, the real world invades the world of the raft, and the latter loses forever the dream-like and idyllic quality it has often had for the two voyagers. The climax of Huck's lyric praise of the river comes significantly just before this mood is shattered forever by the arrival of the Duke and Dauphin.

Parallel to this pattern of the ever-increasing engagement of the world of the shore with that of the raft is a pattern which begins with Huck's pretended death, a death which is actual to all the world but Huck and Jim. The symbolic fact of his death accomplished, Huck must find an identity with which he can face the real world. His assumptions of various such identities forms a significant pattern. The various masks he assumes, starting with that of a girl, as far removed from the reality as possible, gradually draw back nearer the truth. Huck's final disguise, as Tom Sawyer, is only slightly removed from his real self. When he is about to reveal this real self and is instead taken for Tom, Huck almost recognizes the meaning of his journey. For he says to himself, "But if they was joyful, it warn't nothing to what I was; for it was like being born again, I was so glad to find out who I was."

This, then, is the allegory of *Huckleberry Finn*. Dying symbolically almost at the opening of the novel, Huck journeys through the world of the spirit, ever working out a pattern of increasing involvement with the world of reality and with his own self, both cast aside at the beginning of the journey. Only when he is finally forced to assume this real self in the eyes of the world, through the sudden arrival of Aunt Polly, is he allowed to learn the all-important truth Jim has kept from him throughout the novel, that his Pap, "ain't comin back no mo." We cannot say that Huck has undergone a total initiation and is now fully prepared to take on adulthood, but neither can we doubt that he has undergone a knowledgeful and maturing experience. And at the end of the story he is about to undertake another journey, this time to the west, in search of further experience and further knowledge.

In this essay, Lane evaluates *Huckleberry Finn* by examining it according to several clearly stated criteria: the significance of its themes, its scope, and its allegorical pattern. By analyzing the novel according to these criteria, the author is able to show us why the novel is a great one.

WRITING STRATEGIES

Part of writing an evaluation is choosing words that accurately communicate the judgment you are making. Creating a list of possible words to use to make the judgment can be helpful. Write down the subject of the evaluation and use free association (putting down on paper whatever comes to mind) to create a list of words that express your judgment.

Consider these questions as you create an evaluation.

- How is the subject to be evaluated presented to the reader? (What other patterns of organization are used?)
- What judgment or judgments are you making about the subject?
- What criteria are you using to make the judgment?
- How can you defend the criteria?
- How does your presentation fit the characteristics of your primary purpose?

PROCESS
Part 3

Ideas
Details
Focus
Refinement

Ideas

The writing process usually begins before you actually start putting words down. Before you can do anything else, you must have an idea. Depending on the occasion that has prompted your writing, your idea may take one of two different forms: it may be rather vague and undefined, or it may be fairly well focused on a general subject or even on a specific topic. Your use of the techniques suggested in this chapter will vary depending on how far along you are in shaping your topic. If your idea is vague and undefined, you will probably need to use a number of the strategies suggested in this chapter to define the subject a little more clearly. These strategies include using techniques of free association, working with your journal, and doing background research.

If you have already decided on a general subject, you will need to narrow the the scope of the subject so that it is a manageable topic. As your topic becomes more clearly defined, you may still use the techniques suggested in this chapter, but in more definitive way. For instance, you would probably start a free association activity with an explicit focus in mind. Similarly, research, rather than being concerned with general background information, would become more precise in its focus.

FREE ASSOCIATION

One of the most straightforward ways to get ideas is by using one of several different free association activities. These activities allow you to gain access to the creative flow of ideas in your mind.

BRAINSTORMING

Brainstorming is the most unstructured of all free association activities. It can be done individually or in a group. (Group brainstorming has the advantage of bringing a broad range of perspectives to bear on a topic.) Anything goes in brainstorming. You may jot down words and phrases or even draw pictures and doodle. No possible avenue of exploration should be rejected. Brainstorming will open up your mind to whatever resources you have available. After you have made some notes (10 minutes is usually enough), you can go back and restructure, or you can start over again and explore the subject from a different perspective.

LISTING

Listing is a bit more structured than brainstorming. The advantage is that you can generate quite a lot of relevant information quickly. The list can be totally random, or it can begin from a general subject, of even a specific topic.

An Example of Listing on the Topic of Bird Watching

colors
feathers
shapes of birds—pelicans, woodpeckers…
drab colored birds
camouflage
brightly colored birds
mating
feathers for flight
feathers for warmth
structure of the body
how they fly
songs
identifying birds—by songs, by shape, by flight
field guides
notebooks
observing—how to observe, what to look for
habitat—trees, water, ground
habits—breeding, migration, nesting

ecology—range
distribution of birds over the world
classification of birds
evolution

MAPPING

Mapping (also called clustering) allows you to explore your ideas graphically. You simply put an idea down in the middle of a page and then
begin to put down associated ideas around it. You can show a number
of relationships between the ideas on the page by drawing lines to
show connections.

An Example of Mapping on the Topic of Bird Watching

FREEWRITING

Freewriting is, in effect, "talking on paper." It is an attempt to capture in written form the natural, spontaneous flow of conversation. As with other forms of free association, you follow wherever the associations take you, but freewriting is in sentence form. Often, freewriting can open you up to the flow of ideas as no other technique can because freewriting stimulates thinking in terms that can be translated immediately into writing. It can also be a kind of "warmup" to prepare you for writing a draft, or it may even be a part of the initial draft itself. Freewriting is such a versatile technique that you can use it anytime you get stuck and need to start the flow of words again.

An Example of Freewriting

When I was a child the world of nature was a playground and a context for the world of fantasy that was my main preoccupation. I romped with playmates, both real and imaginary, and had imaginary adventures with toys of all kinds. I'm thinking about my stuffed animals and my legos and my action figures. It was a time of freedom and happiness. Later I became aware of nature and found that the natural world was as fascinating as the imaginary world I had created.

The example of freewriting above illustrates what happens when a writer simply lets associations occur freely. But freewriting can also be more focused. Focused freewriting lets you get at your ideas about a specific topic. You begin the process with a focus, a thesis or a claim, or a sentence from a previous freewriting activity. You then follow the same pattern as with freewriting discussed above by simply letting your mind go and putting together the associations you have. What makes focused freewriting different from unfocused freewriting is that you keep your focus always in mind. If you begin to go too far afield, you will need to come back to the focus.

An Example of Focused Freewriting on the Topic of the Outdoors

I have always been interested in the outdoors. As a child most of my play time was spent outdoors, weather permitting, and even sometimes when it didn't, much to Mom's dismay. As I grew up the kind of outdoor activity changed. In contrast to the wild, exuberant unstructured play of childhood, I began as an adolescent to enjoy more purposeful activities like fishing and hunting. Now as an adult I have discovered other outdoor pastimes, less aggressive. These turn out to be both physical and intellectual. Like, last year I took up bird watching. I have found that bird watching fulfills my desire for enjoying the world of nature, while, at the same time allowing me to assemble a body of knowledge about that world.

Focused freewriting can be repeated again and again by looping back to another focus. Simply identify a new focus and begin again. The following is an example of a focused freewriting activity that begins with the sentence *last year I took up bird watching* taken from the previous exercise.

Last year I took up bird watching. I guess I have always been a bird watcher to some degree. It is something children do naturally. When we were children, we didn't find it necessary to label ourselves as much as we do when we are adults. I find it necessary to call myself a bird watcher, perhaps as a way of committing to the activity and justifying myself in doing it. If you buy binoculars and a field guide and tramp around in the woods looking for birds, then you must be a bird watcher. I mean, I kind of feel guilty spending all this time and money—so I better have a good reason—like being a bird watcher. But the activity itself should, and does for most people who do it, come from an abiding interest in and a curiosity about the natural environment. Finding and identifying birds in some ways is an excuse for indulging an interest in natural science. For some people it is a hobby; for others, a sport; and for still others, almost a religion. Like Bill who's making a pilgrimage to Alaska to see a bird he's never seen. But bird watchers all share a common bond—a fascination with the working of nature, and birds are perhaps the most fascinating of the earth's fauna: after all, they can actually fly.

You could keep going with this kind of activity by identifying a phrase in the previous exercise and using it as the focus of a new freewriting activity.

THE JOURNAL

Another source of ideas is the journal. Many writers keep personal journals in which they record reactions to what is happening to them, ideas of interest, and explorations of the self. The section on the personal perspective of expressive writing in Chapter 1 explains the characteristics of the journal.

Keeping a personal journal will allow you to experiment with style, explore ideas for your writing assignments, and become more comfortable with writing. Even if your writing instructor doesn't require you to keep a journal, you should consider doing it on your own. You may be surprised at what you discover.

RESEARCH

If you are searching for ideas, casual exploration can help you uncover things that interest you and help you shape your ideas. Watching television, reading the newspaper, surfing the net, or simply talking with friends can all be sources of material to include in your writing projects. This kind of background research can be used as a stimulus for free association or for journal writing. It may help you remember things that you had forgotten. So even if your topic is personal in nature, some background research may be beneficial.

If you already have a subject or a topic in mind, your research will be more focused than it would be if you were doing background research. Gathering information through focused research enables you to explore ideas systematically that are relevant to your topic. Some general sources, like encyclopedias and almanacs, may give you an initial overview of your topic, but chances are you will need to consult other sources, like books on the topic and articles in periodicals.

Research may simply help you understand your topic better, or it may become an integral part of your composition. How you use research information will, of course, depend on your topic, your purpose, and your audience.

NARROWING A SUBJECT

When you first get an idea, you may have a subject that is too broad. You will need to narrow it to a topic that is manageable. Usually, this means making the topic more specific and concrete. You may discover ways to narrow your topic while you are doing free association activities, as you are doing research, or while you are writing in your journal.

Creating a ladder can help you narrow a subject that is too general. Begin with the general subject and list below it more specific and concrete topics.

AN EXAMPLE

- The Environment
- Pollution
- Air Pollution
- Sources of Air Pollution

Each related idea above is more specific than the one above it. *The environment* is a broad concept that suggests related ideas like the general subject *pollution*. *Air pollution* is more specific than *pollution* and more general than *sources of air pollution*.

Details

O nce you have a manageable topic, you will need to add details to it. You may not always know in advance that the topic is manageable until you begin working with it by generating detail. If it is still too broad, you may need to go back and try to narrow it more.

In this part of the writing process, you will be interested in translating your ideas into words. You may have already begun to do that if you used freewriting and journal entries as a way of exploring a topic that were discussed in the previous chapter. Other techniques discussed in this chapter such as asking questions and using specific kinds of elaboration are also helpful techniques that will enable you to generate details.

QUESTIONS

In one sense, writing is answering questions that arise naturally in relation to the topic you are considering. Journalists' questions and logical questions can help you create content for your paper. Your response to questions will determine in part the pattern of organization you will use.

JOURNALISTIC QUESTIONS

In putting together news stories, journalists often rely on a questioning technique to make sure that they have all the facts necessary. They ask who? what? when? where? how? and why?

These questions are especially helpful when your topic is an informative narrative because they will help you achieve the comprehensiveness usually required in informative writing. In other words, if you answer these six questions, you can be sure that all essential information will be included in your paper.

LOGICAL QUESTIONS

Logical questions are those that grow naturally out of the topic. You will notice that the questions in the following lists suggest a number of the patterns of organization discussed in Chapters 5–8.

A Person (e.g., a relative or a celebrity)
What does he or she look like?
What does he or she do?
How does he or she behave?
What is his or her personality like?
What is unusual or notable about him or her?

A Place (e.g., a city or a landmark)
Where is it?
What are its characteristics?
What is it similar to?
How is it unusual?
How old is it?

A Thing (e.g., a car or a painting)
What is it made of?
What are its parts?
How is it used?
What is it similar to?
Where did it come from?

An Event (e.g., an athletic event or the French Revolution)
Where did it happen?
When did it happen?
What happened before and after it?
What caused it?
What is its significance?

A Process (e.g., cooking or working out)
What are its steps?
What is it similar to?
How difficult is it?
What causes it to happen?
What are its consequences?

An Abstraction (e.g., freedom or justice)
What is its definition?
What is its significance?
What is it similar to?
What forms does it take?
What is it related to?

A Problem (e.g., overpopulation or drug abuse)
What causes it?
Why does it occur?
Who or what does it affect?
What are some related problems?
What are some possible solutions?

QUESTIONS ABOUT CATEGORIES

Classification allows you to explore a topic by asking questions about the categories related to your topic. By shifting the basis of classification, you can very often come up with other patterns of classification that you may not have considered initially. (See the discussion of basis of classification in Chapter 5.)

Tree diagrams are useful tools for exploring topics that are organized by classification. The three diagrams that follow are interconnected and illustrate how classification can be used to explore a topic. Look at them and study the connections among them.

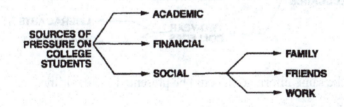

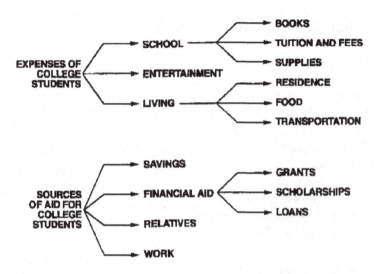

THE OUTLINE

The outline is a common way of representing classification systems. For example, the topic "Kinds of Post-Secondary Education" could be represented by the following tree diagram.

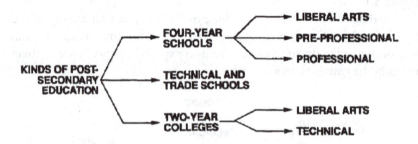

Or the same information could be presented as an outline.

   I. Universities and Colleges
      A. Liberal Arts
      B. Pre-Professional
      C. Professional

  II. Business, Industrial, Technical, and Trade Schools

III. Two-Year Colleges
      A. Liberal Arts
      B. Technical

ELABORATION

Elaboration means that you need to make sure that you have said enough about the topic. There are four ways that you can add depth to any given piece of writing: reiteration, generalization, contrast, and exemplification.

Consider the following sentence:

Air pollution adversely affects almost everybody.

Any sentence that follows it will elaborate in one of four ways mentioned above.

The following sentence is a reiteration or restatement of the same idea:

It creates a problem for our society.

Notice that this sentence is at roughly the same level of generality as the first one. It simply restates in other words, the same idea. This kind of elaboration will not produce the kind of detail that you need in most situations, so it has limitations.

Another way to elaborate on the idea in the first sentence is by generalization:

All environmental problems create problems for our society.

This sentence is more general than the first one, but it too has limitations as a method of elaboration. Usually the most general statement in a paragraph or in a paper will be the main idea and, as a result, will need to be developed by statements that follow it. General statements like this frequently appear at the beginning of a paper as part of the introduction or perhaps at the end as part of the conclusion.

A third way to elaborate on an idea is by contrast, as in the following sentence:

However, the problem is usually worse in large cities.

Developing by contrast takes the ideas off in a different direction.

The fourth way to elaborate on an idea is by exemplification, as in this sentence:

On days when the levels are high, especially in the summer, some people cannot engage in outdoor activities.

This sentence is more specific than the first one. It gives a specific example of the idea in the first sentence. Exemplification is the most common method of elaborating detail. Writing that moves back and forth between general and specific statements is usually easier for the reader to follow.

RESEARCH

At this stage in the process if your paper includes research, you will need to identify specific sources that you intend to use in your paper. You will also need to look for information in those sources that you can incorporate into your paper. Identifying possible quotations and paraphrases will help you decide if you need to do additional research, identify more sources, and collect more information. At this point the process is still quite fluid and you can still change directions if the initial draft proves to be unmanageable.

For some investigative topics, in addition to using secondary sources, like books, periodicals and websites, you may find it helpful to generate information from primary sources. In particular, interviews or surveys provide original research information that is unavailable from any other sources.

PRINT SOURCES

When you are researching a topic, it is important that you use a wide variety of sources. These sources could include books, articles from periodicals, or websites. A good place to begin looking for these sources is your college or local library, so make sure to plan a visit and talk to a librarian. Consulting a librarian about your research project will probably save you a lot of time and effort because librarians will be able to direct you to books and other sources relevant to your research topic. Your librarian will be able to show you how to use the library catalogue to find books and locate them using their call numbers on the library shelves.

Other than books, some of the most common sources that yield information for a research topic are articles from journals. Most libraries subscribe to databases that would allow you to find articles from newspapers, periodicals, and academic or technical journals. Some examples of these databases are *Proquest, Academic Search Complete, JSTOR,* and *SciTech.* Databases organized by subject too can be found on your college library's website. However, one of the challenges one faces is searching through these databases to find appropriate sources for your topic. You can search the databases by using what's called a "keyword" search. A keyword is a term pertaining to your topic. For example, if you are researching a topic associated with air pollution, appropriate keyword searches would include terms like *smog, emissions, particulates,* etc. This is where talking to a librarian about your topic and asking for help with using the database would reduce the time spent searching for the appropriate sources for your topic.

Once you have identified the sources you want to use for your project, the librarian would be able to save the call numbers and bibliographic information, so that you have easy access to the sources you've identified for your project.

INTERVIEWS

Interviewing (gathering information from a single person) is an established method of collecting primary data on a topic. It is still used widely because of its flexibility. An interview is usually more informal than other methods of data collection and so allows an interviewer to elaborate on a question that is not clear.

Unstructured interviews provide the freedom to explore a topic and allow for some spontaneity in following up on questions. Such an approach is often valuable at the beginnings of a research project when the researcher is trying to determine what questions should be addressed in a study.

Structured interviews (often used if there is more than one informant) require a well-defined format. As a result, they can be somewhat more formal the unstructured interviews. This approach will yield consistent information that can be readily analyzed and incorporated into a final study.

SURVEYS

Surveys (or questionnaires) are a more efficient method of gathering research information from groups of people than interviewing, which can be time consuming. Surveys offer the advantage of allowing the researcher to gather information in a form that can be easily converted into statistics. However, the questions used in a survey must be carefully constructed so that respondents can understand without confusion. In addition, the number of questions asked must be carefully considered.

THE INITIAL DRAFT

An initial draft is a first attempt to put ideas into words in a way that roughly approximates what the final paper will be like. It may begin as a freewriting activity, but will probably be a bit more unified.

As you write the rough draft, you will become aware of an emerging main idea. Depending on the purpose, the main idea will be a self-definition (expressive writing), a theme (literary writing), a claim (persuasive writing), or a thesis (referential writing). (See the discussion of purpose in the introductory chapter.) If the main idea is actually stated in the paper, it will be in the form of a generalization.

The nature of an initial draft will vary from person to person and from paper to paper for the same writer. At times an initial draft will be more highly developed than at others depending on how familiar the writer is with the topic and under what circumstances the paper is being produced.

AN EXAMPLE

Take a look at the following passage:

> Look at the problems with the environment. Like air pollution. Air pollution adversely affects almost everybody. Just look at the smog that covers our cities like a blanket. It's stifling. Smoke stacks are belching out toxic wastes. On bad smog days, I can hardly breath. Fish are dying in the oceans. We should really try to do something about it before it destroys the earth. I mean, this is a serious problem that many people aren't even aware of. Acid rain kills trees in the forests.

This passage from an initial draft represents the writer's effort to get something down in writing. The writer reflects some personal experiences by saying, "I can hardly breath," as well as showing values by saying, "I mean, this is a serious problem." These examples reflect the writer's initial conception of purpose. The style is natural and conversational, and so we might assume that the writing is going to be controlled by an expressive purpose. However, a persuasive intent has caused the writer to characterize the issue as a "problem" and to make an appeal to "do something about it." An awareness of the potential audience is revealed by the sentence, "Air pollution adversely affects almost everybody."

Focus

Although you may engage in focusing activities at all stages of of the writing process, usually you will do more of it in the intermediate drafts. After all, you can't really focus ideas, structure details, and clarify points if you don't have something to work with. This focusing can be explained by three concepts: clarity, unity, and coherence.

CLARITY

Clarity means that the individual sentences and the ideas presented are clear to the reader. As you are drafting, especially the initial draft, you may create sentences that are not as clear as they could be. As you are revising your work, you will want to make sure that all sentences are as clear as you can make them.

Although you may need to consult a handbook in order to figure out how to solve some problems, often you will be able to see the solutions by simply reading your work aloud. Sometimes we fall into traps by trying to impress the reader with words and phrases we may not feel comfortable with. Try first to communicate your ideas clearly and simply. Save stylistic niceties for later drafts once you have said what you want to say.

UNITY

Unity means that everything included in a piece of writing relates to the main idea (the self-definition in expressive writing, the theme in literary writing, the claim in persuasive writing, or the thesis in referential writing). Any sentence that isn't related to the main idea in some way will distract the reader.

In addition, each paragraph in a piece of writing will have a main idea, sometimes called a topic sentence. Each sentence in the paragraph should be related to that topic sentence.

Notice how the writer of the following passage maintains unity:

> That sandwich man I'd replaced had little chance of getting his job back. I went bellowing up and down those train aisles. I sold sandwiches, coffee, candy, cake, and ice cream as fast as the railroad's commissary department could supply them. It didn't take me a week to learn that all you had to do was give white people a show and they'd buy anything you offered them. It was like popping your shoeshine rag. The dining car waiters and Pullman porters knew it too, and they faked their Uncle Tomming to get bigger tips. We were in that world of Negroes who are both servants and psychologists, aware that white people are so obsessed with their own importance that they will pay liberally, even dearly, for the impression of being catered to and entertained.
>
> —Malcolm X, with the assistance of Alex Haley,
> *The Autobiography of Malcolm X*

The first six sentences in this passage lead up to and contribute to our understanding of the paragraph's main idea stated in the last sentence.

COHERENCE

Coherence means that the sentences are connected to each other in a natural way and that the movement from one sentence to the next is smooth and easy for the reader to follow. Coherence can be increased in three ways: by using transitional words and phrases, by using pronouns, and by repeating key words and phrases.

TRANSITIONS

Transitional words and phrases show relationships between sentences and ideas. Typically, they appear at the beginning of a sentence and indicate what kind of relationship it has to sentences that preceded it. Some commonly used transitions and their functions follow:

> To indicate an addition: *again, and, also, finally, furthermore, in addition, likewise, moreover, next, second, similarly, then*

To introduce a contrast: *but, conversely, however, instead, or, nevertheless, nor, on the contrary, on the other hand, still*

To mark a conclusion: *accordingly, as a result, consequently, in conclusion, in other words, then, therefore, thus*

To introduce an example: *for example, for instance, in other words, namely, that is, thus*

Notice how transitions are used in the following example:

In all our literary experience there are two kinds of response. There is the direct experience of the work itself, while we're reading a book or seeing a play, especially for the first time. The experience is uncritical, or rather pre-critical, so it's not infallible. If our experience is limited, we can be roused to enthusiasm or carried away by something that we can later see to have been second-rate or even phony. Then there is the conscious, critical response we make after we've finished reading or left the theatre, where we compare what we've experienced with other things of the same kind, and form a judgment of value and proportion on it. This critical response, with practice, gradually makes our pre-critical responses more sensitive and accurate, or improves our taste, as we say. But behind our responses to individual works, there's a bigger response to our literary experience as a whole, as a total possession.

—Northrop Frye, *The Educated Imagination*

Frye has used three transitions (*so, then,* and *but*) to help maintain coherence. Especially important is his use of the word *then* to mark the second of the two kinds of response.

PRONOUNS

Pronouns will help you achieve coherence in papers because they tie together the pronouns and the words they refer back to.

Notice how pronouns are used to create coherence in the following passage:

No matter how far-ranging some of the mental probes that man has philosophically devised, by his own created nature he is forced to hold the specious and emerging present and transform it into words. The words are startling in their immediate effectiveness, but at the same time they are always finally imprisoning because man has constituted himself a prison keeper. He does so out of no conscious intention, but because for immediate purposes he has created an unnatural world of his own, which he calls the cultural world, and in which he feels at home. It defines his needs and allows him to lay a small immobilizing spell upon the nearer portions of his universe. Nevertheless, it transforms that universe into a cosmic prison house which is no sooner mapped than man feels its inadequacy and his own.

—Loren Eiseley, *The Invisible Pyramid*

In this passage Eiseley uses twelve personal pronouns to refer to the word *man*. He uses the word *it* three times, once to refer to the word *present* and twice to refer to the word *world*. Finally, he uses the words *they* and *their* to refer to the word *words*.

REPETITION

Although the repetition of words can be monotonous if used clumsily, when used skillfully, repetition can help achieve coherence.

Notice how repetition is used in the following passage:

Our lives are completely dominated by the fundamental rhythms. My breathing, my pulse, my unconscious processes of digestion, my hearing, my eyesight, my sense of touch, my speech, my thought—all are matters of rhythm. Life is governed by the rhythms. The female animal has rhythmic periods of fertility. The sex act of fertilization is rhythmic. Birth is accomplished in rhythmic labor. And all the rhythmic processes in us, pulse to speech, are a part of growth, maturity, life's continuation. When they cease, a unit of life has come to its physical end. When my pulse stops, I die. But my progeny, in whom the rhythm continues, live on, the next step, the next beat, in the rhythm of life.

—Hal Borland, *What We Save Now*

Borland uses the repetition of forms of the word *rhythm* nine times. In this passage it does not seem to be excessive, but rather allows the reader to see the connections more clearly.

AN EXAMPLE

Notice how the following passage illustrates all three techniques of achieving coherence:

> The good educator is very serious but also very sensible. And somewhere in his soul there is a saving lightness. He understands, to begin with, the meaning of a recent remark: "Not everything can be learned." Some things are never taught; they are simply known. Other things cannot in the nature of things be known, either by student or by teacher. And then there is that endless series of knowable things only a few of which can be bestowed upon the student during the fragment of his life he spends in school.
>
> —Mark Van Doren, *Liberal Education*

The personal pronouns *his* and *he* refer back to the word *educator*. The phrases *some things* and *other things* are a repetition of *everything*. In addition, Van Doren uses the transitions *and* and *and then* to show relationships between his ideas.

RESEARCH

At this point in the writing process, if you are writing a paper in which you are using sources, you will be ready to include some quotations and paraphrases in your drafts.

The information given below should be used as a guideline when using longer direct quotations and indirect quotations in your essays. The following passage from Lauriat Lane, Jr.'s "Why Huckleberry Finn's a Great World Novel," which can be found in Chapter 8 of this book, will be used as an example to demonstrate different methods for quoting and paraphrasing:

> Allegory may be defined simply as the representation of one thing in the form of another. A second definition, more germane to literature, is that allegory is a process by which the spiritual is embodied in the physical. To go one step further, the main purpose of allegory is somehow to embody a spiritual action in a physical action. By making a suitable physical object stand for some metaphysical one, or at least for one which cannot be contained in the terms of normal everyday

life, the writer carries out one of the main purposes of all art, which is to bring to its audience, through the representation of real objects, an awareness and knowledge which transcend the limitations of such reality. Allegory, that is, deals primarily with matters of the spirit.

EMBEDDING THE QUOTATION

When using quotations, you must try to incorporate the source material smoothly and elegantly into your own sentences. One way to ensure that your quotation is integrated nicely into your writing is to embed the quotation between an introductory phrase and an interpretation. Failing to properly introduce and interpret the quotation will make your writing seem choppy and unclear.

Begin by introducing the quotation with a "signal phrase." The signal phrase provides context for the quote and also indicates to the reader that a quotation is forthcoming. After writing the signal phrase, enclose the quote within quotation marks making sure to cite the page number in parentheses at the end of the sentence. Next, interpret the quotation to justify your rationale for using this piece of evidence from the text as in the following example.

> In his essay, Lauriat Lane, Jr. provides an explanation for the allegory's role in the world of literature: "the main purpose of allegory is somehow to embody a spiritual action in a physical action" (223). He asserts that the real function of the allegory is to convey abstract truths through the use of the commonplace and the familiar.

> If you can make your point by using just the signal phrase and the quotation, then you do not need to follow up with an interpretation.

USING SHORT QUOTATIONS

Integrate short quotations directly into your sentences. You can embed the phrase between an introduction and follow-up phrase. Your voice guiding us to an author's opinion can be quite effective, as long as you do not distort the original thought. You must then cite the page number in parentheses at the end of your sentence. Notice the following example.

> Lane suggests that the allegory addresses "matters of the spirit" through its use of the familiar and the commonplace (223).

USING LONG QUOTATIONS

Quotations longer than four lines should start on a new line and be indented 10 spaces. You do not use quotation marks when setting off longer indented quotations. Avoid using too many long quotations as a way of filling space in your paper. On occasion, however, longer quotations are necessary to present an author's complex point. This principle is illustrated by the following example.

> In his essay, "Why Huckleberry Finn's a Great World Novel" Lauriat Lane, Jr. addresses how allegories are used by writers to convey larger, more abstract truths about the human experience:
> By making a suitable physical object stand for some meta-physical one, or at least for one which cannot be contained in the terms of normal everyday life, the writer carries out one of the main purposes of all art, which is to bring to its audience, through the representation of real objects, an awareness and knowledge which transcend the limitations of such reality. Allegory, that is, deals primarily with matters of the spirit. (223)

ALTERING AND CONDENSING LONG QUOTATIONS

Sometimes long quotations can be edited and condensed. Doing this can actually make your writing more concise and elegant. The original quote can be altered as long as you correctly indicate to the reader the changes you have made to the actual quotation.

The two common techniques used by writers to alter quotations are through the use of square brackets and ellipses. Square brackets can be used to insert your own words and letters into the original quote. You can do this in order to preserve grammatical correctness when you integrate the quotation directly into your sentence. You can also condense a long quote by using ellipses to indicate that words were deleted from the original quotation. You must ensure, however, that your edited version is grammatically correct. Notice the following example.

> In his essay, Lauriat Lane, Jr. asserts that the true function of the allegory is the use of common everyday objects to convey to the reader larger and more abstract concerns: "By making a suitable physical object stand for some metaphysical one...the writer...bring[s] to [his or her] audience...an awareness and knowledge which transcend the limitations of such reality" (223).

PARAPHRASING

Paraphrasing is the method where you rewrite the source material in your own words. This is a very effective way to combine both the original evidence and your interpretation of the material into your own writing. Use this technique if you find that the source material cannot be quoted in a concise manner and if the longer indented quotation seems excessive and unnecessary. If you do paraphrase, however, you must cite the page number and include the author's name if you have not indicated it in a signal phrase. Paraphrasing is illustrate by the following example.

> Lauriat Lane Jr. in his essay, "Why Huckleberry Finn's a Great World Novel" tackles the idea that the allegory functions as a way for the writer to convey the larger, more abstract truths about the human experience. He begins by defining the allegory as simply a symbol, but then expands this definition into the realm of literature, where he characterizes the allegorical as a physical representation of a spiritual, more abstract notion. Lane sees the writer as fulfilling in the allegory one of the primary purposes of art: the ability to let the audience experience the profound in ordinary, commonplace objects and actions. Allegory, he emphasizes, broaches the metaphysical through the depiction of the materialistic (223).

INTERMEDIATE DRAFTS

Intermediate drafts, and there may be several of them, can be thought of as the essential building blocks that create the final product. Each time you do an intermediate draft, you will no doubt add something essential to the work, change what you have already written, or delete material altogether.

In intermediate drafts you may still be creating ideas and generating details as well as focusing what you have already done. If you do generate detail at this stage, it will probably take on a character different from the previously produced work in that it will in some way be related to that original material and will serve to make the work clearer, more unified, or more coherent.

AN EXAMPLE

Consider this revision of the previous draft in Chapter 10:

> Never before have we had such problems with the quality of our environment. Air pollution in particular affects all of us. For example, just look at the smog that covers cities like a blanket. It's stifling. Smoke stacks and exhaust pipes are belching out toxic wastes. On bad smog days, I can hardly breath. We should really try to do something about it before it destroys the earth. I mean, this is a serious problem that many people aren't even aware of. We should enact some laws that restrict the use of fossil fuels.

You will notice that this draft, in contrast to the one in Chapter 10, is more unified and more coherent. The ideas have been arranged into a more understandable pattern and the main idea, "We should enact some laws that restrict the use of fossil fuels" has been added to clarify the meaning. Because the main idea reflects a persuasive intent, the purpose has been made clearer by this more explicit statement. The phrase "exhaust pipes" has been added to make the statement about emissions more complete and more understandable. The second sentence was created by combining two sentences, thus giving more power and clarity to the idea that air pollution affects everybody. The addition of the phrase "for example" in the third sentence makes the passage more coherent. Two sentences from the previous draft that were not relevant to the topic, "Fish are dying in the oceans" and "Acid rain is killing trees in the forests," have been deleted. Leaving them in this part of paper would have distracted the reader from the main idea, which addresses air pollution only.

Refinement

U sually toward the end of the drafting process, but not exclusively, you will begin to refine the work. That is, you will begin to be more concerned about stylistic details than you were in earlier drafts. In this final revision of your work, you will make fewer changes in content. Rather you do a kind of fine tuning, making adjustments in the way you say what you have already decided you are going to say.

In some cases you will streamline what you have said by making the language used more economical. In other cases you will embellish by adding variety to sentence structure. Finally, you will need to be attentive to the requirements of mechanics, grammar, and usage that are appropriate to your writing project.

STYLE

When writers give special attention to language itself, regardless of the primary purpose of the writing, we often refer to that feature as style. For example, articles in newspapers and news magazines are usually more stylistically sophisticated than information that comes from a wire service reporting the basic facts of a story. Similarly, events recorded in expressive works like autobiographies or memoirs usually show more attention to stylistic considerations than do the same events reported in a journal or a diary. This attention to style results in writing that is more interesting and generally more pleasing to read than a collection of bare facts or random observations would be.

The discussions of economy and variety that follow will enable you to make some stylistic decisions about your work as you revise. Although that kind of refinement often comes at the end of the writing process, you may find that you will make use of some of these principles while you are working on initial drafts.

ECONOMY

Sometimes you say too much in the early drafts and the extraneous material will need to be cut away. In a sense, this process is the opposite of elaboration. You may have already done some deleting in the intermediate drafts, but in the final draft, it becomes even more important.

Some words communicate very little information and so should be cut. You will want to become sensitive to words that take up space but contribute little to either the meaning or the readability of what you have written. The following suggestions will help you make your work more concise.

NOUNS

- You should try to figure out ways to eliminate vague nouns like these: *area, aspect, concept, condition, consideration, factor, indication, infrastructure, parameter, phase,* and *situation.*

- You will make your work more readable if you eliminate nouns created from verbs. When these nouns create wordy verb phrases, replace them with the original verbs.

  give consideration to: consider
  give encouragement to: encourage
  is reflective of: reflects
  is representative of: represents
  make adjustments: adjust
  make an approximation of: approximate

MODIFIERS

- Other wordy phrases can also be replaced by single words.

  at the present time: now
  due to the fact that: because
  during the course of: during
  for the simple reason that: because
  in a very real sense: truly
  in spite of the fact: although

in view of the fact: since
on the part of: by
owing to the fact that: because

- Some modifiers that carry very little meaning can usually be eliminated from your drafts: *absolutely, basically, certainly, definitely, incredibly, intensely, just, of course, perfectly, positively, quite, really, simply,* and *very.*
- A cliché is an overused expression. They were once original metaphors, but they have now lost that freshness. They should be eliminated from your drafts. Some examples follow: *quick as a cat, strong as an ox, sly as a fox,* and *green as grass.*

VERBS

When you revise, you will find that in some cases simply changing verbs can make a real difference in the impact of sentences. In particular, you should pay attention to forms of the verb *to be (be, been, being, am, is, are, was,* and *were).* *To be* verbs create passive voice, linking constructions, and the progressive tense. These three forms have legitimate uses and certainly writers use them all the time. But, as a general rule, eliminating *to be* verbs will make your writing more effective.

The following sentence is written in the passive voice:

Stress can be reduced by exercise.

The more straightforward active voice is probably better:

Exercise can reduce stress.

Occasionally, the passive may be preferable if, for example, the receiver of the action is more important than the doer of the action, as in the following sentence:

The house has just been remodeled.

The passive may also be preferable if the action itself is more important than the doer of the action, as in this sentence:

Talking is not allowed during the performance.

Look carefully at each *to be* verb as you proofread. If you don't have a specific reason for keeping it, you will probably improve the sentence by changing it.

VARIETY

A monotonous presentation will make any piece of writing more difficult for the reader, so it is important to for you to consider ways of creating variety. You can accomplish this in two ways, by varying sentence length and by varying sentence structure.

LENGTH

Readers can begin to lose track of the content if the sentences in a paragraph are all the same length.

Notice the following paragraph:

> Pollution is a problem. It seems to be getting worse. Cars are a major source of air pollution. There are many cars in the world. They are increasing in number. They emit carbon dioxide. Carbon dioxide is a greenhouse gas. Greenhouse gases contribute to the greenhouse effect. The greenhouse effect causes global warming.

Obviously, this is not an effectively written paragraph. Try your hand at rewriting it. Simply combining a few sentences will make a noticeable difference in readability.

On the other hand, sentences that are overly long my obscure information and so create problems for the reader. Using a variety of sentence lengths helps the reader focus on important ideas more easily.

SENTENCE STRUCTURE

By paying attention to the structure of sentences, you can make your writing more interesting and more accurate. With more highly structured sentences, it is possible to show relationships between ideas that would be impossible in simple sentences.

Notice how the following base sentence can be changed by the addition of a variety of sentence elements.

The bridge collapsed.

Adjective
The **ancient** bridge collapsed.

Adverb
The bridge collapsed **violently**.

Prepositional Phrases
After the snow, the bridge collapsed **in a heap**.

Participial Phrases
Weakened by time, the bridge collapsed, **tumbling into
the chasm**.

Appositive
The bridge, **a crumbling eyesore,** collapsed.

Absolute Phrase
Metal twisting and snapping, the bridge collapsed.

Adverbial Clause
**Because time and the elements had weakened the sup-
porting structures,** the bridge collapsed.

Adjective Clause
The bridge, **which spans a wild river,** collapsed.

MECHANICS, GRAMMAR, AND USAGE

The following discussions will help you proofread your drafts more effectively. As you proofread your final draft, you may need to pay attention to
some of the following problems that often plague first-year college writers.

SENTENCES

A sentence expresses a complete thought.

> *It rained all night.*

> *The streets were flooded.*

> *I wasn't able to go to school.*

> *The rain continued throughout the night, flooding streets all over the city, so that most commuters found it impossible to get anywhere the next morning.*

Each of the preceding sentences expresses a complete thought. Occasionally, you may write a sentence that creates problems for the reader because it doesn't express a complete thought. When you are proofreading, you should be able to find those sentences and rewrite them.

Fused sentences

Consider the following sentence.

> *It rained all night I was not able to go to school the next morning.*

The preceding sentence is a fused sentence. Two independent clauses (complete thoughts) are fused together without any punctuation. Such sentences can be corrected in a number of different ways. You can simply divide it into two sentences.

> *It rained all night. I was not able to go to school the next morning.*

You could create a complex sentence by subordinating one clause to the other.

> *Because it rained all night, I was not able to go to school the next morning.*

You could create a compound sentence by inserting a semicolon or a coordinating conjunction between the two independent clauses.

> *It rained all night; I was not able to go to school the next morning.*

> *It rained all night, and I was not able to go to school the next morning.*

> *It rained all night, so I was not able to go to school the next morning.*

If you use a comma without a conjunction, you will have created a comma splice. See below.

Comma Splices

> *It rained all night, I was not able to go to school the next morning.*

In the sentence above, the two independent clauses have been connected by a comma; a comma splice results. A comma splice can be corrected in a number of different ways. You can simply make two separate sentences.

> *It rained all night. I was not able to go to school the next morning.*

You could create a complex sentence by subordinating one clause to the other.

> *Because it rained all night, I was not able to go to school the next morning.*

You could create a compound sentence by inserting a semicolon or a coordinating conjunction between the two independent clauses.

> *It rained all night; I was not able to go to school the next morning.*

It rained all night, and I was not able to go to school the next morning.

It rained all night, so I was not able to go to school the next morning.

Fragments

Fragments are incomplete sentences. Look at the following:

Running through the woods. He tripped over a root.

He fell down. Because he tripped over a root.

To correct the two fragments above, you would need to attach the fragment to the independent clasue.

Running through the woods, he tripped over a root.

He fell down because he tripped over a root.

PRONOUNS

Pronoun Agreement

When a student decides to study abroad, they must confirm that all proposed classes meet the college's degree plan requirements.

In the sentence above, the pronoun used is "they." However, the antecedent or the noun that this pronoun is replacing is the word "student," which is singular, whereas the pronoun "they" is plural. Pronouns and their antecedents must agree, so you can do one of two things to correct this problem.

You can change the pronoun to the singular, "he or she." You will notice, however, that doing this makes the sentence wordy and somewhat clunky.

When a student decides to study abroad, he or she
must confirm that all proposed classes meet the college's degree
plan requirements.

A more elegant solution is to change the antecedent to its plural form.
You also want to make sure to change the verb to agree with the subject, so
"decides" becomes "decide."

When students decide to study abroad, they must confirm that
all proposed classes meet the college's degree plan requirements.

Pronoun Reference

Susan went with Emma to her father's funeral.

In this sentence, it is not clear which antecedent the pronoun "her" is
referring to. Is it Emma's father's funeral or Susan's father's? Changing the
vague pronoun "her" to a definite antecedent would clarify the confusion
created by the vague pronoun reference as shown below.

Susan went with Emma to Emma's father's funeral.

Notice the use of pronouns in the following paragraph.

The main character in the story, "Not Human Beings" by
Etgar Keret is Shmulik Stein, an Israeli conscript who is exposed to
the brutal realities of armed conflict in the Gaza Strip. In the begin-
ning of the story, he is portrayed as a young soldier, whose bravado
conceals the naïve youthfulness lurking underneath. By the end of
the story, however, after witnessing acts of brutality committed by
members of the military unit he has been assigned to, he is forced
to confront the dehumanizing nature of war, which results in the
character's devastating loss of innocence.

In the passage above, the writer only mentions the main character once in the opening sentence. After that, every subsequent reference to the main character, Shmulik Stein, is through the use of the pronoun "he." Because the antecedent is farther and farther removed from the pronouns in the subsequent sentences, the passage tends to lose its focus. Consider reminding the reader of the antecedent as in the revision of the original passage below.

> *The main character in the story, "Not Human Beings" by Etgar Keret is Shmulik Stein, an Israeli conscript who is exposed to the brutal realities of armed conflict in the Gaza Strip. In the beginning of the story, Stein is portrayed as a young soldier, whose bravado conceals the naïve youthfulness lurking underneath. By the end of the story, however, after witnessing acts of brutality committed by members of the military unit he has been assigned to, Stein is forced to confront the dehumanizing nature of war, which results in the character's devastating loss of innocence.*

YOU

Trying to figure out when to use the pronoun *you* can be perplexing when you are proofreading your papers. In general in referential forms of writing you should use the third person, *he, she,* or *they*—someone other than the writer, *I,* or the reader, *you*—or you can use nouns like *students, professors,* or *employees* and proper nouns like *John, Mary,* or *Americans.* In persuasive writing when the writer is addressing the reader directly, obviously the word *you* must be used. Even in some referential forms like informative narration of process the second person is mandatory. Consider the following imperative sentence: Put the red wire in the red slot. There is an implied *you*: (You) put the red wire in the red slot. Obviously you must use the second person when you are giving directions.

We tend to use *you* so extensively in conversation that we may be tempted to use *you* without thinking about it when we write. The difficulty arises with the so-called indefinite *you*, that is, using *you* to refer to "anybody." Consider the following sentence: During the Puritan rule in England, you could not go to the theater. The "you" in that sentence cannot possibly be the reader. To correct that sentence, you would simply substitute a word like *people* for the word *you.* Some uses of the indefinite *you* are less obvious. Consider this sentence: Because mystics report experiences that are completely subjective, you have no way to validate their assertions.

VERBS

Verb Endings

An –ed ending creates the past tense and an –s ending creates the present tense. In the drafting process, occasionally you may fail to put an ending on a verb. When you are proofreading and revising your work, make sure to check the verb endings.

> *They are supposed to go with us.*

> *He asked about the assignment.*

> *He feels he should make an effort to catch up.*

> *She hopes she can make it to the meeting.*

> *The dog wants to go for a walk.*

Subject-Verb Agreement

> *The student make very few mistakes.*

The preceding sentence has a problem with subject-verb agreement. With a singular noun or a third person singular pronoun (*he, she, it*), a verb in the present tense adds an –s to the base form of the verb. So the sentence should read like this:

> *The student makes very few mistakes.*

With a plural noun or a plural third person pronoun (*they*), a verb in the present tense will not have the –s.

> *The students make very few mistakes.*

Occasionally, when several words separate subject from the verb, confusion can occur.

The mall with the largest number of stores usually attract the largest crowds.

In this sentence the word *mall*, the singular subject, is separated from the verb *attract*. As a result, the writer has made an error in agreement by failing to put the –s on the verb. The sentence should read:

The mall with the largest number of stores usually attracts the largest crowds.

RESEARCH

If you have used sources in your paper and have included parenthetical citations, make sure that you have a list of works cited at the end of the paper. The following is a sample list of works cited. Note: Your list of works cited should be put in alphabetical order without the headings. The headings are included here as information only and should not appear in a list of works cited.

WORKS CITED

The following are some samples of work cited entries for different types of entries. For examples of how to set up a works cited page in a paper, see "Beauty Becomes the Beast" and "Crime Scene Investigations and Forensic Analysis" in Chapter 14.

Book

Plath, Sylvia. *The Bell Jar.* Harper Perennial, 2005.

Periodical Article

Smith, Jennie Erin. "A State of Nature." *The New Yorker* 22 Apr. 2013 pp. 58–63.

Article in an Online Magazine

Rosenberg, David. "What Does Your Kitchen Say About You." Slate.com. 30 Apr. 2013, http://www.slate.com/blogs/behold/2013/04/30/erik_klein_wolterink_kitchen_portraits_examines_the_multicultural_reality.html. Accessed 1 May, 2013.

Selection in an Anthology

Lane Jr., Lauriat. "Why Huckleberry Finn's a Great World Novel." *Purpose, Pattern, and Process,* Edited by Lennis Polnac, Kendall Hunt, 2011. pp. 219–225.

Advertisement

Love You, Skinny Cow by Nestlé. Advertisement. *Cooking Light* Mar. 2011. pp. 61

Film

Django Unchained. Directed by Quentin Tarantino. Performances by Jaime Fox, Christof Waltz, and Leonardo DiCaprio. The Weinstein Company, 2012.

Article from a Website

Levin, David. "The Risks of Automated Flights." *Nova,* http://www. pbs.org/wgbh/nova/space/automation-voss-au.html 16 Feb. 2011. http://www.pbs.org/wgbh/nova/space/automation-voss-au.html. Accessed 21 Feb. 2017.

Article from an Online Database

Applbaum, Kalman D. "Marriage with the Proper Stranger: Arranged Marriage in Metropolitan Japan." *Ethnology,* vol. 34, no. 1, 1995, pp. 37–51. JSTOR, www.jstor.org/stable/3773862.

An Entry in a Blog

Sullivan, Andrew. "The View From Your Window." *The Dish* 25 Jan. 2015, http://dish.andrewsullivan.com/2015/01/25/the-view-from-your-window-795/. Accessed Sept. 5, 2016.

ADDITIONAL READINGS & STUDENT WRITING

Part 4

Additional Readings

T he readings in this chapter are grouped by cultural themes and offer a variety of discussion questions and writing assignments related to those topics.

SOCIAL PROCESSES AND RELATIONSHIPS

THE HANDS OF POVERTY

JANE ADDAMS

Jane Addams was a social activist and reformer in late nineteenth century America. She founded Hull House in the slums of Chicago in 1889 to help those in poverty, especially newly arrived immigrants. She was the first American woman to receive the Nobel Peace Prize. This excerpt taken from Chapter 4 of her book Twenty Years at Hull-House, *published in 1912, recounts a visit to London, England where she observes appalling conditions of poverty in the East End. Notice in particular her use of descriptive detail.*

One of the most poignant of these experiences, which occurred during the first few months after our landing upon the other side of the Atlantic, was on a Saturday night, when I received an ineradicable impression of the wretchedness of East London, and also saw for the first time the overcrowded quarters of a great city at midnight. A small party of tourists were taken to the East End by a city missionary to witness the Saturday night sale of decaying vegetables and fruit, which, owing to the Sunday laws in London, could not be sold until Monday, and, as they were beyond safe keeping, were disposed of at auction as late as possible on Saturday night. On Mile End Road, from the top of an omnibus which paused at the end of a dingy street lighted by only occasional flares of gas, we saw two huge masses of ill-clad people clamoring around two hucksters' carts. They were bidding their farthings and ha'pennies for a vegetable held up by the auctioneer, which he at last scornfully flung, with a gibe for its cheapness, to the successful bidder. In the momentary pause only one man detached himself from the groups. He had bidden on a cabbage, and when it struck his hand, he instantly sat down on the curb, tore it with his teeth, and hastily devoured it, unwashed and uncooked as it was. He and his fellows were types of the "submerged tenth," as our missionary guide told us, with some little satisfaction in the then new phrase, and he further added that so many of them could scarcely be seen in one spot save at this Saturday night auction, the desire for cheap food being apparently the one thing which could move them simultaneously. They were huddled into ill-fitting, cast-off clothing, the ragged finery which one sees only in East London. Their pale faces were dominated by that most unlovely of human expressions, the cunning and shrewdness of the bargain-hunter who starves if he cannot make a successful trade, and yet the final impression was not of ragged, tawdry clothing nor of pinched and sallow faces, but of myriads of hands, empty, pathetic, nerveless and workworn, showing white in the uncertain light of the street, and clutching forward for food which was already unfit to eat.

Perhaps nothing is so fraught with significance as the human hand, this oldest tool with which man has dug his way from savagery, and with which he is constantly groping forward. I have never since been able to see a number of hands held upward, even when they are moving rhythmically in a calisthenic exercise, or when they belong to a class of chubby children who wave them in eager response to a teacher's query, without a certain revival of this memory, a clutching at the heart reminiscent of the despair and resentment which seized me then.

For the following weeks I went about London almost furtively, afraid to look down narrow streets and alleys lest they disclose again this hideous human need and suffering. I carried with me for days at a time that curious surprise we experience when we first come back into the streets after days given over to sorrow and death; we are bewildered that the world should be going on as usual and unable to determine which is real, the inner pang or the outward seeming. In time all huge London came to seem unreal save the poverty in its East End.

1910

DISCUSSION QUESTIONS

1. Discuss Addams' descriptive imagery. How does it reinforce her main idea?
2. Discuss the emotional effect of the descriptions.
3. Explain how the central symbol of the hand reinforces her main idea.

WRITING ASSIGNMENTS

PERSONAL. Tell about an example of poverty (may include homelessness) that you have seen.

RESEARCH. In a documented paper discuss the kinds of assistance available to people in the United States whose income is below poverty level.

PERSUASIVE. In a persuasive paper argue that government should provide more (or less) assistance to people in poverty than it currently does.

ANALYTICAL. Write a paper analyzing Addams' use of description.

INVESTIGATIVE. Conduct a study of the attitudes of people about receiving assistance from the government or from charities.

THE RIGHTS OF WOMEN

MARY WOLLSTONECRAFT

> *The mother of Mary Shelley (the author of Frankenstein), Mary Wollstonecraft was an early voice advocating equality for women. This excerpt is from* A Vindication of the Rights of Women, *published in 1792, one of the first great works of feminist literature.*

My own sex, I hope, will excuse me, if I treat them like rational creatures, instead of flattering their *fascinating* graces, and viewing them as if they were in a state of perpetual childhood, unable to stand alone. I earnestly wish to point out in what true dignity and human happiness consists—I wish to persuade women to endeavour and acquire strength, both of mind and body, and to convince them that the soft phrases, susceptibility of heart, delicacy of sentiment, and refinement of taste, are almost synonymous with epithets of weakness, and that those beings who are only the objects of pity and that kind of love, which has been termed its sister, will soon become objects of contempt.

Dismissing then those pretty feminine phrases, which the men condescendingly use to soften our slavish dependence, and despising that weak elegancy of mind, exquisite sensibility, and sweet docility of manners, supposed to be the sexual characteristics of the weaker vessel, I wish to shew that elegance is inferior to virtue, that the first object of inaudable ambition is to obtain a character as a human being, regardless of the distinction of sex; and that secondary views should be brought to this simple touchstone.

This is a rough sketch of my plan; and should I express my conviction with the energetic emotions that I feel whenever I think of the subject, the dictates of experience and reflection will be felt by some of my readers. Animated by this important object, I shall disdain to cull my phrases or polish my style;—I aim at being useful, and sincerity will render me unaffected; for, wishing rather to persuade by the force of my arguments, than dazzle by the elegance of my language, I shall not waste my time in rounding periods, or in fabricating the turgid bombast of artificial feelings, which, coming from the head, never reach the heart.—I shall be employed about things, not words!—and, anxious to render my sex more respectable members of society, I shall try to avoid that flowery diction which has slided from essays into novels, and from novels into familiar letters and conversation.

These pretty superlatives, dropping glibly from the tongue, vitiate the taste, and create a kind of sickly delicacy that turns away from simple unadorned truth; and a deluge of false sentiments and overstretched feelings stifling the natural emotions of the heart, render the domestic pleasures insipid, that ought to sweeten the exercise of those severe duties, which educate a rational and immortal being for a nobler field of action.

The education of women has, of late, been more attended to than formerly; yet they are still reckoned a frivolous sex, and ridiculed or pitied by the writers who endeavor by satire or instruction to improve them. It is acknowledged that they spend many of the first years of their lives in acquiring a smattering of accomplishments; meanwhile strength of body and mind are sacrificed to libertine notions of beauty, to the desire of establishing themselves,—the only way women can rise in the world,—by marriage. And this desire making mere animals of them, when they marry they act as such children may be expected to act:—they dress; they paint, and nickname God's creatures.—Surely these weak beings are only fit for a seraglio!—Can they be expected to govern a family with judgment, or take care of the poor babes whom they bring into the world?

If then it can be fairly deduced from the present conduct of the sex; from the prevalent fondness for pleasure which takes place of ambition and those nobler passions that open and enlarge the soul; that the instruction which women have hitherto received has only tended, with the constitution of civil society to render them insignificant objects of desire—mere propagators of fools!—if it can be proved that in aiming to accomplish them, without cultivating their understandings, they are taken out of their sphere of duties, and made ridiculous and useless when the short-lived bloom of beauty is over, I presume that *rational* men will excuse me for endeavouring to persuade them to become more masculine and respectable.

Indeed the word masculine is only a bugbear: there is little reason to fear that women will acquire too much courage or fortitude; for their apparent inferiority with respect to bodily strength, must render them, in some degree, dependent on men in the various relations of life; but why should it be increased by prejudices that give a sex to virtue, and confound simple truths with sensual reveries?

Women are, in fact so much degraded by mistaken notions of female excellence, that I do not mean to add a paradox when I assert that this artificial weakness produces a propensity to tyrannize, and gives birth to cunning, the natural opponent of strength, which leads them to play off those contemptible infantine airs that undermine esteem even whilst they excite desire. Let men become more chaste and modest, and if women do not grow wiser in the same ratio, it will be clear that they have weaker understandings.

It seems scarcely necessary to say, that I now speak of the sex in general. Many individuals have more sense than their male relatives; and, as nothing preponderates where there is a constant struggle for an equilibrium, without it has naturally more gravity, some women govern their husbands without degrading themselves, because intellect will always govern.

DISCUSSION QUESTIONS

1. Rodriguez begins with an anecdote before stating his main idea. Why is this effective?

2. In what ways do the examples provided by Rodriguez heighten the contrast between a private and a public language? Does he make a strong case against bilingual education?

3. Rodriguez's essay reminds the reader of the distinctions in our private (intimate) versus public lives. Besides language, what other elements can you think of that define our public and private selves? In what ways are the lines between the public and private behavior becoming more blurred?

WRITING ASSIGNMENTS

PERSONAL. Tell about an experience you have had when the language you used as a child seemed out of place.

RESEARCH. Write a paper based on research explaining the principles and strategies used to teach children in bilingual education.

PERSUASIVE. Write a paper supporting the position that bilingual education should (or should not) be used in public schools.

ANALYTICAL. Write a paper analyzing the different ways Rodriguez communicates his values.

INVESTIGATIVE. Interview a number of friends and classmates who have similar interests. Collect examples of words and expressions that are unique to a particular subculture. Write a paper reporting your findings.

THE POWER OF MERELY REQUESTING A FAVOR

Simon Blanchard

> *In this essay, Simon Blanchard, assistant professor of marketing at Georgetown University's Mcdonough School of Business, explores the effects of the so called Benjamin Franklin effect. This principle, explained in the excerpt in Chapter 7 under persuasive narrative, has been the subject of a number of psychological studies.*
>
> You can access this reading with the following link: https://www.psychologytoday.com/us/blog/the-initiative/201605/the-power-merely-requesting-favor or you can find it by entering the author's name and the title of the reading in your search engine.

DISCUSSION QUESTIONS

1. Explain how the fictional narratives help explain Blanchard's main idea?
2. Discuss the overall organization of the reading.
3. What are the psychological effects of the strategies Blanchard suggests?

WRITING ASSIGNMENTS

PERSONAL. Tell about an experience you have had that involved financial dealings. Explain your emotional reaction to the transaction.

RESEARCH. Write a paper explaining different kinds of strategies for selling products. Document your sources

PERSUASIVE. Write a paper defending or refuting the idea that manipulative strategies in interpersonal relations are unethical and should not be used.

ANALYTICAL. Write a paper analyzing Blanchard's use of hypothetical narratives in his explanation.

INVESTIGATIVE. Try out the strategy of asking for a favor on several of your acquaintances. Keep a journal recording your observations of any changes in behavior as a result of the experiment.

THE INDIVIDUAL AND IDENTITY

WHERE I HAVE LIVED, AND WHAT I LIVED FOR

HENRY DAVID THOREAU

Walden, *an account of Thoreau's two-year stay in the woods near* Walden Pond *just outside Concord, Massachusetts, is the acknowledged classic of American nature writing. In this selection, the second chapter of the work, we encounter Thoreau's wide-ranging and challenging observations about himself and his culture. Many of his assertions are as surprising to us now as they were to his contemporaries.*

At a certain season of our life we are accustomed to consider every spot as the possible site of a house. I have thus surveyed the country on every side within a dozen miles of where I live. In imagination I have bought all the farms in succession, for all were to be bought, and I knew their price. I walked over each farmer's premises, tasted his wild apples, discoursed on husbandry with him, took his farm at his price, at any price, mortgaging it to him in my mind; even put a higher price on it,— every thing but a deed of it,—took his word for his deed, for I dearly love to talk,—cultivated it, and him too to some extent, I trust, and withdrew when I had enjoyed it long enough, leaving him to carry it on. This experience entitled me to be regarded as a sort of real estate broker by my friends. Wherever I sat, there I might live, and the landscape radiated from me accordingly. What is a house but a sedes, a seat?—better if a country seat. I discovered many a site for a house not likely to be *soon* improved, which some might have thought too far from the village, but to my eyes the village was too far from it. Well, there I might live, I said; and there I did live, for an hour, a summer and a winter life; saw how I could let the years run off, buffet the winter through, and see the spring come in. The future inhabitants of this region wherever they may place their houses may be sure that they have been anticipated. An afternoon sufficed to lay out the land into orchard woodlot, and pasture, and to decide what fine oaks or pines should be left to stand before the door, and whence each blasted tree could he seen to the best advantage; and then I let it lie, fallow perchance, for a man is rich in proportion to the number of things which he can afford to let alone.

My imagination carried me so far that I even had the refusal of several farms,—the refusal was all I wanted, I never got my fingers burned by actual possession. The nearest that I came to actual possession was when I bought the Hollowell place, and had begun to sort my seeds, and collected materials with which to make a wheelbarrow to carry it on or off with; but before the owner gave me a deed of it, his wife—every man has such a wife—changed her mind and wished to keep it, and he offered me ten dollars to release him. *Now*, to speak the truth, I had but ten cents in the world, and it surpassed my arithmetic to tell, if I was that man who had ten cents, or who had a farm, or ten dollars, or all together. However, I let him keep the ten dollars and the farm too, for I had carried it far enough; or rather, to be generous, I sold him the farm for just what I gave for it, and, as he was not a rich man, made him a present of ten dollars, and still had my ten cents, and seeds, and materials for a wheelbarrow left. I found thus that I had been a rich man without any damage to my poverty. But I retained the landscape, and I have since annually carried off what it yielded without a wheelbarrow. With respect to landscapes,—

I am monarch of all I *survey*, My right there is none to dispute."

I have frequently seen a poet withdraw, having enjoyed the most valuable part of a farm, while the crusty farmer supposed that he had got a few wild apples only. Why, the owner does not know it for many years when a poet has put his farm in rhyme, the most admirable kind of invisible fence, has fairly impounded it, milked it, skimmed it, and got all the cream, and left the farmer only the skimmed milk.

The real attractions of the Hollowell farm, to me, were; its complete retirement, being about two miles from the village, half a mile from the nearest neighbor, and separated from the highway by a broad field; its bounding on the river, which the owner said protected it by its fogs from frosts in the spring, though that was nothing to me; the gray color and ruinous state of the house and barn, and the dilapidated fences, which put such an interval between me and the last occupant; the hollow and lichen-covered apple trees, gnawed by rabbits, showing what kind of neighbors

I should have; but above all, the recollection I had of it from my earliest voyages up the river, when the house was concealed behind a dense grove of red maples, through which I heard the house-dog bark. I was in haste to buy it, before the proprietor finished getting out some rocks, cutting down the hollow apple trees, and grubbing up some young birches which had sprung up in the pasture, or, in short, had made any more of his improvements. To enjoy these advantages I was ready to carry it on; like Atlas, to take the world on my shoulders,—I never heard what compensation he received for that,—and do all those things which had no other motive or excuse but that I might pay for it and be unmolested in my possession of it; for I knew all the while that it would yield the most abundant crop of the kind I wanted if I could only afford to let it alone. But it turned out as I have said.

All that I could say, then, with respect to farming on a large scale, (I have always cultivated a garden,) was, that I had had my seeds ready. Many think that seeds improve with age. I have no doubt that time discriminates between the good and the bad; and when at last I shall plant, I shall be less likely to be disappointed. But I would say to my fellows, once for all, As long as possible live free and uncommitted. It makes but little difference whether you are committed to a farm or the county jail.

Old Cato, whose "De Re Rusticâ" is my "Cultivator," says, and the only translation I have seen makes sheer nonsense of the passage, "When you think of getting a farm, turn it thus in your mind, not to buy greedily; nor spare your pains to look at it, and do not think it enough to go round it once. The oftener you go there the more it will please you, if it is good." I think I shall not buy greedily, but go round and round it as long as I live, and be buried in it first, that it may please me the more at last.

The present was my next experiment of this kind, which I purpose to describe more at length; for convenience, putting the experience of two years into one. As I have said, I do not propose to write an ode to dejection, but to brag as lustily as chanticleer in the morning, standing on his roost, if only to wake my neighbors.

When first I took up my abode in the woods, that is, began to spend my nights as well as days there, which, by accident, was on Independence day, or the fourth of July, 1845, my house was not finished for winter, but was merely a defence against the rain, without plastering or chimney, the walls being of rough weather-stained boards, with wide chinks, which made it cool at night.

The upright white hewn studs and freshly planed door and window casings gave it a clean and airy look, especially in the morning, when its timbers were saturated with dew, so that I fancied that by noon some sweet gum would exude from them. To my imagination it retained throughout the day more or less of this auroral character, reminding me of a certain house on a mountain which I had visited the year before. This was an airy and unplastered cabin, fit to entertain a travelling god, and where a goddess might trail her garments. The winds which passed over my dwelling were such as sweep over the ridges of mountains bearing the broken strains, or celestial parts only, of terrestrial music. The morning wind forever blows the poem of creation is uninterrupted, but few are the ears that hear it Olympus is but the outside of the earth every where.

The only house I had been the owner of before, if I except a boat, was a tent, which I used occasionally when making excursions in the summer, and this is still rolled up in my garret; but the boat, after passing from hand to hand, has gone down the stream of time. With this more substantial shelter about me, I had made some progress toward settling in the world. This frame, so slightly clad, was a sort of crystallization around me, and reacted on the builder. It was suggestive somewhat as a picture in outlines. I did not need to go out doors to take the air, for the atmosphere within had lost none of its freshness. It was not so much within doors as behind a door where I sat, even in the rainiest weather. The Harivansa says, "An abode without birds is like a meat without seasoning." Such was not my abode, for I found myself suddenly neighbor to the birds; not by having imprisoned one, but having caged myself near them. I was not only nearer to some of those which commonly frequent the garden and the orchard, but to those wilder and more thrilling songsters of the forest which never, or rarely, serenade a villager,—the wood-thrush, the veery, the scarlet tanager, the field-sparrow, the whippoorwill, and many others.

I was seated by the shore of a small pond, about a mile and a half south of the village of Concord and somewhat higher than it, in the midst of an extensive wood between that town and Lincoln, and about two miles south of that our only field known to fame, Concord Battle Ground; but I was so low in the woods that the opposite shore, half a mile off, like the rest, covered with wood, was my most distant horizon. For the first week, whenever I looked out on the pond it impressed me like a tarn high up on the side of a mountain, its bottom far above the surface of other lakes, and, as the sun arose, I saw it throwing off its nightly clothing of mist, and here and there, by degrees, its soft ripples or its smooth reflecting surface was revealed, while the mists, like ghosts, were stealthily withdrawing in every direction into the woods, as at the breaking up of some nocturnal conventicle. The very dew seemed to hang upon the trees later into the day than usual, as on the sides of mountains.

This small lake was of most value as a neighbor in the intervals of a gentle rain storm in August, when, both air and water being perfectly still, but the sky overcast, mid-afternoon had all the serenity of evening, and the wood-thrush sang around, and was heard from shore to shore. A lake like this is never smoother than at such a time; and the clear portion of the air above it being shallow and darkened by clouds, the water, full of light and reflections, becomes a lower heaven itself so much the more important. From a hill top near by, where the wood had been recently cut off, there was a pleasing vista southward across the pond, through a wide indentation in the hills which form the shore there, where their opposite sides sloping toward each other suggested a stream flowing out in that direction through a wooded valley, but stream there was none. That way I looked between and over the near green hills to some distant and higher ones in the horizon, tinged with blue. Indeed, by standing on tiptoe I could catch a glimpse of some of the peaks of the still bluer and more distant mountain ranges in the north-west, those true-blue coins from heaven's own mint, and also of some portion of the village. But in other directions, even from this point, I could not see over or beyond the woods which surrounded me. It is well to have some water in your neighborhood to give buoyancy to and float the earth. One value even of the smallest well is, that when you look into it you see that earth is not continent but insular. This is as important as that it keeps butter cool. When I looked across the pond from this peak toward the Sudbury meadows, which in time of flood I distinguished elevated perhaps by a mirage in their seething valley, like a coin in a basin, all the earth beyond the pond appeared like a thin crust insulated and, floated even by this small sheet of intervening water, and I was reminded that this on which I dwelt was but dry land. [...]

Every morning was a cheerful invitation to make my life of equal simplicity, and I may say innocence, with Nature herself. I have been as sincere a worshipper of Aurora as the Greeks. I got up early and bathed in the pond; that was a religious exercise, and one of the best things which I did. They say that characters were engraven on the bathing tub of king Tching-thang [Confucius] to this effect: "Renew thyself completely each day; do it again, and again, and forever again." I can understand that Morning brings back, the heroic ages. I was as much affected by the faint hum of a mosquito making its invisible and unimaginable tour through my apartment at earliest dawn, when I was sitting with door and windows open, as I could be by any trumpet that ever sang of fame. It was Homer's requiem; itself an Iliad and Odyssey in the air, singing its own wrath and wanderings. There was something cosmical about it; a standing advertisement, till forbidden, of the everlasting vigor and fertility of the world. The morning, which is the most memorable season of the day, is the awakening hour. Then there is least somnolence in us; and for an hour, at least, some part of us awakes which slumbers all the rest of the day and night. Little is to be expected of that day, if it can be called a day, to which we are not awakened by our Genius, but by the mechanical nudgings of some servitor, are not awakened by our own newly-acquired force and aspirations from within, accompanied by the undulations of celestial music, instead of factory bells, and a fragrance filling the air—to a higher life than we fell asleep from; and thus the darkness bear its fruit, and prove itself to be good, no less than the light. That man who does not believe that each day contains an earlier, more sacred, and auroral hour than he has yet profaned, has despaired of life, and is pursuing a descending and darkening way. After a partial cessation of his sensuous life, the soul of man, or its organs rather, are reinvigorated each day, and his Genius tries again what noble life it can make. All memorable events, I should say, transpire in morning lime and in a morning atmosphere. The Vedas say, "All intelligences awake with the morning." Poetry and art, and the fairest and most memorable of the actions of men, date from such an hour. All poets and heroes, like Memnon, are the children of Aurora, and emit their music at sunrise. To him whose elastic and vigorous thought keeps pace with the sun, the day is a perpetual morning. It matters not what the clocks say or the attitudes and labors of men. Morning is when I am awake and there is a dawn in me. Moral reform is the effort to throw off sleep. Why is it that men give so poor an account of their day if they have not been slumbering? They are not such poor calculators. If they had not been overcome with drowsiness they would have performed something. The millions are awake enough for physical labor; but only one in a million is awake enough for effective intellectual exertion, only one in a hundred millions to a poetic or divine life. To be awake is to be alive. I have never yet met a man who was quite awake. How could I have looked him in the face?

We must learn to reawaken and keep ourselves awake, not by mechanical aids, but by an infinite expectation of the dawn, which does not forsake us in our soundest sleep. I know of no more encouraging fact than the unquestionable ability of man to elevate his life by a conscious endeavor. It is something to be able to paint a particular picture, or to carve a statue, and so to make a few objects beautiful; but it is far more glorious to carve and paint the very atmosphere and medium through which we look, which morally we can do. To affect the quality of the day, that is the highest of arts. Every man is tasked to make his life, even in its details, worthy of the contemplation of his most elevated and critical hour. If we refused, or rather used up, such paltry information as we get, the oracles would distinctly inform us how this might be done.

I went to the woods because I wished to live deliberately, to front only the essential facts of life, and see if I could not learn what it had to teach, and not, when I came to die, discover that I had not lived. I did not wish to live what was not life, living is so dear; nor did I wish to practise resignation, unless it was quite necessary. I wanted to live deep and suck out all the marrow of life, to live so sturdily and Spartan-like as to put to rout all that was not life, to cut a broad swath and shave close, to drive life into a corner, and reduce it to its lowest terms, and, if it proved to be mean, why then to get the whole and genuine meanness of it, and publish its meanness to the world; or if it were sublime, to know it by experience, and be able to give a true account of it in my next excursion. For most men, it appears to me, are in a strange uncertainty about it, whether it is of the devil or of God, and have somewhat hastily concluded that it is the chief end of man here to "glorify God and enjoy him forever."

Still we live meanly, like ants; though the fable tells us that we were long ago changed into men; like pygmies we fight with cranes; it is error upon error, and clout upon clout, and our best virtue has for its occasion a superfluous and evitable wretchedness. Our life is frittered away by detail. An honest man has hardly need to count more than his ten fingers, or in extreme cases he may add his ten toes, and lump the rest. Simplicity, simplicity, simplicity! I say, let your affairs be as two or three, and not a hundred or a thousand; instead of a million count half a dozen, and keep your accounts on your thumb nail. In the midst of this chopping sea of civilized life, such are the clouds and storms and quicksands and thousand-and-one items to be allowed for, that a man has to live, if he would not founder and go to the bottom and not make his port at all, by dead reckoning, and he must be a great calculator indeed who succeeds. Simplify, simplify. Instead of three meals a day, if it be necessary eat but one; instead of a hundred dishes, five; and reduce other things in proportion. Our life is like a German Confederacy, made up of petty states, with its boundary forever fluctuating, so that even a German cannot tell you how it is bounded at any moment. The nation itself, with all its so called internal improvements, which, by the way, are all external and superficial, is just such an unwieldy and overgrown establishment, cluttered with furniture and tripped up by its own traps, ruined by luxury and heedless expense, by want of calculation and a worthy aim, as the million households in the land; and the only cure for it as for them is in a rigid economy, a stern and more than Spartan simplicity of life and elevation of purpose. It lives too fast. Men think that it is essential that the Nation have commerce, and export ice, and talk through a telegraph, and ride thirty miles an hour, without a doubt, whether they do or not; but whether we should live like baboons or like men, is a little uncertain. If we do not get out sleepers, and forge rails, and devote days and nights to the work, but go to tinkering upon our lives to improve them, who will build railroads? And if railroads are not built, how shall we get to heaven in season? But if we stay at home and mind our business, who will want railroads? We do not ride on the railroad; it rides upon us. Did you ever think what those sleepers are that underlie the railroad? Each one is a man, an Irishman, or a Yankee man. The rails are laid on them, and they are covered with sand, and the cars run smoothly over them. They are sound sleepers, I assure you. And every few years a new lot is laid down and run over; so that, if some have the pleasure of riding on a rail, others have the misfortune to be ridden upon. And when they run over a man that is walking in his sleep, a supernumerary sleeper in the wrong position, and wake him up, they suddenly stop the cars, and make a hue and cry about it, as if this were an exception. I am glad to know that it takes a gang of men for every five miles to keep the sleepers down and level In their beds as it is, for this is a sign that they may sometime get up again.

Why should we live with such hurry and waste of life? We are determined to be starved before we are hungry. Men say that a stitch in time saves nine, and so they take a thousand stitches to day to save nine to-morrow. As for work, we haven't any of any consequence. We have the Saint Vitus' dance, and cannot possibly keep our heads still. If I should only give a few pulls at the parish bell-rope, as for a fire, that is, without setting the bell, there is hardly a man on his farm in the outskirts of Concord, notwithstanding that press of engagements which was his excuse so many times this morning, nor a boy, nor a woman, I might almost say, but would forsake all and follow that sound, not mainly to save property from the flames, but, if we will confess the truth, much more to see it burn, since burn it must, and we, be it known, did not set it on fire,—or to see it put out, and have a hand in it, if that is done as handsomely; yes, even if it were the parish church itself. Hardly a man takes a half hour's nap after dinner, but when he wakes he holds up his head and asks, "What's the news?" as if the rest of mankind had stood his sentinels. Some give directions to be waked every half hour, doubtless for no other purpose; and then, to pay for it, they tell what they have dreamed. After a night's sleep the news is as indispensable as the breakfast. "Pray tell me any thing new that has happened to a man any where on this globe,"— and he reads it over his coffee and rolls, that a man has had his eyes gouged out this morning on the Wachito River; never dreaming the while that he lives in the dark unfathomed mammoth cave of this world, and has but the rudiment of an eye himself.

For my part, I could easily do without the post-office. I think that there are very few important communications made through it. To speak critically, I never received more than one or two letters in my life—I wrote this some years ago—that were worth the postage. The penny-post is, commonly, an institution through which you seriously offer a man that penny for his thoughts which is so often safely offered in jest. And I am sure that I never read any memorable news in a newspaper. If we read of one man robbed, or murdered, or killed by accident, or one house burned, or one vessel wrecked, or one steamboat blown up, or one cow run over on the Western Railroad, or one mad dog killed, or one lot of grasshoppers in the winter,—we never need read of another. One is enough. If you are acquainted with the principle, what do you care for a myriad instances and applications? To a philosopher all news, as it is called, is gossip, and they who edit and read it are old women over their tea Yet not a few are greedy after this gossip. There was such a rush, as I hear, the other day at one of the offices to learn the foreign news by the last arrival, that several large squares of plate glass belonging to the establishment were broken by the pressure,—news which I seriously think a ready wit might write a twelve-month or twelve years beforehand with sufficient accuracy. [...]

Shams and delusions are esteemed for soundest truths, while reality is fabulous. If men would steadily observe realities only, and not allow themselves to be deluded, life, to compare it with such things as we know, would be like a fairy tale and the Arabian Nights' Entertainments. If we respected only what is inevitable and has a right to be, music and poetry would resound along the streets. When we are unhurried and wise, we perceive that only great and worthy things have any permanent and absolute existence,—that petty fears and petty pleasures are but the shadow of the reality. This is always exhilarating and sublime. By closing the eyes and slumbering, and consenting to be deceived by shows, men establish and confirm their daily life of routine and habit every where, which still is built on purely illusory foundations. Children, who play life, discern its true law and relations more clearly than men, who fail to live it worthily, but who think that they are wiser by experience, that is, by failure. I have read in a Hindoo book, that "there was a king's son, who, being expelled in infancy from his native city, was brought up by a forester, and, growing up to maturity in that state, imagined himself to belong to the barbarous race with which he lived. One of his father's ministers having discovered him, revealed to him what he was, and the misconception of his character was removed, and he knew himself to be a prince. So soul," continues the Hindoo philosopher, "from the circumstances in which it is placed, mistakes its own character, until the truth is revealed to it by some holy teacher, and then it knows itself to be *Brahme*." I perceive that we inhabitants of New England live this mean life that we do because our vision does not penetrate the surface of things. We think that that *is* which *appears* to be. If a man should walk through this town and see only the reality, where, think you, would the "Mill— dam" go to? If he should give us an account of the realities he beheld there, we should not recognize the place in his description. Look at a meeting-house, or a court-house, or a jail, or a shop, or a dwelling-house, and say what that thing really is before a true gaze, and they would all go to pieces in your account of them. Men esteem truth remote, in the outskirts of the system, behind the farthest star, before Adam and after the last man. In eternity there is indeed something true and sublime. But all these times and places and occasions are now and here. God himself culminates in the present moment, and will never be more divine in the lapse of all the ages. And we are enabled to apprehend at all what is sublime and noble only by the perpetual instilling and drenching of the reality that surrounds us. The universe constantly and obediently answers to our conceptions; whether we travel fast or slow, the track is laid for us. Let us spend our lives in conceiving then. The poet or the artist never yet had so fair and noble a design but some of his posterity at least could accomplish it.

Let us spend one day as deliberately as Nature, and not be thrown off the track by every nutshell and mosquito's wing that falls on the rails. Let us rise early and fast, or break fast, gently and without perturbation; let company come and let company go, let the bells ring and the children cry,—determined to make a day of it. Why should we knock under and go with the stream? Let us not be upset and overwhelmed in that terrible rapid and whirlpool called a dinner, situated in the meridian shallows. Weather this danger and you are safe, for the rest of the way is down hill. With unrelaxed nerves, with morning vigor, sail by it, looking another way, tied to the mast like Ulysses. If the engine whistles, let it whistle till it is hoarse for its pains. If the bell rings, why should we run? We will consider what kind of music they are like. Let us settle ourselves, and work and wedge our feet downward through the mud and slush of opinion, and prejudice, and tradition, and delusion, and appearance, that alluvion which covers the globe, through Paris and London, through New York and Boston and Concord, through church and state, through poetry and philosophy and religion, till we come to a hard bottom and rocks in place, which we can call reality, and say, This is, and no mistake; and then begin, having a point d'appui [base], below freshet and frost and fire, a place where you might found a wall or a state, or set a lamp post safely, or perhaps a gauge, not a Nilometer, but a Realometer, that future ages might know how deep a freshet of shams and appearances had gathered from time to time. If you stand right fronting and face to face to a fact, you will see the sun glimmer on both its surfaces, as if it were a cimeter, and feel its sweet edge dividing you through the heart and marrow, and so you will happily conclude your mortal career. Be it life or death, we crave only reality. If we are really dying, let us hear the rattle in our throats and feel cold in the extremities; if we are alive, let us go about our business.

Time is but the stream I go a-fishing in. I drink at it; but while I drink I see the sandy bottom and detect how shallow it is. Its thin current slides away, but eternity remains. I would drink deeper; fish in the sky, whose bottom is pebbly with stars. I cannot count one. I know not the first letter of the alphabet. I have always been regretting that I was not as wise as the day I was born. The intellect is a cleaver; it discerns and rifts its way into the secret of things. I do not wish to be any more busy with my hands than is necessary. My head is hands and feet. I feel all my best faculties concentrated in it. My instinct tells me that my head is an organ for burrowing, as some creatures use their snout and fore-paws, and with it I would mine and burrow my way through these hills. I think that the richest vein is somewhere hereabouts; so by the divining rod and thin rising vapors I judge; and here I will begin to mine.

DISCUSSION QUESTIONS

1. What is Thoreau's attitude toward property?
2. How does Thoreau characterize the idea of progress? What examples would he use if he were writing about today's society?
3. How does Thoreau define himself in relation to nature?

WRITING ASSIGNMENTS

PERSONAL. Write about an experience you have had when your possessions have proved to be a burden.

RESEARCH. Explain the effects of a technological innovation that has created problems for the modern world. Document your sources.

PERSUASIVE. Defend the claim that people should simplify their lives. Use examples from your own experience and knowledge.

ANALYTICAL. Write a paper explaining how Thoreau reveals the essential details of his value system and his identity through his use of narrative.

INVESTIGATIVE. Examine your life style. Identify those aspects of your life that are unnecessarily complicated. Interpret the meaning of your findings in a paper.

ON ANDROGYNY

Virginia Woolf

Virginia Woolf was one of the most innovative writers of the 20th century. Her use of a "stream of consciousness" technique in her novels allowed her to explore the inner workings of the minds of her characters. In this except from Woolf's extended essay "A Room of One's Own," published in 1929, she muses on the dual nature of the human mind.

Now it was bringing from one side of the street to the other diagonally a girl in patent leather boots, and then a young man in a maroon overcoat; it was also bringing a taxi-cab; and it brought all three together at a point directly beneath my window; where the taxi stopped; and the girl and the young man stopped; and they got into the taxi; and then the cab glided off as if it were swept on by the current elsewhere.

The sight was ordinary enough; what was strange was the rhythmical order with which my imagination had invested it; and the fact that the ordinary sight of two people getting into a cab had the power to communicate something of their own seeming satisfaction. The sight of two people coming down the street and meeting at the corner seems to ease the mind of some strain, I thought, watching the taxi turn and make off. Perhaps to think, as I had been thinking these two days, of one sex as distinct from the other is an effort. It interferes with the unity of the mind. Now that effort had ceased and that unity had been restored by seeing two people come together and get into a taxi-cab. The mind is certainly a very mysterious organ, I reflected, drawing my head in from the window, about which nothing whatever is known, though we depend upon it so completely. Why do I feel that there are severances and oppositions in the mind, as there are strains from obvious causes on the body? What does one mean by "the unity of the mind," I pondered, for clearly the mind has so great a power of concentrating at any point at any moment that it seems to have no single state of being. It can separate itself from the people in the street, for example, and think of itself as apart from them, at an upper window looking down on them. Or it can think with other people spontaneously, as, for instance, in a crowd waiting to hear some piece of news read out. It can think back through its fathers or through its mothers, as I have said that a woman writing thinks back through her mother. Again if one is a woman one is often surprised by a sudden splitting off of consciousness, say in walking down Whitehall, when from being the natural inheritor of that civilisation, she becomes, on the contrary, outside of it, alien and critical. Clearly the mind is always altering its focus, and bringing the world into different perspectives. But some of these states of mind seem, even if adopted spontaneously, to be less comfortable than others. In order to keep oneself continuing in them one is unconsciously holding something back, and gradually the repression becomes an effort. But there may be some state of mind in which one could continue without effort because nothing is required to be held back. And this perhaps, I thought, coming in from the window, is one of them. For certainly when I saw the couple get into the taxi-cab the mind felt as if, after being divided, it had come together again in a natural fusion. The obvious reason would be that it is natural for the sexes to co-operate. One has a profound, if irrational, instinct in favour of the theory that the union of man and woman makes for the greatest satisfaction, the most complete happiness. But the sight of the two people getting into the taxi and the satisfaction it gave me made me also ask whether there are two sexes in the mind corresponding to the two sexes in the body, and whether they also require to be united in order to get complete satisfaction and happiness. And I went on amateurishly to sketch a plan of the soul so that in each of us two powers preside, one male, one female: and in the man's brain, the man predominates over the woman, and in the woman's brain, the woman predominates over the man. The normal and comfortable state of being is that when the two live in harmony together, spiritually co-operating. If one is a man, still the woman part of the brain must have effect; and a woman also must have intercourse with the man in her. Coleridge perhaps meant this when he said that a great mind is androgynous. It is when this fusion takes place that the mind is fully fertilised and uses all its faculties.

DISCUSSION QUESTIONS

1. What is Woolf's main idea?
2. Discuss Woolf's emotional responses.
3. What is implication of the reference to Coleridge in the last paragraph?

WRITING ASSIGNMENTS

PERSONAL. Write a paper explaining how your behaviors and attitudes reflect male and/or female characteristics.

RESEARCH. Write a research paper exploring the development of androgynous fashion during the 20th century. (You may want to look at celebrities and pop culture during the period for ideas.)

PERSUASIVE. Write a persuasive paper arguing that androgyny in fashion should be encouraged, or conversely, that traditional male and female conventions of dress should be maintained.

ANALYTICAL. Write a paper analyzing Woolf's narrative point of view (her position as an observer in relation to the action of the narrative).

INVESTIGATIVE. Create a working definition of androgynous fashion by collecting images and explaining the features of androgynous fashion they illustrate. Go to a number of clothing retailers (either in store or online) and analyze the presence of androgynous fashion. Report your findings in a paper.

LIFE WITHOUT GENDER?

Barbara Kantrowitz

A graduate of Cornell University and the Columbia University School of Journalism, Barbara Kantrowitz is an award-winning journalist, formerly a senior editor with Newsweek. *Her work, covering many cultural issues, has appeared in a number of national publications. She is co-author, with Pat Wingert, of* The Menopause Book *(2009). This article appeared in the Culture section of* Newsweek *on August 16, 2010. In it Kantrowitz explores the challenging question of gender identity.*

You can access this reading with the following link: https://www.newsweek.com/life-without-gender-71847 or you can find it by entering the author's name and the title of the reading in your search engine.

DISCUSSION QUESTIONS

1. Discuss the effect of the first three paragraphs.
2. Explain the importance of accurate definitions in discussing controversial issues.
3. Discuss Kantrowitz's use of quotations from authorities. What do they add to her explanations?

WRITING ASSIGNMENTS

PERSONAL. Write a paper discussing traits of the opposite sex you have observed in yourself or someone you know well.

RESEARCH. Write a documented paper identifying and explaining the problems faced by LGBT people in mainstream society.

PERSUASIVE. Write a persuasive paper arguing that a particular social policy that has a negative impact on transsexuals should be changed.

ANALYTICAL. Write a paper analyzing Kantrowitz's use of examples to develop her main idea.

INVESTIGATIVE. Create a survey to find out how your classmates or members of another peer group feel about transsexual issues. Write a paper explaining your findings.

EDUCATION AND HUMAN DEVELOPMENT

A LIBERAL EDUCATION

THOMAS HENRY HUXLEY

> *Thomas Henry Huxley was a nineteenth century biologist and is best known as an early supporter of Darwin's theory of evolution. This excerpt, taken from an essay titled "A Liberal Education; and Where to Find It," was delivered at the South London Working Men's College in 1868.*

> By way of a beginning, let us ask ourselves—What is education? Above all things, what is our ideal of a thoroughly liberal education?—of that education which, if we could begin life again,

we would give ourselves—of that education which, if we could mould the fates to our own will, we would give our children? Well, I know not what may be your conceptions upon this matter, but I will tell you mine, and I hope I shall find that our views are not very discrepant.

Suppose it were perfectly certain that the life and fortune of every one of us would, one day or other, depend upon his winning or losing a game of chess. Don't you think that we should all consider it to be a primary duty to learn at least the names and the moves of the pieces; to have a notion of a gambit, and a keen eye for all the means of giving and getting out of check? Do you not think that we should look with a disapprobation amounting to scorn, upon the father who allowed his son, or the state which allowed its members, to grow up without knowing a pawn from a knight?

Yet it is a very plain and elementary truth, that the life, the fortune, and the happiness of every one of us, and, more or less, of those who are connected with us, do depend upon our knowing something of the rules of a game infinitely more difficult and complicated than chess. It is a game which has been played for untold ages, every man and woman of us being one of the two players in a game of his or her own. The chessboard is the world, the pieces are the phenomena of the universe, the rules of the game are what we call the laws of Nature. The player on the other side is hidden from us. We know that his play is always fair, just, and patient. But also we know, to our cost, that he never overlooks a mistake, or makes the smallest allowance for ignorance. To the man who plays well, the highest stakes are paid, with that sort of overflowing generosity with which the strong shows delight in strength. And one who plays ill is checkmated—without haste, but without remorse.

My metaphor will remind some of you of the famous picture in which Retzsch has depicted Satan playing at chess with man for his soul. Substitute for the mocking fiend in that picture a calm, strong angel who is playing for love, as we say, and would rather lose than win—and I should accept it as an image of human life.

Well, what I mean by Education is learning the rules of this mighty game. In other words, education is the instruction of the intellect in the laws of Nature, under which name I include not merely things and their forces, but men and their ways; and the fashioning of the affections and of the will into an earnest and loving desire to move in harmony with those laws. For me, education means neither more nor less than this. Anything which professes to call itself education must be tried by this standard, and if it fails to stand the test, I will not call it education, whatever may be the force of authority, or of numbers, upon the other side.

It is important to remember that, in strictness, there is no such thing as an uneducated man. Take an extreme case. Suppose that an adult man, in the full vigour of his faculties, could be suddenly placed in the world, as Adam is said to have been, and then left to do as he best might. How long would he be left uneducated? Not five minutes. Nature would begin to teach him, through the eye, the ear, the touch, the properties of objects. Pain and pleasure would be at his elbow telling him to do this and avoid that; and by slow degrees the man would receive an education which, if narrow, would be thorough, real, and adequate to his circumstances, though there would be no extras and very few accomplishments.

And if to this solitary man entered a second Adam or, better still, an Eve, a new and greater world, that of social and moral phenomena, would be revealed. Joys and woes, compared with which all others might seem but faint shadows, would spring from the new relations. Happiness and sorrow would take the place of the coarser monitors, pleasure and pain; but conduct would still be shaped by the observation of the natural consequences of actions; or, in other words, by the laws of the nature of man.

To every one of us the world was once as fresh and new as to Adam. And then, long before we were susceptible of any other modes of instruction, Nature took us in hand, and every minute of waking life brought its educational influence, shaping our actions into rough accordance with Nature's laws, so that we might not be ended untimely by too gross disobedience. Nor should I speak of this process of education as past for any one, be he as old as he may. For every man the world is as fresh as it was at the first day, and as full of untold novelties for him who has the eyes to see them. And Nature is still continuing her patient education of us in that great university, the universe, of which we are all members—Nature having no Test-Acts.

Those who take honours in Nature's university, who learn the laws which govern men and things and obey them, are the really great and successful men in this world. The great mass of mankind are the "Poll," who pick up just enough to get through without much discredit. Those who won't learn at all are plucked; and then you can't come up again. Nature's pluck means extermination.

Thus the question of compulsory education is settled so far as Nature is concerned. Her bill on that question was framed and passed long ago. But, like all compulsory legislation, that of Nature is harsh and wasteful in its operation. Ignorance is visited as sharply as wilful disobedience—incapacity meets with the same punishment as crime. Nature's discipline is not even a word and a blow, and the blow first; but the blow without the word. It is left to you to find out why your ears are boxed.

The object of what we commonly call education—that education in which man intervenes and which I shall distinguish as artificial education—is to make good these defects in Nature's methods; to prepare the child to receive Nature's education, neither incapably nor ignorantly, nor with wilful disobedience; and to understand the preliminary symptoms of her pleasure, without waiting for the box on the ear. In short, all artificial education ought to be an anticipation of natural education. And a liberal education is an artificial education which has not only prepared a man to escape the great evils of disobedience to natural laws, but has trained him to appreciate and to seize upon the rewards, which Nature scatters with as free a hand as her penalties.

That man, I think, has had a liberal education who has been so trained in youth that his body is the ready servant of his will, and does with ease and pleasure all the work that, as a mechanism, it is capable of; whose intellect is a clear, cold, logic engine, with all its parts of equal strength, and in smooth working order; ready, like a steam engine, to be turned to any kind of work, and spin the gossamers as well as forge the anchors of the mind; whose mind is stored with a knowledge of the great and fundamental truths of Nature and of the laws of her operations; one who, no stunted ascetic, is full of life and fire, but whose passions are trained to come to heel by a vigorous will, the servant of a tender conscience; who has learned to love all beauty, whether of Nature or of art, to hate all vileness, and to respect others as himself.

Such an one and no other, I conceive, has had a liberal education; for he is, as completely as a man can be, in harmony with Nature. He will make the best of her, and she of him. They will get on together rarely; she as his ever beneficent mother; he as her mouthpiece, her conscious self, her minister and interpreter.

DISCUSSION QUESTIONS

1. In this essay Huxley compares life to a game of chess. Discuss the appropriateness of this analogy.
2. How does Huxley distinguish between different kinds of education?
3. How does Huxley define "a liberal education"?

WRITING ASSIGNMENTS

PERSONAL. Write about an experience when you realized that something you learned in school applied to your life outside school.

RESEARCH. Write a paper about different kinds of education. Document your sources.

PERSUASIVE. Write a paper advocating that college courses should have a direct connection to life outside school.

ANALYTICAL. Write a paper analyzing Huxley's use of analogy.

INVESTIGATIVE. Create a survey to discover the courses your classmates think are most practical. Report your findings in a documented paper.

THE POWER OF HABIT

WILLIAM JAMES

> *William James was an American philosopher and psychologist whose writings have influenced thinkers for generations. This excerpt is taken from his* The Principles of Psychology, *Chapter 4 "Habit," written in 1890.*

"Habit a second nature! Habit is ten times nature," the Duke of Wellington is said to have exclaimed; and the degree to which this is true no one can probably appreciate as well as one who is a veteran soldier himself. The daily drill and the years of discipline end by fashioning a man completely over again, as to most of the possibilities of his conduct.

"There is a story, which is credible enough, though it may not be true, of a practical joker, who, seeing a discharged veteran carrying home his dinner, suddenly called out, 'Attention!' whereupon the man instantly brought his hands down, and lost his mutton and potatoes in the gutter. The drill had been thorough, and its effects had become embodied in the man's nervous structure."

Riderless cavalry-horses, at many a battle, have been seen to come together and go through their customary evolutions at the sound of the bugle-call. Most trained domestic animals, dogs and oxen, and omnibus- and car-horses, seem to be machines almost pure and simple, undoubtingly, unhesitatingly doing from minute to minute the duties they have been taught, and giving no sign that the possibility of an alternative ever suggests itself to their mind. Men grown old in prison have asked to be readmitted after being once set free. In a railroad accident to a travelling menagerie in the United States some time in 1884, a tiger, whose cage had broken open, is said to have emerged, but presently crept back again, as if too much bewildered by his new responsibilities, so that he was without difficulty secured.

Habit is thus the enormous fly-wheel of society, its most precious conservative agent. It alone is what keeps us all within the bounds of ordinance, and saves the children of fortune from the envious uprisings of the poor. It alone prevents the hardest and most repulsive walks of life from being deserted by those brought up to tread therein. It keeps the fisherman and the deck-hand at sea through the winter; it holds the miner in his darkness, and nails the countryman to his log-cabin and his lonely farm through all the months of snow; it protects us from invasion by the natives of the desert and the frozen zone. It dooms us all to fight out the battle of life upon the lines of our nurture or our early choice, and to make the best of a pursuit that disagrees, because there is no other for which we are fitted, and it is too late to begin again. It keeps different social strata from mixing. Already at the age of twenty-five you see the professional mannerism settling down on the young commercial traveller, on the young doctor, on the young minister, on the young counsellor-at-law. You see the little lines of cleavage running through the character, the tricks of thought, the prejudices, the ways of the "shop," in a word, from which the man can by-and-by no more escape than his coat-sleeve can suddenly fall into a new set of folds. On the whole, it is best he should not escape. It is well for the world that in most of us, by the age of thirty, the character has set like plaster, and will never soften again.

If the period between twenty and thirty is the critical one in the formation of intellectual and professional habits, the period below twenty is more important still for the fixing of *personal* habits, properly so called, such as vocalization and pronunciation, gesture, motion, and address. Hardly ever is a language learned after twenty spoken without a foreign accent; hardly ever can a youth transferred to the society of his betters unlearn the nasality and other vices of speech bred in him by the associations of his growing years. Hardly ever, indeed, no matter how much money there be in his pocket, can he even learn to *dress* like a gentleman-born. The merchants offer their wares as eagerly to him as to the veriest "swell," but he simply *cannot* buy the right things. An invisible law, as strong as gravitation, keeps him within his orbit, arrayed this year as he was the last; and how his better-bred acquaintances contrive to get the things they wear will be for him a mystery till his dying day.

The great thing, then, in all education, is to *make our nervous system our ally instead of our enemy*. It is to fund and capitalize our acquisitions, and live at ease upon the interest of the fund. *For this we must make automatic and habitual, as early as possible, as many useful actions as we can*, and guard against the growing into ways that are likely to be disadvantageous to us, as we should guard against the plague. The more of the details of our daily life we can hand over to the effortless custody of automatism, the more our higher powers of mind will be set free for their own proper work. There is no more miserable human being than one in whom nothing is habitual but indecision, and for whom the lighting of every cigar, the drinking of every cup, the time of rising and going to bed every day, and the beginning of every bit of work, are subjects of express volitional deliberation. Full half the time of such a man goes to the deciding, or regretting, of matters which ought to be so ingrained in him as practically not to exist for his consciousness at all. If there be such daily duties not yet ingrained in any one of my readers, let him begin this very hour to set the matter right.

DISCUSSION QUESTIONS

1. What is the effect of James' use of examples? How do they substantiate the main idea?

2. Discuss James' use of metaphors like "flywheel" and "orbit." What do they suggest about the nature of his analysis?

3. How does James apply his discussion of habit to education?

WRITING ASSIGNMENTS

PERSONAL. Write about an event in your life when you discovered that a habit was beneficial (or destructive) to you.

RESEARCH. Identify and discuss several different kinds of positive habits that can benefit a student. Document your sources.

PERSUASIVE. Identify a positive habit for a student to have and argue that it should be cultivated.

ANALYTICAL. Analyze James' use of examples.

INVESTIGATIVE. Interview or survey a number of successful students to determine the most beneficial habits for success in school. Report your findings in a paper.

ADVICE, LIKE YOUTH, PROBABLY JUST WASTED ON THE YOUNG

MARY SCHMICH

Mary Schmich has been a columnist at the Chicago Tribune *since 1992. A winner of the Pulitzer Prize for commentary, Schmich uses the form of a commencement address to structure this essay. Schmich's essay circulated widely after it was written and was misattributed to the writer Kurt Vonnegut, who later praised Schmich for her writing. In this essay, Schmich uses an exhortation to her audience to wear sunscreen as a way to dispense advice on how to live a meaningful life.*

You can access this reading with the following link: https://www.chicagotribune.com/columns/chi-schmich-sunscreen-column-column.html or you can find it by entering the author's name and the title of the reading in your search engine.

DISCUSSION QUESTIONS

1. Schmich's title is provocative. In what ways does the title complement what Schmich states in her essay?
2. What examples does Schmich use in her essay to show young people how to live? How do these examples support her main idea?
3. How would you characterize Schmich's tone? In what ways does Schmich's word choice and sentence structure contribute to her tone?

WRITING ASSIGNMENTS

PERSONAL. Reflect on a disappointing experience you had when you were younger. How would you have done things differently, knowing what you know today.

RESEARCH. Do research on the origins of the commencement address. Then write a paper outlining your findings.

PERSUASIVE. Write a paper offering advice on living well to someone who is not from your generation.

ANALYTICAL. Analyze Schmich's use of examples in a paper.

INVESTIGATIVE. Identify a topic that is important to members of your generation. Devise and conduct a survey determining how people from differing generations view this topic. Finally, report your findings in a paper.

HISTORY AND CULTURE

PATRIOTISM AND SPORT

G. K. CHESTERTON

A prolific writer, Chesterton produced a wide range of works including verse, novels, short stories, and essays. His essays cover a variety of topics addressing controversial questions about religion, politics, and cultural beliefs. This selection is taken from one of his most popular collections of essays entitled All Things Considered, *published in 1915.*

I notice that some papers, especially papers that call themselves patriotic, have fallen into quite a panic over the fact that we have been twice beaten in the world of sport, that a Frenchman has beaten us at golf, and that Belgians have beaten us at rowing. I suppose that the incidents are important to any people who ever believed in the self-satisfied English legend on this subject. I suppose that there are men who vaguely believe that we could never be beaten by a Frenchman, despite the fact that we have often been beaten by Frenchmen, and once by a Frenchwoman. In the old pictures in *Punch* you will find a recurring piece of satire. The English caricaturists always assumed that a Frenchman could not ride to hounds or enjoy English hunting. It did not seem to occur to them that all the people who founded English hunting were Frenchmen. All the Kings and nobles who originally rode to hounds spoke French. Large numbers of those Englishmen who still ride to hounds have French names. I suppose that the thing is important to any one who is ignorant of such evident matters as these. I suppose that if a man has ever believed that we English have some sacred and separate right to be athletic, such reverses do appear quite enormous and shocking. They feel as if, while the proper sun was rising in the east, some other and unexpected sun had begun to rise in the north-north-west by north. For the benefit, the moral and intellectual benefit of such people, it may be worth while to point out that the Anglo-Saxon has in these cases been defeated precisely by those competitors whom he has always regarded as being out of the running; by Latins, and by Latins of the most easy and unstrenuous type; not only by Frenchman, but by Belgians. All this, I say, is worth telling to any intelligent person who believes in the haughty theory of Anglo-Saxon superiority. But, then, no intelligent person does believe in the haughty theory of Anglo-Saxon superiority. No quite genuine Englishman ever did believe in it. And the genuine Englishman these defeats will in no respect dismay.

The genuine English patriot will know that the strength of England has never depended upon any of these things; that the glory of England has never had anything to do with them, except in the opinion of a large section of the rich and a loose section of the poor which copies the idleness of the rich. These people will, of course, think too much of our failure, just as they thought too much of our success. The typical Jingoes who have admired their countrymen too much for being conquerors will, doubtless, despise their countrymen too much for being conquered. But the Englishman with any feeling for England will know that athletic failures do not prove that England is weak, any more than athletic successes proved that England was strong. The truth is that athletics, like all other things, especially modern, are insanely individualistic. The Englishmen who win sporting prizes are exceptional among Englishmen, for the simple reason that they are exceptional even among men. English athletes represent England just about as much as Mr. Barnum's freaks represent America. There are so few of such people in the whole world that it is almost a toss-up whether they are found in this or that country.

If any one wants a simple proof of this, it is easy to find. When the great English athletes are not exceptional Englishmen they are generally not Englishmen at all. Nay, they are often representatives of races of which the average tone is specially incompatible with athletics. For instance, the English are supposed to rule the natives of India in virtue of their superior hardiness, superior activity, superior health of body and mind. The Hindus are supposed to be our subjects because they are less fond of action, less fond of openness and the open air. In a word, less fond of cricket. And, substantially, this is probably true, that the Indians are less fond of cricket. All the same, if you ask among Englishmen for the very best cricket-player, you will find that he is an Indian. Or, to take another case: it is, broadly speaking, true that the Jews are, as a race, pacific, intellectual, indifferent to war, like the Indians, or, perhaps, contemptuous of war, like the Chinese: nevertheless, of the very good prize-fighters, one or two have been Jews.

This is one of the strongest instances of the particular kind of evil that arises from our English form of the worship of athletics. It concentrates too much upon the success of individuals. It began, quite naturally and rightly, with wanting England to win. The second stage was that it wanted some Englishmen to win. The third stage was (in the ecstasy and agony of some special competition) that it wanted one particular Englishman to win. And the fourth stage was that when he had won, it discovered that he was not even an Englishman.

This is one of the points, I think, on which something might really be said for Lord Roberts and his rather vague ideas which vary between rifle clubs and conscription. Whatever may be the advantages or disadvantages otherwise of the idea, it is at least an idea of procuring equality and a sort of average in the athletic capacity of the people; it might conceivably act as a corrective to our mere tendency to see ourselves in certain exceptional athletes. As it is, there are millions of Englishmen who really think that they are a muscular race because C.B. Fry is an Englishman. And there are many of them who think vaguely that athletics must belong to England because Ranjitsinhji is an Indian.

But the real historic strength of England, physical and moral, has never had anything to do with this athletic specialism; it has been rather hindered by it. Somebody said that the Battle of Waterloo was won on Eton playing-fields. It was a particularly unfortunate remark, for the English contribution to the victory of Waterloo depended very much more than is common in victories upon the steadiness of the rank and file in an almost desperate situation. The Battle of Waterloo was won by the stubbornness of the common soldier—that is to say, it was won by the man who had never been to Eton. It was absurd to say that Waterloo was won on Eton cricket-fields. But it might have been fairly said that Waterloo was won on the village green, where clumsy boys played a very clumsy cricket. In a word, it was the average of the nation that was strong, and athletic glories do not indicate much about the average of a nation. Waterloo was not won by good cricket-players. But Waterloo was won by bad cricket-players, by a mass of men who had some minimum of athletic instincts and habits.

It is a good sign in a nation when such things are done badly. It shows that all the people are doing them. And it is a bad sign in a nation when such things are done very well, for it shows that only a few experts and eccentrics are doing them, and that the nation is merely looking on. Suppose that whenever we heard of walking in England it always meant walking forty-five miles a day without fatigue. We should be perfectly certain that only a few men were walking at all, and that all the other British subjects were being wheeled about in Bath-chairs. But if when we hear of walking it means slow walking, painful walking, and frequent fatigue, then we know that the mass of the nation still is walking. We know that England is still literally on its feet.

The difficulty is therefore that the actual raising of the standard of athletics has probably been bad for national athleticism. Instead of the tournament being a healthy *melee* into which any ordinary man would rush and take his chance, it has become a fenced and guarded tilting-yard for the collision of particular champions against whom no ordinary man would pit himself or even be permitted to pit himself. If Waterloo was won on Eton cricket-fields it was because Eton cricket was probably much more careless then than it is now. As long as the game was a game, everybody wanted to join in it. When it becomes an art, every one wants to look at it. When it was frivolous it may have won Waterloo: when it was serious and efficient it lost Magersfontein.

In the Waterloo period there was a general rough-and-tumble athleticism among average Englishmen. It cannot be re-created by cricket, or by conscription, or by any artificial means. It was a thing of the soul. It came out of laughter, religion, and the spirit of the place. But it was like the modern French duel in this—that it might happen to anybody. If I were a French journalist it might really happen that Monsieur Clemenceau might challenge me to meet him with pistols. But I do not think that it is at all likely that Mr. C. B. Fry will ever challenge me to meet him with cricket-bats.

DISCUSSION QUESTIONS

1. Discuss Chesterton's comments on stereotypes.
2. How does Chesterton depict the national character of England?
3. How do modern athletic events support or refute Chesterton's idea?

WRITING ASSIGNMENTS

PERSONAL. Write a narrative about a sporting event you have seen that had national implications.

RESEARCH. Write a paper discussing different kinds of international sporting events. Document your sources.

PERSUASIVE. Write a paper arguing that the number of international sporting events should be expanded.

ANALYTICAL. Write a paper discussing Chesterton's use of irony.

INVESTIGATIVE. Look at the coverage of an international sporting event in news reports from several different countries. Identify and analyze differences in reporting.

MY KIOWA GRANDMOTHER

N. Scott Momaday

N. Scott Momaday is a Native American writer best known for two works: House Made of Dawn *written in 1968, which won the Pulitzer prize for Fiction, and* The Way to Rainy Mountain, *a collection of Kiowa tales written in 1969. This excerpt is taken from* The Way to Rainy Mountain.

A single knoll rises out of the plain in Oklahoma, north and west of the Wichita Range. For my people, the Kiowas, it is an old landmark, and they gave it the name Rainy Mountain. The harest weather in the world is there. Winter brings blizzards, hot tornadic winds arise in the spring, and in summer the prairie is an anvil's edge. The grass turns brittle and brown, and it cracks beneath your feet. There are green belts along the rivers and creeks, linear groves of hickory and pecan, willow and witch hazel. At a distance in July or August the steaming foliage seems almost to writhe in fire. Great green and yellow grasshoppers are everywhere in the tall grass, popping up like corn to sting the flesh, and tortoises crawl about on the red earth, going nowhere in the plenty of time. Loneliness is an aspect of the land. All things in the plain are isolate; there is no confusion of objects in the eye, but one hill or one tree or one man. To look upon that landscape in the early morning, with the sun at your back, is to lose the sense of proportion. Your imagination comes to life, andthis, you think, is where Creation was begun.

I returned to Rainy Mountain in July. My grandmother had died in the spring, and I wanted to be at her grave. She had lived to be very old and at last infirm. Her only living daughter was with her when she died, and I was told that in death her face was that of a child.

I like to think of her as a child. When she was born, the Kiowas were living the last great moment of their history. For more than a hundred years they had controlled the open range from the Smoky Hill River to the Red, from the headwaters of the Canadian to the fork of the Arkansas and Cimarron. In alliance with the Comanche, they had ruled the whole of the southern Plains. War was their sacred business, and they were among the finest horsemen the world has ever known. But warfare for the

Kiowas was preeminently a matter of disposition rather than of survival, and they never understood the grim, unrelenting advance of the U.S. Cavalry. When at last, divided and ill-provisioned, they were driven onto the Staked Plains in the cold rains of autumn, they fell into panic. In Palo Duro Canyon they abandoned their crucial stores to pillage and had nothing then but their lives. In order to save themselves, they surrendered to the soldiers at Fort Sill and were imprisoned in the old stone corral that now stands as a military museum. My grandmother was spared the humiliation of those high gray walls by eight or ten years, but she must have known from birth the affliction of defeat, the dark brooding of old warriors.

Her name was Aho, and she belonged to the last culture to evolve in North America. Her forebears came down from the high country in western Montana nearly three centuries ago. They were a mountain people, a mysterious tribe of hunters whose language has never been positively classified in any major group. In the late seventeenth century they began a long migration to the south and east. It was a journey toward the dawn, and it led to a golden age. Along the way the Kiowas were befriended by the Crows, who gave them the culture and religion of the Plains. They acquired horses, and their ancient nomadic spirit was suddenly free of the ground. They acquired Tai-me, the sacred Sun Dance doll, from that moment the object and symbol of their worship, and so shared in the divinity of the sun. Not least, they acquired the sense of destiny, therefore courage and pride. When they entered upon the southern Plains they had been transformed. No longer were they slaves to the simple necessity of survival; they were a lordly and dangerous society of fighters and thieves, hunters and priests of the sun. According to their origin myth, they entered the world through a hollow log. From one point of view, their migration was the fruit of an old prophecy, for indeed they emerged from a sunless world.

Although my grandmother lived out her long life in the shadow of Rainy Mountain, the immense landscape of the continental interior lay like memory in her blood. She could tell of the Crows, whom she had never seen, and of the Black Hills, where she had never been. I wanted to see in reality what she had seen more perfectly in the mind's eye, and traveled fifteen hundred miles to begin my pilgrimage.

Yellowstone, it seemed to me, was the top of the world, a region of deeplakes and dark timber, canyons and waterfalls. But, beautiful as it is, one might have the sense of confinement there. The skyline in all directions is close at hand, the high wall of the woods and deep cleavages of shade. There is a perfect freedom in the mountains, but it belongs to the eagle and the elk, the badger and the bear. The Kiowas reckoned their stature by the distance they could see, and they were bent and blind in the wilderness.

Descending eastward, the highland meadows are a stairway to the plain.In July the inland slope of the Rockies is luxuriant with flax and buckwheat, stonecrop and larkspur. The earth unfolds and the limit of the land recedes. Clusters of trees, and animals grazing far in the distance, cause the vision to reach away and wonder to build upon the mind. The sun follows a longer course in the day, and the sky is immense beyond all comparison. The great billowing clouds that sail upon it are shadows that move upon the grain like water, dividing light. Farther down, in the land of the Crows and Blackfeet, the plain is yellow. Sweet clover takes hold of the hills and bends upon itself to cover and seal the soil. There the Kiowas paused on their way; they had come to the place where they must change their lives. The sun is at home on the plains. Precisely there does it have the certain character of a god. When the Kiowas came to the land of the Crows, they could see the dark lees of the hills at dawn across the Bighorn River, the profusion of light on the grain shelves, the oldest deity ranging after the solstices. Not yet would they veer southward to the caldron of the land that lay below; they must wean their blood from the northern winter and hold the mountains a while longer in their view. They bore Tai-me in procession to the east.

A dark mist lay over the Black Hills, and the land was like iron. At the top of a ridge I caught sight of Devil's Tower upthrust against the gray sky as if in the birth of time the core of the earth had broken through its crust and the motion of the world was begun. There are things in nature that engender an awful quiet in the heart of man; Devil's Tower is one of them. Two centuries ago, because they could not do otherwise, the Kiowas made a legend at the base of the rock. My grandmother said:

> Eight children were there at play, seven sisters and their brother. Suddenly the boy was struck dumb; he trembled and began to run upon his hands and feet. His fingers became

claws, and his body was covered with fur. Directly there was a bear where the boy had been. The sisters were terrified; they ran, and the bear after them. They came to the stump of a great tree, and the tree spoke to them. It bade them climb upon it, and as they did so it began to rise into the air. The bear came to kill them, but they were just beyond its reach. It reared against the tree and scored the bark all around with its claws. The seven sisters were borne into the sky, and they became the stars of the Big Dipper.

From that moment, and so long as the legend lives, the Kiowas have kinsmen in the night sky. Whatever they were in the mountains, they could be no more. However tenuous their well-being, however much they had suffered and would suffer again, they had found a way out of the wilderness.

My grandmother had a reverence for the sun, a holy regard that now is all but gone out of mankind. There was a wariness in her, and an ancient awe. She was a Christian in her later years, but she had come a long way about, and she never forgot her birthright. As a child she had been to the Sun Dances; she had taken part in those annual rites, and by them she had learned the restoration of her people in the presence of Tai-me. She was about seven when the last Kiowa Sun Dance was held in 1887 on the Washita River above Rainy Mountain Creek. The buffalo were gone. In order to consummate the ancient sacrifice—to impale the head of a buffalo bull upon the medicine tree—a delegation of old men journeyed into Texas, there to beg and barter for an animal from the Goodnight herd. She was ten when the Kiowas came together for the last time as a living Sun Dance culture. They could find no buffalo; they had to hang an old hide from the sacred tree. Before the dance could begin, a company of soldiers rode out from Fort Sill under orders to disperse the tribe. Forbidden without cause the essential act of their faith, having seen the wild herds slaughtered and left to rot upon the ground, the Kiowas backed away forever from the medicine tree. That was July 20, 1890, at the great bend of the Washita. My grandmother was there.Without bitterness, and for as long as she lived, she bore a vision of deicide.

Now that I can have her only in memory, I see my grandmother in the several postures that were peculiar to her: standing at the wood stove on a winter morning and turning meat in a great iron skillet; sitting at the south window, bent above her bead work, and afterwards, when her vision failed, looking down for a long time into the fold of her hands; going out upon a cane, very slowly as she did when the weight of age came upon her; praying. I remember her most often at prayer. She made long, rambling prayers out of suffering and hope, having seen many things. I was never sure that I had the right to hear, so exclusive were they of all mere custom and company. The last time I saw her she prayed standing by the side of her bed at night, naked to the waist, the light of a kerosene lamp moving upon her dark skin. Her long, black hair, always drawn and braided in the day, lay upon her shoulders and against her breasts like a shawl. I do not speak Kiowa, and I never understood her prayers, but there was something inherently sad in the sound,some merest hesitation upon the syllables of sorrow. She began in a high and descending pitch, exhausting her breath to silence; then again and again—and always the same intensity of effort, of something that is, and is not, like urgency in the human voice. Transported so in the dancing light among the shadows of her room, she seemed beyond the reach of time. But that was illusion;I think I knew then that I should not see her again.

Houses are like sentinels in the plain, old keepers of the weather watch. There, in a very little while, wood takes on the appearance of great age. All colors wear soon away in the wind and rain, and then the wood is burned gray and the grain appears and the nails turn red with rust. The windowpanes are black and opaque; you imagine there is nothing within, and indeed there are many ghosts, bones given up to the land. They stand here and there against the sky, and you approach them for a longer time than you expect. They belong in the distance; it is their domain.

Once there was a lot of sound in my grandmother's house, a lot of coming and going, feasting and talk. The summers there were full of excitement and reunion. The Kiowas are a summer people; they abide the cold and keep to themselves, but when the season turns and the land becomes warm and vital they cannot hold still; an old love of going returns upon them. The aged visitors who came to my grandmother's house when I was a child were made of lean and leather, and they bore themselves upright. They wore great black hats and bright ample shirts that shook in the wind. They rubbed fat upon their hair and wound their braids with strips of colored cloth. Some of them painted their faces and carried the scars of old and cherished enmities. They were an old council of warlords, come to remind and be reminded of who they were. Their wives and daughters served them well. The women might indulge themselves; gossip was at once the mark and compensation of their servitude. They made loud and elaborate talk among themselves, full of jest and gesture, fright and false alarm. They went abroad in fringed and flowered shawls, bright beadwork and German silver. They were at home in the kitchen, and they prepared meals that were banquets.

There were frequent prayer meetings, and great nocturnal feasts. When I was a child I played with my cousins outside, where the lamplight fell upon the ground and the singing of the old people rose up around us and carried away into the darkness. There were a lot of good things to eat, a lot of laughter and surprise. And afterwards, when the quiet returned, I lay down with my grandmother and could hear the frogs away by the river and feel the motion of the air.

Now there is funeral silence in the rooms, the endless wake of some final word. The walls have closed in upon my grandmother's house. When I returned to it in mourning, I saw for the first time in my life how small it was. It was late at night, and there was a white moon, nearly full. I sat for a long time on the stone steps by the kitchen door. From there I could see out across the land; I could see the long row of trees by the creek, the low light upon the rolling plains, and the stars of the Big Dipper. Once I looked at the moon and caught sight of a strange thing. A cricket had perched upon the handrail, only a few inches away from me. My line of vision was such that the creature filled the moon like a fossil. It had gone there, I thought, to live and die, for there, of all places, was its small definition made whole and eternal. A warm wind rose up and purled like the longing within me.

The next morning I awoke at dawn and went out on the dirt road to Rainy Mountain. It was already hot, and the grasshoppers began to fill the air. Still, it was early in the morning, and the birds sang out of the shadows. The long yellow grass on the mountain shone in the bright light, and a scissortail hied above the land. There, where it ought to be, at the end of a long and legendary way, was my grandmother's grave. Here and there on the dark stones were ancestral names. Looking back once, I saw the mountain and came away.

DISCUSSION QUESTIONS

1. Momaday combines personal experience, biography, myth, and historical information in his essay. What is the effect of his combining these
varied narratives?

2. There are two travel narratives at play in this essay: Momaday's personal journey and the migration of the Kiowas from Western Montana
to Oklahoma. How are these journeys presented? Which one seems
more compelling?

3. Momaday chooses to begin and end his essay with geographical description. What similarities do you notice between his opening and ending
paragraphs? What differences?

WRITING ASSIGNMENTS

PERSONAL. Recount an experience when you have learned something
important about your ancestry.

RESEARCH. Write a research paper about the causes of immigration.
Document your sources.

PERSUASIVE. Write a paper arguing that people should find out as much as
possible about their family histories.

ANALYTICAL. Write a paper discussing the different kinds of narratives
Momaday uses.

INVESTIGATIVE. Find out about your family history. Report your findings
in a paper.

ALL MEN CAN'T JUMP

David Stipp

*David Stipp has written extensively about science in a number
of national publications, including* The Wall Street Journal, Salon,
and Science. *In 1998 he won a National Association of Science Writers'
award for best magazine article. In this article, published in the online
magazine* Slate *in 2012, Stipp explores human nature as it is revealed
in our athletic abilities.*

You can access this reading with the following link: https://slate.com/culture/2012/06/long-distance-running-and-evolution-why-humans-can-outrun-horses-but-cant-jump-higher-than-cats.html or you can find it by entering the author's name and the title of the reading in your search engine.

DISCUSSION QUESTIONS

1. What is the significance of the title?
2. How does Stipp get the reader's attention in the first paragraph?
3. How does Stipp use narration to substantiate his main idea?

WRITING ASSIGNMENTS

PERSONAL. Write a paper telling a story about an athletic event you have participated in.

RESEARCH. Write a documented paper discussing various kinds of fitness training.

PERSUASIVE. Write a paper advocating that a person should use some particular method of fitness training.

ANALYTICAL. Write a paper analyzing Stipp's use of cause and effect.

INVESTIGATIVE. Conduct a survey to find out the most popular kinds of fitness training among college students. Report your findings in a documented paper.

ECONOMICS AND BUSINESS

THE EMPLOYMENT OF CAPITAL

ADAM SMITH

The Wealth of Nations, a book by the Scottish philosopher Adam Smith (1723-90), was published in 1776 and is generally regarded as the classic work explaining how the free market capitalistic economy works. It also played a key role in establishing economics as an area of study in its own right. It was the first major work in the science of economics and most discussions of economic theory since its publication have been influenced by Smith's theories. This excerpt reveals some of the basic assumptions Smith makes about the way markets work.

Though all capitals are destined for the maintenance of productive labour only, yet the quantity of that labour which equal capitals are capable of putting into motion, varies extremely according to the diversity of their employment; as does likewise the value which that employment adds to the annual produce of the land and labour of the country.

A capital may be employed in four different ways; either, first, in procuring the rude produce annually required for the use and consumption of the society; or, secondly, in manufacturing and preparing that rude produce for immediate use and consumption; or, thirdly in transporting either the rude or manufactured produce from the places where they abound to those where they are wanted; or, lastly, in dividing particular portions of either into such small parcels as suit the occasional demands of those who want them. In the first way are employed the capitals of all those who undertake improvement or cultivation of lands, mines, or fisheries; in the second, those of all master manufacturers; in the third, those of all wholesale merchants; and in the fourth, those of all retailers. It is difficult to conceive that a capital should be employed in any way which may not be classed under some one or other of those four.

Each of those four methods of employing a capital is essentially necessary, either to the existence or extension of the other three, or to the general conveniency of the society.

Unless a capital was employed in furnishing rude produce to a certain degree of abundance, neither manufactures nor trade of any kind could exist.

Unless a capital was employed in manufacturing that part of the rude produce which requires a good deal of preparation before it can be fit for use and consumption, it either would never be produced, because there could be no demand for it; or if it was produced spontaneously, it would be of no value in exchange, and could add nothing to the wealth of the society.

Unless a capital was employed in transporting either the rude or manufactured produce from the places where it abounds to those where it is wanted, no more of either could be produced than was necessary for the consumption of the neighbourhood.

The capital of the merchant exchanges the surplus produce of one place for that of another, and thus encourages the industry, and increases the enjoyments of both.

Unless a capital was employed in breaking and dividing certain portions either of the rude or manufactured produce into such small parcels as suit the occasional demands of those who want them, every man would be obliged to purchase a greater quantity of the goods he wanted than his immediate occasions required. If there was no such trade as a butcher, for example, every man would be obliged to purchase a whole ox or a whole sheep at a time. This would generally be inconvenient to the rich, and much more so to the poor. If a poor workman was obliged to purchase a month's or six months' provisions at a time, a great part of the stock which he employs as a capital in the instruments of his trade, or in the furniture of his shop, and which yields him a revenue, he would be forced to place in that part of his stock which is reserved for immediate consumption, and which yields him no revenue. Nothing can be more convenient for such a person than to be able to purchase his subsistence from day to day, or even from hour to hour, as he wants it. He is thereby enabled to employ almost his whole stock as a capital. He is thus enabled to furnish work to a greater value; and the profit which he makes by it in this way much more than compensates the additional price which the profit of the retailer imposes upon the goods. The prejudices of some political writers against shopkeepers and tradesmen are altogether without foundation. So far is it from being necessary either to tax them, or to restrict their numbers, that they can never be multiplied so as to hurt the public, though they may so as to hurt one another. The quantity of grocery goods, for example, which can be sold in a particular town, is limited by the demand of that town and its neighbourhood. The capital, therefore, which can be employed in the grocery trade, cannot exceed what is sufficient to purchase that quantity. If this capital is divided between two different grocers, their competition will tend to make both of them sell cheaper than if it were in the hands of one only; and if it were divided among twenty, their competition would be just so much the greater, and the chance of their combining together, in order to raise the price, just so much the less. Their competition might, perhaps, ruin some of themselves; but to take care of this, is the business of the parties concerned, and it may safely be trusted to their discretion. It can never hurt either the consumer or the producer; on the contrary, it must tend to make the retailers both sell cheaper and buy dearer, than if the whole trade was monopolized by one or two persons. Some of them, perhaps, may sometimes decoy a weak customer to buy what he has no occasion for. This evil, however, is of too little importance to deserve the public attention, nor would it necessarily be prevented by restricting their numbers. It is not the multitude of alehouses, to give the must suspicious example, that occasions a general disposition to drunkenness among the common people; but that disposition, arising from other causes, necessarily gives employment to a multitude of alehouses.

The persons whose capitals are employed in any of those four ways, are themselves productive labourers. Their labour, when properly directed, fixes and realizes itself in the subject or vendible commodity upon which it is bestowed, and generally adds to its price the value at least of their own maintenance and consumption. The profits of the farmer, of the manufacturer, of the merchant, and retailer, are all drawn from the price of the goods which the two first produce, and the two last buy and sell. Equal capitals, however, employed in each of those four different ways, will immediately put into motion very different quantities of productive labour; and augment, too, in very different proportions, the value of the annual produce of the land and labour of the society to which they belong.

The capital of the retailer replaces, together with its profits, that of the merchant of whom he purchases goods, and thereby enables him to continue his business. The retailer himself is the only productive labourer whom it immediately employs. In his profit consists the whole value which its employment adds to the annual produce of the land and labour of the society.

The capital of the wholesale merchant replaces, together with their profits, the capital's of the farmers and manufacturers of whom he purchases the rude and manufactured produce which he deals in, and thereby enables them to continue their respective trades. It is by this service chiefly that he contributes indirectly to support the productive labour of the society, and to increase the value of its annual produce. His capital employs, too, the sailors and carriers who transport his goods from one place to another; and it augments the price of those goods by the value, not only of his profits, but of their wages. This is all the productive labour which it immediately puts into motion, and all the value which it immediately adds to the annual produce. Its operation in both these respects is a good deal superior to that of the capital of the retailer.

Part of the capital of the master manufacturer is employed as a fixed capital in the instruments of his trade, and replaces, together with its profits, that of some other artificer of whom he purchases them. Part of his circulating capital is employed in purchasing materials, and replaces, with their profits, the capitals of the farmers and miners of whom he purchases them. But a great part of it is always, either annually, or in a much shorter period, distributed among the different workmen whom he employs. It augments the value of those materials by their wages, and by their masters' profits upon the whole stock of wages, materials, and instruments of trade employed in the business. It puts immediately into motion, therefore, a much greater quantity of productive labour, and adds a much greater value to the annual produce of the land and labour of the society, than an equal capital in the hands of any wholesale merchant.

No equal capital puts into motion a greater quantity of productive labour than that of the farmer. Not only his labouring servants, but his labouring cattle, are productive labourers. In agriculture, too, Nature labours along with man; and though her labour costs no expense, its produce has its value, as well as that of the most expensive workmen. The most important operations of agriculture seem intended, not so much to increase, though they do that too, as to direct the fertility of Nature towards the production of the plants most profitable to man. A field overgrown with briars and brambles, may frequently produce as great a quantity of vegetables as the best cultivated vineyard or corn field. Planting and tillage frequently regulate more than they animate the active fertility of Nature; and after all their labour, a great part of the work always remains to be done by her. The labourers and labouring cattle, therefore, employed in agriculture, not only occasion, like the workmen in manufactures, the reproduction of a value equal to their own consumption, or to the capital which employs them, together with its owner's profits, but of a much greater value. Over and above the capital of the farmer, and all its profits, they regularly occasion the reproduction of the rent of the landlord. This rent may be considered as the produce of those powers of Nature, the use of which the landlord lends to the farmer. It is greater or smaller, according to the supposed extent of those powers, or, in other words, according to the supposed natural or improved fertility of the land. It is the work of Nature which remains, after deducting or compensating every thing which can be regarded as the work of man. It is seldom less than a fourth, and frequently more than a third, of the whole produce. No equal quantity of productive labour employed in manufactures, can ever occasion so great reproduction. In them Nature does nothing; man does all; and the reproduction must always be in proportion to the strength of the agents that occasion it. The capital employed in agriculture, therefore, not only puts into motion a greater quantity of productive labour than any equal capital employed in manufactures; but in proportion, too, to the quantity of productive labour which it employs, it adds a much greater value to the annual produce of the land and labour of the country, to the real wealth and revenue of its inhabitants. Of all the ways in which a capital can be employed, it is by far the most advantageous to society.

The capitals employed in the agriculture and in the retail trade of any society, must always reside within that society. Their employment is confined almost to a precise spot, to the farm, and to the shop of the retailer. They must generally, too, though there are some exceptions to this, belong to resident members of the society.

The capital of a wholesale merchant, on the contrary, seems to have no fixed or necessary residence anywhere, but may wander about from place to place, according as it can either buy cheap or sell dear.

The capital of the manufacturer must, no doubt, reside where the manufacture is carried on; but where this shall be, is not always necessarily determined. It may frequently be at a great distance, both from the place where the materials grow, and from that where the complete manufacture is consumed. Lyons is very distant, both from the places which afford the materials of its manufactures, and from those which consume them. The people of fashion in Sicily are clothed in silks made in other countries, from the materials which their own produces. Part of the wool of Spain is manufactured in Great Britain, and some part of that cloth is afterwards sent back to Spain.

Whether the merchant whose capital exports the surplus produce of any society, be a native or a foreigner, is of very little importance. If he is a foreigner, the number of their productive labourers is necessarily less than if he had been a native, by one man only; and the value of their annual produce, by the profits of that one man. The sailors or carriers whom he employs, may still belong indifferently either to his country, or to their country, or to some third country, in the same manner as if he had been a native. The capital of a foreigner gives a value to their surplus produce equally with that of a native, by exchanging it for something for which there is a demand at home. It as effectually replaces the capital of the person who produces that surplus, and as effectually enables him to continue his business, the service by which the capital of a wholesale merchant chiefly contributes to support the productive labour, and to augment the value of the annual produce of the society to which he belongs.

DISCUSSION QUESTIONS

1. Explain how Smith uses classification to organize his explanation.
2. Explain how Smith uses narration of process.
3. Discuss Smith's use of examples to support his main idea.

WRITING ASSIGNMENTS

PERSONAL. Tell about a memorable experience you have had buying or selling something.

RESEARCH. Write a paper discussing the effects of the free market.

PERSUASIVE. Write a paper arguing that an economy should have no governmental controls or conversely that it should have some governmental controls.

ANALYTICAL. Write a paper analyzing Smith's use of examples.

INVESTIGATIVE. Interview the owners or managers of stores in your area to find out the relationship between wholesale and retail process and to determine how profit margins are calculated (either in one particular industry or several).

CONSPICUOUS CONSUMPTION

Thorstein Veblen

Thorstein Veblen is best known for his book The Theory of the Leisure Class *(1899), from which the following excerpt is taken. The book is a devastating analysis of the causes of social pretense and snobbery. Although his work is a reflection of American society at the end of the nineteenth century, it is still relevant to contemporary society. He introduced the term "conspicuous consumption" into our vocabulary. Veblen struggled for acceptance during his lifetime, teaching at a number of different universities. Neither the university administrators nor the students were willing to accommodate his eccentric personality. Nevertheless, his contributions to an understanding of human behavior are still highly regarded.*

During the earlier stages of economic development, consumption of goods without stint, especially consumption of the better grades of goods—ideally all consumption in excess of the subsistence minimum—pertains normally to the leisure class. This restriction tends to disappear, at least formally, after the later peaceable stage has been reached, with private ownership of goods and an industrial system based on wage labor or on the petty household economy. But during the earlier quasi-peaceable stage, when so many of the traditions through which the institution of a leisure class has affected the economic life of later times were taking form and consistency, this principle has had the force of a conventional law. It has served as the norm to which consumption has tended to conform, and any appreciable departure from it is to be regarded as an aberrant form, sure to be eliminated sooner or later in the further course of development.

The quasi-peaceable gentleman of leisure, then, not only consumes of the staff of life beyond the minimum required for subsistence and physical efficiency, but his consumption also undergoes a specialization as regards the quality of the goods consumed. He consumes freely and of the best, in food, drink, narcotics, shelter, services, ornaments, apparel, weapons and accoutrements, amusements, amulets, and idols or divinities. In the process of gradual amelioration which takes place in the articles of his consumption, the motive principle and the proximate aim of innovation is no doubt the higher efficiency of the improved and more elaborate products for personal comfort and well-being. But that does not remain the sole purpose of their consumption. The canon of reputability is at hand and seizes upon such innovations as are, according to its standard, fit to survive. Since the consumption of these more excellent goods is an evidence of wealth, it becomes honorific; and conversely, the failure to consume in due quantity and quality becomes a mark of inferiority and demerit.

This growth of punctilious discrimination as to qualitative excellence in eating, drinking, etc., presently affects not only the manner of life, but also the training and intellectual activity of the gentleman of leisure. He is no longer simply the successful, aggressive male—the man of strength, resource, and intrepidity. In order to avoid stultification he must also cultivate his tastes, for it now becomes incumbent on him to discriminate with some nicety between the noble and the ignoble in consumable goods. He becomes a connoisseur in creditable viands of various degrees of merit, in manly beverages and trinkets, in seemly apparel and architecture, in weapons, games, dances, and the narcotics. This cultivation of the aesthetic faculty requires time and application, and the demands made upon the gentleman in this direction therefore tend to change his life of leisure into a more or less arduous application to the business of learning how to live a life of ostensible leisure in a becoming way. Closely related to the requirement that the gentleman must consume freely and of the right kind of goods, there is the requirement that he must know how to consume them in a seemly manner. His life of leisure must be conducted in due form. Hence arise good manners in the way pointed out in an earlier chapter. High-bred manners and ways of living are items of conformity to the norm of conspicuous leisure and conspicuous consumption.

Conspicuous consumption of valuable goods is a means of reputability to the gentleman of leisure. As wealth accumulates on his hands, his own unaided effort will not avail to sufficiently put his opulence in evidence by this method. The aid of friends and competitors is therefore brought in by resorting to the giving of valuable presents and expensive feasts and entertainments. Presents and feasts had probably another origin than that of naive ostentation, but they acquired their utility for this purpose very early, and they have retained that character to the present; so that their utility in this respect has now long been the substantial ground on which these usages rest. Costly entertainments, such as the potlatch or the ball, are peculiarly adapted to serve this end. The competitor with whom the entertainer wishes to institute a comparison is, by this method, made to serve as a means to the end. He consumes vicariously for his host at the same time that he is a witness to the consumption of that excess of good things which his host is unable to dispose of singlehanded, and he is also made to witness his host's facility in etiquette.

In the giving of costly entertainments other motives, of a more genial kind, are of course also present. The custom of festive gatherings probably originated in motives of conviviality and religion; these motives are also present in the later development, but they do not continue to be the sole motives. The latter-day leisure-class festivities and entertainments may continue in some slight degree to serve the religious need and in a higher degree the needs of recreation and conviviality, but they also serve an invidious purpose; and they serve it none the less effectually for having a colorable non-invidious ground in these more avowable motives. But the economic effect of these social amenities is not therefore lessened, either in the vicarious consumption of goods or in the exhibition of difficult and costly achievements in etiquette.

As wealth accumulates, the leisure class develops further in function and structure, and there arises a differentiation within the class. There is a more or less elaborate system of rank and grades. This differentiation is furthered by the inheritance of wealth and the consequent inheritance of gentility. With the inheritance of gentility goes the inheritance of obligatory leisure; and gentility of a sufficient potency to entail a life of leisure may be inherited without the complement of wealth required to maintain a dignified leisure. Gentle blood may be transmitted without goods enough to afford a reputably free consumption at one's ease. Hence results a class of impecunious gentlemen of leisure, incidentally referred to already. These half-caste gentlemen of leisure fall into a system of hierarchical gradations. Those who stand near the higher and the highest grades of the wealthy leisure class, in point of birth, or in point of wealth, or both, outrank the remoter-born and the pecuniarily weaker. These lower grades, especially the impecunious, or marginal, gentlemen of leisure, affiliate themselves by a system of dependence or fealty to the great ones; by so doing they gain an increment of repute, or of the means with which to lead a life of leisure, from their patron. They become his courtiers or retainers, servants; and being fed and countenanced by their patron they

are indices of his rank and vicarious consumers of his superfluous wealth. Many of these affiliated gentlemen of leisure are at
the same time lesser men of substance in their own right; so that
some of them are scarcely at all, others only partially, to be rated as
vicarious consumers. So many of them, however, as make up the
retainers and hangers-on of the patron may be classed as vicarious
consumers without qualification. Many of these again, and also
many of the other aristocracy of less degree, have in turn attached
to their persons a more or less comprehensive group of vicarious
consumers in the persons of their wives and children, their servants, retainers, etc.

Throughout this graduated scheme of vicarious leisure and
vicarious consumption the rule holds that these offices must be
performed in some such manner, or under some such circumstance
or insignia, as shall point plainly to the master to whom this leisure or consumption pertains, and to whom therefore the resulting
increment of good repute of right inures. The consumption and leisure executed by these persons for their master or patron represents
an investment on his part with a view to an increase of good fame.
As regards feasts and largesses this is obvious enough, and the
imputation of repute to the host or patron here takes place immediately, on the ground of common notoriety. Where leisure and
consumption is performed vicariously by henchmen and retainers,
imputation of the resulting repute to the patron is effected by their
residing ilear his person so that it may be plain to all men from
what source they draw. As the group whose good esteem is to be
secured in this way grows larger, more patent means are required
to indicate the imputation of merit for the leisure performed, and
to this end uniforms, badges, and liveries come into vogue. The
wearing of uniforms or liveries implies a considerable degree of
dependence, and may even be said to be a mark of servitude, real
or ostensible. The wearers of uniforms and liveries may be roughly
divided into two classes-the free and the servile, or the noble and
the ignoble. The services performed by them are likewise divisible
into noble and ignoble. Of course the distinction is not observed
with strict consistency in practice; the less debasing of the base
services and the less honorific of the noble functions are not infrequently merged in the same person. But the general distinction is
not on that account to be overlooked. What may add some per-
plexity is the fact that this fundamental distinction between noble
and ignoble, which rests on the nature of the ostensible service

performed, is traversed by a secondary distinction into honorific and humiliating, resting on the rank of the person for whom the service is performed or whose livery is worn. So, those offices which are by right the proper employment of the leisure class are noble; such as government, fighting, hunting, the care of arms and accoutrements, and the like—in short, those which may be classed as ostensibly predatory employments. On the other hand, those employments which properly fall to the industrious class are ignoble; such as handicraft or other productive labor, menial services and the like. But a base service performed for a person of very high degree may become a very honorific office; as for instance the office of a Maid of Honor or of a Lady in Waiting to the Queen, or the King's Master of the Horse or his Keeper of the Hounds. The two offices last named suggest a principle of some general bearing. Whenever, as in these cases, the menial service in question has to do directly with the primary leisure employments of fighting and hunting, it easily acquires a reflected honorific character. In this way great honor may come to attach to an employment which in its own nature belongs to the baser sort.

In the later development of peaceable industry, the usage of employing an idle corps of uniformed men-at-arms gradually lapses. Vicarious consumption by dependents bearing the insignia of their patron or master narrows down to a corps of liveried menials. In a heightened degree, therefore, the livery comes to be a badge of servitude, or rather of servility. Something of a honorific character always attached to the livery of the armed retainer, but this honorific character disappears when the livery becomes the exclusive badge of the menial. The livery becomes obnoxious to nearly all who are required to wear it. We are yet so little removed from a state of effective slavery as still to be fully sensitive to the sting of any imputation of servility. This antipathy asserts itself even in the case of the liveries or uniforms which some corporations prescribe as the distinctive dress of their employees. In this country the aversion even goes the length of discrediting-in a mild and uncertain way-those government employments, military and civil, which require the wearing of a livery or uniform.

With the disappearance of servitude, the number of vicarious consumers attached to anyone gentleman tends, on the whole, to decrease. The like is of course true, and perhaps in a still higher degree, of the number of dependents who perform vicarious leisure for him. In a general way, though not wholly nor consistently, these two groups coincide. The dependent who was first delegated for these duties was the wife, or the chief wife; and, as would be expected, in the later development of the institution, when the number of persons by whom these duties are customarily performed gradually narrows, the wife remains the last. In the higher grades of society a large volume of both these kinds of service is required; and here the wife is of course still assisted in the work by a more or less numerous corps of menials. But as we descend the social scale, the point is presently reached where the duties of vicarious leisure and consumption devolve upon the wife alone. In the communities of the Western culture, this point is at present found among the lower middle class.

And here occurs a curious inversion. It is a fact of common observance that in this lower middle class there is no pretense of leisure on the part of the head of the household. Through force of circumstances it has fallen into disuse. But the middle-class wife still carries on the business of vicarious leisure, for the good name of the household and its master. In descending the social scale in any modern industrial community, the primary fact-the conspicuous leisure of the master of the household-disappears at a relatively high point. The head of the middle-class household has been reduced by economic circumstances to turn his hand to gaining a livelihood by occupations which often partake largely of the character of industry, as in the case of the ordinary business man of today. But the derivative fact-the vicarious leisure and consumption rendered by the wife, and the auxiliary vicarious performance of leisure by menials-remains in vogue as a conventionality which the demands of reputability will not suffer to be slighted. It is by no means an uncommon spectacle to find a man applying himself to work with the utmost assiduity, in order that his wife may in due form render for him that degree of vicarious leisure which the common sense of the time demands.

The leisure rendered by the wife in such cases is, of course, not a simple manifestation of idleness or indolence. It almost invariably occurs disguised under some form of work or household duties or social amenities, which prove on analysis to serve little or no ulterior end beyond showing that she does not occupy herself with anything that is gainful or that is of substantial use. As has already been noticed under the head of manners, the greater part of the customary round of domestic cares to which the middle-class housewife gives her time and effort is of this

character. Not that the results of her attention to household matters, of a decorative and mundificatory character, are not pleasing
to the sense of men trained in middle-class proprieties; but the
taste to which these effects of household adornment and tidiness
appeal is a taste which has been formed under the selective guidance of a canon of propriety that demands just these evidences
of wasted effort. The effects are pleasing to us chiefly because we
have been taught to find them pleasing. There goes into these
domestic duties much solicitude for a proper combination of form
and color, and for other ends that are to be classed as aesthetic
in the proper sense of the term; and it is not denied that effects
having some substantial aesthetic value are sometimes attained.
Pretty much all that is here insisted on is that, as regards these
amenities of life, the housewife's efforts are under the guidance
of traditions that have been shaped by the law of conspicuously
wasteful expenditure of time and substance. If beauty or comfort
is achieved—and it is a more or less fortuitous circumstance if
they are—they must be achieved by means and methods that
commend themselves to the great economic law of wasted effort.
The more reputable, "presentable" portion of middle-class household paraphernalia are, on the one hand, items of conspicuous
consumption, and on the other hand, apparatus for putting in
evidence the vicarious leisure rendered by the housewife.

The requirement of vicarious consumption at the hands of
the wife continues in force even at a lower point in the pecuniary
scale than the requirement of vicarious leisure. At a point below
which little if any pretense of wasted effort, in ceremonial clean-
ness and the like, is observable, and where there is assuredly no
conscious attempt at ostensible leisure, decency still requires the
wife to consume some goods conspicuously for the reputability
of the household and its head. So that, as the latter-day outcome
of this evolution of an archaic institution, the wife, who was at
the outset the drudge and chattel of the man, both in fact and in
theory-the producer of goods for him to consume-has become the
ceremonial consumer of goods which he produces. But she still
quite unmistakably remains his chattel in theory; for the habitual
rendering of vicarious leisure and consumption is the abiding mark
of the unfree servant.

This vicarious consumption practiced by the household of the
middle and lower classes can not be counted as a direct expression

of the leisure-class scheme of life, since the household of this pecuniary grade does not belong within the leisure class. It is rather
that the leisure-class scheme of life here comes to an expression
at the second remove. The leisure class stands at the head of the
social structure in point of reputability; and its manner of life and
its standards of worth therefore afford the norm of reputability for
the community. The observance of these standards, in some degree
of approximation, becomes incumbent upon all classes lower in the
scale. In modern civilized communities the lines of demarcation
between social classes have grown vague and transient, and wherever this happens the norm of reputability imposed by the upper
class extends its coercive influence with but slight hindrance down
through the social structure to the lowest strata; The result is· that
the members of each stratum accept as their ideal of decency the
scheme of life in vogue in the next higher stratum, and bend their
energies to live up to that ideal. On pain of forfeiting their good
name and their self-respect in case of failure, they must conform to
the accepted code, at least in appearance.

The basis on which good repute in any highly organized
industrial community ultimately rests is pecuniary strength; and
the means of showing pecuniary strength, and so of gaining or
retaining a good name, are leisure and a conspicuous consumption of goods. Accordingly, both of these methods are in vogue as
far down the scale as it remains possible; and in the lower strata
in which the two methods are employed, both offices are in great
part delegated to the wife and children of the household. Lower
still, where any degree of leisure, even ostensible, has become
impracticable for the wife, the conspicuous consumption of goods
remains and is carried on by the wife and children. The man of the
household also can do something in this direction, and indeed,
he commonly does; but with a still lower descent into the levels
of indigence—along the margin of the slums—the man, and
presently also the children, virtually cease to consume valuable
goods for appearances, and the woman remains virtually the sole
exponent of the household's pecuniary decency. No class of society,
not even the most abjectly poor, forgoes all customary conspicuous
consumption. The last items of this category of consumption are
not given up except under stress of the direst necessity. Very much
of squalor and discomfort will be endured before the last trinket or
the last pretense of pecuniary decency is put away. There is no class

and no country that has yielded so abjectly before the pressure of physical want as to deny themselves all gratification of this higher or spiritual need.

From the foregoing survey of the growth of conspicuous leisure and consumption, it appears that the utility of both alike for the purposes of reputability lies in the element of waste that is common to both. In the one case it is a waste of time and effort, in the other it is a waste of goods. Both are methods of demonstrating the possession of wealth, and the two are conventionally accepted as equivalents. The choice between them is a question of advertising expediency simply, except so far as it may be affected by other standards of propriety, springing from a different source. On grounds of expediency the preference may be given to the one or the other at different stages of the economic development. The question is, which of the two methods will most effectively reach the persons whose convictions it is desired to affect. Usage has answered this question in different ways under different circumstances.

So long as the community or social group is small enough and compact enough to be effectually reached by common notoriety alone-that is to say, so long as the human environment to which the individual is required to adapt himself in respect of reputability is comprised within his sphere of personal acquaintance and neighborhood gossip-so long the one method is about as effective as the other. Each will therefore serve about equally well during the earlier stages of social growth. But when the differentiation has gone farther and it becomes necessary to reach a wider human environment, consumption begins to hold over leisure as an ordinary means of decency. This is especially true during the later, peaceable economic stage. The means of communication and the mobility of the population now expose the individual to the observation of many persons who have no other means of judging of his reputability than the display of goods (and perhaps of breeding) which he is able to make while he is under their direct observation.

The modern organization of industry works in the same direction also by another line. The exigencies of the modern industrial system frequently place individuals and households in juxtaposition between whom there is little contact in any other sense than that of juxtaposition. One's neighbors, mechanically speaking, often are socially not one's neighbors, or even acquaintances; and still their transient good opinion has a high degree of utility. The only practicable means of impressing one's pecuniary ability on these unsympathetic observers of one's everyday life is an unremitting demonstration of ability to pay. In the modern community there is also a more frequent attendance at large gatherings of people to whom one's everyday life is unknown; in such places as churches, theaters, ballrooms, hotels, parks, shops, and the like. In order to impress these transient observers, and to retain one's self-complacency under their observation, the signature of one's pecuniary strength should be written in characters which he who runs may read. It is evident, therefore, that the present trend of the development is in the direction of heightening the utility of conspicuous consumption as compared with leisure.

It is also noticeable that the serviceability of consumption as a means of repute, as well as the insistence on it as an element of decency, is at its best in those portions of the community where the human contact of the individual is widest and the mobility of the population is greatest. Conspicuous consumption claims a relatively larger portion of the income of the urban than of the rural population, and the claim is also more imperative. The result is that, in order to keep up a decent appearance, the former habitually live hand-to-mouth to a greater extent than the latter. So it comes, for instance, that the American farmer and his wife and daughters are notoriously less modish in their dress, as well as less urbane in their manners, than the city artisan's family with an equal income. It is not that the city population is by nature much more eager for the peculiar complacency that comes of a conspicuous consumption, nor has the rural population less regard for pecuniary decency. But the provocation to this line of evidence, as well as its transient effectiveness, is more decided in the city. This method is therefore more readily resorted to, and in the struggle to outdo one another the city population push their normal standard of conspicuous consumption to a higher point, with the result that a relatively greater expenditure in this direction is required to indicate a given degree of pecuniary decency in the city. The requirement of conformity to this higher conventional standard becomes mandatory. The standard of decency is higher, class for class, and this requirement of decent appearance must be lived up to on pain of losing caste.

Consumption becomes a larger element in the standard of living in the city than in the country. Among the country population its place is to some extent taken by savings and home comforts known through the medium of neighborhood gossip sufficiently to serve the like general purpose of pecuniary repute. These home comforts and the leisure indulged in—where the indulgence is found—are of course also in great part to be classed as items of conspicuous consumption; and much the same is to be said of the savings. The smaller amount of the savings laid by by the artisan class is no doubt due, in some measure, to the fact that in the case of the artisan the savings are a less effective means of advertisement, relative to the environment in which he is placed, than are the savings of the people living on farms and in the small villages. Among the latter, everybody's affairs, especially everybody's pecuniary status, are known to everybody else. Considered by itself simply-taken in the first degree-this added provocation to which the artisan and the urban laboring classes are exposed may not very seriously decrease the amount of savings; but in its cumulative action, through raising the standard of decent expenditure, its deterrent effect on the tendency to save cannot but be very great.

DISCUSSION QUESTIONS

1. What is Veblen's thesis? What proof of the thesis does he offer?
2. How does Veblen show the relationship between economics and cultural values?
3. What historical influences does Veblen explain? How does Veblen's theory operate in contemporary culture?

WRITING ASSIGNMENTS

PERSONAL. Write a paper telling about time when you have bought something to impress your friends or neighbors.

RESEARCH. Write a research paper about different ways to spend leisure time. Document your sources.

PERSUASIVE. Write a persuasive paper defending the position that people need leisure activities if they are to be successful and happy or that people should avoid wasting time.

ANALYTICAL. Write a paper analyzing the validity of Veblen's evidence.

INVESTIGATIVE. Identify clothes, cars, and/or other products that are designed to impress other people. How are these items marketed? Report your findings in a paper.

BLUE-COLLAR BRILLIANCE
MIKE ROSE

Mike Rose is an American educator and author of the best-selling book, Lives on the Boundaries. *He is currently a research professor at the Graduate School of Education and Information Studies at UCLA. He is the author of 12 books, most recently a 10th-anniversary edition of* The Mind at Work. *In this piece, Rose, using the examples of the members of his family, explores the analytical rigor, the cognitive processes, and ultimately, the intellectual value behind blue-collar work.*

You can access this reading with the following link: https://theamericanscholar.org/blue-collar-brilliance/#.Xpx_3i2ZOEI or you can find it by entering the author's name and the title of the reading in your search engine.

DISCUSSION QUESTIONS

1. Discuss the purpose and effectiveness of Rose's first three paragraphs.
2. Rose uses members of his family as examples to make his point. Identify some of these examples, and explain how each supports Rose's main idea.
3. What conclusions does Rose draw from comparing the cognitive processes involved in white and blue-collar work?

WRITING ASSIGNMENTS

PERSONAL. Write about a personal experience you had working a blue-collar job.

RESEARCH. Write a paper exploring the cultural perceptions of blue-collar work in contemporary life.

PERSUASIVE. Write a paper arguing for the idea that blue-collar work deserves the same compensation and benefits as white-collar work.

ANALYTICAL. Write a paper analyzing Rose's use of comparison and contrast in this essay.

INVESTIGATIVE. Interview people you know and get their opinions about blue-collar work. Can you classify these observations by the survey participants' economic class, race, education, vocation, etc.?

POLITICS AND LAW

COYOTE VS. ACME

IAN FRAZIER

In this clever fictional lawsuit filed by Wile E. Coyote, humorist Ian Frazier makes us aware of the subtle connections between life and art.

In the United States District Court, Southwestern District, Tempe, Arizona
Case No. B19294, Judge Joan Kujava, Presiding

WILE E. COYOTE, Plaintiff
-v.-
ACME COMPANY, Defendant

Opening Statement of Mr. Harold Schoff, attorney for Mr. Coyote: My client, Mr. Wile E. Coyote, a resident of Arizona and contiguous states, does hereby bring suit for damages against the Acme Company, manufacturer and retail distributor of assorted merchandise, incorporated in Delaware and doing business in every state, district, and territory. Mr. Coyote seeks compensation for personal injuries, loss of business income, and mental suffering, caused as a direct result of the actions and/or gross negligence of said company, under Title 15 of the United States Code, Chapter 47, section 2072, subsection (a), relating to product liability.

Mr. Coyote states that on eighty-five separate occasions he has purchased of the Acme Company (hereinafter, "Defendant"), through that company's mail-order department, certain products which did cause him bodily injury due to defects in manufacture or improper cautionary labelling. Sales slips made out to Mr. Coyote as proof of purchase are at present in the possession of the Court, marked Exhibit A. Such injuries sustained by Mr. Coyote have temporarily restricted his ability to make a living in his profession of predator. Mr. Coyote is self-employed and thus not eligible for Workmen's Compensation.

Mr. Coyote states that on December 13th he received of Defendant via parcel post one Acme Rocket Sled. The intention of Mr. Coyote was to use the Rocket Sled to aid him in pursuit of his prey. Upon receipt of the Rocket Sled Mr. Coyote removed it from its wooden shipping crate and, sighting his prey in the distance, activated the ignition. As Mr. Coyote gripped the handlebars, the Rocket Sled accelerated with such sudden and precipitate force as to stretch Mr. Coyote's forelimbs to a length of fifty feet. Subsequently, the rest of Mr. Coyote's body shot forward with a violent jolt, causing severe strain to his back and neck and placing him unexpectedly astride the Rocket Sled. Disappearing over the horizon at such speed as to leave a diminishing jet trail along its path, the Rocket Sled soon brought Mr. Coyote abreast of his prey. At that moment the animal he was pursuing veered sharply to the right. Mr. Coyote vigorously attempted to follow this maneuver but was unable to, due to poorly designed steering on the Rocket Sled and a faulty or nonexistent braking system. Shortly there-after, the unchecked progress of the Rocket Sled brought it and Mr. Coyote into collision with the side of a mesa.

Paragraph One of the Report of Attending Physician (Exhibit B), prepared by Dr. Ernest Grosscup, M.D., D.O., details the multiple fractures, contusions, and tissue damage suffered by Mr. Coyote as a result of this collision. Repairof the injuries required a full bandage around the head (excluding the ears), a neck brace, and full or partial casts on all four legs.

Hampered by these injuries, Mr. Coyote was nevertheless obliged to support himself. With this in mind, he purchased of Defendant as an aid to mobility one pair of Acme Rocket Skates. When he attempted to use this product, however, he became involved in an accident remarkably similar to that which occurred with the Rocket Sled. Again, Defendant sold over the counter, without caveat, a product which attached powerful jet engines (in this case, two) to inadequate vehicles, with little or no provision for passenger safety. Encumbered by his heavy casts, Mr. Coyote lost control of the Rocket Skates soon after strapping them on, and collided with a roadside billboard so violently as to leave a hole in the shape of his full silhouette.

Mr. Coyote states that on occasions too numerous to list in this document he has suffered mishaps with explosives purchased of Defendant: the Acme "Little Giant" Firecracker, the Acme Self-Guided Aerial Bomb, etc. (For a full listing, see the Acme Mail Order Explosives Catalogue and attached deposition, entered in evidence as Exhibit C.) Indeed, it is safe to say that not once has an explosive purchased of Defendant by Mr. Coyote per-formed in an expected manner. To cite just one example: At the expense of much time and personal effort, Mr. Coyote constructed around the outer rim of a butte a wooden trough beginning at the top of the butte and spiralling downward around it to some few feet above a black X painted on the desert floor. The trough was designed in such a way that a spherical explosive of the type sold by Defendant would roll easily and swiftly down to the point of detonation indicated by the X. Mr. Coyote placed a generous pile of birdseed directly on the X, and then, carrying the spherical Acme Bomb (Catalogue # 78-832), climbed to the top of the butte. Mr. Coyote's prey, seeing the birdseed, approached, and Mr. Coyote proceeded to light the fuse. In an instant, the fuse burned down to the stem, causing the bomb to detonate.

In addition to reducing all Mr. Coyote's careful preparations to naught, the premature detonation of Defendant's product resulted in the following disfigurements to Mr. Coyote:

1. Severe singeing of the hair on the head, neck, and muzzle.

2. Sooty discoloration.

3. Fracture of the left ear at the stem, causing the ear to dangle in the aftershockwith a creaking noise.

4. Full or partial combustion of whiskers, producing kinking, frazzling, and ashy disintegration.

5. Radical widening of the eyes, due to brow and lid charring.

We come now to the Acme Spring-Powered Shoes. The remains of a pair of these purchased by Mr. Coyote on June 23rd are Plaintiff's Exhibit D. Selected fragments have been shipped to the metallurgical laboratories of the University of California at Santa Barbara for analysis, but to date no explanation has been found for this product's sudden and extreme malfunction. As advertised by Defendant, this product is simplicity itself: two wood-and-metal sandals, each attached to milled-steel springs of high tensile strength and compressed in a tightly coiled position by a cocking device with a lanyard release. Mr. Coyote believed that this product would enable him to pounce upon his prey in the initial moments of the chase, when swift reflexes are at a premium.

To increase the shoes' thrusting power still further, Mr. Coyote affixed them by their bottoms to the side of a large boulder. Adjacent to the boulder was a path which Mr. Coyote's prey was known to frequent. Mr. Coyote put his hind feet in the wood-and-metal sandals and crouched in readiness, his right forepaw holding firmly to the lanyard release. Within a short time Mr. Coyote's prey did indeed appear on the path coming toward him. Unsuspecting, the prey stopped near Mr. Coyote, well within range of the springs at full extension. Mr. Coyote gauged the distance with care and proceeded to pull the lanyard release.

At this point, Defendant's product should have thrust Mr. Coyote forward and away from the boulder. Instead, for reasons yet unknown, the Acme Spring-Powered Shoes thrust the boulder away from Mr. Coyote. As the intended prey looked on unharmed, Mr. Coyote hung suspended in air. Then the twin springs recoiled, bringing Mr. Coyote to a violent feet-first collision with the boulder, the full weight of his head and forequarters falling upon his lower extremities.

The force of this impact then caused the springs to rebound, whereupon Mr. Coyote was thrust skyward. A second recoil and collision followed. The boulder, meanwhile, which was roughly ovoid in shape, had begun to bounce down a hillside, the coiling and recoiling of the springs adding to its velocity. At each bounce, Mr. Coyote came into contact with the boulder, or the boulder came into contact with Mr. Coyote, or both came into contact with the ground. As the grade was a long one, this process continued for some time. The sequence of collisions resulted in systemic physical damage to Mr. Coyote, viz., flattening of the cranium, sideways displacement of the tongue, reduction of length of legs and upper body, and compression of vertebrae from base of tail to head. Repetition of blows along a vertical axis produced a series of regular horizontal folds in Mr. Coyote's body tissues—a rare and painful condition which caused Mr. Coyote to expand upward and contract downward alternately as he walked, and to emit an off-key, accordionlike wheezing with every step. The distracting and embarrassing nature of this symptom has been a major impediment to Mr. Coyote's pursuit of a normal social life.

As the Court is no doubt aware, Defendant has a virtual monopoly of manufacture and sale of goods required by Mr. Coyote's work. It is our contention that Defendant has used its market advantage to the detriment of the consumer of such specialized products as itching powder, giant kites, Burmese tiger traps, anvils, and two-hundred-foot-long rubber bands. Much as he has come to mistrust Defendant's products, Mr. Coyote has no other domestic source of supply to which to turn. One can only wonder what our trading partners in Western Europe and Japan would make of such a situation, where a giant company is allowed to victimize the consumer in the most reckless and wrongful manner over and over again.

Mr. Coyote respectfully requests that the Court regard these larger economic implications and assess punitive damages in the amount of seventeen million dollars. In addition, Mr. Coyote seeks actual damages (missed meals, medical expenses, days lost from professional occupation) of one million dollars; general damages (mental suffering, injury to reputation) of twenty million dollars; and attorney's fees of seven hundred and fifty thousand dollars. Total damages: thirty-eight million seven hundred and fifty thousand dollars. By awarding Mr. Coyote the full amount, this Court will censure Defendant, its directors, officers, shareholders, successors, and assigns, in the only language they understand, and reaffirm the right of the individual predator to equal protection under the law.

DISCUSSION QUESTIONS

1. How does our familiarity with the cartoon characters affect our reading of the essay?
2. How is the humor created? What makes it different from the humor in a cartoon?
3. What is the effect of Frazier's use of concrete details in his descriptions of Wile E. Coyote.

WRITING ASSIGNMENTS

PERSONAL. Write a paper about some physical injury you have suffered.

RESEARCH. Write a paper about the most common kinds of defects in products.

PERSUASIVE. Write a paper advocating that companies should be held responsible for the malfunction of their products or conversely that the buyer should exercise care when buying products.

ANALYTICAL. Write a paper analyzing the various techniques Frazier used to create humor.

INVESTIGATIVE. Go to an outdoor store like REI and identify products that are potentially dangerous. Write a paper analyzing the problems.

CONCERNING THE WAY IN WHICH PRINCES SHOULD KEEP FAITH

NICCOLÒ MACHIAVELLI

Chapter 28 of Machiavelli's The Prince, *written in 1513, shows why the term Machiavellianism has such a negative connotation and why this chapter in particular has offended political idealists. Machiavelli's defense of political realism and pragmatic morality contradicts most commonly accepted ideals of ethical behavior.*

Every one admits how praiseworthy it is in a prince to keep faith, and to live with integrity and not with craft. Nevertheless our experience has been that those princes who have done great things have held good faith of little account, and have known how to circumvent the intellect of men by craft, and in the end have overcome those who have relied on their word. You must know there are two ways of contesting, the one by the law, the other by force; the first method is proper to men, the second to beasts; but because the first is frequently not sufficient, it is necessary to have recourse to the second. Therefore it is necessary for a prince to understand how to avail himself of the beast and the man. This has been figuratively taught to princes by ancient writers, who describe how Achilles and many other princes of old were given to the Centaur Chiron to nurse, who brought them up in his discipline; which means solely that, as they had for a teacher one who was half beast and half man, so it is necessary for a prince to know how to make use of both natures, and that one without the other is not durable. A prince, therefore, being compelled knowingly to adopt the beast, ought to choose the fox and the lion; because the lion cannot defend himself against snares and the fox cannot defend himself against wolves. Therefore, it is necessary to be a fox to discover the snares and a lion to terrify the wolves. Those who rely simply on the lion do not understand what they are about. Therefore a wise lord cannot, nor ought he to, keep faith when such observance may be turned against him, and when the reasons that caused him to pledge it exist no longer. If men were entirely good this precept would not hold, but because they are bad, and will not keep faith with you, you too are not bound to observe it with them. Nor will there ever be wanting to a prince legitimate reasons to excuse this non-observance. Of this endless modern examples could be given, showing how many treaties and engagements have been made void and of no effect through the faithlessness of princes; and he who has known best how to employ the fox has succeeded best.

But it is necessary to know well how to disguise this characteristic, and to be a great pretender and dissembler; and men are so simple, and so subject to present necessities, that he who seeks to deceive will always find someone who will allow himself to be deceived. One recent example I cannot pass over in silence. Alexander the Sixth did nothing else but deceive men, nor ever thought of doing otherwise, and he always found victims; for there never was a man who had greater power in asserting, or who with greater oaths would affirm a thing, yet would observe it less; nevertheless his deceits always succeeded according to his wishes, because he well understood this side of mankind.

Therefore it is unnecessary for a prince to have all the good qualities I have enumerated, but it is very necessary to appear to have them. And I shall dare to say this also, that to have them and always to observe them is injurious, and that to appear to have them is useful; to appear merciful, faithful, humane, religious, upright, and to be so, but with a mind so framed that should you require not to be so, you may be able and know how to change to the opposite.

And you have to understand this, that a prince, especially a new one, cannot observe all those things for which men are esteemed, being often forced, in order to maintain the state, to act contrary to fidelity, friendship, humanity, and religion. Therefore it is necessary for him to have a mind ready to turn itself accordingly as the winds and variations of fortune force it, yet, as I have said above, not to diverge from the good if he can avoid doing so, but, if compelled, then to know how to set about it.

For this reason a prince ought to take care that he never lets anything slip from his lips that is not replete with the above-named five qualities, that he may appear to him who sees and hears him altogether merciful, faithful, humane, upright, and religious. There is nothing more necessary to appear to have than this last quality, inasmuch as men judge generally more by the eye than by the hand, because it belongs to everybody to see you, to few to come in touch with you. Every one sees what you appear to be, few really know what you are, and those few dare not oppose themselves to the opinion of the many, who have the majesty of the state to defend them; and in the actions of all men, and especially of princes, which it is not prudent to challenge, one judges by the result.

For that reason, let a prince have the credit of conquering and holding his state, the means will always be considered honest, and he will be praised by everybody; because the vulgar are always taken by what a thing seems to be and by what comes of it; and in the world there are only the vulgar, for the few find a place there only when the many have no ground to rest on.

One prince of the present time, whom it is not well to name, never preaches anything else but peace and good faith, and to both he is most hostile, and either, if he had kept it, would have deprived him of reputation and kingdom many a time.

DISCUSSION QUESTIONS

1. Explain the effect of Machiavelli's reference to "ancient writers.
2. Discuss the tone of Machiavelli's work. Some critics have suggested that Machiavelli is being ironic. Is this reading of his work justified?
3. Discuss examples of modern politicians who seem to be following Machiavelli's advice.

WRITING ASSIGNMENTS

PERSONAL. Write a paper about an experience you have had when someone you trusted deceived you.

RESEARCH. Write a documented paper discussing the effects of deception.

PERSUASIVE. Write a paper arguing that leaders in government should always fulfill their promises or conversely that leaders sometimes need to break their promises.

ANALYTICAL. Write a paper discussing Machiavelli's use of examples.

INVESTIGATIVE. Conduct a survey to discover the attitudes of fellow students about the ethics of deception.

THE HISTORY OF THE EQUAL RIGHTS AMENDMENT

Tara Law

> *Tara Law is a journalist based in New York City and works for* Time Magazine. *She writes about health, world news, and politics in the United States. In this piece, Law outlines the history of the Equal Rights Amendment (ERA), which tries to guarantee the sexes equal protection under the law. The ERA gained new prominence after Virginia became the 38th state to pass the amendment in 2020, 97 years after the original text of the ERA was proposed in 1923.*
>
> You can access this reading with the following link: https://time.com/5657997/equal-rights-amendment-history/ or you can find it by entering the author's name and the title of the reading in your search engine.

DISCUSSION QUESTIONS

1. Discuss how Law chooses to organize her article. How does her use of historical examples support her central premise that the US Constitution does not guarantee women equal rights?

2. Law brings up the example of Phyllis Schlafly who opposed the Equal Rights Amendment by noting that the ERA would cause women to lose their special status in society. Do you agree with Schlafly's argument that a "woman should have the right to be in the home as a wife and mother?" Why or why not?

3. Based on the information provided by Law, do you think that the Equal Rights Amendment could still be ratified today? Or would the process need to be initiated all over again?

WRITING ASSIGNMENTS

PERSONAL. Write about an experience when you or a woman you know faced discrimination based on their gender.

RESEARCH. Research the historical origins of the ERA, and write a paper outlining the how the amendment came to be written. Document your sources.

PERSUASIVE. Write a persuasive paper arguing for or against the case that passing the ERA is necessary to guarantee equal rights for men and women.

ANALYTICAL. Write a paper discussing the patterns of organization that Law uses to support her thesis.

INVESTIGATIVE. Interview friends and classmates to determine how they feel about the ratification of the ERA. Report your findings in a paper.

LANGUAGE AND THE ARTS

THE REALISTS

GUY DE MAUPASSANT

Known for his cleverly plotted short stories, Guy de Maupassant was a nineteenth century French writer generally associated with literary realism. This except is taken from the Preface to his novel titled Pierre and Jean *published in 1888.*

The novelist...who professes to give us an exact image of life ought carefully to avoid every concatenation of events that seems exceptional. His object is not to tell a story, to amuse us, to touch our pity, but to compel us to think, and to understand the deep, hidden meaning of events. Through having seen and meditated, he looks at the universe, things, facts and men, in a manner peculiar to himself, the result of the combined effect of observation and reflection. He seeks to impart to us this personal vision of the world by reproducing it in his book. In order to move us as he himself has been moved by the spectacle of life, he must reproduce it before our eyes with scrupulous accuracy. He will have, then, to compose his work so skillfully, with such apparent simplicity, as to conceal his plot and render it impossible to discover his intentions.

Instead of taking an incident and developing it in a manner to render it interesting down to the dénoûment, he will introduce his character or characters at a certain period of their lives, and conduct them, by natural transitions, down to the following period. In this way he will show, at times, how minds are modified under the influence of surrounding circumstances; and, again, how sentiments and passions are developed, how we love, hate, combat each other, in all social conditions; how business interests, money interests, family interests, and political interests, all vie with one another.

The skillful execution of his plan, then, will not consist in emotion or charm, in a fascinating beginning or an affecting catastrophe, but in the adroit grouping of everyday facts from which the definitive meaning of the work may be gathered. If, in three hundred pages, he can portray ten years of a life for the purpose of showing its peculiar and characteristic significance in relation to all the beings that surrounded it, he ought to know how to eliminate, among the innumerable little daily events, all those which are useless to him, and to place in a strong and distinct light all those which would have remained unperceived by less clear-sighted observers, and which give his book its power and its value as a whole.

One can understand how such a manner of composition, so different from the old method, apparent to all eyes, often bewilders the critics, and that they do not discover the fine, secret, almost invisible threads employed by certain modern artists in place of the single thread which was called "the plot."

In brief, if the novelist of yesterday selected and related the crises of life, the poignant emotions of soul and heart, the novelist of to-day writes the history of the heart, the soul, and the intellect, in their normal condition. To produce the effect he aims at, that is, the feeling of simple reality, and to bring out the artistic lesson which he desires to draw from it, that is, the revelation of the real contemporary man before his eyes, he must employ only actual and incontestable facts. But if we place ourselves at the very point of view of those realistic artists, we must discuss and contest their theory, which seems to be summed up in these words, "The whole truth, and nothing but the truth."

Their intention being to bring out the philosophy of certain current everyday facts, they are often obliged to change events in the interest of probability and to the detriment of truth, for "Truth may sometimes be improbable."

The realist, if he is an artist, will seek, not to show us a vulgar photograph of life, but to give us a more complete, striking and convincing vision of life than the reality itself.

It would be impossible to narrate everything, for it would require at least a volume a day to enumerate the multitude of insignificant incidents that fill up our existence.

Some selection is therefore imposed on the writer, and this is the first blow at the theory of the "whole truth."

Life, besides, is composed of the most different, most unforeseen, most contrary, and most incongruous things; it is brutal, without sequence or connection, full of inexplicable, illogical and contradictory catastrophes which ought to be classed under the heading, "Various Events."

That is why the artist, having chosen his theme, selects in this life, incumbered as it is with accidents and trivialities, only those characteristic details necessary to his subject, and will cast all the rest aside.

One example out of a thousand. The number of people in the world who die every day by accident is considerable. But we cannot make a tile fall on the head of a principal character, or throw him under the wheels of a carriage in the middle of a story, under pretext that it is necessary to introduce an accident.

Life, again, leaves everything just as it finds it, precipitates action, or drags it out indefinitely. Art, on the contrary, consists in using forethought and care in elaboration, bringing into prominence, through sheer skill in composition, the essential incidents, and in giving to all the rest the degree of prominence proportioned to their importance, in order to produce a convincing impression of the special truth it seeks to portray.

To make things real consists, therefore, in giving a complete similitude of truth according to the ordinary logical sequence of facts, and not in transcribing them, servilely, one after another, in the order of their successive occurrence.

Hence, I conclude that the realists of art ought rather to call themselves the illusionists.

DISCUSSION QUESTIONS

1. What does Maupassant say the object of the novelist is?
2. How does Maupassant contrast the differences between "the novelist of yesterday" and the "realistic artists" in their approach to plot?
3. What are the implications of Maupassant's statement, "Truth may sometimes be improbable"?

WRITING ASSIGNMENTS

PERSONAL. In this reading Maupassant says, "Truth may sometimes be improbable. " Write about an experience you have had that illustrates that concept.

RESEARCH. Identify kinds of historical literary movements and write a documented paper explaining them.

PERSUASIVE. Write a paper advocating that writers of fiction should write stories that are realistic.

ANALYTICAL. Write a paper analyzing Maupassant's use of narration of process.

INVESTIGATIVE. Create a survey to find out what kinds of popular literature (mysteries, romances, westerns, sci-fi, fantasy, etc.) your classmates prefer. Report your findings in a paper.

THE HERESY OF THE DIDACTIC

Edgar Allan Poe

Most people think of Edgar Allan Poe as a writer of haunting poems like "The Raven" and "Annabel Lee" as well as Gothic short stories like "The Fall of the House of Usher" and "The Cask of Amontillado." He was, however, also an important literary critic and literary theorist. This excerpt comes from "The Philosophy of Composition" first published in Graham's Magazine *in 1846.*

. . . . It has been assumed, tacitly and avowedly, directly and indirectly, that the ultimate object of all Poetry is Truth. Every poem, it is said, should inculcate a moral; and by this moral is the poetical merit of the work to be adjudged. We Americans especially have patronized this happy idea; and we Bostonians, very especially, have developed it in full. We have taken it into our heads that to write a poem simply for the poem's sake, and to acknowledge such to have been our design, would be to confess ourselves radically wanting in the true Poetic dignity and force:—but the simple fact is, that, would we permit ourselves to look into our own souls, we should immediately there discover that under the sun there exists nor *can* exist any work more thoroughly dignified—more supremely noble than this very poem—this poem *perse*—this poem which is a poem and nothing more—this poem written solely for the poem's sake.

With as deep a reverence for the True as ever inspired the bosom of man, I would, nevertheless, limit, in some measure, its modes of inculcation. I would limit to enforce them. I would not enfeeble them by dissipation. The demands of Truth are severe. She has no sympathy with the myrtles. All *that* which is so indispensable in Song, is precisely all *that* with which *she* has nothing whatever to do. It is but making her a flaunting paradox, to wreathe her in gems and flowers. In enforcing a truth, we need severity rather than efflorescence of language. We must be simple, precise, terse. We must be cool, calm, unimpassioned. In a word, we must be in that mood which, as nearly as possible, is the exact converse of the poetical. *He* must be blind indeed who does not perceive the radical and chasmal differences between the truthful and poetical modes of inculcation. He must be theory-mad beyond redemption who, in spite of these differences, shall still persist in attempting to reconcile the obstinate oils and waters of Poetry and Truth.

Dividing the world of the mind into its three most immediately obvious distinctions, we have the Pure Intellect, Taste, and the Moral Sense. I place Taste in the middle, because it is just this position which, in the mind, it occupies. It holds intimate relations with wither extreme; but from the Moral Sense is separated by so faint a difference that Aristotle has not hesitated to place some of its operations among the virtues themselves. Nevertheless, we find the offices of the trio marked with a sufficient distinction. Just as the Intellect concerns itself with Truth, so Taste informs us of the Beautiful while the Moral Sense is regardful of Duty. Of this latter, while Conscience teaches the obligation, and Reason the expediency, Taste contents herself with displaying the charms:— waging war upon Vice solely on the ground of her deformity—her disproportion—her animosity to the fitting, to the appropriate, to the harmonious—in a word, to Beauty.

An immortal instinct, deep within the spirit of man, is thus, plainly, a sense of the Beautiful. This is what administers to his delight in the manifold forms, and sounds and odors, and sentiments amid which he exists. And just as the lily is repeated in the lake, or the eyes of Amaryllis in the mirror, so is the mere oral or written repetition of these forms, and sounds, and colors, and odors, and sentiments, a duplicate source of delight. But this mere repetition is not poetry. He who shall simply sing, with however glowing enthusiasm, or with however vivid a truth of description, of the sights, and sounds, and odors, and colors, and sentiments, which greet him in common with all mankind—he, I say, has yet failed to prove his divine title. There is still a something in the distance which he has been unable to attain. We have still a thirst unquenchable, to allay which he has not shown us the crystal springs. This thirst belongs to the immortality of Man. It is at once a consequence and an indication of his perennial existence. It is the desire of the moth for the star. It is no mere appreciation of the Beauty before us—but a wild effort to reach the Beauty above. Inspired by an ecstatic presence of the glories beyond the grave, we struggle, by multiform combinations among the things and thoughts of Time, to attain a portion of Loveliness whose very elements, perhaps, appertain to eternity alone. And thus when by Poetry—or when by Music, the most entrancing of the Poetic moods—we find ourselves melted into tears—we weep then . . . through excess of pleasure, but through a certain, petulant, impatient sorrow at our inability to grasp *now*, wholly, here on earth, at once and forever, those divine and rapturous joys, of which *through* the poem, or *through* the music, we attain to but brief and indeterminate glimpses.

The struggle to apprehend the supernal Loveliness—this struggle, on the part of souls fittingly constituted—has given to the world all *that* which it (the world) has ever been enabled at once to understand and to feel as poetic.

The Poetic Sentiment, of course, may develop itself in various modes—in painting, in Sculpture, in Architecture, in the Dance—very especially in Music—and very peculiarly, and with a wide field, in the composition of the Landscape Garden. Our present theme, however, has regard only to its manifestations in words. And here let me speak briefly on the topic of rhythm. Contenting myself with the certainty that Music, in its various modes of metre, rhythm, and rhyme, is of so vast a moment in Poetry as never to be wisely rejected—is so vitally important an adjunct, that he is simply silly who declines its assistance, I will not now pause to maintain its absolute essentiality. It is in Music, perhaps, that the soul most nearly attains the great end for which, when inspired by the Poetic Sentiment, it struggles—the creation of supernal Beauty. It *may* be, indeed, that here this sublime end is, now and then, attained *in fact*.

We are often made to feel with a shivering delight, that from an earthly harp are stricken notes which *cannot* have been unfamiliar to the angels. And thus there can be little doubt that in the union of Poetry with Music in its popular sense, we shall find the widest field for the Poetic development. The old Bards and Minnesingers had advantages which we do not possess—and Thomas More, singing his own songs, was, in the most legitimate manner, perfecting them as poems.

To recapitulate, then:—I would define, in brief, the Poetry of words as *The Rhythmical Creation of Beauty*. Its sole arbiter is Taste. With the Intellect or with the Conscience, it has only collateral relations. Unless incidentally, it has no concern whatever with Duty or with Truth.

A few words, however, in explanation. *That* pleasure which is at once the most pure, the most elevating, and the most intense, is derived, I maintain, from the contemplation of the Beautiful. In the contemplation of Beauty we alone find it possible to attain that pleasurable elevation, or excitement *of the soul*, which we recognize as the Poetic Sentiment, and which is so easily distinguished from Truth, which is the satisfaction of the Reason, or from passion, which is the excitement of the heart. I make Beauty, therefore—using the word as inclusive of the sublime—I make Beauty the province of the poem, simple because it is an obvious rule of Art that effects should be made to spring as directly as possible from their causes: no one as yet having been weak enough to deny that the peculiar elevation in question is at least *most readily* attainable in the poem. It by no means follows however, that the incitements of Passion, or the precepts of Duty, or even the Lessons of Truth, may not be introduced into a poem, and with advantage; for they may subserve, incidentally, in various ways, the general purposes of the work:—but the true artist will always contrive to tone them down in proper subjection to that *Beauty* which is at atmosphere and the real essence of the poem.

DISCUSSION QUESTIONS

1. What does Poe mean by the term "the poem per se"?
2. What are the implications of Poe's equating poetry with beauty?
3. Why does Poe introduce the term truth into his discussion of poetry and beauty?

WRITING ASSIGNMENTS

PERSONAL. Write a narrative that tells about a time when you were struck by the beauty of something (a poem, a song, a painting, or a sculpture).

RESEARCH. Identify and discuss different kinds of beauty. Document your sources in a research paper.

PERSUASIVE. Write a paper arguing that the arts should be encouraged in public schools.

ANALYTICAL. Analyze Poe's use of definition as a way of explaining his ideas.

INVESTIGATIVE. Go to an art museum and using as many paintings or sculptures as you wish, come up with a definition of beauty.

CULTURE MATTERS! HOW CULTURAL KNOWLEDGE INFLUENCES LANGUAGE

Vyvyan Evans

Vyvyan Evans is a professor of linguistics who has published numerous books and articles about language and communication. In this article he explains the importance of culture to language.

You can access this reading with the following link: https://www.psychologytoday.com/us/blog/language-in-the-mind/201503/culture-matters-how-cultural-knowledge-influences-language or you can find it by entering the author's name and the title of the reading in your search engine.

DISCUSSION QUESTIONS

1. What is Evans' main idea?
2. Discuss the function of his use of examples.
3. How does he use division to organize his essay?

WRITING ASSIGNMENTS

PERSONAL. Tell about a difficult or perplexing encounter you have had with a person or people from a culture different from your own.

RESEARCH. Write a research paper explaining different kinds of languages in the world. Document your sources.

PERSUASIVE. Write a paper defending or refuting the idea that people should broaden their experiences with other cultures.

ANALYTICAL. Write a paper analyzing Evans' use of narration.

INVESTIGATIVE. Create a glossary of terms that require a broad cultural understanding—e.g. Dickensian, Victorian, Orwellian—or terms from a particular culture that have acquired a broader usage—e.g. Olympian, Namaste, _____gate (for a political scandal). You may want to consult a history textbook for ideas.

NATURE AND OTHER HABITATS

THE MYTHOLOGY OF THE AMERICAN WEST

WILLIAM KITTREDGE

William Kittredge, born on his family's cattle ranch in Oregon, returned to it after a time in the service and worked there until it was sold. This selection reflects Kittredge's impressions of agribusiness and the mythology of the West. He taught English and creative writing at the University of Montana until he retired in 1997. As you read this excerpt from his book Owning It All, *note how Kittredge reveals to us the complex relationships between agriculture and the natural environment.*

Agriculture is often envisioned as an art, and it can be. Of course there is always survival, and bank notes, and all that. But your basic bottom line on the farm is again and again some notion of how life should be lived. The majority of agricultural people, if you press them hard enough, even though most of them despise sentimental abstractions, will admit they are trying to create a good place, and to live as part of that goodness, in the kind of connection which with fine reason we call rootedness. It's just that there is good art and bad art.

These are thoughts which come back when I visit eastern Oregon. I park and stand looking down into the lava-rock and juniper-tree canyon where Deep Creek cuts its way out of the Warner Mountains, and the great turkey buzzard soars high in the yellow-orange light above the evening. The fishing water is low, as it always is in late August, unfurling itself around dark and broken boulders. The trout, I know, are hanging where the currents swirl across themselves, waiting for the one entirely precise and lucky cast, the Renegade fly bobbing toward them.

Even now I can see it, each turn of water along miles of that creek. Walk some stretch enough times with a fly rod and its con-figurations will imprint themselves on your being with Newtonian exactitude. Which is beyond doubt one of the attractions of such fishing—the hours of learning, and then the intimacy with a living system that carries you beyond the sadness of mere gaming for sport.

What I liked to do, back in the old days, was pack in some spuds and an onion and corn flour and spices mixed up in a plastic bag, a small cast-iron frying pan in my wicker creel and, in the last twilight on a gravel bar by the water, cook up a couple of rainbows over a fire of snapping dead willow and sage, eating alone while the birds flitted through the last hatch, wiping my greasy fingers on my pants while the heavy trout began rolling at the lower ends of the pools.

The canyon would be shadowed under the moon when I walked out to show up home empty-handed, to sit with my wife over a drink of whiskey at the kitchen table. Those nights I would go to bed and sleep without dreams, a grown-up man secure in the house and the western valley where he had been a child, enclosed in a topography of spirit he assumed he knew more closely than his own features in the shaving mirror.

So, I ask myself, if it was such a pretty life, why didn't I stay? The peat soil in Warner Valley was deep and rich, we ran good cattle, and my most sacred memories are centered there. What could run me off?

Well, for openers, it got harder and harder to get out of bed in the mornings and face the days, for reasons I didn't understand. More and more I sought the comfort of fishing that knowable creek. Or in winter the blindness of television.

My father grew up on a homestead place on the sagebrush flats outside Silver Lake, Oregon. He tells of hiding under the bed with his sisters when strangers came to the gate. He grew up, as we all did in that country and era, believing that the one sure defense against the world was property. I was born in 1932, and recall a life before the end of World War II in which it was possible for a child to imagine that his family owned the world.

Warner Valley was largely swampland when my grandfather bought the M C Ranch with no downpayment in 1936, right at the heart of the Great Depression. The outside work was done mostly by men and horses and mules, and our ranch valley was filled with life. In 1937 my father bought his first track-layer, a secondhand RD6 Caterpillar he used to build a 17-mile diversion canal to carry the spring floodwater around the east side of the valley, and we were on our way to draining all swamps. The next year he bought an RD7 and a John Deere 36 combine which cut an 18-foot swath, and we were deeper into the dream of power over nature and men, which I had begun to inhabit while playing those long-ago games of war.

The peat ground left by the decaying remnants of ancient tule beds was diked into huge undulating grainfields—Houston Swamp with 750 irrigated acres, Dodson Lake with 800—a final total of almost 8,000 acres under cultivation, and for reasons of what seemed like common sense and efficiency, the work became industrialized. Our artistry worked toward a model whose central image was the machine.

The natural patterns of drainage were squared into dragline ditches, the tules and the aftermath of the oat and barley crops were burned—along with a little more of the combustible peat soil every year. We flood-irrigated when the water came in spring, drained in late March, and planted in a 24-hour-a-day frenzy which began around April 25 and ended—with luck—by the 10th of May, just as leaves on the Lombardy poplar were breaking from their buds. We summered our cattle on more than a million acres of Taylor Grazing Land across the high lava rock and sagebrush desert out east of the valley, miles of territory where we owned most of what water there was, and it was ours. We owned it all, or so we felt. The government was as distant as news on the radio.

The most intricate part of my job was called "balancing water," a night and day process of opening and closing pipes and redwood headgates and running the 18-inch drainage pumps. That system was the finest plaything I ever had.

And despite the mud and endless hours, the work remained play for a long time, the making of a thing both functional and elegant. We were doing God's labor and creating a good place on earth, living the pastoral yeoman dream—that's how our mythology defined it, although nobody would ever have thought to talk about work in that way.

And then it all went dead, over years, but swiftly.

You can imagine our surprise and despair, our sense of having been profoundly cheated. It took us a long while to realize some unnamable thing was wrong, and then we blamed it on ourselves, our inability to manage enough. But the fault wasn't ours, beyond the fact that we had all been educated to believe in a grand bad factory-land notion as our prime model of excellence.

We felt enormously betrayed. For so many years, through endless efforts, we had proceeded in good faith, and it turned out we had wrecked all we had not left untouched. The beloved migratory rafts of waterbirds, the green-headed mallards and the redheads and canvasbacks, the cinnamon teal and the great Canadian honkers, were mostly gone along with their swampland habitat. The hunting, in so many ways, was no longer what it had been.

We wanted to build a reservoir, and litigation started. Our laws were being used against us, by people who wanted a share of what we thought of as our water. We could not endure the boredom of our mechanical work, and couldn't hire anyone who cared enough to do it right. We baited the coyotes with 1080, and rodents destroyed our alfalfa; we sprayed weeds and insects with 2-4-D Ethyl and Malathion, and Parathion for clover mite, and we shortened our own lives.

In quite an actual way we had come to victory in the artistry of our playground warfare against all that was naturally alive in our native home. We had reinvented our valley according to the most persuasive ideal given us by our culture, and we ended with a landscape organized like a machine for growing crops and fattening cattle, a machine that creaked a little louder each year, a dreamland gone wrong.

One of my strongest memories comes from a morning when I was maybe 10 years old, out on the lawn before our country home in spring, beneath a bluebird sky. I was watching the waterbirds coming off the valley swamps and grainfields where they had been feeding overnight. They were going north to nesting grounds on the Canadian tundra, and that piece of morning, inhabited by the sounds of their wings and their calling in the clean air, was wonder-filled and magical. I was enclosed in a living place.

No doubt that memory has persisted because it was a sight of possibility which I will always cherish—an image of the great good place rubbed smooth over the years like a river stone, which I touch again as I consider why life in Warner Valley went so seriously haywire. But never again in my lifetime will it be possible for a child to stand out on a bright spring morning in Warner Valley and watch the waterbirds come through in enormous, rafting vee-shaped flocks of thousands—and I grieve.

My father is a very old man. A while back we were driving up the Bitterroot Valley of Montana, and he was gazing away to the mountains. "They'll never see it the way we did," he said, and I wonder what he saw.

We shaped our piece of the West according to the model provided by our mythology, and instead of a great good place such order had given us enormous power over nature, and a blank perfection of fields.

A mythology can be understood as a story that contains a set of implicit instructions from a society to its members, telling them what is valuable and how to conduct themselves if they are to preserve the things they value.

The teaching mythology we grew up with in the American West is a pastoral story of agricultural ownership. The story begins with a vast innocent continent, natural and almost magically alive, capable of inspiring us to reverence and awe, and yet savage, a wilderness. A good rural people come from the East, and they take the land from its native inhabitants, and tame it for agricultural purposes, bringing civilization: a notion of how to live embodied in law. The story is as old as invading armies, and at heart it is a racist, sexist, imperialist mythology of conquest; a rationale for violence—against other people and against nature.

At the same time, that mythology is a lens through which we continue to see ourselves. Many of us like to imagine ourselves as honest yeomen who sweat and work in the woods or the mines or the fields for a living. And many of us are. We live in a real family, a work-centered society, and we like to see ourselves as people with the good luck and sense to live in a place where some vestige of the natural world still exists in working order. Many of us hold that natural world as sacred to some degree, just as it is in our myth. Lately, more and more of us are coming to understand our society in the American West as an exploited colony, threatened by greedy outsiders who want to take our sacred place away from us, or at least to strip and degrade it.

In short, we see ourselves as a society of mostly decent people who live with some connection a holy wilderness, threatened by those who lust for power and property. We look for Shane to come riding out of the Tetons, and instead we see Exxon and the Sierra Club. One looks virtually as alien as the other.

And our mythology tells us we own the West, absolutely and morally—we own it because of our history. Our people brought law to this difficult place, they suffered and they shed blood and they survived, and they earned this land for us. Our efforts have surely earned us the right to absolute control over the thing we created. The myth tells us this place is ours, and will always be ours, to do with as we see fit.

That's a most troubling and enduring message, because we want to believe it, and we do believe it, so many of us, despite its implicit ironies and wrongheadedness, despite the fact that we took the land from someone else. We try to ignore a genocidal history of violence against the Native Americans.

In the American West we are struggling to revise our dominant mythology, and to find a new story to inhabit. Laws control our lives, and they are designed to preserve a model of society based on values learned from mythology. Only after re-imagining our myths can we coherently remodel our laws, and hope to keep our society in a realistic relationship to what is actual.

In Warner Valley we thought we were living the right lives, creating a great precise perfection of fields, and we found the mythology had been telling us an enormous lie. The world had proven too complex, or the myth too simpleminded. And we were mortally angered.

The truth is, we never owned all the land and water. We don't even own very much of them, privately. And we don't own anything absolutely or forever. As our society grows more and more complex and interwoven, our entitlement becomes less and less absolute, more and more likely to be legally diminished. Our rights to property will never take precedence over the needs of society. Nor should they, we all must agree in our grudging hearts.

Ownership of property has always been a privilege granted by society, and revokable.

DISCUSSION QUESTIONS

1. How does Kittredge characterize farmers? What were the effects of the factory-land notion of farming on the land?
2. How does Kittredge describe the mythology of the west? What does he say is the flaw in that mythology?
3. What is Kittredge's view of property ownership? How does your view of the mythology of the West, farm life, and property ownership compare to Kittredge's? What experiences have affected your views?

WRITING ASSIGNMENTS

PERSONAL. Write about an experience you have had in a rural area.

RESEARCH. Write a paper explaining how a particular aspect of land use in some region of the U.S. (water use, livestock grazing, planting crops, logging, etc.) may affect the natural environment.

PERSUASIVE. Write a persuasive paper advocating that a particular use of land that is damaging the environment should be discontinued or curtailed.

ANALYTICAL. Write a paper analyzing Kittredge's use of personal experience as an appeal in his argument. How does he create a compelling narrative?

INVESTIGATIVE. Interview classmates and friends to find out what they believe to be the American Myth of the west. Report your findings.

THE WOODS AND THE PACIFIC

Robert Louis Stevenson

> *Robert Louis Stevenson is certainly best known for his novels, especially his two classics* Treasure Island *(1883) and* Dr Jekyll and Mr Hyde *(1886). The reading that follows is an excerpt from* Across the Plains, *a travel memoir about a trip across America by train from New York to San Francisco in 1879. It was first published in 1883.*

The Bay of Monterey has been compared by no less a person than General Sherman to a bent fishing-hook; and the comparison, if less important than the march through Georgia, still shows the eye of a soldier for topography. Santa Cruz sits exposed at the shank; the mouth of the Salinas river is at the middle of the bend; and Monterey itself is cosily ensconced beside the barb. Thus the ancient capital of California faces across the bay, while the Pacific Ocean, though hidden by low hills and forest, bombards her left flank and rear with never-dying surf. In front of the town, the long line of sea-beach trends north and north-west, and then westward to enclose the bay. The waves which lap so quietly about the jetties of Monterey grow louder and larger in the distance; you can see the breakers leaping high and white by day; at night, the outline of the shore is traced in transparent silver by the moonlight and the flying foam; and from all round, even in quiet weather, the distant, thrilling roar of the Pacific hangs over the coast and the adjacent country like smoke above a battle.

These long beaches are enticing to the idle man. It would be hard to find a walk more solitary and at the same time more exciting to the mind. Crowds of ducks and sea-gulls hover over the sea. Sandpipers trot in and out by troops after the retiring waves, trilling together in a chorus of infinitesimal song. Strange sea- tangles, new to the European eye, the bones of whales, or sometimes a whole whale's carcase, white with carrion-gulls and poisoning the wind, lie scattered here and there along the sands. The waves come in slowly, vast and green, curve their translucent necks, and burst with a surprising uproar, that runs, waxing and waning, up and down the long key-board of the beach. The foam of these great ruins mounts in an instant to the ridge of the sand glacis, swiftly fleets back again, and is met and buried by the next breaker. The interest is perpetually fresh. On no other coast that I know shall you enjoy, in calm, sunny weather, such a spectacle of Ocean's greatness, such beauty of changing colour, or such degrees of thunder in the sound. The very air is more than usually salt by this Homeric deep.

Inshore, a tract of sand-hills borders on the beach. Here and there a lagoon, more or less brackish, attracts the birds and hunters. A rough, undergrowth partially conceals the sand. The crouching, hardy live-oaks flourish singly or in thickets—the kind of wood for murderers to crawl among—and here and there the skirts of the forest extend downward from the hills with a floor of turf and long aisles of pine-trees hung with Spaniard's Beard. Through this quaint desert the railway cars drew near to Monterey from the junction at Salinas City—though that and so many other things are now for ever altered—and it was from here that you had the first view of the old township lying in the sands, its white windmills bickering in the chill, perpetual wind, and the first fogs of the evening drawing drearily around it from the sea.

The one common note of all this country is the haunting presence of the ocean. A great faint sound of breakers follows you high up into the inland canons; the roar of water dwells in the clean, empty rooms of Monterey as in a shell upon the chimney; go where you will, you have but to pause and listen to hear the voice of the Pacific. You pass out of the town to the south-west, and mount the hill among pine-woods. Glade, thicket, and grove surround you. You follow winding sandy tracks that lead nowhither. You see a deer; a multitude of quail arises. But the sound of the sea still follows you as you advance, like that of wind among the trees, only harsher and stranger to the ear; and when at length you gain the summit, out breaks on every hand and with freshened vigour that same unending, distant, whispering rumble of the ocean; for now you are on the top of Monterey peninsula, and the noise no longer only mounts to you from behind along the beach towards Santa Cruz, but from your right also, round by Chinatown and Pinos lighthouse, and from down before you to the mouth of the Carmello river. The whole woodland is begirt with thundering surges. The silence that immediately surrounds you where you stand is not so much broken as it is haunted by this distant, circling rumour. It sets your senses upon edge; you strain your attention; you are clearly and unusually conscious of small sounds near at hand; you walk listening like an Indian hunter; and that voice of the Pacific is a sort of disquieting company to you in your walk.

DISCUSSION QUESTIONS

1. Discuss Stevenson's use of figurative imagery.
2. How does Stevenson introduce tension into his descriptions.
3. How does the central image of the ocean control the descriptions in this selection?

WRITING ASSIGNMENTS

PERSONAL. Tell about an experience you have had in a scenic place.

RESEARCH. Write a research paper about the most popular kinds of destinations for outdoor vacations.

PERSUASIVE. Write a paper arguing that people should spend time in contact with nature.

ANALYTICAL. Analyze Stevenson's use of descriptive imagery.

INVESTIGATIVE. Go to a scenic place. Identify its unique qualities. Report your findings in a paper.

BUILDING MORE SUSTAINABLE CITIES

WILLIAM E. REES

William E. Rees is Professor Emeritus at the University of British Columbia's School of Community and Regional Planning in Vancouver, Canada. Rees is best known for his innovative work in the field of ecological economics, where he, along with a former student of his, developed "ecological footprint analysis." Today, eco-footprint analysis is perhaps the best-known indicator for sustainability. In this essay, Rees argues that the city of the future must be re-envisioned as "bio-regional city states" in order to reduce our urban ecological footprint.

You can access this reading with the following link: https://www.scientificamerican.com/article/building-more-sustainable-cities/ or you can find it by entering the author's name and the title of the reading in your search engine.

DISCUSSION QUESTIONS

1. How does Rees establish himself as an authority on the subject of sustainability?

2. In what ways does Rees create a sense of urgency through his use of examples?

3. Rees identifies certain historical trends in urban planning that led to the current state of the North American city. How does Rees use cause and effect in his piece?

WRITING ASSIGNMENTS

PERSONAL. Write about your experience with living in an urban environment, or about a visit to a city.

RESEARCH. Research ways in which people in an urban environment can live in a more sustainable fashion. Record your findings in a research paper.

PERSUASIVE. Write a paper arguing that a better way to address the problems with climate change is to create a sustainable urban environment, or make the argument that it is better to leave city life in order to mitigate the effects of climate change.

ANALYTICAL. Write a paper analyzing Rees' use of appeals.

INVESTIGATIVE. Identify features of the city or town you live in that reflect sustainability. Report you findings in a paper.

SCIENCE AND TECHNOLOGY

IS GOOGLE MAKING US STUPID?

Nicholas Carr

Nicholas Carr's articles about technology and culture have been published in a number of prominent national periodicals. This article originally appeared in the Atlantic *in 2008 and was later expanded into a book* The Shallows: What the Internet Is Doing to Our Brains, *a* New York Times *bestseller and a finalist for the Pulitzer Prize.*

"Dave, stop. Stop, will you? Stop, Dave. Will you stop, Dave?" So the supercomputer HAL pleads with the implacable astronaut Dave Bowman in a famous and weirdly poignant scene toward the end of Stanley Kubrick's *2001: A Space Odyssey.* Bowman, having nearly been sent to a deep-space death by the malfunctioning machine, is calmly, coldly disconnecting the memory circuits that control its artificial "brain." "Dave, my mind is going," HAL says, forlornly. "I can feel it. I can feel it."

I can feel it, too. Over the past few years I've had an uncomfortable sense that someone, or something, has been tinkering with my brain, remapping the neural circuitry, reprogramming the memory. My mind isn't going—so far as I can tell—but it's changing. I'm not thinking the way I used to think. I can feel it most strongly when I'm reading. Immersing myself in a book or a lengthy article used to be easy. My mind would get caught up in the narrative or the turns of the argument, and I'd spend hours strolling through long stretches of prose. That's rarely the case anymore. Now my concentration often starts to drift after two or three pages. I get fidgety, lose the thread, begin looking for something else to do. I feel as if I'm always dragging my wayward brain back to the text. The deep reading that used to come naturally has become a struggle.

I think I know what's going on. For more than a decade now, I've been spending a lot of time online, searching and surfing and sometimes adding to the great databases of the Internet. The Web has been a godsend to me as a writer. Research that once required days in the stacks or periodical rooms of libraries can now be done in minutes. A few Google searches, some quick clicks on hyperlinks, and I've got the telltale fact or pithy quote I was after. Even when I'm not working, I'm as likely as not to be foraging in the Web's info-thickets, reading and writing e-mails, scanning headlines and blog posts, watching videos and listening to podcasts, or just tripping from link to link to link. (Unlike footnotes, to which they're sometimes likened, hyperlinks don't merely point to related works; they propel you toward them.)

For me, as for others, the Net is becoming a universal medium, the conduit for most of the information that Hows through my eyes and ears and into my mind. The advantages of having immediate access to such an incredibly rich store of information are many, and they've been widely described and duly applauded. "The perfect recall of silicon memory," *Wired's* Clive Thompson has written, "can be an enormous boon to thinking." But that boon comes at a price. As the media theorist Marshall McLuhan pointed out in the 1960s, media are not just passive channels of information. They supply the stuff of thought, but they also shape the process of thought. And what the Net seems to be doing is chipping away my capacity for concentration and contemplation. My mind now expects to take in information the way the Net distributes it: in a swiftly moving stream of particles. Once I was a scuba diver in the sea of words. Now I zip along the surface like a guy on a Jet Ski.

I'm not the only one. When I mention my troubles with reading to friends and acquaintances—literary types, most of them—many say they're having similar experiences. The more they use the Web, the more they have to fight to stay focused on long pieces of writing. Some of the bloggers I follow have also begun mentioning the phenomenon. Scott Karp, who writes a blog about online media, recently confessed that he has stopped reading books altogether. "1 was a lit major in college, and used to be [a] voracious book reader," he wrote. "What happened?" He speculates on the answer: "What if I do all my reading on the Web not so much because the way I read has changed, i.e., I'm just seeking convenience, but because the way I THINK has changed?"

Bruce Friedman, who blogs regularly about the use of computers in medicine, also has described how the Internet has altered his mental habits. "I now have almost totally lost the ability to read and absorb a longish article on the Web or in print," he wrote earlier this year. A pathologist who has long been on the faculty of the University of Michigan Medical School, Friedman elaborated on his comment in a telephone conversation with me. His thinking, he said, has taken on a "staccato" quality, reflecting the way he quickly scans short passages of text from many sources online. "I can't read *War and Peace* anymore," he admitted. "I've lost the ability to do that. Even a blog post of more than three or four paragraphs is too much to absorb. I skim it."

Anecdotes alone don't prove much. And we still await the long-term neurological and psychological experiments that will provide a definitive picture of how Internet use affects cognition. But a recently published study of online research habits, conducted by scholars from University College London, suggests that we may well be in the midst of a sea change in the way we read and think. As part of the five-year research program, the scholars examined computer logs documenting the behavior of visitors to two popular research sites, one operated by the British Library and one by a U.K. educational consortium, that provide access to journal articles, e-books, and other sources of written information. They found that people using the sites exhibited "a form of skimming activity," hopping from one source to another and rarely returning to any source they'd already visited. They typically read no more than one or two pages of an article or book before they would "bounce" out to another site. Sometimes they'd save a long article, but there's no evidence that they ever went back and actually read it. The authors of the study report:

> It is clear that users are not reading online in the traditional sense; indeed there are signs that new forms of "reading" are emerging as users "power browse" horizontally through titles, contents pages and abstracts going for quick wins. It almost seems that they go online to avoid reading in the traditional sense.

Thanks to the ubiquity of text on the Internet, not to mention the popularity of text-messaging on cell phones, we may well be reading more today than we did in the 1970s or 1980s, when television was our medium of choice. But it's a different kind of reading, and behind it lies a different kind of thinking—perhaps even a new sense of the self. "We are not only *what* we read," says Maryanne Wolf, a developmental psychologist at Tufts University and the author of *Proust and the Squid: The Stoiy and Science of the Reading Brain.* "We are *how* we read." Wolf worries that the style of reading promoted by the Net, a style that puts "efficiency" and "immediacy" above all else, may be weakening our capacity for the kind of deep reading that emerged when an earlier technology, the printing press, made long and complex works of prose commonplace. When we read online, she says, we tend to become "mere decoders of information." Our ability to interpret text, to make the rich mental connections that form when we read deeply and without distraction, remains largely disengaged.

Reading, explains Wolf, is not an instinctive skill for human beings. It's not etched into our genes the way speech is. We have to teach our minds how to translate the symbolic characters we see into the language we understand. And the media or other technologies we use in learning and practicing the craft of reading play an important part in shaping the neural circuits inside our brains. Experiments demonstrate that readers of ideograms, such as the Chinese, develop a mental circuitry for reading that is very different from the circuitry found in those of us whose written language employs an alphabet. The variations extend across many regions of the brain, including those that govern such essential cognitive functions as memory and the interpretation of visual and auditory stimuli. We can expect as well that the circuits woven by our use of the Net will be different from those woven by our reading of books and other printed works.

Sometime in 1882, Friedrich Nietzsche bought a type-writer—a Malling-Hanscn Writing Ball, to be precise. His vision was failing, and keeping his eyes focused on a page had become exhausting and painful, often bringing on crushing headaches. He had been forced to curtail his writing, and he feared that he would soon have to give it up. The typewriter rescued him, at least for a time. Once he had mastered touch-typing, he was able to write with his eyes closed, using only the tips of his fingers. Words could once again (low from his mind to the page.

But the machine had a subtler effect on his work. One of Nietzsche's friends, a composer, noticed a change in the style of his writing. His already terse prose had become even tighter, more telegraphic. "Perhaps you will through this instrument even take to a new idiom," the friend wrote in a letter, noting that, in his own work, his "'thoughts' in music and language often depend on the quality of pen and paper."

"You are light," Nietzsche replied, "our writing equipment takes part in the forming of our thoughts." Under the sway of the machine, writes the German media scholar Friedrich A. Kittler, Nietzsche's prose "changed from arguments to aphorisms, from thoughts to puns, from rhetoric to telegram style."

The human brain is almost infinitely malleable. People used to think that our mental meshwork, the dense connections formed among the 100 billion or so neurons inside our skulls, was largely fixed by the time we reached adulthood. But brain researchers have discovered that that's not the case. James Olds, a professor of neuroscience who directs the Krasnow Institute lor Advanced Study at George Mason University, says that even the adult mind "is very plastic." Nerve cells routinely break old connections and form new ones. "The brain," according to Olds, "has the ability to reprogram itself on the lly, altering the way it functions."

As we use what the sociologist Daniel Bell has called our "intellectual technologies"—the tools that extend our mental rather than our physical capacities—we inevitably begin to take on the qualities of those technologies. The mechanical clock, which came into common use in the 14th century, provides a compelling example. In *Technics and Civilization*, the historian and cultural critic Lewis Mumford described how the clock "disassociated time from human events and helped create the belief in an independent world of mathematically measurable sequences." The "abstract framework of divided time" became "the point of reference for both action and thought."

The clocks methodical ticking helped bring into being the scientific mind and the scientific man. But it also took something away. As the late MIT computer scientist Joseph Weizenbaum observed in his 1976 book, *Computer Power and Human Reason: From Judgment to Calculation*, the conception of the world that emerged from the widespread use of timekeeping instruments "remains an impoverished version of the older one, for it rests on a rejection of those direct experiences that formed the basis lor, and indeed constituted, the old reality." In deciding when to eat, to work, to sleep, to rise, we stopped listening to our senses and started obeying the clock.

The process of adapting to new intellectual technologies is reflected in the changing metaphors we use to explain ourselves to ourselves. When the mechanical clock arrived, people began thinking of their brains as operating "like clockwork." Today, in the age of software, we have come to think of them as operating "like computers." But the changes, neuroscience tells us, go much deeper than metaphor. Thanks to our brain's plasticity, the adaptation occurs also at a biological level.

The Internet promises to have particularly far-reaching effects on cognition. In a paper published in 1936, the British mathematician Alan Turing proved that a digital computer, which at the time existed only as a theoretical machine, could be programmed to perform the function of any other information-processing device. And that's what we're seeing today. The Internet, an immeasurably powerful computing system, is subsuming most of our other intellectual technologies. It's becoming our map and our clock, our printing press and our typewriter, our calculator and our telephone, and our radio and TV.

When the Net absorbs a medium, that medium is re-created in ' the Net's image. It injects the medium's content with hyperlinks, blinking ads, and other digital gewgaws, and it surrounds the content with the content of all the other media it has absorbed. A new e-mail message, for instance, may announce its arrival as we're glancing over the latest headlines at a newspaper's site. The result is to scatter our attention and diffuse our concentration.

The Net's influence doesn't end at the edges of a computer screen, either. As people's minds become attuned to the crazy quilt of Internet media, traditional media have to adapt to the audience's new expectations. Television programs add text crawls and pop-up ads, and magazines and newspapers shorten their articles, introduce capsule summaries, and crowd their pages with easy-to-browse info-snippets. When, in March of this year, the *New York Times* decided to devote the second and third pages of every edition to article abstracts, its design director, Tom Bodkin, explained that the "shortcuts" would give harried readers a quick "taste" of the day's news, sparing them the "less efficient" method of actually turning the pages and reading the articles. Old media have little choice but to play by the new-media rules.

Never has a communications system played so many roles in our lives—or exerted such broad influence over our thoughts—as the Internet does today. Yet, for all that's been written about the Net, there's been little consideration of how, exactly, it's reprogramming us. The Net's intellectual ethic remains obscure.

About the same time that Nietzsche started using his typewriter, an earnest young man named Frederick Winslow Taylor carried a stopwatch into the Midvale Steel plant in Philadelphia and began a historic series of experiments aimed at improving the efficiency of the plant's machinists. With the approval of Midvale's owners, he recruited a group of factory hands, set them to work on various metalworking machines, and recorded and timed their every movement as well as the operations of the machines. By breaking down every job into a sequence of small, discrete steps and then testing different ways of performing each one, Taylor created a set of precise instructions—an "algorithm," we might say today—for how each worker should work. Midvale's employees grumbled about the strict new regime, claiming that it turned them into little more than automatons, but the factory's productivity soared.

More than a hundred years after the invention of the steam engine, the Industrial Revolution had at last found its philosophy and its philosopher. Taylor's tight industrial choreography—his "system," as he liked to call it—was embraced by manufacturers throughout the country and, in time, around the world. Seeking maximum speed, maximum efficiency, and maximum output, factory owners used time-and-motion studies to organize their work and configure the jobs of their workers. The goal, as Taylor defined it in his celebrated 1911 treatise, *The Principles of Scientific Management*, was to identify and adopt, for every job, the "one best method" of work and thereby to effect "the gradual substitution of science for rule of thumb throughout the mechanic arts." Once his system was applied to all acts of manual labor, Taylor assured his followers, it would bring about a restructuring not only of industry but of society, creating a Utopia of perfect efficiency. "In the past the man has been first," he declared; "in the future the system must be first."

Taylors system is still very much with us; it remains the ethic of industrial manufacturing. And now, thanks to the growing power that computer engineers and software coders wield over our intellectual lives, Taylor's ethic is beginning to govern the realm of the mind as well. The Internet is a machine designed for the efficient and automated collection, transmission, and manipulation of information, and its legions of programmers are intent on finding the "one best method"—the perfect algorithm—to carry out every mental movement of what we've come to describe as "knowledge work."

Google's headquarters, in Mountain View, California—the Googleplex—is the Internet's high church, and the religion practiced inside its walls is Taylorism. Google, says its chief executive, Eric Schmidt, is "a company that's founded around the science of measurement," and it is striving to "systematize everything" it does. Drawing on the terabytes of behavioral data it collects through its search engine and other sites, it carries out thousands of experiments a day, according to the *Harvard Business Review*, and it uses the results to refine the algorithms that increasingly control how people find information and extract meaning from it. What Taylor did for the work of the hand, Google is doing for the work of the mind.

The company has declared that its mission is "to organize the world's information and make it universally accessible and useful." It seeks to develop "the perfect search engine," which it defines as something that "understands exactly what you mean and gives you back exactly what you want." In Google's view, information is a kind of commodity, a utilitarian resource that can be mined and processed with industrial efficiency. The more pieces of information we can "access" and the faster we can extract their gist, the more productive we become as thinkers.

Where does it end? Sergey Brin and Larry Page, the gifted young men who founded Google while pursuing doctoral degrees in computer science at Stanford, speak frequently of their desire to turn their search engine into an artificial intelligence, a HAL-like machine that might be connected directly to our brains. "The ultimate search engine is something as smart as people—or smarter," Page said in a speech a few years back. "For us, working on search is a way to work on artificial intelligence." In a 2004 interview with *Newsweek*, Brin said, "Certainly if you had all the world's information directly attached to your brain, or an artificial brain that was smarter than your brain, you'd be better off." Last year, Page told a convention of scientists that Google is "really trying to build artificial intelligence and to do it on a large scale."

Such an ambition is a natural one, even an admirable one, for a pair of math whizzes with vast quantities of cash at their disposal and a small army of computer scientists in their employ. A fundamentally scientific enterprise, Google is motivated by a desire to use technology, in Eric Schmidt's words, "to solve problems that have never been solved before," and artificial intelligence is the hardest problem out there. Why wouldn't Brin and Page want to be the ones to crack it?

Still, their easy assumption that we'd all "be better off" if our brains were supplemented, or even replaced, by an artificial intelligence is unsettling. It suggests a belief that intelligence is the output of a mechanical process, a series of discrete steps that can be isolated, measured, and optimized. In Google's world, the world we enter when we go online, there's little place for the fuzziness of contemplation. Ambiguity is not an opening for insight but a bug to be fixed. The human brain is just an outdated computer that needs a faster processor and a bigger hard drive.

The idea that our minds should operate as high-speed dataprocessing machines is not only built into the workings of the Internet, it is the network's reigning business model as well. The faster we surf across the Web—the more links we click and pages we view—the more opportunities Google and other companies gain to collect information about us and to feed us advertisements. Most of the proprietors of the commercial Internet have a financial stake in collecting the crumbs of data we leave behind as we flit from link to link—the more crumbs, the better. The last thing these companies want is to encourage leisurely reading or slow, concentrated thought. It's in their economic interest to drive us to distraction.

Maybe I'm just a worrywart. Just as there's a tendency to glorify technological progress, there's a countertendency to expect the worst of every new tool or machine. In Plato's *Phaedrus*, Socrates bemoaned the development of writing. He feared that, as people came to rely on the written word as a substitute for the knowledge they used to carry inside their heads, they would, in the words of one of the dialogue's characters, "cease to exercise their memory and become forgetful." And because they would be able to "receive a quantity of information without proper instruction," they would "be thought very knowledgeable when they are for the most part quite ignorant." They would be "filled with the conceit of wisdom instead of real wisdom." Socrates wasn't wrong—the new technology did often have the effects he feared—but he was shortsighted. He couldn't foresee the many ways that writing and reading would serve to spread information, spur fresh ideas, and expand human knowledge (if not wisdom).

The arrival of Gutenberg's printing press, in the 15th century, set off another round of teeth gnashing. The Italian humanist Hieronimo Squarciafico worried that the easy availability of books would lead to intellectual laziness, making men "less studious" and weakening their minds. Others argued that cheaply printed books and broadsheets would undermine religious authority, demean the work of scholars and scribes, and spread sedition and debauchery. As New York University professor Clay Shirky notes, "Most of the arguments made against the printing press were correct, even prescient." But, again, the doomsayers were unable to imagine the myriad blessings that the printed word would deliver.

So, yes, you should be skeptical of my skepticism. Perhaps those who dismiss critics of the Internet as Luddites or nostalgists will be proved correct, and from our hyperactive, datastoked minds will spring a golden age of intellectual discovery and universal wisdom. Then again, the Net isn't the alphabet, and although it may replace the printing press, it produces something altogether different. The kind of deep reading that a sequence of printed pages promotes is valuable not just for the knowledge we acquire from the author's words but for the intellectual vibrations those words set off within our own minds. In the quiet spaces opened up by the sustained, undistracted reading of a book, or by any other act of contemplation, for that matter, we make our own associations, draw our own inferences and analogies, foster our own ideas. Deep reading, as Maryanne Wolf argues, is indistinguishable from deep thinking.

If we lose those quiet spaces, or fill them up with "content," we will sacrifice something important not only in our selves but in our culture. In a recent essay, the playwright Richard Foreman eloquently described what's at stake:

> I come from a tradition of Western culture, in which the ideal (my ideal) was the complex, dense and "cathedral-like" structure of the highly educated and articulate personality—a man or woman who carried inside themselves a personally constructed and unique version of the entire heritage of the West. [But now] I see within us all (myself included) the replacement of complex inner density with a new kind of self—evolving under the pressure of information overload and the technology of the "instantly available."

As we are drained of our "inner repertory of dense cultural inheritance," Foreman concluded, we risk turning into "'pancake people'—spread wide and thin as we connect with that vast network of information accessed by the mere touch of a button."

I'm haunted by that scene in *2001*. What makes it so poignant, and so weird, is the computer's emotional response to the disassembly of its mind: its despair as one circuit after another goes dark, its childlike pleading with the astronaut—"I can feel it. I can feel it. I'm afraid"—and its final reversion to what can only be called a state of innocence, HAL'S outpouring of feeling contrasts with the emotionlessness that characterizes the human figures in the film, who go about their business with an almost robotic efficiency. Their thoughts and actions feel scripted, as if they're following the steps of an algorithm. In the world of *2001*, people have become so machinelike that the most human character turns out to be a machine. That's the essence of Kubrick's dark prophecy: as we come to rely on computers to mediate our understanding of the world, it is our own intelligence that flattens into artificial intelligence.

DISCUSSION QUESTIONS

1. What is the effect of the opening paragraph?
2. What is Carr's attitude toward technological progress? How is that attitude related to his main idea?
3. What is the significance of the image "pancake people"?

WRITING ASSIGNMENTS

PERSONAL. Tell about an experience you have had when your use of the Internet has made you feel positive (or negative) about it.

RESEARCH. Write a research paper discussing the various uses of the Internet in modern society.

PERSUASIVE. Write a persuasive paper advocating that people should resist (or fully embrace) the use of the Internet in their daily lives.

ANALYTICAL. Write a paper analyzing Carr's use of narration to substantiate his main idea.

INVESTIGATIVE. Interview friends and classmates to discover their attitudes about using the Internet. Report your findings in a paper.

LOOK AT YOUR FISH!

SAMUEL SCUDDER

In this essay first published in 1874, Samuel Scudder, an entomologist and paleontologist, records his experience at Harvard as a student of the biologist Louis Agassiz. The method of observation and analysis taught by Agassiz illustrates the application of inductive reasoning.

It was more than fifteen years ago that I entered the laboratory of Professor Agassiz, and told him I had enrolled my name in the scientific school as a student of natural history. He asked me a few questions about my object in coming, my antecedents generally, the mode in which I afterwards proposed to use the knowledge I might acquire, and finally, whether I wished to study any special branch. To the latter I replied that while I wished to be well grounded in all departments of zoology, I purposed to devote myself specially to insects.

"When do you wish to begin?" he asked.

"Now," I replied.

This seemed to please him, and with an energetic "Very well," he reached from a shelf a huge jar of specimens in yellow alcohol.

"Take this fish," said he, "and look at it; we call it a haemulon; by and by I will ask what you have seen."

With that he left me, but in a moment returned with explicit instructions as to the care of the object entrusted to me.

"No man is fit to be a naturalist," said he, "who does not know how to take care of specimens."

I was to keep the fish before me in a tin tray, and occasionally moisten the surface with alcohol from the jar, always taking care to replace the stopper tightly. Those were not the days of ground glass stoppers, and elegantly shaped exhibition jars; all the old students will recall the huge, neckless glass bottles with their leaky, wax-besmeared corks, half eaten by insects and begrimed with cellar dust. Entomology was a cleaner science than ichthyology, but the example of the professor, who had unhesitatingly plunged to the bottom of the jar to produce the fish, was infectious; and though this alcohol had "a very ancient and fish-like smell," I really dared not show any aversion within these sacred precincts, and treated the alcohol as though it were pure water. Still I was conscious of a passing feeling of disappointment, for gazing at a fish did not commend itself to an ardent entomologist. My friends at home, too, were annoyed, when they discovered that no eau de cologne would drown the perfume which haunted me like a shadow.

In ten minutes I had seen all that could be seen in that fish, and started in search of the professor, who had however left the museum; and when I returned, after lingering over some of the odd animals stored in the upper apartment, my specimen was dry all over. I dashed the fluid over the fish as if to resuscitate the beast from a fainting fit, and looked with anxiety for a return of the normal, sloppy appearance. This little excitement over, nothing was to be done but return to a steadfast gaze at my mute companion. Half an hour passed—an hour—another hour; the fish began to look loathsome. I turned it over and around; looked it in the face—ghastly; from behind, beneath, above, sideways, at a three-quarters view—just as ghastly. I was in despair; at an early hour I concluded that lunch was necessary; so, with infinite relief, the fish was carefully replaced in the jar, and for an hour I was free.

On my return, I learned that Professor Agassiz had been at the museum, but had gone and would not return for several hours. My fellow-students were too busy to be disturbed by continued conversation. Slowly I drew forth that hideous fish, and with a feeling of desperation again looked at it. I might not use a magnifying glass; instruments of all kinds were interdicted. My two hands, my two eyes, and the fish: it seemed a most limited field. I pushed my finger down its throat to feel how sharp the teeth were. I began to count the scales in the different rows until I was convinced that that was nonsense. At last a happy thought struck me—I would draw the fish; and now with surprise I began to discover new features in the creature. Just then the professor returned.

"That is right," said he; "a pencil is one of the best of eyes. I am glad to notice, too, that you keep your specimen wet, and your bottle corked."

With these encouraging words, he added, "Well, what is it like?"

He listened attentively to my brief rehearsal of the structure of parts whose names were still unknown to me; the fringed gill-arches and movable operculum; the pores of the head, fleshy lips and lidless eyes; the lateral line, the spinous fins, and forked tail; the compressed and arched body. When I had finished, he waited as if expecting more, and then, with an air of disappointment: "You have not looked very carefully; why," he continued, more earnestly, "you haven't even see one of the most conspicuous features of the animal, which is as plainly before your eyes as the fish itself; look again, look again!" and he left me to my misery.

I was piqued; I was mortified. Still more of that wretched fish! But now I set myself to my task with a will, and discovered one new thing after another, until I saw how just the professor's criticism had been. The afternoon passed quickly, and when, towards its close, the professor inquired:

"Do you see it yet?"

"No," I replied, "I am certain I do not, but I see how little I saw before."

"That is the next best," said he earnestly, "but I won't hear you now; put away your fish and go home; perhaps you will be ready with a better answer in the morning. I will examine you before you look at the fish."

This was disconcerting; not only must I think of my fish all night, studying without the object before me, what this unknown but most visible feature might be; but also, without reviewing my new discoveries, I must give an exact account of them the next day. I had a bad memory; so I walked home by the Charles River in a distracted state, with my two perplexities.

The cordial greeting from the professor the next morning was reassuring; here was a man who seemed to be quite as anxious as I that I should see for myself what he saw.

"Do you perhaps mean," I asked, "that the fish has symmetrical sides with paired organs?"

His thoroughly pleased "Of course! of course!" repaid the wakeful hours of the previous night. After he had discoursed most happily and enthusiastically—as he always did—upon the importance of this point, I ventured to ask what I should do next.

"Oh, look at your fish!" he said, and left me again to my own devices. In a little more than an hour he returned and heard my new catalogue.

"That is good, that is good!" he repeated; "but that is not all; go on"; and so for three long days he placed that fish before my eyes; forbidding me to look at anything else, or to use any artificial aid. "Look, look, look," was his repeated injunction.

This was the best entomological lesson I ever had—a lesson, whose influence has extended to the details of every subsequent study; a legacy the professor has left to me, as he has left it to many others, of inestimable value, which we could not buy, with which we cannot part.

A year afterward, some of us were amusing ourselves with chalking outlandish beasts upon the museum blackboard. We drew prancing star-fishes; frogs in mortal combat; hydra-headed worms; stately crawfishes, standing on their tails, bearing aloft umbrellas; and grotesque fishes with gaping mouths and staring eyes. The professor came in shortly after and was as amused as any at our experiments. He looked at the fishes.

"Haemulons, every one of them," he said; "Mr. _____ drew them."

True; and to this day, if I attempt a fish, I can draw nothing but haemulons.

The fourth day, a second fish of the same group was placed beside the first, and I was bidden to point out the resemblances and differences between the two; another and another followed, until the entire family lay before me, and a whole legion of jars covered the table and surrounding shelves; the odor had become a pleasant perfume; and even now, the sight of an old, six-inch, worm eaten cork brings fragrant memories!

The whole group of haemulons was thus brought in review; and, whether engaged upon the dissection of the internal organs, the preparation and examination of the bony framework, or the description of the various parts, Agassiz's training in the method of observing facts and their orderly arrangement, was ever accompanied by the urgent exhortation not to be content with them.

"Facts are stupid things," he would say, "until brought into connection with some general law."

At the end of eight months, it was almost with reluctance that I left these friends and turned to insects; but what I had gained by this outside experience has been of greater value than years of later investigation in my favorite groups.

DISCUSSION QUESTIONS

1. Discuss the structure of Scudder's narrative.
2. Discuss Scudder's illustration of the process of inductive reasoning.
3. What does the narrative suggest about the nature of teaching and learning?

WRITING ASSIGNMENTS

PERSONAL. Write a paper about an experience you have had in a science lab.

RESEARCH. Write a documented paper about the uses of scientific investigation.

PERSUASIVE. Write a paper arguing that students should approach their studies systematically.

ANALYTICAL. Write a paper discussing Scudder's use of dialogue.

INVESTIGATIVE. Use the method suggested by Scudder to draw some general conclusions about some aspect of your environment (your home, your neighborhood, or some public area).

BY ANY OTHER NAME

Neil deGrasse Tyson

Neil deGrasse Tyson is an astrophysicist ad is Frederick P. Rose Director of New York City's Hayden Planetarium. Beginning in the fall of 2006, Tyson hosted the PBS series NOVA ScienceNow. *In 2012 he edited and hosted the thirteen-part series* Cosmos: A SpaceTime Odyssey, *a continuation of Carl Sagan's celebrated television series. His latest book (his tenth)* Space Chronicles: Facing the Ultimate Frontier *reveals his insights about the past, present, and future of space exploration. This article was first published in Natural History Magazine,* July/August 2001.

You can access this reading with the following link: https://www.haydenplanetarium.org/tyson/essays/2001-07-by-any-other-name.php or you can find it by entering the author's name and the title of the reading in your search engine.

DISCUSSION QUESTIONS

1. What is the effect of Tyson's opening sentence—the comparison of the big toe to the Big Bang, not the epigraph attributed to Galen.

2. Discuss Tyson's use of humor. Does it add to or detract from his discussion?

3. Discuss the effectiveness of the examples Tyson uses.

WRITING ASSIGNMENTS

PERSONAL. Write a paper about an experience in school when you tried to learn the specialized vocabulary used in a course you were taking.

RESEARCH. Write a documented paper examining the various languages that have given rise to scientific terminology.

PERSUASIVE. Write a paper arguing that academic disciplines should simplify the technical language they use.

ANALYTICAL. Write a paper analyzing Tyson's use of examples to support his main idea.

INVESTIGATIVE. Create a survey to find out how your classmates view courses in the sciences in regard to difficulty, interest, opportunity for creativity, relevance, for example.

PHILOSOPHY AND RELIGION

DISCOURSE FOUR

René Descartes

René Descartes is often called the "Father of Modern Philosophy" because he emphasized the use of reason as a way of discovering knowledge. He used this rational approach in trying to discover the meaning of the natural world. The famous quote "I think; therefore I am" is found in this excerpt from Part IV of Discourse on the Method of Rightly Conducting the Reason, and Seeking Truth in the Sciences *(1641).*

I am in doubt as to the propriety of making my first meditations in the place above mentioned matter of discourse; for these are so metaphysical, and so uncommon, as not, perhaps, to be acceptable to every one. And yet, that it may be determined whether the foundations that I have laid are sufficiently secure, I find myself in a measure constrained to advert to them. I had long before remarked that, in relation to practice, it is sometimes necessary to adopt, as if above doubt, opinions which we discern to be highly uncertain, as has been already said; but as I then desired to give my attention solely to the search after truth, I thought that a procedure exactly the opposite was called for, and that I ought to reject as absolutely false all opinions in regard to which I could suppose the least ground for doubt, in order to ascertain whether after that there remained aught in my belief that was wholly indubitable. Accordingly, seeing that our senses sometimes deceive us, I was willing to suppose that there existed nothing really such as they presented to us; and because some men err in reasoning, and fall into paralogisms, even on the simplest matters of geometry, I, convinced that I was as open to error as any other, rejected as false all the reasonings I had hitherto taken for demonstrations; and finally, when I considered that the very same thoughts (presentations) which we experience when awake may also be experienced when we are asleep, while there is at that time not one of them true, I supposed that all the objects (presentations) that had ever entered into my mind when awake, had in them no more truth than the illusions of my dreams. But immediately upon this I observed that, whilst I thus wished to think that all was false, it was absolutely necessary that I, who thus thought, should be somewhat; and as I observed that this truth, I think, therefore I am (COGITO ERGO SUM), was so certain and of such evidence that no ground of doubt, however extravagant, could be alleged by the sceptics capable of shaking it, I concluded that I might, without scruple, accept it as the first principle of the philosophy of which I was in search.

In the next place, I attentively examined what I was and as I observed that I could suppose that I had no body, and that there was no world nor any place in which I might be; but that I could not therefore suppose that I was not; and that, on the contrary, from the very circumstance that I thought to doubt of the truth of other things, it most clearly and certainly followed that I was; while, on the other hand, if I had only ceased to think, although all the other objects which I had ever imagined had been in reality existent, I would have had no reason to believe that I existed; I thence concluded that I was a substance whose whole essence or nature consists only in thinking, and which, that it may exist, has need of no place, nor is dependent on any material thing; so that "I," that is to say, the mind by which I am what I am, is wholly distinct from the body, and is even more easily known than the latter, and is such, that although the latter were not, it would still continue to be all that it is.

After this I inquired in general into what is essential to the truth and certainty of a proposition; for since I had discovered one which I knew to be true, I thought that I must likewise be able to discover the ground of this certitude. And as I observed that in the words I think, therefore I am, there is nothing at all which gives me assurance of their truth beyond this, that I see very clearly that in order to think it is necessary to exist, I concluded that I might take, as a general rule, the principle, that all the things which we very clearly and distinctly conceive are true, only observing, however, that there is some difficulty in rightly determining the objects which we distinctly conceive.

DISCUSSION QUESTIONS

1. Discuss Descartes' reason for his exploration.
2. Discuss Descartes' notion of the relationship between mind and body.
3. Discuss Descartes' requirement for truth.

WRITING ASSIGNMENTS

PERSONAL. Write a paper about an experience you have had when you have felt uncertain about something you had previously believed.

RESEARCH. Write a documented paper discussing the different kinds of sense impressions.

PERSUASIVE. Write a paper arguing that we should constantly examine our beliefs or conversely that we should rely on authority for the answers to some questions.

ANALYTICAL. Write a paper analyzing Descartes' use of deductive logic.

INVESTIGATIVE. Create a survey use it to discover what beliefs students have changed after they have entered college. Report your findings in a paper.

THE ALLEGORY OF THE CAVE

Plato

> *Plato is perhaps the most famous philosopher in history. Alfred North Whitehead said, "The safest general characterization of European philosophical tradition is that it consists of a series of footnotes to Plato." This famous passage is from Book VII of Plato's* The Republic *written in 360 B.C.E. It is a conversation between Socrates and Glaucon, Plato's older brother.*

And now, I said, let me show in a figure how far our nature is enlightened or unenlightened:—Behold! human beings living in a underground den, which has a mouth open towards the light and reaching all along the den; here they have been from their childhood, and have their legs and necks chained so that they cannot move, and can only see before them, being prevented by the chains from turning round their heads. Above and behind them a fire is blazing at a distance, and between the fire and the prisoners there is a raised way; and you will see, if you look, a low wall built along the way, like the screen which marionette players have in front of them, over which they show the puppets.

I see.

And do you see, I said, men passing along the wall carrying all sorts of vessels, and statues and figures of animals made of wood and stone and various materials, which appear over the wall? Some of them are talking, others silent.

You have shown me a strange image, and they are strange prisoners.

Like ourselves, I replied; and they see only their own shadows, or the shadows of one another, which the fire throws on the opposite wall of the cave?

True, he said; how could they see anything but the shadows if they were never allowed to move their heads?

And of the objects which are being carried in like manner they would only see the shadows?

Yes, he said.

And if they were able to converse with one another, would they not suppose that they were naming what was actually before them?

Very true.

And suppose further that the prison had an echo which came from the other side, would they not be sure to fancy when one of the passers-by spoke that the voice which they heard came from the passing shadow?

No question, he replied.

To them, I said, the truth would be literally nothing but the shadows of the images.

That is certain.

And now look again, and see what will naturally follow it' the prisoners are released and disabused of their error. At first, when any of them is liberated and compelled suddenly to stand up and turn his neck round and walk and look towards the light, he will suffer sharp pains; the glare will distress him, and he will be unable to see the realities of which in his former state he had seen the shadows; and then conceive some one saying to him, that what he saw before was an illusion, but that now, when he is approaching nearer to being and his eye is turned towards more real existence, he has a clearer vision, -what will be his reply? And you may further imagine that his instructor is pointing to the objects as they pass and requiring him to name them, -will he not be perplexed? Will he not fancy that the shadows which he formerly saw are truer than the objects which are now shown to him?

Far truer.

And if he is compelled to look straight at the light, will he not have a pain in his eyes which will make him turn away to take and take in the objects of vision which he can see, and which he will conceive to be in reality clearer than the things which are now being shown to him?

True, he said.

And suppose once more, that he is reluctantly dragged up a steep and rugged ascent, and held fast until he 's forced into the presence of the sun himself, is he not likely to be pained and irritated? When he approaches the light his eyes will be dazzled, and he will not be able to see anything at all of what are now called realities.

Not all in a moment, he said.

He will require to grow accustomed to the sight of the upper world. And first he will see the shadows best, next the reflections of men and other objects in the water, and then the objects themselves; then he will gaze upon the light of the moon and the stars and the spangled heaven; and he will see the sky and the stars by night better than the sun or the light of the sun by day?

Certainly.

Last of he will be able to see the sun, and not mere reflections of him in the water, but he will see him in his own proper place, and not in another; and he will contemplate him as he is.

Certainly.

He will then proceed to argue that this is he who gives the season and the years, and is the guardian of all that is in the visible world, and in a certain way the cause of all things which he and his fellows have been accustomed to behold?

Clearly, he said, he would first see the sun and then reason about him.

And when he remembered his old habitation, and the wisdom of the den and his fellow-prisoners, do you not suppose that he would felicitate himself on the change, and pity them?

Certainly, he would.

And if they were in the habit of conferring honours among themselves on those who were quickest to observe the passing shadows and to remark which of them went before, and which followed after, and which were together; and who were therefore best able to draw conclusions as to the future, do you think that he would care for such honours and glories, or envy the possessors of them? Would he not say with Homer,

Better to be the poor servant of a poor master, and to endure anything, rather than think as they do and live after their manner?

Yes, he said, I think that he would rather suffer anything than entertain these false notions and live in this miserable manner.

Imagine once more, I said, such an one coming suddenly out of the sun to be replaced in his old situation; would he not be certain to have his eyes full of darkness?

To be sure, he said.

And if there were a contest, and he had to compete in measuring the shadows with the prisoners who had never moved out of the den, while his sight was still weak, and before his eyes had become steady (and the time which would be needed to acquire this new habit of sight might be very considerable) would he not be ridiculous? Men would say of him that up he went and down he came without his eyes; and that it was better not even to think of ascending; and if any one tried to loose another and lead him up to the light, let them only catch the offender, and they would put him to death.

No question, he said.

This entire allegory, I said, you may now append, dear Glaucon, to the previous argument; the prison-house is the world of sight, the light of the fire is the sun, and you will not misapprehend me if you interpret the journey upwards to be the ascent of the soul into the intellectual world according to my poor belief, which, at your desire, I have expressed whether rightly or wrongly God knows. But, whether true or false, my opinion is that in the world of knowledge the idea of good appears last of all, and is seen only with an effort; and, when seen, is also inferred to be the universal author of all things beautiful and right, parent of light and of the lord of light in this visible world, and the immediate source of reason and truth in the intellectual; and that this is the power upon which he who would act rationally, either in public or private life must have his eye fixed.

I agree, he said, as far as I am able to understand you.

Moreover, I said, you must not wonder that those who attain to this beatific vision are unwilling to descend to human affairs;

for their souls are ever hastening into the upper world where they desire to dwell; which desire of theirs is very natural, if our allegory may be trusted.

Yes, very natural.

And is there anything surprising in one who passes from divine contemplations to the evil state of man, misbehaving himself in a ridiculous manner; if, while his eyes are blinking and before he has become accustomed to the surrounding darkness, he is compelled to fight in courts of law, or in other places, about the images or the shadows of images of justice, and is endeavouring to meet the conceptions of those who have never yet seen absolute justice?

Anything but surprising, he replied.

Any one who has common sense will remember that the bewilderments of the eyes are of two kinds, and arise from two causes, either from coming out of the light or from going into the light, which is true of the mind's eye, quite as much as of the bodily eye; and he who remembers this when he sees any one whose vision is perplexed and weak, will not be too ready to laugh; he will first ask whether that soul of man has come out of the brighter light, and is unable to see because unaccustomed to the dark, or having turned from darkness to the day is dazzled by excess of light. And he will count the one happy in his condition and state of being, and he will pity the other; or, if he have a mind to laugh at the soul which comes from below into the light, there will be more reason in this than in the laugh which greets him who returns from above out of the light into the den.

That, he said, is a very just distinction.

DISCUSSION QUESTIONS

1. What does the allegory imply about the nature of our perceptions of reality?

2. What does the allegory tell us about the nature of social interaction?

3. Why did Plato use the dialogue structure?

WRITING ASSIGNMENTS

PERSONAL. Write about a time when you have experienced an awakening, when you discovered something significant that you hadn't known before.

RESEARCH. Identify other belief systems that seek to explain a truth beyond reality. Report your findings in a documented paper.

PERSUASIVE. Write a paper arguing that students should search for eternal truths rather than being satisfied with learning facts.

ANALYTICAL. Analyze the structure and effect of the dialogue.

INVESTIGATIVE. Create a survey and use it to discover the core beliefs most students hold. Report your findings in a paper.

METAPHYSICAL MISTAKE

KAREN ARMSTRONG

Karen Armstrong, author of more than 20 books on religion and faith, is a leading authority on comparative religion and the history of the major Abrahamic traditions. In this essay she challenges the reader to consider the role of religion in the modern world.

You can access this reading with the following link: https://www.theguardian.com/commentisfree/belief/2009/jul/12/religion-christianity-belief-science or you can find it by entering the author's name and the title of the reading in your search engine.

DISCUSSION QUESTIONS

1. What is Armstrong's main idea?
2. Discuss Armstrong's use of cause and effect in her historical analysis.
3. At the end of her essay, Armstrong asks the question, "how can we extricate ourselves from the religious cul-de-sac we entered about 300 years ago?" How would you answer the question?

WRITING ASSIGNMENTS

PERSONAL. Write a paper telling about your attitude toward organized religion.

RESEARCH. Write a research paper comparing two religious traditions. Document your sources.

PERSUASIVE. Write a paper defending or refuting the idea that people should follow a religious tradition.

ANALYTICAL. Write a paper analyzing Armstrong's use of historical analysis.

INVESTIGATIVE. Interview friends and classmates who consider themselves to be religious and find our what their religious practices are. Report your findings in a paper.

Student Writing

This chapter contains samples of student-written papers of various kinds.

AN OUTSTANDING SELECTION FOR AUSTIN AREA LANDSCAPER

JANECE FEATHER

Visiting Austin, Texas, or just driving along its streets, one can't help noticing the plethora of native plants growing in the area. Wildflowers boast exuberant colors while native shrubs and trees demonstrate incredible strength with their sturdy forms. The viewer gets a genuine "sense of place" when greeted and surrounded by these treasures. The citizens of Austin are fortunate in that there is a heightened awareness in the community of the value of native plants, possibly attributable to the fact that the Lady Byrd Johnson National Wildflower Center is located here. The public is increasingly better informed about plant choices and plant nurseries are stocked with more native plants for the buying public. In my years of gardening and perusing plant nurseries in the Austin area, one native plant has emerged as a clear favorite. Autumn sage (*Salvia greggii*) is known by other common names such as Gregg salvia, and cherry sage. It is a superb native plant for use in Austin area landscapes based on its adaptability to local soil and weather conditions, its ability to provide color and structure over several seasons, and its availability in local nurseries.

Autumn sage does extremely well in the soils around the Austin area. According to Sally and Andy Wasowski in *Native Texas Plants: Landscaping Region by Region*, its growing range includes the Edwards Plateau where "you can find caliche slopes, limestone escarpments, and thin clay soils barely covering caliche and rock" (41). Autumn sage reportedly does well also in sand and clay soils which are found in the Post Oak Savannah region of Austin (Wasowski 23) and the Blackland region (Wasowski 33), respectively. Autumn sage is suitable for weather conditions in Austin. It is winter-hardy here and thrives even in near-drought conditions. Anyone familiar with Austin's summer temperatures knows of the intense heat that we must endure here. Plants are no exception. I have about ten autumn sage plants in my own garden that have survived since being planted three or four years ago, despite two summers with drought-like conditions. Aside from rainfall, these plants have required minimal supplemental watering beyond the first few weeks after planting and rarely show signs of withering. Autumn sage thrives in both full sun and part shade.

Plants that provide color or structure in gardens through several seasons are welcomed by landscapers. Autumn sage is one such plant. Flower colors can be red, pink, white, or coral and usual bloom time is from spring to frost (Wasowski 260). As explained by Sally and Andy Wasowski, "although it is called autumn sage, Gregg salvia blooms as prolifically in the spring and summer as it does in the fall. If you keep snipping off the tips, it will bloom constantly from spring to frost" (260). My own regimen of cutting the plants back in January, May, and August, causes near-constant bloom, even in winter months. One thing that I especially appreciate about this plant is that it flowers even when located in partial shade. Plants that hold their leaves through winter months or have strong shapes or branch structures provide interest in gardens in colder months when many annual and perennial plants are dormant. Sydney Eddison in *The Unsung Season: Gardens and Gardeners in Winter*, discusses her efforts over thirty-odd years to have "something to look at in every season" (xi). Eddison says, "Garden pleasures don't stop when the leaves fall. Some of the most beautiful and startling effects result from this annual phenomenon" (xi). Sally and Andy Wasowski claim that autumn sage is almost evergreen (260). I was under the impression that autumn sage was fully evergreen as my own plants steadfastly provide structure with their green color every winter while other perennials slumber peacefully through the season. With its color and shrub-like structure, autumn sage also works well with other native plants in the landscape. A very popular combination is to pair the pink or red varieties with Mealy blue sage, a plant with "dark blue blooms on 3 to 9 inch spikes" (Wasowski 208).

It would be foolish to recommend a plant for area landscapes if that plant was difficult to acquire. Sally and Andy Wasowski claim that autumn sage "has become one of our most widely used natives" (260). That, coupled with the public's growing knowledge and appreciation of native plants, has helped to ensure that stocks of autumn sage are plentiful and available. Three to four years ago, I had to go to one of the area nurseries that specializes in native plants to find an abundance of autumn sage specimens from which to choose. Trips to a nearby Home Depot nursery left me with little or no choice at all during spring planting months. I saw maybe one or two autumn sage plants in pot sizes too large for my needs and prices too high for my budget. During fall months, there may have been only a few plants of the size I needed and they were only available on one color. Trips to the same Home Depot nursery during this past spring, summer, and fall, showed that autumn sage plants are well-stocked there. I was delighted to find dozens of plants in at least three colors: red, pink, and white. These plants were available in my favorite size: one-gallon containers. Cost was about $3.99. Recent phone calls to some area native plant nurseries revealed that they, too, have stocks of autumn sage. Garden-Ville has one-gallon plants at a cost of $5.99 each. Barton Springs Nursery has one-gallon plants for $4.99 and 4-inch pots for $1.89 each. Residents can appreciate having these plants readily available throughout the Austin area in a variety of sizes and price ranges. The availability of autumn sage plants at the Home Depot nursery is beneficial to those like me who don't want to drive clear across town and pay extra money for their native plants.

Austin is a beautiful city with tree-covered hills, limestone cliffs, and prairie land, interspersed with winding rivers and creeks. It is made all the more beautiful with a vast array of native plants. It is encouraging to see more and more native plants being used on commercial properties and in homeowners' landscapes. An outstanding selection for area landscapes is autumn sage. It thrives in Austin soils and endures intense summertime heat and sporadic rainfall. It provides brilliant color and sturdy structure in gardens throughout all seasons and is found in plentiful supply at numerous garden centers for most of the year. When it comes to choosing plants for Austin area landscapes, autumn sage deserves a place at the top of anyone's list.

Works Cited

Eddison, Sydney. *The Unsung Season: Gardens and Gardeners in Winter.* Boston: Houghton Mifflin Company, 1995.

Wasowski, Sally and Andy. *Native Texas Plants: Landscaping Region by Region.* Houston: Gulf Publishing Company, 1991.

AMSTERDAM

JAMES HENDERSON

Amsterdam is a world class city with some truly unique characteristics perhaps found nowhere else in the world. The city is extremely beautiful and historic. Having been built largely in the 1600s, Amsterdam was designed with a system of canals that traverse the city allowing for both commercial transport and leisure travel by boat. Often it has been referred to as the "Venice of the North." Located in the Netherlands, the city of Amsterdam has a government that invests extensively in its people while emphasizing personal freedoms, tolerance, and diversity to a level found nowhere on earth. This noble endeavor is reflected throughout society including its accommodations, entertainment, and especially, its people.

When visiting Amsterdam, a guest in the city has an extraordinary range of choices for accommodation. Like all major metropolitan areas, there are many hotels to choose from, and some of Amsterdam's are among the best I've seen. With European amenities and impeccable service, there is no lack of comfort. Many of these hotels are historic and the Dutch architecture offers an ambiance and atmosphere characteristic of the region.

Many tourists choose to stay in the city's wonderful canal homes. Often run as "bed and breakfasts," many of these houses are older than the hotels and, as a result, offer more insight into traditional Dutch life in Amsterdam. Generally, they are tall, thin buildings with ornate triangular upper facades. Perhaps the most unusual features of these homes are the staircases. Many of the stairs are so thin and curving that furniture is hoisted up and through the large windows that overlook the trees and canals. Individually, these homes cater to different kinds of tourists. Some have a family clientele, while others cater especially to young party people, business people, the elderly tourist, gay people, or people of various nationalities. The choices are unlimited.

Perhaps the most interesting choice of accommodation is staying on a canal boat. Waking in the morning, opening the cabin porthole and listening to the waves lap against the hull while watching other boats go by is an experience not soon forgotten.

Amsterdam provides an array of entertainment unmatched elsewhere. The city is full of historical sites ranging from the Royal Palace to the city's old churches, including *Oude Kerk* (Old Church), the city's oldest cathedral which was built in the 1300s. Monuments erected over the centuries are found everywhere as are some very ornate medieval clock towers. One of the best ways to take the sights in is to take the canal tour. Day or night, the canal tour offers spectacular sights, during the day, the architectural details and at night, the lighted facades.

For the traveler who wishes to be pampered, the European spas are a must. They offer seemingly every service imaginable to enhance the way people look and feel.

Nightlife in Amsterdam is extremely festive and draws people from around the world. Music and dancing in the clubs goes on until the early hours of the morning and the sense of abandon is possibly the most carefree anywhere. There are many theaters and music venues that attract acting troups and bands from all over Europe and the world.

The city seems to operate on the principle that there's a time and place for everything and that people can do what they want just as long as it doesn't hurt anybody. The red light district (absolutely legal) is a case in point. It even attracts sightseers who have no interest in participating in the activities associated with the area.

Of all of the wonders of Amsterdam, its greatest treasure is its people. Having traveled to a great many places, I've never been more warmly received than in Amsterdam. Perhaps the great diversity of the populous breeds tolerance and acceptance. Perhaps liberal politics that champions freedom breeds cohesion. Whatever the case, the genuine hospitality of the people of Amsterdam puts so many of the world's travel destinations to shame, making Amsterdam one of the world's greatest places to visit.

With so much to offer the tourist—accommodations, entertainment, and hospitality—its no wonder so many people visit Amsterdam each year. Its uniqueness makes it a refreshing stop in anyone's itinerary and one that will be remembered for many years. Amsterdam is certainly one of the best destinations for anyone visiting Europe.

BEAUTY BECOMES THE BEAST

Sarah Matthes

Throughout the generations, women have been regarded as the fairer of the sexes. While many have seen this as a point of pride, it has also created an obligation to maintain this standard of beauty and near perfection. This in and of itself is not such a terrible thing. However, over time it has created impossible standards, unrealistic ideas of beauty, and a sense of dissatisfaction among millions of women. Instead of fixating on flaws, we should redefine our society's idea of beauty and focus more on what we like about ourselves and other women, even daring to go beyond just the physical aspects of beauty. By changing the way we view it, we can turn beauty into something to be found within us, instead of an impossible goal, always just beyond our reach.

In 2009 almost 9.9 million Americans received plastic surgery, and that included roughly 311,000 breast augmentations and 243,000 liposuctions ("2009 Top 5"). In other words, over half a million women have felt so pressured by societal requirements for women to have small waists and large breasts that they were willing to undergo invasive surgery in order to conform to these ideals. Over the years the quest for beauty has made women do ugly things. However, some women have managed to strike the balance, something we all should try to achieve. "Like French women, we, too, need to understand that a healthy approach to beauty is neither pretending it's unnecessary or unimportant nor making it important beyond all else" (Alkon 2).

The question now becomes, how do we break this cycle of vicious self-attack and the insatiable desire to achieve perfection? The answer lies in a shift in thought. Instead of seeing our differences as imperfections, we must learn to see them as aspects of ourselves that make us unique and add diversity to physical appearance. When I was in middle school, people made fun of me because of how skinny I was. I used to eat and eat and eat in hopes of filling out to stop all the teasing. As I grew older though, people treated it differently, some even envied my figure, something I wasn't used to. More importantly though, I learned to accept my own slenderness, even like it, regardless of what I saw in other people. I received the same ridicule and felt the same way about my freckles as well. But as time went by, I saw them less as a telltale sign of a nerd, and more of a sign of distinction, one more thing that made me different from everybody else. If everyone learned to appreciate the little things about themselves instead of covering them up, women in general would be much happier about the way they see themselves.

Along with impossible comparisons come the impossible attempts to change ourselves to meet those standards set for us. This is what drives women to anorexia, bulimia, and extreme exercise. The focus is always on making ourselves look like somebody else, when instead it should be on making you into a better version of yourself. The primary goal should always be on being healthy and fit. If this does not turn you into a size 0 supermodel, *that is okay*.

Perhaps a more extreme shift in thought, women should also learn to see beauty as more than the sum of physical aspects. It is also the spirit of a woman, her kindness, her humor that grants her the title of beautiful. In a study conducted by Dove, researchers found a correlation between a woman's perception of her own beauty and what she considered beautiful. Those who were dissatisfied with their appearance seemed to think that cosmetics and physical perfection make a woman beautiful, while women who found themselves beautiful placed importance on happiness, kindness, confidence, humor, and intelligence (Etcoff and Orbach). These are the legacies that should be passed down from mothers to daughters, and these are the attributes of beauty that will free women from the beauty trap that tells us we must be a slave to our own good looks. In her essay "Beauty," Susan Sontag observes that beauty is "a crude trap" that makes it easy to define "women as caretakers of their surfaces" and then "disparage them (or find them adorable) for being 'superficial'" (134).

Many women feel that being attractive is the only way to appeal to men. While it is true that men are visually wired, they are not completely oblivious to a girl's personality. I do not suggest that women completely ignore their hygiene and overall appearance, but a relationship formed solely on the basis of attraction will have no depth or substance; it would be like buying a house just because you like the color of the paint. Other women feel that there is no beauty trap from which to escape. The system allows women to use their looks as a leverage to get ahead, and this can't be such a bad thing. I cannot argue with any woman who is willing to promote herself through her vanity; that is her own prerogative. I can warn her, however, that her success may not bring her the fulfillment she expects. Success rarely brings happiness unless it is achieved through values that one can be proud of, values that are consequently connected to the true idea of beauty.

With media bombarding our culture with images of anatomically ideal models, women have come to look in the mirror with dread as they prepare to analyze everything that needs to change in order to meet the criteria. Before society becomes a congregation of "beautiful" drones, we must teach ourselves to look in the mirror and see the good-hearted, unique, capable, and funny woman. We must teach the next generation of women to see themselves in this way as well, before the next vicious cycle of self-degradation begins and it is too late.

Works Cited

"2009 Top 5 Cosmetic Surgeries." *American Society for Aesthetic Plastic Surgery*. 2009. Graph. Web. 12 March 2011.

Alkon, Amy. "The Truth About Beauty." *Psychology Today*. November 2010. 1–2. Web. 3/12/11.

Etcoff, Nancy, and Susie Orbach. "The Real Truth About Beauty: A Global Report." *Dove, a Unilever Beauty Brand*. September 2004. 1–48. Web. 12 March 2011.

Sontag, Susan. "Beauty." *75 Readings: A Freshman Anthology*. Ed. Emily G. Barrose. New York: McGraw-Hill, 1987. 132–34. Rpt. of "Women's Beauty: Put Down or Power Source." 1975. Print.

THE HOUSE

KIM KRUPP PEPE

The house sits on the highest hill in the county. It's a big old two story structure of no discernable architectural style. It was built in stages over the last few centuries and is a series of styles from different times. The huge trees in the lawn cover the house and grass in dappled shade. The breeze constantly rolls over the emerald farmland and meets on the hilltop to make the sunlight dance and play over everything. It's a very pleasant place. My sisters and brother and I grew up there, and my memories still live here.

As I walk up the driveway, I glance at one of my old climbing trees. When I was little, I'd climb up into the giant maple to read. I'd lay myself on one of the massive branches and live many adventures in my mind. Sometimes I'd climb up the branches as high as I could and jump. The dizzying effect is something I can only compare to being pleasantly drunk, just for an instant. I still climb the tree when I go home to see if it feels the same. Of course it doesn't, and I jump down with a half sad smile on my face when I realize that those feelings and adventures are now just a memory.

As I look around, so many memories flood through my head. There's the big boulder that was unearthed one summer when the new septic system was laid. I used to give speeches standing on the top of this rock. Sometimes I'd be Lincoln at Gettysburg or Martin Luther King with a dream or I'd give a talk of my own contrivance about things that were very profound to my young mind. All the solutions seemed simple from the top of that rock. There's the path into the woods where my sister broke her leg one rainy day. The woods also contain a tree with branches very much like parallel bars. Here I was a world class gymnast on afternoons after school. On the far left side of the lawn is a hedge row broken by a tractor path that leads to the back fields, the old barn, and my childhood Shangri-la. Many mornings I remember running barefoot, always barefoot, breathlessly and ceaselessly through the dewy grass to the fields beyond. The sharpness of the newly cut wheat stalks would sometimes cut my feet, all unheeded. If the grain crops were still high, I could swim through them, holding my breath if I fell, as if I were actually in water.

The porch which surrounds the front of the house was the setting for many lazy summer afternoons—eating peaches and swatting flies—and freezing winter mornings waiting for the school bus to arrive. The porch was where my mother gave food to hoboes and then shooed them along before my father saw them. Under the porch I used to hide and secretly look at the world through the gingerbread trim. No one ever found me there.

All my childhood memories still live in that house and out in the fields and woods. When I visit now, many things are much the same, but nothing is exactly the same or nearly as big as I remember them. Now I'm always kind of torn between being sad because I feel like a child and yet knowing I am not and can never be again. Another part of me feels happy for having a place where all my past is stored and secreted away, always waiting for me to come back and make the little girl dance and laugh and run through the dewy grass.

CRIME SCENE INVESTIGATIONS AND FORENSIC ANALYSIS

Marcia Salazar

Most people in today's society are familiar with forensic science and how it relates to crime scene investigations. With television shows like CSI, we are able to get a tiny glimpse of what it takes to solve a crime using forensic science. During a crime scene investigation there are several procedures that must be done in order to ensure that the investigation is conducted properly. The scene must be secured and evidence must be collected in order to establish the nature of the crime that has occurred. Crime scenes are a vital piece of evidence in and of themselves. They must be managed in such a way that nothing gets overlooked. Murder investigations, for example, often use the four most important types of forensic analysis: photography, pathology, toxicology, and anthropology.

The most crucial piece of evidence that can be collected from a crime scene is photographic evidence. A forensic photographer will take accurate pictures depicting exactly what has taken place. It is not a simple as clicking a button and taking a picture. There are several steps involved in the process of crime scene photography.

Taking photographs of the area surrounding the crime scene is very important, but also paperwork must be in place to assure that the information is documented accurately. A photo identifier will be used to and will include the case number, the date the image was taken, the address/location of where the photographs were taken, the name or badge number of the photographer, and the roll number of the film which is being exposed (Robinson 305). There are also other forms that must be used in order to ensure proper documentation. Robinson states in *Crime Scene Photography,* "Every individual photograph should be logged on a photo memo sheet, which is a form to log all specific data related to the camera, film, and specific variables used to capture each individual photograph" (308). Oftentimes these photos are submitted in court; along with the photographs, a witness must testify that the photographs being submitted are authentic and that they accurately portray the crime scene (Buckland 38). Crime scene photographs are long term evidence, making it even more important that they are documented properly.

Another area of forensic analysis that plays a major part in murder investigations is forensic pathology. Prahlow notes that "Forensic pathology represents a subspecialty area within the larger field of pathology that specifically deals with the investigation of sudden, unexpected and/or violent death" (32). In order to be able to determine a cause of death, the forensic pathologist must examine the body. An autopsy has to be conducted which is made up of an external and internal examination of the entire body, but also includes ancillary procedures that must be done. The external examination is more of a visual exam that documents injuries, postmortem changes, and various physical characteristics of the body. The internal examination is much more complicated and involves surgically opening the body and removing the organs. Once the organs are removed they are dissected in order to determine whether or not disease is present. In the process of the autopsy various ancillary procedures may take place as well. One of the major ancillary aspects is toxicology testing, which evaluates the blood and tissue for toxins (Prahlow 33). Toxicology testing must be conducted by a forensic toxicologist.

A forensic pathologist works hand in hand with a toxicologist. A forensic toxicologist can determine whether a toxic substance is present in a human body and if it may have played a part in the death that has occurred. In the reference work *Forensic Science* we find that "In cases of suspicious deaths, pathologists collect at autopsy the specimens that will be subjected to toxicological analysis. In general, the specimens collected from a body for this purpose include urine, blood, stomach and intestinal contents, bile, bone, fat, tissues of the brain and liver, and one whole kidney" ("Forensic Pathology" 542). Once the specimens are collected, the toxicologist will decide what type of testing is needed and will repeat the procedure several times in order to assure that the results are accurate.

Another specialty of forensic science that is sometimes used in crime investigations is forensic anthropology. In *The Use of Forensic Anthropology*, Robert Pickering explains that a "forensic anthropologist can help recover and analyze human remains, particularly those that are decomposed or skeletonized, in a rapid effective manner" (17). The thorough training that forensic anthropologists receive allows them to be able to assist in the reconstruction of the crime scene. Pickering notes, "At minimum, the forensic anthropologist can determine the major biological characteristics, such as age, sex, stature, and possibly race or ethnicity of skeletonized human remains" (15). Although, forensic anthropologists are normally called in to identify remains, they may also aid the pathologist or toxicologist if needed. Many times a forensic anthropologist helps give the skeletal remains an identity by way of facial reconstruction. All of a sudden the bones come to life and are often able to give some insight to the mystery.

A crime scene can be very complicated and as Pickering observes "A forensic investigation requires a team of specialists from many different scientific fields of study along with legal and law enforcement specialists" (xi). These specialists have to work together in order to be able to solve the crime. Televisions shows like CSI can often distort certain aspects of such investigations making it seem that the completion of an investigation is immediate, when in fact it can be a lengthy process. Many crimes would go unsolved if it were not for the several different methods of forensic analysis. Not all methods may be used at once, but there is a good chance that some form of forensic analysis will be used in a crime scene investigation. Although, there are a number of other fields of forensic science, from psychology to accounting, these four—photography, toxicology, pathology, and anthropology—are among the most essential in solving a crime.

Works Cited

Buckland, Gail. *Shots in the Dark*. New York: Bulfinch Press, 2001. Print.

"Forensic Pathology." *Forensic Science*. Ed. Embar-Seddon, Ayn and Allen D. Pass, Vol. 3. Pasadena, CA: Salem Press, 2009. *Gale Virtual Reference Library*. Web. 2 Mar. 2011.

Pickering, Robert B. *The Use of Forensic Anthropology*. Boca Raton: 2nd Ed. CRC Press, 2009. eBook Library. Web. 2 Mar. 2011.

Prahlow, Joseph. *Forensic Pathology for Forensic Scientist, Police, and Death Investigators*. New York: Springer, 2010. eBook Library. Web. 2 Mar. 2011.

Robinson, Edward M. *Crime Scene Photography*. Burlington: 2nd Ed. Academic Press, 2010. eBook Library. Web. 2 Mar. 2011.

THE FORD

Laura Scarborough

I saw my crazed, absent-minded aunt charging full speed in reverse coming straight towards us. I awaited the impact....When metal hit metal, my mom and I were jerked a bit. Not bad. My aunt's sickly yellow, ugly Continental smashed into the side of our huge pickup truck. My aunt didn't bother to use her rearview mirror. Our truck received a smashed-in driver's side door. We never fixed it—my aunt didn't have insurance, it didn't seem worth the money, and it's not the right thing to sue a relative.

Our family pickup truck is a 1974 Ford. All black, red interior. It has this useless "customized" shelf built above the rearview mirror that matches the red design of the inside. It was bought by my father the same year I was born, 1974. I was about eight years old when I started learning how to drive. I'd sit on my mom's lap and steer the truck down a gravel road while she operated the accelerator and brakes. The truck was basically the "second car." We only used it if the other car was in the shop, or if we needed to haul or move something (like picking up hay for the horse). Therefore, the truck stayed in pretty good condition, collected few miles, and ran well.

As I grew older, my fondness for the truck grew less and less. I was turning into a snot-head teenager with an attitude. To me the truck was too outdated, too big, too long, too noisy, too "redneck" looking. When I was nearing sixteen, I started bugging my parents about getting me a car. "Well," they said, "you can drive the truck." I started fuming and argued, "No way! It's ugly! It's a gas guzzler! It only has an AM radio! It's got a smashed door! I'll look stupid being a girl having to drive that big old monster around!"

So, like many parents, they wanted the nagging to cease and wanted to make their (bratty) daughter happy. They bought me a 1987 Nissan Sentra hatchback in royal blue. It was sporty. It had a sunroof. It was soooooo coooool. I immediately had the windows tinted, put in new speakers and a nice tape deck, and spent all this money getting it fixed up "cool." I didn't spend much time or money for oil changes and putting water in. "Just gotta put gas in it," I thought.

Time went on and my teenage-snot-head self ragged out and abused that wimpy Japanese contraption until it finally overheated so badly (because of the lack of oil) that the engine warped and was destroyed. We spent $1300 to put another engine in it. Within two weeks it overheated, warped, and was destroyed. A couple months later we got the money together to put in engine #3. Eventually, that engine also overheated and warped. Mommy and Daddy finally realized—no more of this. The insurance was taken off, and the dead Nissan still sits under a tree in my parents' yard.

Being without a car for a year and a half taught me that one must respect the transportation they own. I also learned that Nissans are pieces of dookie even despite my bad maintenance. When I moved to South Austin six months ago, I was stuck. I had to persuade my boyfriend to be may chauffeur to and from school, or I had to take two hour bus trips (each way) to get to ACC. I whined and complained to my parents until they gave me the same offer: "You can drive the truck." So I did.

Now, I really appreciate and enjoy driving my baby (as I call it). It still has a smashed-in door and still guzzles gas. In fact, it only gets 8–10 miles per gallon, so I spend a fortune on gasoline. I deserve it, for wasting so much of my parents' money on that worthless Nissan.

I feel a bond with all the other early Ford truck drivers I see. They look at me and I look at them. Occasionally, some wave. It's weird. I get more looks from people at gas stations than I ever did driving a Nissan. People just don't expect a girl in a long flowery skirt and Dock Martins to jump out of a dented up, old Ford truck.

I'm not worried when I drive on the roads. I'm not an obvious cop magnet. I feel safe being surrounded by one ton of American-made steel. Other car owners know they would suffer a lot more than I would if we were to have a collision. So they stay away from me and my smelly pollutant exhaust.

I'm a good driver. Driving such a huge, long massive machine makes you a good driver. It's taught me to judge distances better. If I can parallel park in one try, I know I'm doing something admirable.

I've learned about car maintenance. I know that automobiles need gas, oil, water, brake fluid, etc. (gee, I'm a genius). Since I give the truck a lot of care and love, it has never failed to start since it's been with me in Austin. It's reliable, safe, and very special. I find it ironic that I'm the person it ended up with after all these years—especially since I had the worst attitude towards it in my high school daze. I'll be holding on to my baby for awhile because I'm happy with it and wouldn't really want anything else. So, if you see a girl cruising down Lamar in a big black Ford with a smashed-in driver's door, you know it's me.

AN ANALYSIS OF "ON ANDROGYNY"

SARAH TORRES

Virginia Woolf's "On Androgyny" is a referential, although personal, examination and analysis of human mental processes and the role of gender in the human psyche. Woolf relies on her own mental reactions to the scene of a man and woman coming to-gether in a street to demonstrate her viewpoints and explain her conclusions.

Woolf's primary purpose is referential because she purports to reveal certain innate characteristics of the human psyche by using herself as an example. She relates that "the ordinary sight of two people getting into a cab had the power to communicate something of their own seeming satisfaction," and that, "to think …of one sex as distinct from the other…interferes with the unity of the mind." She conveys detailed information as she deciphers human mental processes, and she reports each step of her mental journey to certain conclusions. Although she often expresses an idea as a personal "feeling," she merely uses this characterization as an initial vehicle for ultimately stating her viewpoints as acceptable and reliable information. For example, Woolf says, "Why do I feel that there are severances and oppositions in the mind, as there are strains from obvious causes on the body?" Although here she expresses this idea as a subjective personal feeling, she proceeds to rely on this idea as established fact in her following statements. On another subject, she explains as a matter of fact that, "the mind has so great a power of concentrating at any point at any moment that it seems to have no single state of being. It can separate itself from the people in the street, for example...Again if one is a woman one is often surprised by a sudden splitting off of consciousness, say in walking down Whitehall, when from being the natural inheritor of that civilisation, she becomes, on the contrary, outside of it, alien and critical." She also informs us, "Clearly the mind is always altering its focus, and bringing the world into different perspectives."

Woolf's secondary purpose is to persuade the reader that her viewpoints and conclusions are reliable and acceptable. First, she uses her personal mental reactions as a sort of primary source example to support the statements she makes about the human mind in general: "When I saw the couple get into the taxi-cab the mind felt as if, after being divided, it had come together again in a natural fusion. The obvious reason would be that it is natural for the sexes to cooperate." Second, she follows a methodical path of purportedly supporting logic. First attaching much significance to the natural mental reaction that occurs when she witnesses the man and woman, she notes, "The sight of two people coming down the street and meeting at the corner seems to ease the mind of some strain..." and from there begins to conclude, "Perhaps to think...of one sex as distinct from the other is an effort." She says that making this distinction "interferes with the unity of the mind." Woolf then uses the universal sense of "satisfaction" derived from the physical union of a man and woman to support her idea that each individual's satisfaction requires a mental union of the male and female genders: "in each of us two powers preside, one male, one female..."

Woolf uses narration as her primary writing pattern. Beginning by describing the street scene she witnesses from her window, she tells a chronological story of how and when she came to think certain thoughts, have certain impressions, or conclude certain concepts: "The mind is certainly a very mysterious organ, I reflected...." And later: "For certainly when I saw the couple get into the taxi-cab the mind felt as if, after being divided, it had come together again in a natural fusion." In her concluding sentences she says, "And I went on amateurishly to sketch a plan of the soul...."

Within a narrative framework, Woolf organizes her information by classification. In explaining what she means by the "unity of the mind," she uses examples to categorizes the various types of mental states the mind can adopt which change one's perspective of the world: "[The mind] can separate itself from the people on the street...and think of itself as apart from them....Or it can think with other people spontaneously, as, for instance, in a crowd waiting to hear some piece of news read out. It can think back through its fathers or through its mothers...." She distinguishes two main types of mental states: "some of these states of mind seem...to be less comfortable than others," but "there may be some state of mind in which one could continue without effort...And this perhaps...is one of them." She also categorizes where male and female powers ought to reside within men as opposed to women: "two powers preside, one male, one female: and in the man's brain, the man predominates over the woman, and in the woman's brain, the woman predominates over the man...If one is a man, still the woman part of the brain must have effect; and a woman also must have intercourse with the man in her."

Woolf ultimately concludes that it is with the "fusion" of male and female "powers" within a single individual that the mind is "fully fertilised and uses all its faculties" and that "the normal and comfortable state of being is that when the two [powers] live in harmony together, spiritually cooperating." Using metaphorical symbols of the physical union of a man and a woman, she seems to say that as the unity of a man and woman succeeds, so succeeds the unity of mind in each individual—with the fusion of male and female powers. While the train of thought that leads Woolf to her conclusions is in a sense only as persuasive as the reader can relate to her experiences or accept her logic, and while in most cases Woolf's logical path seems heavily subject to her personal mental experiences and impressions, her intent seems to be merely to use what information is available to her by direct analysis of personal mental experiences to conclude certain truths about human nature. She appears to consider herself a reliable source at least for attempting to glean information about the human mind in general. Woolf's mental journey is intriguing because the reader is given a way to systematically examine ideas regarding male and female powers from a personal perspective and also because the reader is indirectly offered a deep window into the mind and philosophy of Virginia Woolf, however limited the topic, and often subtly given a uniquely sympathetic perspective of how she views herself in the world.

A RARE FIND

Chris Woffenden

Living in Texas, it's never hard to find a Tex-Mex restaurant around. You run into them on just about every other street corner it seems. I have eaten at many Tex-Mex joints, and I'll say that most of them have been decent. *Decent.* It's very rare that you come across a restaurant that captures the taste of Mom's home cooking, whether it's Mexican food, Chinese, or just a plain ol' steak house. It was only by chance that I found this perfect Tex-Mex restaurant. It's the closest thing to my mother's cooking I have ever tasted. It's a little pink house on East Seventh Street, just east of the Interstate, across from the downtown area. Angie's Mexican Restaurant delivers a combination of service, taste, and atmosphere like no other restaurant I have ever set foot in. Let me tell you about the magic that is Angie's.

The service is superb. As soon as you walk through the door, you are greeted with a smile by one of about five or six servers who work there. Having such a small wait staff all but eliminates the possibility of getting bad service. I know each one of them and have always been treated like a special guest. Barring weekday lunch hours, it never takes more than about five minutes to get a table. The staff is fast and friendly and does a wonderful job of keeping your glass full and a smile on your face with pleasant conversation. Even the busboy there is a delight to talk to. Each time I eat there, he comes out from the back room and says hello and chats with me a bit, usually about cars or football. I have never been to a restaurant with a staff that, as a whole, is as friendly as Angie's. They make you feel as if you are a long-lost cousin visiting from a distant city. They are open every day from 7 a.m. to 4 p.m. and are closed on Tuesday. They are just as happy to see you at ten 'til 4 as they are at opening time.

Once you are seated, you'll get started with chips and salsa, a custom at just about any Mexican restaurant. But this is not your average salsa. Oh, no. It is a perfect blend of tomatoes, jalapenos, and onions that'll set your mouth on fire. After munching on the appetizer and sipping your iced tea for a short time, you get to the real good stuff. There are a number of platters to choose from including tacos, chalupas, and enchiladas. Any of these delicious dishes come with corn tortillas that are made right in the back of the restaurant every day. If you choose the enchilada or taco platter, you have a choice of beef or chicken, either of which are perfectly seasoned with salt, ground cominos, and diced bell pepper. The chalupas are pretty messy, but definitely worth the wash your hands will need afterward. All platters are served with beans, rice, and two hot flour tortillas. My personal favorite is the beef enchilada platter. When the plate comes, it is steaming hot, and the cheese melts in with the chili sauce to form an enchilada base that has no equal. For dessert you can choose from any of the common goodies they serve like cobbler, pecan pie, etc. But if you want to finish the meal off right, have a bowl of homemade flan. It's a custard-like dessert topped with a vanilla liqueur. Simply delicious! By the way, anything on the menu is all available for take-out if you are in a rush, and you can pay by check or credit card if you are short on cash.

As you sit, savoring each bite of this authentic Mexican food, you will also be treated to traditional Mexican surroundings. The limited space of Angie's always gives me a feeling that I'm back home eating freshly cooked food at my mom's small kitchen table. The tables are situated fairly close together giving it a very intimate setting. The building is an old house that was converted into a restaurant, so it's got a very homey feel. It's not fancy, but it is very clean and attractive. And if, for some reason, you do not care for the interior of Angie's, you can request outdoor seating which is situated right under a cluster of nice shade trees. They always have beautiful Mexican music playing, and the sound of accordion and Spanish guitar fill the room. There is nothing quite like feasting on a tasty Mexican meal and listening to Ana

Gabriel while you enjoy every last morsel. On one of the walls in the restaurant there is a mural of the skyline of Austin that was painted by an employee there. Looking out the west window, you have a beautiful view of the real Austin skyline. On the ceiling, there are paintings of the constellations, which may sound a bit strange. But all these things combine to put forth a very unpretentious setting that is very relaxing.

A few days ago, some friends of mine came into town and were in the mood for some good Mexican cooking. Since my mother lives in Abilene, the choice was clear. Without disagreement, we decided on Angie's not only for the excellent food, but also for the stellar service and comfortable setting. So, if you are ever in the mood for authentic Mexican food and you're in the downtown area, give Angie's a try. Heck, even if you aren't downtown, make the trip. You won't be disappointed.

Credits

Page No.

22 From *Hard Scrabble* by John Graves, copyright © 1973, 1974 by John Graves. Used by permission of Alfred A. Knopf, a division of Random House, Inc.

41 From *Georgia O'Keefe: Art and Letters* (Little, Brown & Co., 1987).

48 From *October Light* by John Gardner. Copyright © 1976 by Boskydell Artists, Ltd. Reprinted by permission of Georges Borchardt, Inc. for the Estate of John Gardner.

53 From *Text & Commentary: My First Nine Lives* by Lyman Grant. Copyright © 1993 by Lyman Grant. Reprinted by permission.

55 Excerpted from *Lord Jim* by Joseph Conrad, 1900.

60 Copyright © by W. Joe Hoppe. Reprinted by permission.

66 "Life in the 30's" from *The New York Times*, September 17, 1986 by Anna Quindlen. Copyright © 1986 by The New York Times. Reprinted by permission.

70 From *Unbought and Unbossed* by Shirley Chisholm. Copyright © 1970 by Shirley Chisholm. Originally published in *McCalls*, August 1970. Reprinted by permission of the author.

80 Radio Address on January 29, 2009 by U.S. President Barack Obama.

84 Courtesy The Territory Ahead.

92 "Where the Sequoia Grows" by John Muir, 1901.

96 Excerpt from *Wild Heritage* by Sally Carrighar. Copyright © 1965 by Sally Carrighar. Reprinted by permission of Houghton Mifflin Harcourt Publishing Company. All rights reserved.

107 From *Saturday Review*, December 14, 1974. Reprinted by permission of the publisher.

110 © 2016 The Atlantic Media Co., as first published in The Atlantic Magazine. All rights reserved. Distributed by Tribune Content Agency, LLC.

234   From *How Do They Do That?*, pp. 89–91, by Caroline Sutton. Copyright © 1981 by Hilltown Books. Reprinted by permission of HarperCollins Publishers, William Morrow.

238   How Flowers Changed the World from *Immense Journey* by Loren Eiseley, Copyright © 1946, 1950, 1951, 1953, 1955, 1956, 1957 by Loren Eiseley. Used by permission of Random House, an imprint of The Random House Publishing Group, a division of Random House LLC. All rights reserved.

243   From *Soul on Ice* by Eldridge Cleaver. Copyright © 1968 by Eldridge Cleaver. Reprinted by permission.

243   Reprinted with permission of the students.

243   "Why I left the U.S. and Why I am Returning" from *Target Zero: A Life in Writing*, by Eldridge Cleaver, edited by Kathleen Cleaver, published by Palgrave Macmillan, copyright © 2006 by The Estate of Eldridge Cleaver. Reprinted by the estate of Eldridge Cleaver.

245   From *Collected Essays and Occasional Writings* of Katherine Anne Porter. Copyright © 1948 by Katherine Anne Porter. Reprinted by permission of Delacorte Press/Syemour Lawrence.

250   From *Voice of the Desert*, pp. 190–6, by Joseph Wood Krutch. Copyright © 1954, 1955 by Joseph Wood Krutch. Renewed 1992 by Marcella Krutch. Reprinted by permission of HarperCollins Publishers, William Morrow.

252   "Wilderness", pp 188–200 from *A Sand County Almanac, 2/e* by Aldo Leopold. Copyright © 1949, 1977 by Oxford University Press, Inc. Reprinted by permission of Oxford University Press USA.

254   From *The Frontier in American History* by Frederick Jackson Turner, 1921.

270   Republished with permission of The Economist Group Limited, from *The Economist, March/April 2012* by Robert Lane Greene. Copyright © 2012 The Economist Group Limited. Permission conveyed through Copyright Clearance Center, Inc.

275   From *College English*, October 1955 by Lauriat Lane, Jr.

334   Where Have I Lived, and What I Lived For by Henry David Thoreau, 1845.

346   Excerpt from *A Room of One's Own* by Virginia Woolf, copyright 1929 by Houghton Mifflin Harcourt Publishing Company and renewed 1957 by Leonard Woolf, reprinted by permission of the publisher.

Index

G

H

I

S